HEIR TO THE DARKMAGE

LISA CASSIDY

Tate House

National Library of Australia Cataloguing-in-Publication entry

Creator: Cassidy, Lisa, 2021 - author.

Title: Heir to the Darkmage

ISBN: 978-1-922533-01-2

Subjects: Young Adult fantasy

Series: Heir to the Darkmage

First published 2021 by Tate House

Cover artwork and design by Jeff Brown Graphics

CHAPTER 1
BEFORE

Bitter, aching cold.

It was her first clear memory, before hunger or affection or fear. The type of cold that digs deep into your bones and won't let go.

It came in the draughts that whispered through every crack in the walls of the hut she and her mother lived in. It crept through the floor under her bare feet, the straw mattress of her bed, the surface of everything she touched. And with cold came the stark white of the snow carpeting the world outside her home.

Hunger came next, a constant dull ache in the pit of her stomach, and after that... fear. The fear in her mother's eyes when she looked at her sometimes. Or drawn tight in her features when she left the hut early each morning to work or hunt.

She didn't remember much before the night her mother died. Those memories held a fuzzy, dreamlike quality. Impressions mostly. Her mother's laugh. The way her embrace could dispel the aching cold, if only for a brief moment. A snatch of brown hair, light, coppery, like the leaves floating to the ground before the merciless winter came.

But she remembered that day like it had been yesterday. The glow of the sunset lighting the unbroken white outside the hut aflame in orange. The way she'd shivered as any warmth the day had held faded with it. She remembered watching as the sun finally slid below the horizon and the shadows crept further and further across the floor toward her... remembered staring out that window. Waiting. For her mother to return with the night as she always did.

But she hadn't come, no matter how long she waited.

She'd almost frozen to death in the early hours before dawn, too young to know how to start a fire or make dinner, too young to know what to do about the fact her mother hadn't come home like she was supposed to.

The night had been unending.

Fear of the dark swamped her. The walls of the tiny hut closed in until she felt she couldn't breathe. Every sound outside caused her to start in fright, the pressure in her chest at the dark and the small space growing tighter and tighter until it hurt. Until she was taking quick, panting breaths, numb fingers clenched painfully tight in the thread-bare fabric of the blanket she'd wrapped around herself.

She'd huddled on her straw bed and shivered from cold and terror until morning light had crept under the door and through the windows, slowly dispelling the darkness. By then her hands and feet were numb and she was so stiff she could barely move.

With the day came the slowing of her breath, an easing in her chest. Fear had not defeated her. She had survived.

She had decided then and there that she would bury that fear and dread so far away that she would never have to re-live it. Never have to remember the horror of that night, how she'd whimpered and trembled and begged for it all to be over. Whatever it took. Even if she was already afraid of what would happen when the sun set once again and darkness returned.

So bit by bit she packed it away, let the daylight banish the shadows, and then she forced herself to her feet. Eventually her stiff limbs cooperated, and she tidied the hut as she knew her mother would want her to, even though they barely had any possessions. Then she curled up on her straw bed and continued waiting. Her mother would come eventually.

Not long after sunrise a visitor came. Stomping feet sounded through the snow outside and then an impatient knock came at the door, hard enough to make it rattle on its hinges. It startled her from the daze of hunger and exhaustion she'd fallen into, and her heart quickened in fear when a second knock thudded on the wood.

She forced herself off the bed, stumbling and falling when cold-stiffened limbs refused to work properly. Gritting her teeth, she'd heaved herself off the floor and gone to answer the knock.

A big, bearded, man stood there, towering over her. She'd seen him before at the village market. The grim look on his weathered face marked itself in her memory for always... but it wasn't the news he brought that made her remember it with such clarity. It was the flash of fear in his eyes when she opened the door and he saw her standing there.

"You survived the night," he'd muttered, mostly to himself. If anything, the fear on his face grew starker at the fact of her survival. "I didn't expect that, it was a cold one."

She stared at him, uncomprehending.

"Your mother is dead. Someone will be here soon to collect you and take you away. You're not wanted here."

Before she could process that, could think to ask any questions, he'd turned and stomped away. She'd stared after him for a long time. Cold wind swept around her shivering body, toyed with the strands of her lank hair. Death was a concept she vaguely understood, enough to know her mother wasn't coming back.

Where would they take her?

Eventually closing the door, she'd turned and looked at the inside of their hut. At the unlit fire and the old chest holding her and her mother's belongings. Hunger ached in her stomach, but that wasn't a new sensation, and she pushed it aside.

If her mother was dead, where would she get food? She had no way of paying for it. She couldn't even light the fire to make herself warm. Not that there was much kindling left. Would they take her some-where where there was food? The girl made herself walk over to the chest and open it up. She owned only one change of clothes, as tattered and worn as the ones she had on, but she pulled them out anyway. That was what Mother wanted her to do each day. Dress in clean clothes.

She'd only just finished putting her old clothing in the pail near the fire to be washed when a second banging came at the door. A different villager was outside this time. He hid his fear better, but it was still there in the way he took an unconscious step back when she opened the door.

"What happened to my mother?" She hadn't quite *felt* yet that her mother wasn't ever returning, even though she knew it must be true.

"She's gone. Best not to dwell on it, girl," he said, his voice blunt but not unkind. "You'll be better off away from here."

"Why?"

"Your kind isn't wanted here," he said gruffly. "We tolerated your mother because she had none of his... but you do and it's best you be gone before you bring trouble down on us all. I'm off to Dirinan to sell my carvings, and it's been decided you'll come with me. Come along now."

Five years old and she'd closed the door of her home behind her for the final time, small feet trudging through the thick snow towards the man's cart. It was already loaded with crates, so she climbed up and perched between two of them, curling her body in an attempt to stay warm.

The journey had taken all day and night. He hadn't spoken a word to her the entire day, apart from when he tossed her a hunk of bread and a blanket once night fell.

They'd entered Dirinan not long after dawn. Freezing, hungry, and exhausted, she hadn't taken in much of the port city, her gaze unseeing as the cart moved through quiet cobblestoned streets. Her mother was gone. That realisation had slowly sunk in during the long night. A shudder racked her frame.

Her mother was gone, and she'd never see her again. Nobody wanted her now. Tears iced on her cheek, but she barely noticed. The pain inside was much worse than the discomfort on the outside.

The man didn't say anything when he'd stopped the cart in front of a grey stone building either. She'd waited, shivering, while he went inside. When he came back out, he'd told her to get out of his cart, go inside, and never come back to the village.

Not knowing what else to do, she'd climbed down from the cart. He clicked his tongue and the cart took off. He didn't look back. Shoulders hunched against the icy air, she turned and went inside the building.

The woman waiting beyond the front doors told her she was at an orphanage, a home for motherless children, and that she would be living there until she was old enough to leave.

"What's your name, girl?"

"Lira."

"You have a last name?"

Lira had shrugged, unsure what that was. "Mama called me Lira."

The woman masked her fear better than the villagers, but the man had clearly told the woman who she was, because the girl could see wariness in the stiffness of her shoulders and the way she held herself back, as if the girl carried some kind of disease. It was a familiar sight.

Five years old and already they were afraid of Shakar's grand-daughter.

CHAPTER 2

"We could take them if we wanted. The Mage Council is only growing stronger, and we need to move before they become too powerful to bring down. The Shadowcouncil should give the order now."

A ripple of scornful laughter ran through the gathering, and the young man who'd spoken hunched down into his chair, cheeks flushed, a scowl on his face. Lira shifted, crossing and uncrossing her legs, trying to keep her impatience from becoming noticeable to those seated nearby.

She was so bored.

Once, she'd tried entertaining herself by keeping count of how many of these meetings she'd attended without anything actually happening, but they'd begun to blur together, and she'd stopped bothering. It was always the same thing over and over. Lots of talking and not much else.

"The Mage Council has been unassailably strong since Shakar was destroyed," an impatient voice countered. It came from an older woman sitting on a crate towards the front of the room. Grey streaked her messily bound hair and dark soot smudged her jaw. "And the Darkmage was a mage of the higher order with multiple powerful magic abilities. Only a fool would think we're strong enough to go at the council head on."

Murmured agreement swept the gathering. It quickly cut off when the man standing at the head of the room lifted his hand. "As much as I appreciate your eagerness, Tornaal, Alegra is right. We still have a ways to go yet."

Lira's bored gaze shifted to the leader of the Karonan cell of Underground, the secretive group answering to the even more secretive Shadowcouncil. He called himself Greyson, but she doubted it was his real name. His words were the same old spiel, amounting to nothing more than a meaningless pat on Tornaal's head. She wanted to understand why, what exactly the Shadowcouncil were waiting for before they actually did *something*.

In the twenty-odd years since the war with the Darkmage had ended, the Mage Council had only grown stronger under the stewardship of its Magor-lier, Tarrick Tylender. The kingdoms of Tregaya and Rionn were firmly aligned with the council, Zandia nearly as close. Only Shivasa—the single kingdom to rally behind the Darkmage in a bid for greater land and power—remained a wary ally at best. Old wounds had proved hard to heal.

Mage apprentices still chose to swear allegiance to either the council or their respective monarchs after passing their trials, but the kingdoms had learned their lessons well from war. The balance of power between mage and civilian leadership was steady and relatively frictionless.

At least, that's what everyone lauded as the great success of the post-war years. The Shadowcouncil sneered at such balance, their followers contemptuous of the way the council allowed its power to be suborned by non-mage monarchs and their sovereign rule. And Shivasa, still far from a full recovery after the ravages of war, was the perfect breeding ground for their followers. Many Shiven still held grudges. None had liked losing. Some thought they should have fought on despite Shakar's defeat, and installed another powerful mage to lead them.

Those people didn't consider the war to be over.

Lira wondered what her grandfather would think of the pretty names and the stultifying boredom of these endless meetings. She doubted he'd tolerate the lack of action, but then, he'd lost in the end. Maybe a ridiculous level of caution *was* the right approach.

"No we don't," Tornaal persisted, an angry flush on his face, bringing Lira sharply back to the present. It was rare for anyone to push once Greyson had shut a topic down. "We've got Shakar's grand-daughter, don't we, his only living heir? We should start now before it's too late and the council consolidate their strength further. All we ever do is talk—I've had enough of talking."

Every gaze in the room shifted to Lira. Even though she sympa-thised with Tornaal's sentiments, she needed to stay on Greyson's good side, so she narrowed her eyes, made her voice waspish. "My grandfa-ther didn't get so close to bringing down the entire mage council and annexing three kingdoms by being a fool. If we move before we're ready, it will all be for nothing. Unless you've come up with a way of bringing down Alyx Egalion—the council's pet mage of the higher order who is ten times more powerful than any other mage alive—that you haven't shared with us yet?"

Those sitting closest to Tornaal muttered in discontent. But none other than Tornaal were brave enough to gainsay her. He scowled. "You are his heir. You should be able to bring her down."

"Tornaal, enough!" Greyson's voice whipped out before Lira could respond, and the interruption both relieved and annoyed her. She hated being reined in like a dog on a leash, but if he hadn't cut in then, she'd have likely unleashed the fury surging in her chest at Tornaal's words and risked losing his loyalty. The anger didn't subside easily either, bubbling in her chest and leaving a burning sensation at the back of her throat. How *dare* that boy challenge her strength?

The entire room froze at the command in Greyson's voice, but as quick as he'd been to employ the control he held over them, his features softened almost as fast into a paternal smile. "Patience. I promise you will one day get everything you desire," Greyson said. The smile and the warm understanding in his tone served to calm the young man and ease the restlessness rising in the room. "Now, are there any more questions before we finish up?"

Greyson was the oldest in the group by far—few of those old

enough to remember the war were willing to start another one, even if they did sympathise with Underground's sentiments. He was cell leader for a reason, with his silver-grey hair and pale brown eyes that could turn from warm and accommodating to firm and sharp in a blink. Lira had to regularly remind herself never to relax around him.

Her gaze ran over the gathering, studying it carefully. Underground liked to keep an air of mystery and secrecy to their meetings, hence their location in the cellar of a tailor's shop—a space that was poorly lit and full of shadows. Attendees sat on a motley collection of uncomfortable chairs, stools, and crates, or stood along the walls.

Without exception, the group's members were as ragged as the cellar. Their clothes were worn and plain, and dirt creased their pale Shiven skin. No doubt a glance at their fingers and palms would reveal dirty, chipped, fingernails and callouses born of hard work. Lira deliberately dressed the same way for these meetings—sliding into a skin that had once been hers and that allowed these people to feel she was one of them.

Which she was.

Her gaze lingered on one figure standing in the deepest shadow at the corner of the room. Whoever it was—Lira hadn't gotten close enough to catch a glimpse of their face—was new tonight. She didn't like it, had told Greyson so, but Greyson had assured her the individual was trusted. He wouldn't tell her more than that, which had reinforced to Lira how little *she* was trusted.

She walked a fine line. As boring and useless as these meetings felt, she couldn't afford to forget how precarious her position with Underground was. How important it was for her ends that they did trust her, *follow* her eventually. It could all go wrong very quickly if she wasn't careful.

"Our notices in the south of the city near the causeway were taken down almost as soon as we put them up." A young woman in the back spoke. "It's like the city guard knew as soon as we did it."

"We might have a spy." The man beside her spoke loudly, a note of accusation in his voice.

Ugly muttering broke out through the space, only quieting when Greyson lifted his hand again. "It's a possibility," he agreed. "For that reason, the Shadowcouncil has dispatched the Darkhand to Karonan to investigate."

A shiver of fear rippled through the room. Lira's eyes narrowed. Her heartbeat quickened, a small thrill going through her before she quickly quashed it. Finally, an interesting development. The Darkhand —right hand and executioner of the Shadowcouncil—was in Karonan.

"The Shiven leader has a strong focus on wiping us out, as you all know, no thanks to General Caverlock and the council constantly whispering in his ear," Greyson continued. "The city guard can keep taking the notices down, but we will keep putting them up. And if there's a spy, the Darkhand will quickly take care of it."

Mention of the Darkhand had quelled the room, adding a layer of fear and unease to the proceedings, but one of the braver attendees soon rallied. "We've already gotten three new recruits over the past two months from our notices," he said proudly.

Lira held back the desire to roll her eyes at the clapping that rippled through the room, Greyson following suit with a proud smile on his face. If posting notices recruiting for new members was the only thing the Shadowcouncil was up to, they certainly wouldn't be taking over the council in her lifetime. Yet that was all these meetings gave her insight into. But if the Darkhand was here... she doubted it was just to round up a potential spy. Maybe more was afoot than she'd realised.

"That will do for tonight," Greyson said once the applause died. "You all have your jobs. Go to them."

Stifling a sigh, Lira rose to go and stand beside Greyson near the exit, allowing everyone the opportunity to give her a nod or a wave or quick word as they filed out. Greyson liked to have her on display like that. He wanted them all to be reminded of their one shining symbol.

The heir to the Darkmage.

She bore the scrutiny with a faint smile and straight shoulders, making sure she didn't seem too approachable. Too nice and she'd lose the mystique of being the feared scion of Shakar. And if she lost that, then she'd lose her utility to the group—the one thing she couldn't afford to lose. The hooded person that made Lira uneasy passed by without a word, not even looking in her direction.

The second last to leave, a young man who'd been sitting next to Tornaal, shook her hand eagerly, leaning in, his eyes alight at having her attention. Lira's practised gaze caught the flash of the pocket watch tucked into his unbuttoned vest, and her free hand was halfway to it before she ruthlessly stopped herself.

That wasn't her anymore. Even so, the urge was strong, and she was glad when he let go of her hand and headed up the stairs, removing temptation.

Once the last person had left, Lira turned to Greyson. She kept her voice casual, careful not to sound too interested. "What Tornaal said, he has a point. But I assume there are things happening in the background you don't make them aware of. The Darkhand isn't here to hunt down someone reporting notices to the city authorities, I'm guessing?"

The Darkhand was the blade of the Shadowcouncil. The one who carried out their most important, and dangerous, tasks. Those that crossed Underground found themselves at the mercy of the Darkhand, and the Darkhand gave none.

He frowned. "There are always things happening in the background. I thought you understood that our plans wouldn't progress quickly."

"I do." She shrugged. "I guess I'm wondering when you're going to start trusting me a little more. It's hard to be the symbol you need me to be when I don't know any more about what's going on than Tornaal and his friends."

"It's not a matter of trust. It's a matter of discretion. What you don't know can't be leaked if you're caught, or if your mind is read by a telepath mage."

"Fair. But I'm not just anyone. I would never betray the Shadowcouncil's confidence. And I can help—more than just showing up at meetings and being on display for you." She pushed a little.

"You will. It won't be long now." He smiled that warm paternal smile. She fought not to roll her eyes again—did he really think that worked on her? "In fact, we have a task for you."

She tried not to let her leap of interest show on her face, was pretty sure she'd managed it. "Whatever you ask, it will be done."

"The council representative in Karonan, Rawlin Duneskal, you know him?"

"Not personally, but I know who he is." Lira made it her business to know everything she could about the eight mages sitting on the Mage Council. The Duneskals were an old and powerful pureblood family. Rawlin's younger brother, Cario, had been killed by one of the Darkmage's Hunters during the war.

"He's been undertaking some work on behalf of Finn A'ndreas. He recently sent a report to the man. We need you to get your hands on it and bring it to me." Greyson lowered his voice, even though they were alone. "The Shadowcouncil needs this done as soon as possible. This is important, Lira."

The reason Lira was being asked to do this was abundantly clear. She was the only Underground member with any kind of access to Finn A'ndreas. Still, the apparent urgency of the task was odd. "What do they care about work being done by Temari Hall's master librarian?" she asked in puzzlement.

"Even if I knew, I wouldn't tell you. Can you do this? If you can't, say so now and I'll find another way." He turned grim, hesitating briefly. "You know the consequences of failure."

"I can do it." She replied without hesitation. She'd been wanting deeper access into the group, and this was her opportunity. Pull off this task successfully and she'd win the trust she needed.

"And quickly?" Greyson emphasised. "The Shadowcouncil need that report before A'ndreas can do anything with it."

"I can get it to you within a week," she promised, even though she had no idea whether that would be possible. She'd figure out a way. "Though it would help if I knew more about this report. What was it on? How long is it?"

"I can't tell you." He turned grim. "Just find a recent letter from Councillor Duneskal in A'ndreas' office and bring it to me. That is all."

"Consider it done," she said confidently.

"Are you sure? Because—"

"I know what the Shadowcouncil does with those who fail it," she reassured him. "It's one of the things that impresses me most about them. We need soldiers who know how to succeed."

He smiled a little, that paternal smile once more. "I knew I could count on you."

She hesitated, hoping her agreement had won her a little latitude. "Can you tell me why the Shadowcouncil has dispatched the Darkhand here?" A shiver went through her at the thought of him in Karonan, paying attention to her activities. At the same time, he would be *her* Darkhand someday, and he was another key part of the mysterious Shadowcouncil she hadn't been granted access to yet.

Greyson glanced up the stairs, then back at her. "Thanks for coming tonight."

The polite dismissal sent irritation spiking through her. She briefly considered pressing harder for more information, but she hadn't liked that little frown on his face at her questions, and she didn't want them developing a hint of doubt about how loyal she was. It wasn't like subtlety or patience were her greatest qualities, so she smiled instead. "I'll get that information to you as soon as I can."

"No more than a week, Lira." He spoke with finality. "If you don't have Duneskal's report to me by then..."

"I will." She left without another word, taking the narrow, rickety staircase leading up to the ground floor two steps at a time. Her boots thumped on the wood, echoing in the darkness, but there was no audience above to hear her coming. It was late. The tailor shop had closed hours ago.

Outside, an icy breeze whispered through the Karonan streets, lifting fallen leaves and other debris, sending them rustling across the hardpacked dirt under her feet. This was her favourite part of going to the Underground meetings—the walk back afterwards, where it was just her and the mostly empty streets. Streets that were dark and shadowed in this part of the city after the sun had set for the day. No street lanterns burning all night like they did closer to the centre of Karonan, just the faint moonlight that did nothing to hide the rundown nature of the buildings or the occasional sight of a rat digging through debris gathered on the sides of the road.

It wasn't a safe area to be walking in so late, but the solitude reminded her of the vague impressions she had of the time *before*. Memories of quiet and peace. Before the orphanage and sharing living space with thirty other children who either hated or feared her or both. Before... She swallowed, forcing that memory away before it could ache enough to ruin the peace of her walk.

Besides, it had been a *very* long time since Lira had been afraid of dark streets and shadowy corners. She'd almost welcome an attempted mugging or enterprising pick-pocketer; it would be a break from the boredom and restlessness that plagued her much of the time, no matter how hard she fought to pretend otherwise.

Three blocks away from the tailor's shop she ducked into an abandoned property between two failing businesses. Avoiding the interior —used as a squat by a group of homeless beggar children—she walked around to the ragged garden out the back.

After ensuring she was alone, she reached under a thick bush growing against the rotting wooden back fence. Her fingers closed over the rough weave of the plain duffel she kept there and dragged it out. Shivering, she tugged off the tattered shirt, jacket, and breeches she'd worn to the meeting. From the bag she pulled out much finer breeches and a long-sleeved tunic—both in grey—as well as her grey robe and staff.

She shrugged the robe on, belted it around her waist, then slid the staff into its holster down her back before reaching up to deftly weave the strands of her shoulder-length chestnut hair into a short braid.

It was only the work of moments to slide the Underground skin off and put her usual one back on.

After doing another check to ensure nobody was around to see her, she shoved the duffel with her Underground clothing back under the bush, then slipped through a gap in the fence into another narrow street. From there she headed for the main road leading to the northern causeway.

Lanterns lit the road here, and even this late a few riders and carriages moved in both directions along the causeway. Four of them— one for each direction of the compass—stretched across the lake surrounding the city and linked Karonan to the rest of Shivasa.

The city guards posted at the gates saw her robe and staff and waved her through with a friendly greeting. She gave them a nod of acknowledgement but didn't otherwise return their greetings. Her strides lengthened past the gates, a vain attempt to keep warm. The cold wind was stronger out over the frozen lake and tugged relentlessly at her robe and hair.

The further she walked, the more the relaxation of her solitary journey faded and a familiar tightness began creeping through her muscles, coalescing in a faint pressure in her chest. That tightness was an old friend now, one she was rarely free of.

At the end of the causeway she turned left into a wide road leading a short distance towards a high stone wall. The main gates stood open, as always, lamps burning merrily in welcome, and the sight of them removed all remaining vestiges of the peace of her walk. Through the gates she caught glimpses of the sprawling grounds along the northern shore of the lake.

Movement stirred in the shadows beyond the lit torches at the entrance as the two apprentices on guard duty stepped out to see who was approaching. They wore the same grey robes and tunic as she did, the same wooden staffs hanging between their shoulder blades. A large, shaggy dog—one of the handful that added to the protection of the grounds—padded at their side. He seemed utterly uninterested in Lira as he yawned, revealing long, sharp teeth that would tear an intruder to shreds if he was given the order.

"You're out late, Spider," one of the apprentices called, the mocking tone in his voice a reminder that the nickname wasn't a friendly one. His companion gave her a suspicious look. She ignored them both and walked through the gates.

Into Temari Hall and her life as a mage apprentice.

CHAPTER 3
BEFORE

The mages in their blue cloaks arrived at the orphanage several months after Lira had been dropped there like she was a sack of mouldy potatoes nobody wanted.

Not that the orphanage had wanted her any more than the villagers had. Word had quickly spread through the other children living there —Lira suspected one of them had been eavesdropping at the orphanage matron's door when she arrived—that she was Shakar's granddaughter.

She didn't understand why the villager had told the matron who she was. Why he hadn't kept the secret the entire village had been keeping, her mother included.

Her mother had always stayed away from the village as much as she could. Their hut was a long walk from the centre of town, and they only travelled to market when they had coin for food—and they only had coin when her mother managed to bring down a deer or other forest creature with a hide valuable enough to sell.

But on the rare occasion they did go into the village, Lira had seen the fear and reserve on the faces of the villagers. She'd sensed the stiffening of her mother's shoulders, heard the whispers behind their backs, had noticed that she was never invited to play in the games the other children enjoyed in the street, their laughter bright and happy.

When her mother eventually tried to explain why this was the case, she told Lira that her grandfather had been a bad man who had hurt a lot of people.

"He died before you were born, but people around here have long memories." Resignation and a hint of something else—anger?—filled her mother's eyes. "They followed him, gave their lives for him, but he failed them. When something hurts you badly, Lira, it's very hard to forget it. People find different ways to try and make the hurting stop. Sometimes they try to keep fighting for what they lost, never giving up on getting it back." A shadow had rippled over her mother's face at this. "And sometimes, like the people here, they get angry and blame their hurt on someone else."

"But you said he died, Mama." Lira tried to understand. "Why are they afraid of us?"

Her mother had looked away, eyes dropping to the floor. "They're worried we might be like him. That we might do what he did. They're afraid of getting hurt again."

"Why don't we leave? If they don't want us here, we could go away. Where you were before you came here to have me."

"They don't want us either." The bitterness in her mother's voice had made Lira flinch, but her mother hadn't even noticed. She'd gone somewhere else in her mind. "Those council mages and their fine clothes and lives of comfort. He just..." Her mother had blinked, coming back to herself abruptly, the look in her face vanishing as if it had never been there. "We have each other, all right?"

Lira had nodded.

Her mother had pulled her close. "I know it's hard, but the real danger you have to be careful of is those who *would* welcome us. Those who want to fight on. You stay away from those people, Lira. You understand me?"

Lira didn't understand, not really, though she pretended she did for her mother's sake. Lira didn't even know this bad man. What did the bad things he'd done have to do with either of them?

After long contemplation, she'd eventually decided the why didn't matter. It just was what it was. Like the endless cold and the relentless hunger in her belly. There was nothing to be done but simply bear it. Still, it taught her how people behaved when they were truly afraid of something. A lesson she resolved not to forget.

But the word *welcome* stayed with her for a long time after. Would it be so bad, to find the people that *would* want them? It might be nice. To be wanted.

IN SOME WAYS, amidst such unwelcoming new surroundings, Lira found the wariness and instant dislike she faced at the orphanage almost comforting in their familiarity. In other ways, it was worse than the village, because there was no isolated hut to retreat to with her mother where they could hide from the world together. Where Lira could forget the looks and her mother's unease. Where she felt loved.

At the orphanage there was no escape from any of it. Nobody to seek solace from. Only the long, draughty room she shared with ten other girls of various ages who took one look at Lira and decided she was an outcast.

A big, yawning chasm had opened in Lira's chest since her mother's death, and she became terrified that she might fall into it one day and never come out again. It made her afraid to sleep, to be still too long, to let quiet settle around her when the chasm would grow bigger and bigger until her breath came in panicked gasps and her fingers clenched and unclenched at her sides. She slept as little as she could and made sure to always stay busy, keeping her thoughts occupied, away from the hole in her chest or memories of her mother.

When the mages came, the matron brought Lira downstairs to a reception area. It was usually used to display the orphanage's attractive and better-behaved children when childless couples came to adopt. Lira had never been taken to that room, and she knew she never would —not even desperate parents would want the grandchild of such a bad man—so being escorted there had raised a flame of surprised hope in her chest.

Maybe there would be escape from this never-ending loneliness after all. Maybe a home and a family would close the hole and she could stop being afraid of it.

A fire crackled in the hearth, and Lira angled her body toward it when the matron left her standing there with a sharp instruction to be quiet and wait. It was the first time she'd ever been in a properly warm room. The winters in far north Shivasa were brutal, and the orphanage didn't spend what little coin they had on any more than the bare minimum for the children they housed. Her muscles loosened, and a languid sort of contentment spread through her body. It was the nicest thing she'd felt since leaving the village.

When the door opened, she spun guiltily away from the fire, every muscle in her body tensing up. A woman shrouded in a fine blue cloak walked in. Lira knew nothing of mages and magic, but she'd immediately felt *something* in this woman's presence that spoke of power and utter assuredness. She wore it as easily as she wore the perfectly fitted cloak on her shoulders. With her was a tall, broad-shouldered, Shiven man with a magnificent sword at his hip.

The woman paused only for the briefest of seconds, her green eyes narrowing slightly at the sight of Lira before she continued into the room. "Please, sit with me."

Lira took one of the chairs by the fire, perching warily on its edge. Her gaze flicked to the man, who closed the door and remained there, still but watchful.

"You're Lira?" The woman sat in front of her. She had neatly braided brown hair, and while there was little overt warmth or friendliness in her demeanour, Lira didn't feel threat or fear from her either.

That earned the woman a nod.

"I'm Alyx. Councillor Alyx Egalion—I'm the head of Temari Hall, where mages are trained. I also sit on the Mage Council." The woman paused. "Do you have a last name?"

Lira shook her head, glanced over the mage's shoulder. The man seemed calm and very... solid, and her eyes snagged again on the magnificent sword at his hip. The hilt had been dyed a deep midnight blue. Red jewels set into the grip glittered in the firelight, making Lira think of a leaping flame. When he caught her looking at him, he winked. She wasn't sure what to make of that, too unfamiliar with kindness to understand the difference between it and mockery.

"That's Dashan." Alyx gestured to the man at the door. "He's a Taliath. What do you know about mages and Taliath, Lira?"

"Nothing."

A little smile curled at Alyx's mouth, as if Lira's refusal to answer with more than a single word amused, rather than annoyed, her. Yet Alyx and Dashan's lack of obvious fear confused Lira, put her on the back foot. She didn't know how to deal with it.

"I'm told that you are a relative of Shakar, Lira." A shadow passed briefly over Alyx's eyes. "Do you know who that is?"

"A very bad man." She parroted the words her mother had said. "He hurt a lot of people."

Sadness flickered over Alyx's face and her shoulders sagged a little. Over by the door, the man's face turned grim, Shiven eyes dark as coals. Lira retreated further into herself, shoulders hunching. Despite their apparent lack of fear, these people hadn't forgotten the bad things her grandfather had done. They remembered them as clearly as Lira remembered the day her mother had died. So they must hate her then, even if they were pretending not to.

For the first time, she wondered exactly what it was he'd done.

"That's right. He was powerful because he had magic... a lot of magic." Alyx settled back in her chair, calm and composed once again. "Judging by what I've picked up since I walked in here, nobody is comfortable with the fact that you're related to Shakar."

There was still no fear in Alyx Egalion, no wariness, no distrust. Cautiously, Lira spoke. "Mama said people are afraid that we're like him."

Alyx glanced at Dashan, a look of regret on her face. He shrugged. "The Shiven loyal to Shakar suffered, especially the rural populations, and they have long memories. Some don't understand enough about you and how the new council operates to see past their fear. Others just don't want to."

"She's just a child." Alyx sounded exasperated.

"It's not just fear, Aly-girl," Dashan said. "It's anger and grief and bitterness. Shakar is gone, but she's a reminder of what could happen again. We should be grateful she hasn't been placed in the path of those who..." His voice trailed off, as if he suddenly realised Lira could also hear what he was saying.

"Where is your mother, Lira?" Alyx asked gently.

"She died."

"How?"

"I don't know."

"I'm very sorry." Alyx seemed awkward, as if she wasn't comfortable with offering sympathy. "Did she have magic?"

Lira shrugged. She'd never seen her mother use magic, but then she'd never seen anyone use magic. Perhaps it was an invisible thing.

"Did you know that the village where you lived, they kept you a secret, you and your mother both? Nobody knew Shakar had a daughter or a granddaughter, not until you were brought here and they told the matron." Alyx paused. "It seems Shakar kept his daughter a secret too."

Lira still said nothing. None of this meant anything to her, though there was an odd intensity in Alyx's voice which made her curious.

"We spoke with the villagers. They said your mother left the village after the war, went away and came back when she was pregnant with you. Do you know where she went?"

"No."

"What about your father?"

"I don't know who he is." Lira had no memory of him. She'd known that she must have one, but the one time she'd asked about it her mother had promised to tell her when she was older. "*It will be too hard to understand if I try and explain now. One day, I promise.*"

"*Why isn't he here with us?*" she'd asked.

Her mother had drawn her close, turning her face away. "*He didn't want to be.*"

Alyx let out a breath. She seemed frustrated, impatient, but her annoyance didn't appear to be directed at Lira. "I'm told your magic has broken out."

Lira shook her head.

Alyx frowned. "So it's not true that your hands sometimes glow with a violet light? The villager who brought you here told the matron he'd seen you do it."

"That's not magic." A light was just that, a light. It couldn't do anything useful.

Dashan's chuckle filled the room. "I like this one, Alyx."

"Can you do anything else?" Alyx asked her.

Lira shook her head.

"Are you all right here, Lira? Do you get enough to eat, lessons on reading and writing, that sort of thing?"

"Yes." Even though she still went to bed hungry, she received meals daily at the orphanage, and that hadn't always been the case back in the village.

"That's good. Thank you for talking to me today, Lira." Alyx smiled. "It was nice to meet you. Do you have any questions for me?"

"Why aren't you afraid of me?"

Alyx's smile widened. "Because there's no reason to be. Magic usually breaks out in mages anywhere between thirteen to eighteen years old, although you might be early given you already have the light. When it happens, you'll be welcome at Temari Hall. I'll make sure the matron here knows to send you to us. I look forward to seeing you there."

Dashan had shifted then, opening the door for Alyx as she rose from her chair. His voice dropped to a murmur, but Lira could still hear him. "You don't think we should take her with us?"

"And put her in the middle of all the prying eyes of Karonan? I think that might be even worse than the childhood she'll have here." Alyx had sounded troubled. "You know how some people..." Her voice trailed off, dropping even lower.

"Best word of her not spread further than necessary." Dashan nodded, glanced at Lira before returning to Alyx. "Let's make sure the matron is paid well to keep an eye on her."

"Good idea. And we'll get any mages travelling through Dirinan to drop in and check on her until she breaks out. They can also make sure nobody..."

A brief silence as they began walking away, then Alyx, barely audible: "She has his eyes, Dash. If I had any doubt before I came here about those villagers' claims…"

"She's got more than just his eyes. That look she skewered you with… that was…." Their voices faded away completely then.

Lira waited another moment, then rose from her chair and walked to the window where she could watch as Alyx and Dashan spoke with the matron on the front steps while two other mages lingered in the snowy street. After a few moments they all clambered into a carriage and drove away.

A hunger woke in Lira then, a shaft of hope that pierced the endless dark hole in her and made it briefly less oppressive. A hunger not for food. Or for warmth.

For welcome.

One day she could go to Temari Hall. And they would welcome her. And even if they didn't… well, her mother had spoken of others too, that would want her. If she could find them.

Those who still fought in her grandfather's name.

CHAPTER 4

The familiar mix of wariness and isolation settled over Lira's shoulders as she walked through the gates of Temari Hall. It was an old friend, one as familiar as an old pair of boots, worn and perfectly fitted.

It was well past curfew for initiates, but third and fourth year apprentices were given more leeway than the younger students, and they took full advantage of it. Although in Lira's case, it wasn't to spend her nights hanging out in the tower's common rooms or enjoying the inns of north Karonan.

Beyond the front gates was a circular pebbled drive, wide enough to handle several carriages at once, with a grassy circle and graceful weeping tree in the centre. Lit torches lined the drive, keeping the Temari Hall entry bright and welcoming at all hours of the day and night.

Instinctively uncomfortable with being so visible, Lira turned left once she was through the gates and walked around the outside of the drive, beyond the pools of light cast by the torches. Here it was just soft grass and carefully landscaped gardens.

Alyx Egalion had designed her school for mages as an echo of her Rionnan palace childhood home right on the edge of the Shiven capital. Lira wasn't sure whether that was hubris, homesickness, some misguided attempt to bring the two countries closer together, or all of the above. Either way, nobody in Karonan liked it. Not that anyone said that aloud within hearing distance of mages.

Shiven Leader Tarian Astohar held a firm grip over the city and his governing officials, and he was a close ally of Tregaya and Rionn, the kingdoms he and his rebels had allied with in the war to defeat Shakar and his Shiven army. The Taliath general at his side bolstered his strength and made him almost untouchable. But things were very different outside the city, where Astohar's reach and influence weren't as strong, and where many held allegiances to the way things had been under the previous leader.

Lira had once asked during a strategy class how Astohar maintained power given Shivasa was the only kingdom on the continent that allowed its citizens to vote for their leader.

"Astohar came to power because his rebels, allied with Egalion and her army, defeated the previous Shiven leader and Shakar, and because the kings of Tregaya and Rionn backed him. He's held power since because of creative management of the voting process," her master had answered, then completely lost Lira when he went on to explain the intricacies of how the voting process had been administered so that it skewed in Astohar's favour.

Lira's quick stride brought her around to where the circular drive ended in front of the school's signature building, a graceful tower reaching high into the sky. Two more apprentices stood guard at the top of the steps leading to the open double doors of the tower entrance—where the mage initiates and apprentices slept and studied.

She didn't like the apprentices on guard knowing she'd been out of the grounds late, but being caught sneaking in or out would look even more suspicious. So she'd cultivated a reputation for occasionally taking walks along the river at night—leaning into the general view of her as an aloof and unfriendly student who liked to get away from everyone as much as possible.

One of the guards she didn't recognise, but the other was familiar from her Mapping class. A quick search of memory dragged up the name Perin. She usually didn't bother to take note of her classmates' names but Perin was annoyingly outspoken in class.

"Spider. Out for one of your creepy walks?" Perin gave her a brisk nod, looking her up and down as if to satisfy himself she posed no threat. He was one of the ones that hid his unease around her with bluster and false bravado. The other apprentice stayed well away, shooting her a wary look, but saying nothing.

Lira ignored them both as she walked through the doors and into the hall, heading for the sweeping staircase immediately ahead that would take her up to the higher levels.

Spider. Lira had been bestowed the nickname barely a month after her arrival at the mage academy. It set her apart, made the younger students afraid of her and the older ones keen to challenge her in any competition. It made for no friends.

But that was what you got for being the granddaughter of the most powerful, and evil, mage to ever walk the world. Especially when her hands lit up with the same striking violet as his magic when she used hers—despite having no concussive magic herself.

Especially when she apparently looked just like him.

As she'd grown older and learned more about the Darkmage, Lira had begun to hope that she would have that same power too. That all the hate and fear might be worth something. She'd clung to that hope with everything she had.

If she could be as powerful as him, then she could make them forget about Shakar and remember her instead. She could stop living in the shadow of a man she'd never known. She could take control of her life rather than have it forced upon her.

But she wasn't a mage of the higher order like Shakar.

Accepting that had been so bitterly disappointing it had taken months for the overwhelming despair to settle into a faint but constant ache in her chest, an ache that widened the frightening chasm of emptiness still inside her. Even now the thought made her unhappy, angry, restless. But it was also what pushed her to be better, stronger, to prove that she didn't have to be a mage of the higher order to be the best. And she *would* be the best. It was the only way to wrest her life back under *her* control.

"Late night for you, Lira."

She started from her thoughts at the familiar voice of a fellow third year apprentice leaning against the arch of the library entrance. Mind busy, her feet had carried her along the well-worn path to the second level where the school's library took up most of the floor. An exit at the back of the stacks served as a shortcut up to the eastern side of the fourth floor dormitory level where her room was.

"Is it?" she asked, slowing reluctantly.

"You're normally tucked up in bed at this time, no?" Garan Egalion crossed his arms, lazy smile on his face as he regarded her. His grey apprentice robe was half off one shoulder, and his brown hair was even messier than usual, like he'd been running his hands through it deliberately. Which he probably had. He no doubt thought it made him more charming.

She wasn't charmed.

"While you're normally *anywhere* but in the library," she countered. In fact, she was never in bed at this hour. She usually didn't get to sleep until well after midnight, snatching a few hours' rest before rising at dawn to start the day. But nobody knew that. They thought she retired to her room early each night because she had nothing else to do, and that suited her just fine.

He leaned towards her, voice dropping to a mock-conspiratorial whisper. "I'll tell you my reason if you tell me yours."

"That only works if I'm interested in what you're doing, which I'm not." Irritation rose, and she glanced into the library, wondering if it was worth her dignity to push past him. She decided it wasn't. It crashed down on her then, how much this place wore on her. How inane it so often felt. As quickly as the feeling had come, she pushed it away.

She had a task from the Shadowcouncil now. That was something to focus on. Something to *do*.

His grin only widened. "Are you excited about tomorrow?"

"You mean, am I excited about beating you? Not particularly. It's only an exhibition match." She glanced past him again, wishing he'd stop talking. The fewer people who saw how late she was heading back to her room the better.

He scoffed in disbelief. The exhibition matches were traditionally held the day before mid-winter break, and the inevitable duel between Lira and Garan had been building for the three years they'd been at Temari Hall. The two strongest telekinetic mages at the academy were a drawcard that nobody intended to miss. Lira hadn't been faking her lack of excitement though. The only thing she intended to get out of the match was a decisive win. One step at a time to making them all see *her*. Respect her.

A new voice made them both straighten sharply. "How about you both head off to your rooms and get some rest before the match?"

The mild but firm tone of the master librarian had Lira cursing under her breath—he was the last person she wanted to notice her out of her room so late. Especially since she was going to be robbing him sometime over the next week. Garan was too self-involved to make anything of it, but Master Finn A'ndreas was the smartest man in Karonan. Not even Lira was willing to tangle with him.

"Yes, sir." Lira nodded respectfully.

"Sir," Garan echoed, a sober look squashing the charming grin he'd been wearing.

Lira ducked past A'ndreas to head for her shortcut. She had no desire to prolong their interaction with conversation—it would just make him more likely to remember the encounter later. And she needed him not to be thinking that she'd been behaving oddly when he realised the report he'd gotten from Duneskal was missing.

"Lira?" The master's voice followed her, and she cursed inwardly before turning around.

"Yes, sir?"

"I'll be travelling to Alistriem for the mid-winter break. Is there anything you'd like me to bring back from the palace library?"

King Cayr Llancarvan kept a massive, well-stocked library even more impressive than the one in Temari Hall. It was almost as grand as the one in Carhall, not that Lira had ever seen either. Despite her deliberate aloofness, Master A'ndreas had always welcomed Lira's interest in his library and her voracious reading habit—something he encouraged by bringing books from Alistriem where she had an interest.

He thought she loved knowledge, learning, reading about new things. He had no idea of the real reason behind her interest in his library, and she had no interest in clearing up his misconception. He probably wouldn't even understand it properly if she did.

"No thank you, sir. I've got plenty to read at the moment." She squashed the urge to question him about when exactly he was leaving and how long he'd be gone.

He nodded, eyes creasing a little as if he wanted to say something more, but she walked away without another word, hoping to keep him from speaking further. Finn A'ndreas was a clever man, a firm but kind teacher. But none of that made up for who he was, or what her life had been. She didn't need friends or mentors. It was too late for any of that.

"Night, Lira! See you tomorrow," Garan called out, a laughing note in his voice. Because of course he was amused rather than chastened. It wasn't like *he* would be in trouble for being out after curfew. Not when the library master was also his uncle.

Everything about Garan Egalion was designed to make her dislike him. Son of the influential Ladan Egalion and Dawn A'ndreas, the kingdom of Rionn's Lord-Taliath and Lord-Mage respectively, he was also the nephew of Alyx Egalion, the world's most powerful mage and head of Temari Hall. That meant everything came easy to Garan and always would. He coasted by in his studies and charmed everyone and everything around him. All qualities that she detested.

Yet he was the only apprentice that ever talked to her in a friendly way, seemingly not put off by her name or her determined reluctance to engage with anyone. He treated her like he treated everyone else at Temari. But even that annoyed her—nobody was that friendly, that tolerant. It was a mask he wore just like hers. Only his was formed of ease and privilege, while hers came from constant, desperate clawing for survival.

Lira pushed open the door to her tiny dormitory room, sparing only a brief glance for the empty bed inches apart from her own. She'd not once had a roommate throughout her three years at Temari Hall. Nobody wanted to share a room with Spider.

It was something else to use to her advantage. The last thing she wanted was another person invading her space, making her uncomfortable. Friends were an unnecessary annoyance. It wasn't like you could rely on them.

She'd learned that lesson many times over.

LIRA WOKE at dawn the next day, and made her way along with the rest of the initiates and apprentices down to the dining hall for breakfast. It sat across a pretty garden from the tower's back entrance, the path leading to it wide and surfaced with crushed pink-coloured pebbles. The previous night's snowfall had already been swept to either side of the path.

Her thoughts were busy as she walked, already tackling the problem of getting into Master A'ndreas' private office in the library, and failing finding the report in there, his private rooms on the grounds. Him being away for mid-winter, along with most of the school, was going to make access much easier, but it also worked against her. A'ndreas was a clever man, and when he realised the report was missing, the suspect pool was going to be too small.

She'd already decided she'd have to copy the report and deliver that to Greyson, rather than take the original. That way A'ndreas would never know it was gone.

She'd have to break into his office at night. That would give her time to search and then copy the document out. A little smile tugged at her face at the thought, one she quickly dispelled. She'd promised herself she wouldn't let... But before she could finish that thought, the noise spilling out from the dining hall interrupted her, a welcome distraction as she stepped inside it.

A long, single-story building, it was filled wall to wall with rectangular tables that seated the hundred and twenty-two students living at Temari. It was always a loud and airy space, but today it was even more raucous than usual. The conversation was conducted in excited tones, its noise mixing with trays clattering down on tables, chairs dragging along the stone floor and cutlery ringing against plates and bowls.

Lira lined up for her tray of food—a bowl of oatmeal, two slices of toasted bread, and a small dish of jam—then carried it to a table along the far wall, as far from where everyone else was sitting as possible. There she sat, alone, and ate hungrily.

Nobody looked her way, accustomed by now to Spider's solitary habits. She wondered sometimes how many meals she would have to skip for anyone to notice she was missing.

Loud laughter erupted from the table in the centre of the hall where Garan Egalion sat. His arm was slung around his current girl's shoulder, a laughing grin on his handsome face, his free hand spooning oatmeal and preparing to flick it at one of his friends sitting across from him. The cluster of tables in the middle of the hall was the dais from which the brightest stars of Temari Hall—either pureblood mage lineage or kingdom nobility or both—held court every mealtime.

Everyone else sat at tables further away. How much further was dependent on their status and popularity. At the moment, those sitting along the outer edges of the room were mostly initiates. Only a few months into their first year at Temari, they'd not yet had the opportunity to win accolades or build relationships. Second year apprentices with no pureblood mage connections sat a little closer in, and so forth.

The apprentices gathered at the tables around Garan were laughing along with him, their moods bright and excited. There were no classes today because of the exhibition matches, and then they were all leaving tomorrow, either going home or travelling for the two week midwinter break.

Lira looked away as bitterness swelled in her chest. She was neither nobility nor pureblood mage—Shakar might have been the most powerful mage that ever lived, but he'd been born of non-magic parents. And nobody had a clue who Lira's parents had been. Even if she'd wanted a spot amongst the centre tables, it would never be hers.

They were so carefree, so unaware. She often wondered what it would feel like to have such a golden life unimpeded by needing to worry about staying warm or finding enough food to eat. To feel such simple and unrestrained happiness.

Temari Hall gave her food and clothes now, while she learned there, but never far from her mind was that one day soon she'd graduate as a mage and have to make her own way again. Unrestrained happiness wasn't for people who knew how quickly fortunes could turn bad.

Lira ate as quickly as she could, annoyed and uncomfortable in the raucous holiday atmosphere, and stacked her tray before striding quickly from the hall and back to the tower.

Walking past the main entrance, she slowed at the sight of the courtyard outside busy with people crowding around an ornate carriage and its fine horses. Snow drifted down from the sky in soft flakes. Alyx Egalion and her husband were leaving for Alistriem today, not that Lira could see either of them amongst the blue-cloaked mage warriors and handful of Taliath surrounding the carriage.

The sight made her roll her eyes. What need did Egalion have for a protection detail? She was the most powerful mage alive, not to mention the Taliath invulnerability to magic she'd absorbed from her Taliath husband. No assassin would ever get near her.

Appearances mattered, she supposed, and it probably wouldn't do for a Mage Council member to travel around without visible trappings of their wealth and power. Lira made a note of it. She would need those trappings one day.

Dismissing the activity in the courtyard, she turned and made for the library, already longing for the days ahead. Master A'ndreas would remain for the exhibition matches along with all the other masters, but most of them would leave the next morning. Only one master would be in residence for the next two weeks—to keep an eye on the handful of students staying.

She'd wait a single night after A'ndreas left, to be extra cautious, then she'd make her move the following night. All going well, she'd find what Underground wanted, copy it out before dawn and get it straight to Greyson. If not, she'd have another night to complete the task and still get it to Greyson before a week had passed. She doubted the Shadowcouncil would do anything permanent to harm her if she failed in their task—there weren't any other heirs to the Darkmage lying around, after all—but the consequences would no doubt be unpleasant.

An unbidden spark of excitement flickered in the base of her stomach, one she crushed without thought or hesitation, well-practiced now. Just as smoothly she switched her thoughts back to the next couple of weeks. Free of the tedium of lessons and irritation of other students constantly *around*, Temari Hall would be quiet and free. Avoiding the handful of other students also staying was easy. She could be properly alone. The tightness in her chest loosened a little at the thought.

For now, she planned to use the no-doubt empty library to get a start on homework from Mapping and Languages classes. Not to mention scribble down the notes she needed for her *other* project.

Once that was done, she'd turn her mind to planning out her approach to A'ndreas' office and rooms. It would have to be well-considered. Getting caught would be a disaster in all senses of the word, her plans over before they'd even begun. Part of her remained curious as to why the Shadowcouncil was so interested in whatever Duneskal was doing for him...

Lira dismissed her musings. It didn't matter why they wanted the information. They'd finally given her something meaningful to do, and she had no intention of wasting the opportunity.

CHAPTER 5

Temari Hall was purpose built for the training of mages and Taliath. Constructed after the Darkmage had half-destroyed the previous mage academy, DarkSkull Hall, it even had a space designed specifically for magical duels. A large, domed, chamber sprawling along the southern wall facing the lake, the interior of the duelling building was able—with magical assistance—to withstand extremes of heat, cold, fire, as well as powerful winds and concussive magic.

Mage apprentices planning to become warrior mages trained in there when the weather was bad and they couldn't use the outdoor training courts, but otherwise it was only used for the yearly exhibition day which marked the halfway point of the teaching year and the beginning of mid-winter break.

The final match of the day—as always—would be a battle between Temari Hall's First and Second combat patrols. A holdover from the days before the war ended, the patrols were formed of handpicked students, Temari's strongest apprentices, whose role it would be to help the masters defend Temari Hall if it came under attack.

Lira fought an eyeroll at the thought. The possibility of the mage school being attacked had become so remote since the end of the war that the patrols were now mostly ceremonial.

As were these exhibition matches. They were all for show.

Maybe *that* was what the Shadowcouncil was waiting for. The idea occurred to Lira as she leaned against the back wall watching two second year apprentices battling each other in the raised circular arena at the centre of the dome. Cheering students surrounded it. The place was raucous with noise, but Lira paid no attention to it, instead chasing her thought.

Maybe they were waiting for the experienced mage warriors to lose their edge, their taste for fighting. Their knowledge of how to win a war.

After all, no mage trained at Temari Hall had any battle experience. They knew how to duel in practice conditions, but that was it. They'd never come under threat, seen loved ones, comrades, killed or injured. They were softer. Inexperienced. And eventually those who *had* fought in the war would grow old, die.

The cheering rose to a chaotic pitch, drawing Lira back to the present. The fight ended with the fire mage coming out the victor over her concussive mage opponent. Her friends whooped and whistled as she stepped down. Master Nordan took the steps quickly and strode into the middle of the arena, waiting for the cheers to quiet. Tall, lean, with a narrow face and fair skin, Nordan was another hero of the war. An ice-mage, he'd fought at Alyx Egalion's side, and now held the title of combat master at Temari Hall.

"Apprentices Astor and Egalion, you're up," he said, his expression not changing at the muttered hum of excitement and anticipation that swept through the room. If it wasn't enough that the two strongest telekinetic mages at Temari Hall were about to do battle in public for the first time, then the fact that an Egalion was facing down the Dark-mage's heir was enough to send the tension in the room to a fever pitch.

The moment Garan appeared though, taking the steps two at a time with an ebullient and infectious energy, the cheers went up even louder than before. Lira blocked the noise out as she weaved through the packed bodies and took the steps up onto the opposite side of the platform. There were no matching cheers for her.

The room was so full of students and teachers that the space was warm despite the lack of fireplaces and the bitterly cold winter wind that howled outside. Garan was grinning, lapping up the attention of the crowd, his stance loose and relaxed.

Nordan lifted a hand, and the cheering gradually faded to silence. "You know the rules. No attacks aimed to seriously injure or kill. You win when you force your opponent to surrender. Any questions?"

Lira said nothing, her attention fixed on Garan. The avid gazes of those watching didn't make her nervous or uncomfortable. She *wanted* them watching this. She wanted them to see her beat Garan. More than that, she wanted Nordan and the other masters in the room to see it.

A trickle of excitement went through her, leaking out from behind her hard-won control, and part of her wanted to hold onto it, savouring it like a drink of water after a long trek through the desert. It might just be an exhibition match, completely meaningless, but it was a chance to really use her magic, to feel the sweet thrill of it through her blood.

Instead she closed the excitement down, steadied her breathing and her focus. This had to be done with precision and concentration, no room for mistakes or lapses in control. She had to give them what they wanted to see. A disciplined student.

"Understood, Master Nordan," Garan said.

The expectant hush was almost palpable as Nordan swept off the platform, his mage cloak swinging around his ankles.

Lira's arms hung loosely at her sides, but she allowed a trickle of her magic out, enough to light her hands up in a violet glow. Someone gasped.

"Go!" Nordan barked.

Garan unsheathed his staff in a single, graceful movement, and then he was moving across the platform towards her. Lira met him stride for stride, and the first *crack* of their staffs slamming together ripped through the thick, anticipatory silence.

Garan was strong and confident. Lira was much smaller, had never grown as much as she would have liked, but she was quick and agile. His first near-miss—a blow almost taking out her ankles—had the crowd roaring back to its loud cheering. All of them were shouting Garan's name.

Nobody in that crowd wanted Lira to win.

They surged back and forth for a few minutes, testing each other, settling into the rhythm of staff combat. She welcomed the sheen of sweat on her skin, the quick rasp of her breathing, the warmth of exertion in her muscles. Even better was the hum of magic in her blood, its insistence on coming out, the sweet rush of strength it gave her.

Garan was the first to use magic, tugging at the end of her staff to shift it off course when she tried to sweep it at his head. Lira moved with the momentum, swinging away from him, switching her staff to her left hand and making a sharp tugging motion with her right. Magic surged through the space between them. His staff was ripped from his hands and flew through the air.

He was quick, though, using magic to call his staff back before it was over the crowd, sending it arrowing at Lira's head. She ducked away, spun her staff and swung it towards his ankles. He jumped to avoid the blow, snatched his staff out of the air, and lunged straight at her stomach.

Another burst of magic sent it veering sideways before it could catch her.

The stamping and cheering had become a distant hum, Lira's focus almost entirely on Garan and the fight now. She knew she was good enough to beat him—had spent hours and hours in the training hall and outdoor courts over the past two years to ensure she was good enough to beat anyone at Temari.

But she wanted to do more than beat him. She wanted to do it quickly. No long, drawn-out affair where he could make it look like he was a match for her.

No student at this school was a match for her.

She swung gracefully away from Garan's next swing, a strong but telegraphed attack, her shoulders spinning, staff loose in her grip. And as she swung, her gaze took in the avid expressions of the watching students, the arched windows along the side of the dome, the lightly falling snow, and... Lira stumbled.

Garan didn't hesitate to attack at her mistake, and Lira was on the back foot for the first time, scrambling to clear space for herself while simultaneously trying to get another look out the windows, at the passing figure wheeling a cart of supplies towards the kitchens.

There had been something... she blinked, concentration split between the duel and figuring out what had set her senses alight. There'd been nothing obviously wrong with what she'd seen. Deliveries happened all the time, and each was cleared by the guards on the front gates before entering the compound.

She was being a fool. The fight had dragged out too long already, she needed to finish it now.

Dismissing everything but Garan Egalion from her head, she went at him with a flurry of bows, feet dancing, magic used in quick, targeted bursts to keep him on the defensive, off balance. Neither his strength nor his skill matched hers. Nor could he come close to matching her quickness.

Lira pushed him across the floor, relentless, until he was almost backed against the ropes. By now he'd lost the easy grin and loose stance, his face taut with focus and determination. Right before he hit the ropes she pulled back a little, just the faintest of hesitations, aiming to make him think she was tiring, that he had a chance to force his way out of the corner she was pushing him into.

He fell for it and lunged forward, *almost* too fast for her. She swayed aside as his staff plunged through the space where she'd just been standing, then used his momentum against him and yanked his staff out of his hands with a burst of magic. It flew across the arena at the same moment her leg swept in behind his left ankle, hooking and shoving upwards.

He fell hard to the mats, air whooshing out of his lungs. When he lifted a hand to call for his staff, she channelled more magic, slamming it into his and making it a contest of strength. Some of the cheers changed to cries of shock and surprise when Garan's staff moved further and further out of his reach. Lira's teeth gritted as she used her will and the strength of her magic to utterly dominate his.

Then, while he battled her, uselessly trying to drag his staff back, she spun hers in her free hand and placed it at his throat. "Do you concede?"

He was panting, skin flushed, sweaty tendrils of hair plastered to his forehead. Thwarted frustration flashed over his face for a moment, but then his whole body relaxed and he let out a weary chuckle. "I concede."

Triumph flooded her. A fierce satisfaction. The cheering had faded to a quiet murmur somewhere in the last few moments of the fight when it had become clear Lira was going to win, so Nordan's boots were audible as he climbed the steps into the arena. Lira removed her staff from Garan's throat and walked away.

"That was well done, Lira," Nordan said, wry amusement on his face. "The fastest duel win I've seen here yet, I think."

"Thank you, sir," she said.

Garan clambered to his feet and walked over to pick up his staff. "Well fought, Lira."

She acknowledged him with a nod.

"Right, time for the last match of the day." Nordan's voice grew louder. "First and Second combat patrols up here, please."

As soon as he declared the fight, Lira turned and almost ran down the steps. The crowd parted for her, the looks coming her way the familiar mix of unease and wariness. Some held real fear.

She ignored them, making straight for the exit, the sweat on her skin freezing when the cold wind outside touched it. She barely noticed, boots following the myriad footprints in the snow in the direction of the kitchens. Dinner prep hadn't started yet, so only a single servant was there, sharpening a set of knives.

"Did you just get a delivery?" Lira asked.

He looked up from his work. If he was surprised by a panting, sweaty apprentice asking him questions about deliveries, he didn't show it. "Sure. The usual Sixthday boxes of tapers. We go through them in here like you wouldn't believe, 'specially during winter when it's dark most hours we're working."

"Was it the usual delivery person?"

He shrugged. "Usually a different one every couple weeks."

"Can I see the delivery?"

"Sure." He slid off his chair, led her over to where two large boxes had been stacked just inside the door of the storeroom. "Is there some kind of problem?"

Lira crouched, opened the first box, and saw rows and rows of candles arranged neatly. The faint scent of vanilla wafted up to tease her senses. The second box was identical. "And this was all? Nothing strange about the delivery."

"No, just the usual. She dropped the boxes, took payment, left."

Lira rose to her feet and let out a breath. She was a fool, her brain overtired from long nights and not enough sleep, not to mention the adrenalin of being in the middle of a duel. She'd clearly imagined what she thought she'd seen in the delivery person, a familiarity that didn't exist.

"Sorry to bother you," she muttered.

"Not at all. Gets lonely in here this time of day, don't mind the break." He smiled.

She was halfway back to the tower, intending on more study, when she realised the servant hadn't looked or sounded afraid of her. That almost made her smile. But her thoughts were quickly moving on, already planning her evening.

She would go to the library to study, and at the same time, keep a discreet eye on A'ndreas' office. She'd wait until he left to go back to his rooms, and watch to see where he put the keys to his office. Check that he didn't carry any papers away with him.

The Shadowcouncil were going to get their report.

And she was going to prove her worthiness.

CHAPTER 6
BEFORE

Lira was seven years old the second and third times she almost died.

She'd been at the orphanage almost two years by then. Already small for her age when she'd arrived, she hadn't grown appreciably bigger or displayed any magical abilities beyond the occasional flash of violet light—something she couldn't control.

The matron mostly ignored her. The other adult workers at the orphanage steered clear of her after learning who she was. But the other children, mostly those too old, unruly, or unattractive—or some combination of the three—to ever be chosen for adoption, were emboldened by the growing evidence that Lira might not actually be as dangerous as they had initially feared.

It had started with stares and whispers. Graduated to "accidentally" running into her in the corridor, spilling ink on her work when they were in class—the orphanage didn't make a huge effort at education for their charges, but ensured they could at least read and write—or putting spiders in her bed. Once a rat had been let loose in her chest of belongings.

When none of this resulted in Lira turning into a raging monster and eating them all, when Lira didn't visibly respond at all—apart from to grow even more distant and aloof in the hopes of them leaving her alone—they grew bolder.

She thought of pushing back, of trying to make it stop so that she'd just be left alone, but she didn't know how. She was smaller than them. She didn't know how to fight. She didn't know what words to use that would convince them to stop. Going to the matron wasn't an option—the bullying often happened right in front of her and she did nothing. All she could think to do was to stay silent and hope they got bored of tormenting her.

But her refusal to respond only made them more determined to get some sort of reaction out of her.

Six girls trapped her in the bathing room one morning. It hadn't been about who Lira was by then... it had just been about making her hurt. Turning someone they didn't understand into someone they could control. Someone they could bully into submission. All Lira had felt, though, was terror and despair and a desperate desire for it to end as they shoved her head repeatedly into a bucket of icy water.

They laughed as they did it. Egged each other on. Dared themselves to keep going.

"Go on, beg us," one of them taunted. "Beg us to stop and we will."

Lira fought, struggling bitterly in their bruising hold, but it was no use. They were so much bigger and stronger. One twisted her arm behind her back so painfully she screamed before her cries were muffled by the icy water closing around her head.

Even then she fought. *Kept* fighting. Her jaw smashed against the wooden edge of the bucket, her bare knees scraped repeatedly against the rough stone floor. And the harder she fought, the harder they held onto her, crushing her wrists with how fiercely they gripped them. But a stubborn spark inside her refused to give up.

On the sixth dunking, they held her head just a little too long under the water, and she broke, gasping, sucking water into her lungs. Spots covered her vision. Her lungs burned. Her bitter struggles began to fade. When they yanked her out this time they let go of her arms, allowing her to slump to the ground.

The matron came in as Lira lay sprawled on the floor, choking, blackness closing over her vision. The woman pumped her chest mercilessly, just managing to get Lira to vomit it all back up before she drowned.

But it was a close thing.

The matron carried her out of that room with a bleeding gash on her jaw, knees scraped raw, livid bruises along her arms, a dislocated shoulder, and a cracked rib from the attempts to save her.

THAT NIGHT, when she'd recovered enough strength to get out of bed, she left the orphanage. She didn't tell the matron. She simply wrapped her second set of clothes inside the blanket from her bed, slung it over her shoulder, and limped downstairs once everyone had gone to bed for the night.

The orange glow of firelight spilled into the main foyer from the half-open door of the matron's receiving room. Glancing around to make sure the foyer was empty, Lira limped up to the door, one hand cradling her aching side, and paused in the shadows behind it. Best to make sure those inside were distracted enough not to notice her sneaking past. The sound of two voices speaking softly drifted out. One was the matron, the other an unfamiliar man.

"Last time we spoke you were reluctant to give her up until she was older," he said.

"I get paid well by the council to keep an eye on her." The matron hesitated. "But if she dies under my roof they'll be severely unhappy. I could lose everything. If you pay the fee I'm asking, you can have her. I'll just tell them she ran away."

Lira froze. It was obvious the matron was talking about her.

"The fee is yours," a man's voice replied. "We'll be here to pick her up in the morning."

Lira's heart leapt briefly at her initial thought that someone had come to adopt her. But that hope flicked and died just as quickly. Adoptions didn't happen in whispered conversations after midnight. Nor did the adopting parents bribe the matron to take children. This was something else.

Still, it could be better than staying in this place or braving the streets outside alone.

Turning away, Lira slipped past the door and padded through the hall beyond to the back door out of the kitchens. Nobody saw as she crept out and circled the side of the building to crouch down and linger in the shadows to wait until the front door opened.

When it did, a man of average height, his form hidden beneath a thick cloak, gloves, and scarf, stepped out. The matron closed the door behind him the second he was through it. He glanced around briefly before setting off down the street.

Lira waited until he was almost out of sight, then followed.

The man walked with steady strides, shoulders huddled into his cloak, hands buried deep in his coat pockets for warmth. He paid some attention to his surroundings but never noticed Lira's small form slipping after him in the shadows. This late at night, the streets in this district were empty, its residents long abed, so nobody else saw her either.

He walked for several blocks. Her remaining hopes that he might come from a family that actually wanted to adopt her faded completely as his walk carried him out of the residential area surrounding the orphanage and into a deserted series of streets filled with what looked like warehouses and shops.

Eventually he turned off the street and went into a long, wooden building. A single lantern hung above the front door but otherwise the entire place was cloaked in darkness. She waited until he was inside, made sure nobody else was around, then crept closer. It looked like there might be somewhere to hide down the side of the building where thick shrubbery rustled in the breeze.

Whatever the man wanted her for, it wasn't an adoption. But Lira couldn't stay at the orphanage anymore, not if she wanted to live, and she had nowhere else to go. Maybe he wanted her for some other reason that wasn't bad.

Glancing around, she slipped through the gate, one hand lifting to her nose at the smell emanating from the place. The scent was of blood and dead flesh... one she remembered from the village market when her mother had sold furs to the tanner.

The bushes *were* thick and she pushed through as quietly as she could, moving far back from the street so nobody passing would spot her. Eventually she found a section of glass set into the crumbling wall. It took a moment to realise it was a cellar window; a curtain on the inside had been drawn across it, but some of the glass was cracked and broken. The soft sound of voices from inside the cellar had her crouching beside it to listen.

Though not as bad as out on the windy streets, the cold still sank deep into her, making her ribs throb and body shiver uncontrollably. She covered herself with the blanket and second set of clothes she'd taken with her from the orphanage and settled in to try and hear what was being said.

The sound of chairs sliding across a hard floor came through the broken window first. Then footsteps, too many to count, the murmur of conversation rising, then fading completely as the footsteps moved out of her hearing. None of it was clear enough that she could make out what was being said.

She was considering sneaking inside to get a little closer when the click of a door opening sounded nearby. Her heart thudded and she pressed herself into as tiny a ball as she could manage.

People walked through the bushes right past her, though they moved quietly, as if they didn't want to be noticed either. She was too scared to count them, though not all those leaving walked past her—some were heading away from where she sat. Eventually the door closed with another click, and silence reigned.

The cold of the night was deepening, dangerously so, and Lira had just decided to give up and move on—whatever this was, it didn't feel right—when the voices started up again, this time almost in her ear. She stilled. Whoever was speaking must have moved directly under the window.

"We can get her in the morning as long as we pay the promised fee." It was the voice of the man she'd followed here.

"Good. Make sure you go early, I don't want to lose out on this opportunity." The voice was muffled, indistinct, but sounded female. Maybe whoever it was wore a scarf masking their face. "What news from Lord Anler?"

"They have considered your offer, and it is acceptable to them."

This man had a clean, smooth voice, different from the man Lira had followed. "But they have conditions."

"And those are?"

"Your rabble consults with the network before undertaking any action, and you will report on how and when you use the resources provided."

"You know what resources I'm interested in. I want the children."

"That has already been agreed." A hesitation. "You will need a name, something to inspire interest, loyalty. And you will need..." His voice trailed off, as if he didn't want to say the words aloud.

"I don't take orders from your lord," the woman responded. "If all goes well in the morning, you will be the ones needing *us*."

A long, drawn-out silence.

A sharp gust of wind sprang up, whipping a branch into Lira's face and poking her eye hard. She cried out without thinking at the sudden pain.

"Who's there?" The man's voice was sharp.

"Find them, now." The cold in that muffled voice pierced Lira to her core.

She scrambled to her feet and ran, cursing herself for not having done it sooner. These people were no safer an option than remaining at the orphanage. No, she was on her own.

She was several blocks away before she slowed, out of breath and in pain, her ribs protesting every movement. She forced herself to keep walking, keep moving, wanting to get far away from both the orphanage and whoever those people were.

That night was the third time she almost died.

A bitter wind screamed through the streets, and she walked for miles, not knowing where she was going, only that she needed to get away from everyone who knew her if she wanted to survive. She eventually found herself deep in a much rougher area down near the harbour. It smelled bad. It was darker. The streets turned from cobblestone to mud.

Her hands and feet had gone numb, her body shivering uncontrollably, ribs and shoulder aching unbearably. It sank into her exhausted thoughts at some point that even though she'd run away to survive, she was going to die anyway if she didn't find somewhere warmer to hole up.

Drawn by the lights and noise from the district along the docks, even at this late hour, and their false sense of safety, Lira eventually found a bolt hole in the eaves of a gambling den. It was narrow, and low, and she barely fit inside it. But she burrowed in anyway.

As dawn lit the horizon and the activity in the streets outside slowly faded to stillness, Lira was shivering, in pain all over, and hungry. But she was still alive.

FROM THAT DAY she fought a regular battle with starvation and cold. Every night after, Lira had nightmares of being held down by the stronger girls, of being unable to move, her violet light flashing uselessly from her hands, ice water closing around her face, filling her eyes and nose, sliding down her throat into her lungs.

On those nights the yawning chasm in her chest grew wider and wider, tugging at her relentlessly, threatening to drown her inside it. Those nights were endless, dragging out until she didn't know what she was fighting anymore, or why, just that she had to keep doing it.

Then, gradually, she became good enough at thieving to keep herself fed and warm. She found a slightly larger bolthole which she filled with enough blankets to kept out enough of the cold that she could survive. Just.

Finally, the nightmares stopped after she met *her*. Even the hole closed over a little.

Lira never returned to the orphanage. Alyx Egalion had said she would be welcome at Temari Hall when her magic broke out. But that time was many years and many miles away.

Lira had to survive until then.

CHAPTER 7

Lira's eyes opened to darkness.

She blinked, taking a moment to confirm she was in her bed. In her room. Nothing moved in the dark. No birds sang outside to welcome the dawn. And the air was still... the eerie stillness of the midnight hour. But *something* was different.

For a start, she felt groggy, like she'd woken abruptly from a deep sleep, yet Lira never slept deeply. She'd mastered a light, watchful rest years and years ago. After reminding herself that she was at Temari Hall, and *that* life was far behind her, she rolled over to go back to sleep.

A distant thud sounded, like a door on one of the lower levels had slammed closed. It was likely nothing. But no matter how far behind she'd left that life, no matter how hard she ran from it, Lira was called Spider for a reason. Surviving as a homeless orphan in the lawless districts of a harbour city in far north Shivasa had required developing sharply-honed instincts. Uncanny instincts.

And right now those instincts were sounding a warning gong in the back of her mind. It was a feeling she hadn't had in a long time, not since arriving at Temari Hall. A shiver ran through her muscles and that ever-present pressure in her chest tightened slightly. This wasn't the right place to be having that feeling. She'd left that behind when she'd left Dirinan. Since then she'd had two years of warmth and food and a comfortable bed. Education and proper clothes and the veneer of comfort and safety.

With the rousing of her instincts came the familiar seductive thrill of danger that set her heart beating the slightest bit faster, that made—

She squashed that feeling furiously, literally closing her fingers into tight fists with the force of it. That wasn't her. Not anymore. She swallowed it down, focused her mind on the present, and sat in the darkness and listened.

No other sounds drifted through the night. She was being paranoid. This wasn't Dirinan. But still... she'd been more deeply asleep than she had in years, and something had woken her from it.

Pushing back the covers, Lira swung her legs over the side of her bed, planting her bare feet on the stone floor, the bite of cold against her skin dispelling the last of the grogginess of sleep. It was the work of a minute to dress and lace up her boots before grabbing her staff where it rested by the door and buckling on its holster over her shoulder.

Her fingers curled on the handle of her door, turning it slowly so that it made no noise, before easing the door open. Nothing moved. No sound broke the stillness. She stepped outside, leaving her door ajar, just in case. The rooms of the other third years in her corridor were closed. The space was dark. The handful of lamps left alight each night had burned out.

Or been deliberately doused.

That excitement began curling in her belly again, but she squashed it even faster this time. Now she was being paranoid *and* foolish. This was Temari Hall, home to the most powerful mage alive and her Taliath husband. As if anyone would dare creep inside with nefarious intent.

Except both had left the day before for Alistriem. Along with most of the students. They'd all paraded out that morning after breakfast, leaving the compound empty apart from those few with nowhere to go and Master Alias—too old and infirm to want to leave his comfortable quarters.

A flicker of irritation at herself went through her. She was allowing misplaced yearning to rise up and mess with good sense. Why would anyone creep into a mostly-empty school?

She would go and find out what the noise had been, confirm that she was being an utter fool, then go back to bed. Decision made, she headed towards the narrow side staircase that led down to the library.

The stone steps echoed hollowly under her boots, and without thinking she reverted to the softer tread of her childhood, when sometimes the ability to move with utter silence had meant the difference between living and dying. That old skin slid over her like it had never left and she breathed it in, let it sink through her bones and refused to acknowledge how it made her feel looser, aware, *alive*.

The door to the library opened onto one of the back stacks, sitting dark and empty. Old books, stacked neatly beside rolls and sheaves of parchment, lined the shelf immediately in front of her, lovingly kept in perfect order by Finn A'ndreas. The thought of him brought her mission for the Shadowcouncil to the forefront of her mind—now she was up maybe she'd take a quick look in his office tonight if all was quiet. The quicker she delivered, the more impressed they'd be with her.

Nothing seemed out of place, so Lira increased her pace, winding her way silently through the stacks toward the open atrium at the library's centre. Thick rugs covered the stone floors there to reduce the amount of noise made by those moving through it. Round tables and comfortable chairs filled the space—an area used for study.

Lira paused before leaving the stacks, instinctively surveying the open area before breaking her cover. It was deserted at this hour, chairs sitting empty and alone, tables bare of books or parchment. The grated fireplace and lamps hanging from the ceiling were unlit. That wasn't unusual given it was mid-winter break, but *something* gave Lira pause.

That warning prickle had returned, rippling down the back of her neck. Her heartbeat steadied, smoothed out, readying for whatever came. The air was unnaturally still, and it was cold, colder down here than it had been up in her room. She felt on edge. Like she wasn't in a safe place. Like she needed to keep a constant eye on her surroundings. It was a learned sense, one she'd never failed to trust. But it was so out of place to feel it here that she couldn't be sure of it.

Her sense of danger had grown so strong that she decided to trust it over the logic that wanted to tell her nothing was wrong. Her breathing quickened, her magic tugging at her control, wanting to be let out to play.

She held her focus with an effort, considering what to do next. The thudding she'd heard from her room seemed like it had come from the ground floor. She would exit the library, take the main staircase down, check in with the apprentice on guard. If they hadn't seen anything, she'd search the floor until she found what was tripping her sense of danger.

Then she'd deal with it.

A wide corridor clear of shelves linked the atrium to the front library entrance. In her state of heightened awareness, Lira's roving gaze noted the dark shape on the floor the moment she stepped out of the stacks. Her eyes had adjusted to the moonlight coming through the high glass windows, so she had no trouble making out that the shape was a body.

It sprawled on the stone floor in front of the closed double doors, dark liquid pooling under it, soaking through a grey apprentice robe. Blood. The familiar rusty tang of it teased Lira's senses as she crouched by the body.

It was a girl, lying on her back, blood trickling down her left side from two deep puncture wounds in her chest, either side of her heart. Her brown Zandian skin was oddly pale in the moonlight, but the rest of her appeared untouched. Lira pressed two fingers to her neck, unsurprised to find no pulse. Her skin was still warm though.

The attack had only just happened.

It was then Lira noticed how cold it had gotten, so cold her nose had grown numb, and her breath was steaming in the air with each exhale.

She rose to her feet, no longer interested in the body. Her entire focus was on the shadowy library around her. Whoever had killed the apprentice was probably still here. Slowly, not wanting to draw attention with quick movements, she lifted her left hand to draw her staff. Her fingers closed around the smooth wood.

The cold deepened, biting into her bones. Nothing stirred in the darkness.

But *something* was there. She was certain of it. And it knew she was here. Her neck crawled with the knowledge of being watched. Hunted. Her mouth curled in anger.

She glanced at the doors—at least ten steps away and closed, possibly locked—then back the way she'd come. Her breathing steadied, focused, her body poised to explode into action.

Melt back into the shadows of the stacks and flee?

Or force the killer out of wherever they were hiding and confront them?

The thrill of extreme danger leapt hot and vibrant through Lira's veins. It surged so strongly that it consumed her before she could stop it, and this time she let herself fall into it, into the rush she'd tried to forget, to push out of herself, to pretend no longer existed. Now she welcomed it back with open arms.

And she broke for the main doors.

At the same instant she moved, a dark shape detached from the shadows atop one of the closest stacks and *seethed* into the space between her and the doors, moving so quickly she couldn't get a proper look at it. It let out an eerie sound as it moved, like old chains rattling along a wooden floor. The sound was infused with triumph, like it was thrilled to have captured prey.

There is a monster in the library.

Lira had time for that single, crazy thought and then she stopped all thinking and threw herself completely into the present.

Her searching gaze caught a flash of silver eyes—flickering and vivid like flame—and a writhing dark mass, before a tendril of dark shadow whipped violently towards her head.

Swearing at how fast it moved, she ducked, violet light sparking brilliantly in the darkness, surrounding Lira's hands as she drew on her magic. The *thing* flashed past inches from the top of her head, the light catching on what looked like some sort of hard carapace.

She hadn't had a chance to recover her footing when another tendril of writhing shadow reached out for her ankle. She made a sharp gesture with her right hand, expending far more telekinesis magic than necessary in her shock, but it had no effect.

She froze for the briefest of seconds, heart thudding in her chest.

Her magic hadn't touched it at all.

The moment of inattention cost her. The limb, now solidified, wrapped around her ankle in a painfully tight grip and yanked.

A cry of anger ripped from her throat as her back hit the floor hard, the breath whooshing from her lungs. She tried magic again as her body was dragged along the floor toward the creature's centre of mass. It still seemed to be mostly darkness and shadow, and she was too focused on getting free of its clutches to get a better look.

Her magic failed again. She couldn't wrap her telekinesis around shadows, and even on the solidified carapace holding her ankle, her magic dissolved before it could get close enough to touch.

"Rotted carcasses!" she gasped the curse out unthinkingly, lungs fighting to suck in air. Forgetting about magic, she began struggling, kicking out at the limb with her free leg, but by then she'd been dragged all the way in. The creature loomed over her, the rattling at a higher pitch now, edged with excitement, hunger. A second shadowy limb curled towards her other ankle. At least two more writhed above her, almost completely caging her in. She twisted to avoid the one seeking a grip on her second ankle, only just moving in time.

The creature leaned closer, giving her a clearer look at it. Two long fangs curved down from a narrow, scaled head. The scales were as black as night, swirling with shadow, making the eerie luminescence of the three silver eyes all that much brighter. All she could see in those eyes was hunger... a desperate, furious hunger, one that could never be truly assuaged.

The fangs dripped with fresh blood. The rattling changed in pitch again, chains clashing together. The sound, along with the ravenous hunger in its gaze, struck an instinctive chord of terror deep into Lira's bones, threatening to take all reason with it.

She brought her staff sweeping upwards, a desperate move to try and make the thing back off. The head swung away to avoid her blow and she sat up, twisting so that she could slam the end of her staff down onto the limb locked around her ankle, hitting it with every bit of strength she possessed.

The creature didn't make much of a sound—only a sharp hiss—but temporarily let go.

Lira dropped the staff and scrambled away on hands and knees, dodging as it lunged down at her again, razor-like fangs slashing past inches from her face and tearing a slice through the shoulder of her tunic. Multiple tendrils of darkness swung towards her, twisting, writhing, seeking her with a hunger she could sense. Somehow she managed to get to her feet, and as soon as she did, she called her staff back to her hand and *sprinted* for the cover of the stacks.

A loud, furious rattle echoed through the atrium, the force of it reverberating in her chest. Just as Lira reached the closest stack and ducked around it, a solidified limb crashed into the shelves where her head had been a second earlier. It gouged through wood and books and sent a large chunk of shelving crashing to the floor.

What in a pound of rotting fish carcasses *was* that thing?

Her thoughts slipped back into the street slang of Dirinan as fear and danger entwined, clarified her thinking, gave her the reckless confidence and poise it always had. As she ran, her mind raced, trying to understand. To process. This could not be happening in Temari Hall —she was dreaming, surely? Or having a hallucination. Could there have been something in her food at dinner? What *was* that thing?

She ducked left into a narrow corridor between stacks, her run fast but light-footed and silent. A glance back showed only darkness and silence behind her, but she didn't make the mistake of thinking she'd lost the monster.

The thing was *made* of shadow and darkness. And it moved with a speed she'd never encountered before, so quick it had almost gotten her killed. Fierce determination rose with the seductive heat of coming so close to dying. She was not going to meet her end being torn apart by some monster in the Temari Hall library. She'd survived too much for this to get her.

A plan crystallised in her racing thoughts. She needed to get clear of it, then get out of the library so she could recoup, figure out what was going on and how best to deal with it. She had to be the one with the upper hand before she faced the thing again.

The cold followed her, the warm exhales of her panting breaths steaming in the moonlit passages between the stacks. She took another sharp turn, angling to try and circle around to an exit that connected the library to the second floor classrooms. When she glanced back and saw nothing, she wondered if she *had* lost the thing. But then the rattling came again, only from somewhere up high.

It was climbing the stacks.

A spike of fear shot through her, hot and thrilling, and she took another sharp turn. Breath rasped in her chest, adrenalin flooding her body, but she slid to a halt when she rounded another corner to be faced with a shivering figure in a grey robe pressed against the shelves, seemingly frozen in place. The apprentice looked at Lira, eyes wide with fear, her cheeks streaked with what looked like tears.

"Who are you?" Lira whispered, turning, eyes scanning everywhere for the creature. She swung her staff in her hand, an outlet for the restless energy pouring through her. She detested the feeling of being *hunted*.

The cowering figured *un*-cowered enough to straighten and stare at Lira, displaying more spine than the tears indicated when she spoke in a snappy retort. "You think introductions are really important right now? What in the sake of all magic *is* that thing?"

"Keep your voice down!" Lira hissed.

To her credit, the girl fell quiet, and they both listened hard. For a moment there was nothing, only a heavy silence. Then it sounded.

A soft rattle. Inquisitive. Seeking.

From above and to their right.

Lira hefted her staff. The rattling moved closer, sounding cautious, like it wasn't entirely sure where they were. She had no intention of giving it time to find out. She started moving again, continuing down the dark passage, looking for the turning she knew would take her down to the exit she was aiming for. The apprentice followed, her panicked breathing in the silence making Lira's skin crawl with frustration.

As she ran, an idea came to her. Seconds later, a triumphant rattle echoed loudly through the dark stacks behind them. It had discovered its prey.

Lira ignored the shiver that ran down her spine as the creature closed in on them from atop the massive bookcases. Parchment and books cascaded from shelves, thudding to the floor, the noise growing louder and closer. The cold deepened to a bone-aching chill.

Lira turned right into the corridor she'd been heading for, then stopped, turning to face the direction of the rattling. The other apprentice ran past her, halting when she realised Lira wasn't following. "What are you doing? Run!"

Lira ignored her. This *thing* was not going to defeat her or send her running like a scared child. She stood feet planted, shoulders apart, one hand lifted and *waiting*...

The creature appeared a heartbeat later, a writhing mass of shadow pouring down over the top of the bookcase directly in front of Lira. It was still too dark to make out exactly what it looked like, how solid it was. She waited until it began to coalesce on the ground, two shadowy limbs solidifying into carapace, then flicked her raised hand, summoned her magic, and brought the entire section of shelving down on top of it.

Or at least that was her intention.

Instead she stared in shock as the creature *shifted* out of the way, scant inches from being crushed completely as wooden shelves and books thundered to the ground. It slid up the nearest bookcase, re-formed, then oriented itself back towards Lira with a loud rattle.

Fear pounded through her then, drowning the thrill of danger until it flickered and died, and Lira turned and ran after the apprentice. Her breath burned in her chest from a mixture of cold and exhaustion, legs turning heavy.

"Left and then right. Look for a side exit with a thick wooden door," she shouted.

Angry rattling broke out again as the creature came in pursuit, closing the distance too rapidly. A tendril of shadow curled along the floor to her right, and Lira zigged desperately sideways before it could solidify and grab her leg.

The apprentice reached the door, yanked it open and dived

through. Lira was only a step behind, slamming it closed and turning the lock the moment she was across the threshold.

She braced it with her body just as the creature crashed into it. A grunt escaped her as the force of the blow shuddered through her bones. The apprentice hesitated, glancing further down the corridor, before letting out a sigh and coming to help Lira.

A second later the creature slammed into it again. They both winced at the impact, but gritted their teeth and held their positions. Lira's gaze slid to the hinges on the door. They were solid iron, and the door was made from thick oak. It would stand up better than the library shelves had.

The next slamming impact had them both stumbling back a step. But they both returned, shoulders pressed against the wood. Lira couldn't help but feel a flicker of respect for the girl who wasn't hesitating to help barricade the door from a monstrous creature presumably keen on eating them both.

"I'm Fari Dirsk, to answer your earlier question," she said, panting. "Shouldn't we be running rather than hoping the door holds?"

"You saw how fast it moved. Better to try and contain it in the library than try and outrun it." Lira grunted with effort as the creature slammed again. The door shuddered worryingly in its frame, but seemed to be holding. The scrape of talons or claws or *something* against the wooden surface on the other side was far less reassuring. "Fari, huh? I've never heard of you."

Fari snorted. "Few have."

Lira spared a quick glance for her unlikely companion. Brown Zandian skin, more full-figured than Lira's scrawny frame, and that tell-tale sparkle in her dark eyes that spoke of good humour. It annoyed her on principle. "I thought Zandians were supposed to be stiff and dour and all that."

"Now there's a sweeping generalisation. I could argue that the Shiven are the haughty, dour ones, and we're the reserved, honourable ones, but perhaps that debate is best left for another time." Fari braced as another thudding impact slammed into them.

It went quiet then, and Lira held herself still, all her senses straining to read what was happening on the other side. Fari waited too, eyes wide.

Something moved at their feet, and Lira looked down, swearing at the sight of shadowy tendrils curling under the door. Dread shivered down her spine and she shifted her feet away.

Fari had both palms braced against the wood, shoulders rigid as she watched the shadows twist around the bottom of the door and begin crawling upwards. "I suppose it must be difficult to learn about other cultures when you don't have any friends. What are you, anyway? Tregayan, Rionnan? It's the subject of much gossip around here."

"You nixed introductions, but you're happy to gossip?" Lira had no idea where she was from. She was fair-skinned enough to remove any chance of being Zandian, and though she'd been born and lived in Shivasa all her life, she didn't have their elongated ears, and her skin wasn't pale enough. It left Tregaya or Rionn. But her mother had never said anything to indicate one way or the other.

"I talk a lot when I'm nervous." Fari shifted her position, eyes glazed and fixed on the shadowy limbs climbing inexorably toward her hands. "Think it can get through under the door?"

"I have no idea, but the second they start to solidify, I'm running."

The tendrils crept halfway up the door, then suddenly stopped. Lira's heart was so loud in the quiet she was sure Fari must be able to hear it. Then, slowly, the shadows began to withdraw.

The sudden crashing into the door had Fari screaming in surprise. The rattling grew louder, increasingly frustrated. Lira set her feet and braced her shoulder, absorbing the next impact as best she could. Satisfaction welled in her. "Keep trying, you're not getting to us," she hissed through the door.

After two more hits, everything went quiet again. Lira pressed her ear to the wood and heard nothing but silence on the other side. No rattling, no books falling. A careful inspection showed the hinges in the door remained stable, so she stepped away from it.

The air noticeably warmed from frigid to the biting cold of an unheated hallway on a Shiven winter's night.

She tried to take a steadying breath, but the adrenalin flooding her system mixed with the aftertaste of fear was leaving her jittery. She lowered her hands to hide their trembling and spoke firmly. "We need to get out of here. It's best if we split up, I—"

"Nope, no way." Fari shook her head vehemently, black hair swinging side to side with her movements. "I'm a poor Zandian excuse for a second year apprentice. If there are more of those things out there, I'm going to get eaten in about two minutes on my own. I'm staying with the one apprentice in this place everyone is scared of."

Lira paused, not even sure where to begin with that tumble of words. She wasn't entirely sure she wasn't still hallucinating. Or dreaming. "Poor excuse?"

"I'm a healer. Not an acceptable magic in pureblood Zandian families. I'm terrible at book learning too, so really it's failure all round for my poor parents. Are we going to move, or wait here until the creature comes back with reinforcements?" she demanded, hands on hips.

"You stay quiet and do as I say," Lira snapped, then set off without waiting for the girl to respond.

WITH NO WINDOWS, the back corridor was even darker than the library had been. Lira summoned enough magic to make her hands glow, letting the feel of it soothe the ragged remnants of fear away. Ignoring Fari's sideways glance at the violet colour, she led the way, cutting off the light as soon as they reached a door.

It opened into an empty classroom. In unspoken accord, they moved cautiously through the rectangular room filled with desks and chairs, eyes scanning anxiously for any movement in the shadows.

Once she'd satisfied herself it was empty, Lira turned to Fari, keeping her voice low. "How many students were in the library with you?"

"Just one." Fari shuddered. "Derna."

"She the dead one on the floor by the entrance?"

Fari flinched, biting her lip. Fresh tears welled in her eyes, visible in the faint light coming through the classroom window. "We've been... she asked me to meet her in the library after curfew."

Oh. A romantic interlude. It explained Fari's loose hair and the fact her mage staff wasn't with her either. Still... "At midnight?"

"I fell asleep studying and woke up later than I'd planned, but I went down just in case she was still there waiting for me." Fari swallowed, breath hiccupping as if she held back a sob. "I found her... like that. It was... crouching over her, but it was too dark to see what was happening. I could tell she was dead and..." Fari swallowed, almost as pale as the body had been now. "I ran before it could see me. Then a few minutes later I heard a loud commotion and then you appeared."

"When you say *crouching* over her, was it eating her? Or smelling her? What?"

"What in magical hells does that matter?" Anger roused in the girl's voice.

"I'm trying to work out whether it killed her, or something or someone else did and the monster was just left to guard the body, *or* the entrance."

Fari's eyes widened in horror. "Your mind must be a scary place."

"You're not the first to say it. Well?" she whispered impatiently.

"I don't know, it's not like I've ever seen a dead body before. Especially one being hovered over by a monster straight out of my nightmares. How many dead bodies have *you* seen?"

"Too many to count." Lira reached the classroom door and paused. "Here's the plan. We make straight for the front entrance, warn the apprentices on guard, and then we find Master Alias, who can deal with the monster situation in the library."

There were only two apprentices on guard during mid-winter. And Alias would struggle walking through the snow to the tower from his residence, let alone be capable of dealing with that monster. But in the absence of so many mages there would be Shiven army soldiers guarding the front gates, at least. Alias could draw on them for help.

Either way, Lira's briskly-relayed plan seemed to settle Fari's increasing agitation at talking about what had happened to Derna. The girl braced her shoulders and nodded. "You're getting a lot of points for being calm and thinking clearly in a crisis, Spider. I'll be right behind you."

"A monster loose in the library isn't a crisis," she muttered, trying not to roll her eyes.

"What would you call it then?"

"A challenging obstacle that will be no match for Shiven warriors and trained mages. Do you think you could manage to stay quiet now?"

Fari drew a finger across her lips and gave a firm nod.

Lira turned the handle and opened the door before stepping out into the dim hall. Turning left and then going straight would take them to a wide staircase leading down to the entrance foyer and the main doors. It wasn't far. Everything was still and silent, as it should be.

So why were her instincts still screaming at her that all was not well, despite knowing the monster was contained for the moment?

"Something wrong?" Fari murmured.

Lira shook her head. Gripped her staff. Headed for the stairs with quiet steps. She'd walked the corridors of Temari Hall at night, after curfew, a hundred times. It had never felt like this before. Like the darkness had palpable weight. Like something was lying in wait around every corner.

A smile curled at her mouth without her even realising. She'd missed that feeling so much. Missed how it made her feel alive. It didn't matter how much she'd tried to forget, to pretend she was perfectly content at Temari. She missed it with everything inside her.

Huffing a breath of irritation at herself, Lira sped up, making her strides long and confident. A glow lit up the hall ahead, light from the main foyer reaching up to the landing of the second floor staircase.

Her boots sank into the thick carpet lining the stairs, Fari only half a step behind as they headed for the bottom. The foyer was just as empty as the stairs and corridor had been. A handful of flickering torches lit the cavernous space. Everything looked completely normal.

"Stay here where it's light," she murmured to Fari. "I'm going outside to see if the apprentices are there. If not, I'll go for the Shiven soldiers on the front gates."

Fari glanced towards the windows, which showed only dark night outside, then looked around the foyer. "If I hear one single rattle, I'm coming out there after you."

"If you hear a rattle, hide." She dismissed the girl, reaching to turn the handle of one of the front double doors.

She stepped quickly into the darkness and then closed the door behind her so that she wasn't illuminated by the light of the foyer. The steps were covered in fresh snow, glinting in the moonlight, but there was no challenge from the apprentices that should have been on guard.

She pressed herself against the wall and lowered herself into a crouch so that she was harder to spot. Then, she waited for her eyes to adjust to the dimness and stared around. There was nobody outside. No apprentices. Nothing moved except for the slowly swaying branches of the trees.

Lira's gaze swept across the dark circular drive—the shadowy willow tree in its centre cut off her view of the main gates, but still, she saw nothing amiss. She wavered between running to alert the guards on the gates or heading through the compound to the northern wall, where the residences for the masters sat and where Alias was no doubt sleeping soundly.

It was the missing apprentices that decided her. Whatever was going on, trained Shiven warriors with swords would do much better against the thing in the library than an elderly weather mage.

She gripped her staff, summoned her magic to readiness, and moved down the steps quickly, keeping to the shadows of the trees around the edges of the drive. Here the snow remained unbroken.

A light breeze rustled the branches around her, swirled the hem of her robe around her ankles, cooled the sweat on her skin. She strained her ears, prepared to retreat at the faintest hint of a rattling sound. The darkness settled around her like a worn, well-loved cloak.

The front gates stood closed, the watchhouse beside them dark. Crouching in the shadows of a tree lining the drive, she watched the area for a few moments, seeing no trace of Shiven guards despite the snow around the gates being churned up from several pairs of boots marching through it. But Shiven warriors were elite, well-trained, and they might not necessarily be visible.

Throwing caution to the wind, she rose and jogged for the watch-house. She hit the first body only a few paces away from the open door of the small stone room. A second body lay across the threshold. Dark red blood stained the white snow around them. A short distance away, closer to the gate, two of the school's guard dogs had fallen, also dead.

Glancing around to make sure the area was empty, she knelt by the first Shiven body. Her gaze went instantly to the man's opened throat, the blood pooled on the ground under his head. She'd seen this kind of kill many times before.

A creature hadn't done this. Someone had expertly slit the throat of an elite soldier before he'd even had the chance to draw his sword. Not to mention taking the dogs out before they could raise the alarm.

A shiver of combined excitement and shock whispered down her spine.

Temari Hall had been infiltrated.

CHAPTER 8

L ira rose from where she was crouched over the dead warrior, then moved silently for the front gates, fitting her strides to the snow already churned up by walking boots so as not to make new tracks. The gates were closed and barred, a new chain wrapped around the mechanism to ensure they couldn't be opened.

She couldn't fly. And the walls of Temari Hall were sheer, deliberately designed so they couldn't be climbed. Her telekinetic magic *might* be enough to rip the gates open, but that would make far too much noise, and the distance to run to reach the causeway and help was significant... too far if she were chased. There was another exit from the grounds of Temari Hall, though, a side gate on the western side of the grounds, where she could—

She froze at the realisation her breath was frosting, the sweat on her skin turning to ice as the temperature dropped.

A soft rattle echoed through the stillness from somewhere behind her.

She spun around, heart thudding, gaze searching the darkness. Nothing moved aside from the tree branches swaying in the night's breeze, but Lira was sure she hadn't imagined the sound. Her neck crawled with the sensation of being stalked. Watched.

Mouth curling in anger at the feeling, at knowing her best play was to run, not stand and fight something that would probably kill her if she tried, she sheathed her staff in one quick movement, and then *ran* back for the main entrance.

As she sprinted, she focused her mind on next steps. Get back inside the tower. Go straight to the back entrance, then sneak through the gardens to the western gate out of the academy without being seen. Cross the causeway and fetch help.

Then figure out what in rotted hells was going on.

The moment her boots crunched through the snow on the pebbled surface of the drive, a loud rattling broke out. It was loud against the silence of the night, hungry, crashing against her ear drums. She glanced back, saw shadows stirring where the creature had clearly been sitting, waiting, in the darkness under the willow tree. Flame-like silver eyes blinked open, focusing on hers. A shudder ran through her body and she tore her gaze away.

Had it been waiting for her? Or just keeping watch for whoever had killed the Shiven soldiers guarding the gates?

She pushed herself harder, legs moving in a flat-out sprint for the doors of the academy. Rattling dogged her steps, and she could almost *feel* the shadowy limbs of the monster reaching for her, spilling toward her running feet, solidifying, grabbing, those curved fangs slashing...

One of the double doors swung open as Lira approached, but by then the creature was almost on her. Movement in her peripheral vision was the only warning she had of a dark tendril whipping down to wrap around her neck.

Swearing, she twisted abruptly sideways, swinging away from it. Something rough and hard scraped along the skin of her neck and she staggered, forced herself back into a run. Hitting the steps, she leapt up them, then dived through the open door just as another limb reached for her.

A frustrated rattle tore through the night, so high-pitched she would have winced if she hadn't been so focused on getting clear of the thing. Lira hit the polished floorboards inside the main entrance, rolled, and came straight back to her feet, one arm reaching up to draw her staff in a single movement.

A questing limb followed her through the opening, but Fari was already slamming the door closed. Lira ran to join her, the creature's leg solidifying as it whipped towards her head.

Skidding to the side to avoid the blow, she caught a proper glimpse as it swung over her ducking head. The leg was formed of interlocking scales about the size of her hand in rippling shades of inky black, with whispers of shadow leaking through the almost invisible cracks between them. Then she was righting herself and joining Fari at the door and shoving her shoulder into it.

Running feet sounded, then someone else was throwing their weight into the door. The leg, or tentacle, or whatever the hell it was, dissolved back into shadow and withdrew just before they slammed it shut.

And then silence.

Lira braced, ready for it to try and break through like the one in the library had, but the silence remained. She gave it another long moment, then tentatively stepped back, ready to lunge forward again.

Fari stepped back too. "I think it's gone."

Lira's eyes narrowed as she shifted her attention to the apprentice that had come to help and recognised him instantly. It was Tarion Caverlock, of all people. Cousin to Garan Egalion, son of Alyx Egalion and Dashan Caverlock. Perfect. Just what she needed... another entitled lordling to deal with.

He frowned, glancing between her and the door as he pushed too-long black hair from his eyes. When he spoke, his voice was low, even in the silence of the foyer. "What were you thinking, going out there on your own like that?"

She opened her mouth to respond, but hesitated, gaze sweeping the lit foyer they stood in. It was too open, too visible, and they'd just made quite the noise slamming the front door closed. The sight of the dead soldier's gaping throat flashed through her mind and unease prickled along her skin.

Gesturing for Fari and Tarion to follow, Lira led them over to the cloakroom off to the left side of the main doors, ushering them inside and pulling the door almost all the way closed.

Given most inhabitants had left for the break, only a few coats and cloaks hung on the racks, and there was plenty of space for the three of them. A shaft of light from the crack she'd left in the door was the only illumination, but it was enough that Lira could make out their faces.

She looked at Tarion, answering his question. "I was thinking there's a monster in the library and I'd fetch help to deal with it," she said. "What in rotted hells is going on?"

"You tell us." Fari was wide-eyed. "Did you find anything out there before that thing chased you back inside?"

"The apprentices on guard are missing and there are three dead Shiven soldiers and two dead guard dogs by the front gates. Someone has closed and barred the gates, then chained up the opening mechanism for good measure."

Fari's eyes widened further in horror. Tarion merely frowned. "Were the soldiers killed by whatever that thing is out there?" he asked.

"You first," she said suspiciously. "What are you doing here?"

"Something woke me up—loud thudding coming from below my room, like a door being slammed closed, or someone trying to break though one. I got to the first floor landing and saw Fari opening the door and you flying through with some kind of... monster on your tail, so I ran to help." His hazel eyes darted constantly to the floor as he spoke, as if holding her gaze was too hard. "Is that what woke me? There's another one of those monsters in the library?"

She blinked at him, taken aback. Despite his inability to look at her when talking, he'd spoken like he was describing what he'd eaten for dinner, calm and precise. No trace of panic or fear.

"It's not particularly clear what's going on," Fari answered. "But yes, there's one in the library too. Whatever it is, it's big, extremely fast, and it drinks blood."

"It *what*?" Lira rounded on her.

Fari swallowed. "Derna's body was drained of blood. That's how I knew she was... when I first saw her." At Lira's deepening frown, she scowled. "I'm a healer mage, remember?"

Tarion blinked, seeming to register Fari's presence properly for the first time. "You're Fari, right? A Dirsk—bitter rivals of Uncle Tarrick's family?"

"It's not family reunion time," Lira snapped as Fari opened her mouth, looking offended. "The guards on the gate weren't killed by the monster. They had their throats cut. Execution style. And whoever it was moved fast. None of the three even had time to draw their swords before they were dead. I assume neither of you heard the dogs sounding the alarm either?"

Instantly Tarion and Fari turned to stare out the crack in the door, as if assassins were about to jump out at them.

"There are seven dogs used to guard the grounds. I haven't heard any barking," Tarion said quietly, the implications clear.

"Someone, or some*ones*, is inside the grounds, and my bet is they're using that monster outside to stop anyone escaping," Lira continued. "It didn't even try to break through the front doors to come after us just now. So someone wants us contained in here."

Fari stared at Lira. "Who?"

"How should I know?"

Fari gulped. "So we're under attack?"

"Maybe." Lira wasn't convinced. This felt more like a targeted strike, aimed at something specific. A skilled but small crew. If it were an all-out attack on the mage academy, it would be a much more numerous attack force and they'd likely all be dead by now, like the guards on the gate. And it wouldn't be happening at mid-winter break when nobody was around.

But what was the goal? Were they after something in particular inside Temari Hall? Or someone, perhaps.

"Could it be the trials?" Tarion suggested, referencing the mysterious process by which mage apprentices were tested following completion of their four years at Temari Hall.

Lira considered that. "I'm good enough to sit the trials, but Fari is a second year and from what I've heard the extent of your magic could fit in your little finger, Mage-prince." Tarion flinched, she ignored it. "Plus Derna's dead. Unless we've all been horribly misinformed, apprentices don't die in the trials. Nor do highly-trained Shiven warriors."

"Then whatever is happening, we're in danger," Tarion said soberly. "We need to search the tower and get everyone gathered together in a secure location. Otherwise if that thing gets out of the library, or the one outside finds a way in, they'll be able to pick us off one by one."

"Or the throat-slitting assassins will," Fari pointed out.

"Good, you two do that." Lira moved for the door, glad to be rid of them. Their presence was already stifling. "I'm going to sneak out via the western gate and warn someone who can get the Shiven army in here to hunt the monsters and assassins down." She wasn't cowering in a room somewhere until someone realised what was happening and came to rescue them.

Whoever had gotten inside was good, dangerous even, but they'd made a mistake in not containing everyone in the tower immediately. A full division of fearsome Shiven soldiers was barracked in Karonan, trained by Dashan Caverlock himself—she wished these creatures luck with them.

"I heard you were smart." Fari sighed. "But that's literally the worst idea. You don't know how many monsters are out there, and we've already established we can't use magic on them."

Tarion's head came up sharply. "What?"

"That's right, mage-prince, your lack of ability won't matter a jot if one of these things comes after you," Lira snapped. Frustration surged. Fari had a point. If this crew was as good as she'd guessed, they'd know about the western gate.

"I think there's about twenty or so students staying here over mid-winter break." Tarion's eyebrows were furrowed in thought again. "So maybe we're both right, Lira. If we can gather everyone, it should be enough strength to fight our way out of here together, magic or no."

She hesitated, once again taken aback by his calm reasoning, his willingness to consider her point of view. But she didn't like the idea of remaining within these walls any longer. It felt like a trap, her instincts warning her to get herself out before it closed around her. Still, Lira was nothing if not aware of her limitations. Her grandfather might have been able to take out multiple dangerous monsters without breaking a sweat, but she couldn't. At least not yet. "Fine. We'll start with the initiate floor and work our way down."

"Fast or quiet?" Fari enquired.

"Quiet, and we stick to the unlit areas where possible. We have no way of knowing if whoever killed the guards is inside the tower or somewhere else on the grounds. Either way, without knowing what they're after, best to avoid their notice."

Fari whitened, while Tarion reached back to touch his staff in what seemed like an unconscious gesture. Lira cracked open the door, made sure the foyer was still empty, then slipped out.

Her skin crawled the entire time it took for them to dash across the foyer, hit the stairs, and reach the shadows of the first floor landing. But they made it without incident, pressing against the wall and going still until it was clear they hadn't been seen.

Tarion looked at her. "Move?"

"Let's go."

The first year students at Temari Hall lived in rooms on the floor immediately below the very top level of the tower—forced to travel the longest distance up and down the stairs every morning and night. Second year apprentices had the floor immediately below the initiates, and so on. The seventh and top level was reserved for the offices of Alyx Egalion, Head of Temari Hall.

She could just fly up to her office each day; the most flashy of her multiple magical abilities.

Lira held her staff loose in her left hand as they moved swiftly up the stairs, sticking to the carpeted section down the middle to muffle their footfalls. She tuned out the two apprentices behind her and sank into the razor-sharp focus of her time on the streets, where every one of her senses was poised to read and react to any changes in her surroundings.

Threat hung heavily around them. She could taste it in the air, feel it prickling over her skin, wished it was just her alone so that she could operate without distraction. It had been too long since she'd danced with danger. Swallowing, she buried that thought as quickly as it had come.

The lamps lining the staircase wall were lit intermittently—usual for this hour of the night—but the corridors leading away from each landing were pools of inky darkness.

The thought of one of those shadowy monsters leaping out of the dark to attack them was genuinely terrifying. By tacit agreement, they moved into a run each time they hit a landing, only slowing once they'd crossed the open space and started up towards the next level.

"You said they were impervious to magic?" Tarion asked in a murmur, his long legs taking the stairs two at a time. "Like Taliath?"

"Exactly like," Fari said. "And they're quick. Lira tried to bring a bookcase down on top of the thing but it got out of the way—I've never seen reflexes like that. Not even in a Taliath."

"Quiet!" Lira hissed. When they spoke she couldn't sink her senses into their surroundings like she needed to.

Tarion nodded an apology, looking thoughtful rather than afraid. Lira catalogued that away for future use. As unprepossessing as his general demeanour was, so far he'd maintained an admirably clear head. Even Fari was holding up better than Lira would have expected from any student at Temari who'd never faced anything worse than a broken nail during sparring.

They reached the square gallery on the sixth floor landing and stopped, Fari and Tarion shifting nervously from foot to foot while Lira studied the area. Dark openings yawned in four different directions, the corridors set out like spokes in a wheel joining the gallery to the corridor that surrounded the outer edge of the tower.

Lira spoke in a low murmur. "I'll start from the west side of the floor and work my way back here. Fari, you start on the eastern side and do the same. Tarion, you work through from the north. Whoever finishes first takes the south."

"You want us to split up?" Fari hissed. "What about the knife-wielding killers roaming around?"

Impatience made Lira terse. "You've got magic and your staff, and we need to do this quickly. Yell if you get into trouble."

Not waiting for them to acknowledge her orders or otherwise, Lira curled her fingers tighter around her staff and stepped into the darkness of the corridor to her right.

Several paces in, once she was swallowed by the blackness, she paused, allowing her eyes to adjust to the lack of light. None of the usual lamps were lit. Urgency thrummed in her veins, interfering with her focus. The instinctive urge to get out of the tower was growing stronger. She took deep, steadying breaths, settling into the darkness.

Soon her vision adjusted enough that could make out the faint flow of moonlight from a window set into the tower wall at the far end of the corridor. Apart from the lack of light, everything seemed exactly as it should during mid-winter break. Quiet. Empty.

But the quiet held an edge that thrilled through her. *Something* was out there, and it wasn't just a couple of vicious monsters that looked like they'd stepped directly out of somebody's nightmare.

Reaching the furthest room's door, she turned the handle quietly and pushed it open, blinking until her eyes adjusted to the darkness of the room beyond. All three narrow beds were empty, their sheets neatly made, the curtains drawn firmly across the window.

She crossed to the opposite room. Also empty.

In the third room, a boy slept in one of the three beds. Shiven, from the shape of his visible ear. Leaning over him, she pressed a hand over his mouth and spoke into his ear. "Wake up."

He came awake quickly, as if he hadn't been fully asleep, his gaze landing immediately on her. Wariness flickered over his face when he recognised her, but he didn't struggle in her hold. She ignored the spike of irritation at the familiar expression. "Yes it's me, Spider. I'm not here to eat you, but if you'd like to survive the night, you need to come with me. Now. Not a sound."

When he didn't move, she lifted her hand from his mouth and glanced at the door. "Now!" she hissed. "I'm not messing around, initiate."

He scrambled at the authoritative tone in her voice, reaching for his brown robe and almost falling out of bed in the process, a tangle of lanky limbs. Eventually he righted himself and grabbed his staff—it was so new the wood was still green. She fought not to roll her eyes. So much for breaking out together. This kid was raw and inexperienced, more likely to run at the sight of whatever those creatures were than stand and fight. At least he looked awake and alert.

"Name?" she asked as he tangled with his robe. On his feet he was already taller than her, even though he couldn't be any older than fifteen.

"Lorin," he whispered, then straightened his shoulders. As sleep cleared from his brain he seemed to gather some of that innate Shiven haughtiness. "What is going on?"

"Explanations later, let's go." She made for the door. "Not a sound, remember?"

His touch on her shoulder made her jump, then whirl around in fury. "Do that again and I'll rip it off."

"Where's Haler?" he murmured, undaunted.

"What?" she hissed.

"Haler. His bed is empty." Lorin pointed to another bed in the room. Unlike the third one, the blankets were rumpled, as if they'd been slept in.

Frustration rose in a tide. Wherever Haler was, there wasn't much she could do about it. Maybe they'd find him as they kept searching. "Not my problem right now. Either you come with me or I'm leaving you to get eaten."

He must have hesitated before deciding to follow, because several seconds passed before he followed her out into the hallway. By then she'd checked another empty room and moved on to the next.

"Eaten by what?" Lorin whispered, crowding too close to her.

She ignored him, shoving him away with an elbow.

Her hand was pushing open the next door when she picked up the faint padding of running feet. Bracing herself, she lifted her staff, only to lower it as Tarion appeared around the bend in the hallway. His face was even paler than usual, hazel eyes stark with shock.

"What now?" she asked, dread rising. He'd been so calm until now —what could have set this level of fear into him?

"They're all empty."

Her sense of danger intensified at his grim tone, making her snappish when she hissed. "So? And please try to remember we might not be alone in here and keep your voice down."

His jaw clenched and he moved closer, murmuring this time. "The rooms on the northern side are all empty, every single one. They shouldn't be. I know two initiates who were staying here over the break."

"Haler's missing too," Lorin whispered stubbornly, not looking away when Lira shot him a glare. "What is going on?"

Tarion's eyes flicked to Lorin. "Are you all right?"

"Why wouldn't I be?" Lorin bristled, haughtiness overtaking him now. "If this is some kind of initiate prank—"

"What about Fari?" Lira cut him off, her gaze constantly scanning the dark hallway as they spoke. "Did she find anyone?"

As if on cue, more running feet approached, these louder than Tarion's soft footfalls. Lira's irritation rocketed skywards at the amount of noise they were all making. If the crew behind this was even halfway good at what they did, they'd be on them in moments. She'd just have to hope they were in another part of the school grounds.

When Fari skidded around the corner and propped to a halt beside Tarion, she was gasping for air and her dark Zandian skin was bloodless. "I generally like to put a positive spin on any situation, but we have a serious, *serious* problem. And when I say serious, I mean, like... really serious. Like—"

"Spit it out," Lira snapped. "Were the rooms you checked empty too?"

"Yes, but that's not the problem. Come and see."

Fari turned and began jogging back in the direction she'd come. Lira tossed a considering glance at Lorin as she followed. An entire floor empty except for one boy. That didn't feel like a coincidence. Lira's survival instincts surged again. Maybe she shouldn't be sticking around and looking for reinforcements to fight their way free.

Maybe she should get out before it was too *late* to get out.

Lira trailed behind as Fari entered one of the rooms and crossed to the window, where she'd pulled back the curtains. Lira and Tarion stepped up to the glass at the same time, Lorin hovering at their backs and trying to peer over their shoulders.

As she looked outside, Lira sucked in a breath in shock.

The sky was mostly cloud free and the view out the window showed the moonlit surrounds of Temari Hall and the still surface of the lake surrounding Karonan.

But instead of the hundreds of lights of the biggest city in Shivasa, there was only the silvery midnight glow over dark buildings. No movement on the streets. No guards visible at the closest causeway. Not a single light.

Tarion spoke for all of them. "What happened to Karonan?"

CHAPTER 9
BEFORE

Lira scrambled down the drainpipe, wincing as the ice-cold metal burned the skin of her fingers, and dropped lightly onto the snowdrift piled up against the side of the building.

Night had fallen a short time earlier. It would normally turn this part of Dirinan into a dark and dangerous tangle of streets, but tonight a bright full moon hung in the sky over the city, bathing it in a silvery glow.

Her food had run out two days ago, and her previous day's pick-pocketing attempts had been a miserable failure after she'd been muscled out by older, more experienced thieves operating at the marketplace she'd chosen. Hunger cramped her stomach and exhaustion tugged at her relentlessly—restful sleep was hard to come by when she didn't have enough blankets to stay warm.

If she wanted another blanket and enough food to keep herself alive a little longer, she'd have to venture out into the wealthier part of the city to steal tonight. She preferred operating in the night anyway—it was easier to hide, to sneak around. Nobody saw a too-small eight-year-old girl in the shadows. And ever since her mother... well, she hated sitting alone in the dark and waiting for day to come. It made her feel weak and afraid and she *hated* feeling those things.

A shudder wracked her skinny frame as an icy breeze swept through the alley, a sharp reminder that she needed warmer clothing too, especially if she was going to be hunting more at night.

"You're quite the climber."

Lira started at the rough voice that came out of the darkness, and she instinctively scrambled backwards, stumbling and falling against another snow drift. The alley below her bolt hole was narrow, lined with doors that were the back entrances to a number of shops that only opened during the day, and it only had one exit.

She'd picked it because it was a few blocks away from the harbour district, which consisted of several blocks full of whorehouses, seedy inns, gambling dens, and cheap housing. A number of close calls with gang members unhappy with her infringement on their patch at her previous hiding place had sent her further from the docks in search of shelter. She'd had a few run-ins with the city's nastier and more violent denizens since, but had learned quickly how to stay out of sight and draw no attention, only going out when forced to for food or blankets.

Lira squinted, shivering with a mixture of fear and cold as the speaker moved into sight. He was a thin, rangy man with lank hair, his eyes pools of darkness that were a stark contrast to his almost white Shiven skin. His cheeks had the familiar hollow look of hunger, and his fingers twitched at his sides. "What do we have here?"

Her fear spiked when two more men appeared out of the darkness a pace behind the first one, at his left and right shoulder. They wore the same hungry look, but were taller, broader in the shoulders. All three wore several layers of ragged clothing.

She picked herself up, ignoring how the snow had soaked through the back of her clothes. She was in far more immediate danger from these men than the cold that might kill her if she didn't get warm.

"Do you speak?" the first man barked at her.

She straightened her shoulders, tried to make herself as unthreatening as possible. "I don't want trouble."

"Then you shouldn't have been thieving on our territory yesterday. The rules are clear." A disturbing look crossed his expression then, cunning and avarice in equal measure. "You'll fetch a nice bag of coin from Madam Flower. She needs a new girl, and she likes 'em young too."

"I don't go near the harbour district," she said quickly. Words weren't going to get her out of this, but she had to try.

The man on the left scoffed, ignoring her protest. "She's a bit bony for Flower, don't you think, Mory?"

"She'll fill out with some good meals and a couple years. Most of Flower's customers don't care how they look in the dark anyway." He laughed, and it broke into a hacking cough. "We've decided to extend our boundary to that street back there. You're on our patch."

Lira backed up a step as Mory moved toward her. She couldn't fight off three grown men, but she wasn't just going to let them take her either. After months of desperate struggle to survive each night, her will to live had grown stronger, tempered, like steel. Her gaze flicked from him to the men behind him, to the spaces between them and the alley wall. Maybe she could—

The man on Mory's left grunted, a puzzled look flashing over his face. The moment froze for a heartbeat as Mory and the other man turned toward him, and Lira took advantage of their distraction and shifted another step back.

Before she could think to do anything else, the man swayed on his feet and crumpled to the ground, making no further sounds. Lira stared at the patch of red that spread through the dirty snow under him.

"Hey!" Mory shouted, anger and fear combined, his right hand scrabbling inside his cloak for the knife hanging at his belt.

Before Mory could even close a hand over his knife, his second companion thumped to the ground, throat gaping open and blood spraying from his jugular. Red droplets spattered, steaming, into the white surface of the snow. Their attacker—of small size but moving so quickly it was impossible to get a good look at the person—shifted into sight as Mory drew his blade and swung it viciously. But it did no good. The figure stepped inside his thrust and buried a knife in his heart before yanking it out, so quick it took Lira a moment to figure out what had happened. Mory's breath gargled, he coughed, then he too crashed to the ground.

Silence settled once again over the alley, moonlight casting the three dead bodies in stark relief against the white snow. A soft laugh broke the silence, and the attacker turned away from Mory's body and took a step closer to Lira, head lifting to look at her, giving her a long, assessing glance. Lira's eyes widened.

The killer was a girl.

She was a head taller than Lira, but no more than a year or two older, her hands thrust casually in the pockets of her tattered breeches. Whatever weapon she'd used had already been secreted away somewhere on her person.

A long coat the colour of the sky before a storm hung to her ankles, but its obviously expensive make didn't fool Lira. The girl's raven hair was as tangled as Lira's, and her left boot had a hole in the toe. Her neck and tunic were spattered with blood, and two streaks of the stuff dried on the pale skin of her cheekbone. A silver chain glinted around her neck as it disappeared beneath the collar of her shirt.

Lira blinked, making sure she wasn't dreaming or otherwise seeing things. A girl had just taken down three armed men with an ease Lira found breathtaking.

"They barely put up a fight. How disappointing." The girl spoke, turning back and digging her boot into Mory's ribs, as if hoping he'd come back to life and offer a more challenging fight.

"What do you want?" Lira asked, heart still pounding, part of her realising she might now be in even more danger, the rest of her still struck with awe. "I'm not after any trouble."

"You've been thieving on their patch." The girl took a step closer, her stance nonchalant. Her eyes though... a shiver went through Lira at the look in them, from fear this time, not cold. There was only death, emptiness, in that dark gaze. Somehow, though, it made her bristle too.

"What do you care what I do on their patch?" Lira scoffed before she could stop herself. "You just killed them."

"Because as of now, their patch is my patch." Another step forward, the coat shifting enough to reveal the wicked-looking knife sheathed at the girl's waist. The words were low, edged with threat. Lira's mind flashed back to how easily she'd just killed three men. It had happened so fast. If she'd been asked, Lira wasn't sure she'd be able to describe it in any detail.

The fear came rushing back. "Okay, I know how it works. I'll stop. Find somewhere else to work." Lira lifted her hands in a placating gesture, her heart hammering so hard she worried it might burst. She'd find some other way of getting what she needed, it didn't matter how. Whatever she needed to do to live another day. Just one more day.

The girl's eyebrows shot upwards. "Just like that?"

"All I'm trying to do is survive." Weariness crashed over her shoulders then. Years-long weariness of always having to fight so hard just to live. To not be hungry. To not be cold. A constant, never-ending battle.

"I have to admit, I'm disappointed. A person with your obvious skill for survival, I'd been hoping for a bit more spine. If you want to *keep* surviving, though, you step up when someone comes at you. You don't back down." The girl moved closer, voice lazy, an amused tilt to her mouth. "You back down, you show weakness, and you die. It's that simple."

She was toying with her, like Lira had watched the spiders in her bolthole do with the flies they caught in their webs. That sparked something in her, an ember of defiance returning again, stronger this time. "Maybe, but I've found that killing me is hard to do."

"Is that right?" she murmured, stepping closer, eyes narrowing. "What's your name?"

Danger flooded Lira again at the menace coming from this girl. But instead of fear now, she felt... an odd spark of something uncurling in her belly. Something like challenge. Or anticipation. "Lira."

She studied Lira for a moment, seemingly unbothered by the cold as Lira stood shivering. "Let me guess. You ran away from the orphanage? Or were you just dumped on the streets by your loving parents?"

Lira stiffened, and triumph flashed in the girl's eyes. "Thought so. I'm Ahrin. Ahrin Vensis." She stuck out her hand so abruptly, Lira took a stumbling step backwards, then cursed herself inwardly for it. Her eyes fell on the small black tattoo on the inside of the girl's wrist. It vanished when she dropped her hand, hidden by the sleeve of her coat. Ahrin eyed her. "What's your story?"

"My what?" Lira asked warily. She couldn't tell what this girl wanted, whether she was angry or amused or some mixture of both. Maybe she was just enjoying toying with her prey before killing it. Lira had already encountered predators living on these streets, and young as she was, this girl was a predator.

"You were an extra mouth they couldn't afford? You got sick and they couldn't pay the bills? You cried too much as a baby?" Ahrin elaborated, impatience edging her voice. "How'd you end up orphaned on the streets?"

The threat in this girl's demeanour didn't invite holding back, or wasting her time by hesitating. "My village sent me here after my mother died."

"They didn't take you in?" Ahrin frowned.

"My grandfather did some bad things. They thought I was like him."

Ahrin snorted. "You're not lying to me, are you? Because that's the most creative reason for being abandoned I've heard yet."

"My grandfather was Shakar. The Darkmage. I am his heir." Lira spoke with sudden confidence, relying on the name having its usual effect. It should scare this girl off too, make her leave Lira alone.

Ahrin's midnight-blue eyes widened and she went oddly still. Something rippled over her face. Hunger? No, not quite, but something like it. Whatever it was, it set Lira on edge. "No kidding? Now there's a revelation. *Are* you?"

"Am I what?"

"Like him." Ahrin waved a hand. "Evil, murderous. Do you eat children for breakfast?"

Lira snorted, and a brief smile flickered over Ahrin's face. The coldness was quick to return though, and Lira swallowed. "Maybe, I don't know," she said uncomfortably. Whatever that initial reaction had been, Ahrin didn't seem scared. Or uneasy. Instead, she seemed... almost admiring. Lira wasn't sure how to deal with that.

Ahrin studied Lira a moment longer, and Lira forced herself to keep her shoulders straight and hold that look. After a moment Ahrin turned away. She levered a boot under Mory's cooling body and turned it over, then leaned down and tugged off the coat he'd been wearing. Straightening, she held it out towards Lira. "Here. It's a bit damp and smelly, and you'll want to scrub off the blood, but it'll be warm enough once it dries."

"What do you want in return?" Lira asked warily.

"You're not completely hopeless if you've learned that rule already. Take the coat and come with me, join my crew. Or don't, and we have a problem, because you're working my territory and I don't leave loose ends lying around."

"Your crew?" Disbelief coloured Lira's voice. "You're barely a year older than me."

"So?" Ahrin waved a hand at the three bodies in the snow and lifted her eyebrows. "Something about this make you think I'm not capable of running a crew?"

"I..." Lira's gaze fixated on the coat, and suddenly she was aware of how cold she was, how she hadn't stopped shivering since hopping down from the wall.

Ahrin was clearly dangerous. Not to be trusted. But she didn't fear Lira, and she offered survival, for at least one more night. And Lira had learned to live hour by hour, night by night.

"My arm is getting sore. Take the coat or get out of my patch."

Lira reached out and took the coat. Her eyes studied Ahrin as she buttoned it up. "Where is your place?"

"Not far, inside harbour district. It's small. But it's warm." Ahrin shrugged. "We'll get a bigger place soon."

Ahrin turned and walked away. Lira followed, hesitating for a moment beside Mory's body. Stripped of his coat and lifeless, all threat he'd offered was gone forever. Lira thought about how close she'd been to dying, how in the space of a blink, all three men had been killed instead. And now *she* was alive, she had a coat to warm her, and a new home. She'd defeated death once again.

The spark that had lit in her belly moments earlier strengthened, growing brighter, offering a warmth and light that covered up the gaping chasm in her chest. For the first time since leaving the village, she felt as if she were alive in this moment, *living*, not just existing.

"You coming or not?" Ahrin's voice was sharp, irritated.

Lira turned away from Mory without looking back and jogged until she'd caught up with Ahrin. At the top of the alley, Ahrin suddenly halted, pointing back. "You don't ever leave your back uncovered. You should have made certain the alley was clear before you even started climbing down, and if it wasn't, you should have taken the rooves to get where you were going."

Lira nodded.

"You better be hearing me. I marked you because you've managed to survive despite having no apparent street smarts at all. This is the first lesson you learn, and if you stick with me, you don't ever make that mistake again." Ahrin's gaze bored into hers. "You don't leave a room, an alley, or anyplace without knowing what's outside first."

This seemed to require a verbal response, so Lira settled for, "I understand. Clear a space before entering. I won't forget again."

As they continued walking, she wondered whether following the girl was a mistake. If she'd regret throwing her lot in with others instead of relying on herself alone. But she was barely surviving now. She doubted she'd last another year without help. She told herself she'd take what Ahrin was willing to give, use it to keep herself alive, but never turn her back on the other girl. And once she was big enough and old enough to take care of herself, she'd leave.

Ahrin's voice broke the silence. "It's probably not just the Shakar thing, you know."

"What?" Lira was startled out of her musings.

"Your villagers throwing you out. I assume they didn't want you at the orphanage either, or you wouldn't have run away." Ahrin glanced at her. "You're not Shiven. The war might have ended twenty years ago, but Shivasa and Rionn hated each other for decades before that. That kind of hate doesn't go away quickly or easily. The new Mage Council might have decided to put their fancy new school here, but that's only papered over the massive cracks that already existed."

Lira hadn't exactly had a lot of opportunity to stare at herself in mirrors, but at some point she'd come to a realisation that she wasn't as pale as most of those around her. That she was too small for her age to be Shiven. "How do you know all that?"

Another shrug. Then a quick sideways glance. "My crew do what I say, when I say, and how I say. They don't, and I have no further use for them. You good with that?"

The segue was rapid and sharp, and Lira blinked. "For now."

The smile that spread over Ahrin's face was as dangerous as it was lovely. "Let's not reach a point where you and I are at odds, huh?"

Lira resolved not to let that happen until she was strong enough to come out of that battle the winner. A little thrill went through her again, delighting her, and she sank into it. It made her feel warmer, stronger, filling her with sudden certainty.

The day would come when she was strong enough to match Ahrin. She'd make certain of it.

CHAPTER 10

L ira blinked. Lifted a hand to rub at her eyes. The dark and empty city remained. A flash of lightning flared in the distance from what looked to be an approaching storm. Around her, the other three had fallen silent, even Fari.

Dread whispered through her bones, crawled under her skin. The seductive thrill of the danger she hungered for rose unbidden and entwined with it, leaving her caught wavering on a knife edge of excitement and genuine fear. Not fear of danger, but of the unknown. Of something she didn't understand well enough to be sure that she could fight it and survive. But that was exciting too... a new challenge to pit herself against.

With an effort, she pushed that feeling down, re-buried it—ignored the effort that took—and then she turned and left the room.

The hall outside the dormitory remained dark and still, her tread making no sound as she moved fast and low, turning right at the gallery to head up the stairs to the top level of the tower. Once there, she slid to a halt, faced with a spacious rectangular landing. The lamps here were unlit and night lay a shadowy cloak over the rug filling the middle of the floor and the soft couches lining the edges.

Egalion's formal reception area. Lira had been up here only once before, the day she first arrived at Temari Hall. The unwelcome memory of that day threatened to interrupt her focus, and she ruthlessly shoved it aside, forcing herself into action.

Corridors stretched away into inky blackness to her left and right, leading to offices for those working in the administration of Temari Hall, but Lira ignored them, instead making for the closed double doors directly across the landing. Egalion's office. The doors were unsurprisingly locked.

Without hesitation, Lira pressed a palm over the lock and sent a tiny tendril of her magic sliding inside the mechanism. It wasn't a particularly complex device and it clicked open within seconds.

She was pushing the door open when soft footfalls sounded behind her. She whirled, staff raised and magic ready, but it was just Fari and the others reaching the top of the stairs. Irritation rippled through her and she lowered her staff.

"Why are we breaking into Councillor Egalion's office?" Fari whispered.

Ignoring her, Lira slipped into the massive room, poised to react if anything leapt out. But nothing moved. Moments later, Tarion, Lorin and Fari came piling in behind her.

"Oh, I get it," Fari breathed.

Born a nobleman's daughter, Alyx Egalion liked her palatial creature comforts, and in this case, that meant floor-to-ceiling glass windows filling the entire southern wall of her office, giving her an unobstructed view of Karonan city.

"This can't be possible." Lorin walked straight up to the glass, expression unbelieving as he saw the same thing they were all looking at. The same thing they'd seen from the initiate's room below. The city was utterly dark, lit only by moonlight. Nobody walked the streets. No horse or cart traffic moved through it. There was no movement or light in the guard's huts at the southern causeway entrance.

The storm Lira had seen from below filled the eastern horizon, dark clouds scudding close to the moon. A fork of lightning flashed. As they stood and watched, the clouds covered the moon and the city went completely dark.

"He's right." She spoke more to herself than the others. "It's not physically possible for the entire city to have emptied out in the few hours since we went to bed. And for *all* lights to be out... the coordination needed for that would take an unprecedented amount of planning."

"Leader Astohar doesn't have that level of control over the city," Tarion murmured, barely audible.

"What other explanation could there be?" Lorin was pacing the windows, pausing to stare out every few moments as if hoping to see something different. His voice was steady, though sweat beaded on his forehead and he kept glancing back at the door.

None of the three were panicking, or at least if they were, they were controlling it well. It surprised her, but made her uneasy too, because it didn't quite fit. She hadn't known any of them before this, but the students she *did* know at Temari would be rocking uselessly in a corner by now. Or would have already run screaming out the doors and gotten themselves eaten.

"Magic." Tarion's voice was quiet, as if he spoke to himself rather than them. "Someone might be messing with our heads."

The thought of that sent real terror clawing through Lira's insides for the first time that night, and she instantly checked her mental shields—the first thing she'd taught herself to do on arriving at Temari Hall. They were solid. Flawless. Her shoulders relaxed and she dismissed the fear with a surge of annoyance at herself for feeling it in the first place.

Lira leaned down, yanked the right leg of her breeches up and peered at the skin. Dark bruising mottled the area around her ankle. "The monsters are real. And we didn't imagine that dead body in the library either." She was certain of it. Had seen enough corpses to know.

"Her name was Derna," Fari said coldly.

Lira shrugged. "My point remains."

A frosty silence filled the space. Lira went back to staring at the window, trying to come up with a way forward. Her options were rapidly narrowing. Even if she stuck with these apprentices and tried to round up everyone still alive in the tower, there was no division of

Shiven soldiers to go and fetch. There was *nobody* to get help from. At least not nearby.

Could more people be involved in this than she'd estimated? But if so, who were they to have the necessary resources for all this? And why hadn't they run into any of them yet? "Maybe whatever is going on isn't about Temari Hall."

"You're thinking an invasion of Karonan?" Fari sounded all sorts of sceptical. "Where's the invading army?"

"I'm not suggesting—"

"I want to find Haler," Lorin cut over her, determination in his voice. "I can't just leave him out there alone."

"Yes, well, you wandering around alone looking for him isn't a good idea either," Fari said sharply, but Lorin was already halfway across the room. "Lorin, we have a plan—"

When the rattling whispered through the open door, they all froze. Tarion and Lorin both moved to draw staffs, while Fari backed towards the window. Lira scanned the room for... "Go, under the desk. Now!" she murmured, pointing.

She didn't wait for them to follow her orders, already scrambling into the dark space under Egalion's massive desk and shifting back as far as she could go. Within moments the other three had squeezed in with her.

"Shush!" she hissed at their loud breathing. Panic was clawing at them, she could sense it in the cramped space, tried to keep it from infecting her too. She spoke as much for herself as them when she muttered, "Slow breaths. Stay in control."

"Easier said than done," Fari muttered.

"We could fight our way out," Tarion breathed.

"Maybe, but magic is useless, and we'd make a lot of noise. That will draw any other creatures inside *or* the human killers, or both, and we're stuck on the top floor with no easy way out." Lira shook her head, trying to sound authoritative while whispering. "Better to hide and hope it goes away."

"What if it can smell us?" Fari was barely audible.

"Then we're in trouble. Shush."

Lira sat as still as she could, a stillness she could hold for hours if necessary, her gaze focused on the space beyond the desk. Tarion was pressed up hard against her, Fari beside him, Lorin hunched against the other side of the desk.

Silence reigned, a heavy stillness. The temperature dropped, ice cold slivering through the air. When their breath began visibly steaming, Tarion was the first to cover his mouth with a hand. She gave him an approving nod.

When the next rattle sounded, it was close. Like chains dragging across the threshold of the door... but not quite at the same time.

The thing was inside the room with them.

Her breathing turned shallow. Tarion's shoulder against hers went rigid, his Shiven skin deathly pale. Fari's eyes were closed. Lorin was too much in shadow to see properly.

A long, shadowy tendril curled down from the top of the desk, questing toward the floor. Lira's gaze was caught by the writhing darkness at the core of it, so dense it eclipsed all suggestion of light. Another rattle echoed, even closer. It almost sounded confused.

The cold deepened, and that sense of being hunted, stalked, filled the space. Lira pressed as far back under the desk as she could get. Another shadowy limb probed around the side of the desk, coming within inches of Lorin's boot. Her magic fought her control, wanting to escape, to protect her, but the last thing she could afford was a flash of violet light to give away their position.

Then both tendrils withdrew. Everything went still, like the thing was sitting, waiting, testing the silence for their presence.

Lira swallowed. Kept her breathing even.

The silence lengthened. Drew out. Grew so tense it was palpable.

Lira counted to thirty in her head, waited until the air warmed enough that her breath stopped frosting, then slowly shifted forward. Tarion reached out to grab her arm but she shook it off. Crouching, she inched her head upwards until she could see over the top of the desk.

The room was empty. It had gone. Her shoulders slumped, and she pressed her forehead against the cool wood for a moment. Then, jittery from fading adrenalin, she stood up and padded over to the door to peer outside. Nothing but a dark, empty reception area.

Relaxing, she turned back into the room to see the others climbing out from under the desk, all looking shaky. "That was close," Fari muttered.

Lira looked at the initiate. "Lorin, you're not a telepath, are you?" Maybe they could reach another telepathic mage somehow, ask for help.

He bristled, as if offended by her question. "I have concussive magic. I'm a warrior mage."

Damn.

"Okay, so if it's not someone messing with our heads, maybe we've been moved somewhere else," Tarion suggested, but shook his head as soon as he said it, like he already knew how ridiculous it sounded.

Fari stopped pacing and stared at Tarion like he'd gone mad. "You're suggesting someone *picked up* our tower and *put it down* outside a copy of Karonan?"

His mouth opened. Closed. Then he gave a little shrug.

Fari turned to stare at Lira like she somehow had all the answers. Lira shrugged. "Don't look at me. I'm the evil apprentice, not the authority on geography. But in my experience, I've found the simplest explanation is usually the correct one."

"Good point." Fari took a breath. "If it's not someone messing with our heads magically, then maybe we ate something at dinner and we're hallucinating? Or someone drugged us?"

"You're the healer mage," Lira said. "Is that possible?"

"It's absolutely possible that someone could ingest a drug that causes them to hallucinate and have highly realistic visions." Fari nodded. "But a shared hallucination where all the victims had the exact same vision? I don't know... I'm actually not that good at the book learning stuff." Emotion flashed over the girl's face then, something unhappy, but Lira couldn't work out what it was even if she'd cared to.

"This is ridiculous," Lorin said suddenly, beginning his pacing again. He glanced out the window, then back at the doors. His expression was strained, as if he was fighting to hold on to calm.

"Which part? The vicious monsters trying to eat us, the invisible knife-wielding killers, or the fact that an entire city's population has somehow vanished in the space of a few hours?" Fari asked. She sounded close to hysteria, her eyes tracking Lorin's pacing as if in a daze.

"What if…" Tarion said suddenly, swallowing visibly. "What if we were asleep longer than we thought?"

Lira gave him a sharp look. She *had* felt strange when she'd woken earlier… groggy like she'd been far deeper asleep than normal. A chill closed over her chest at the implications of that. Greyson had given her a week to steal A'ndreas' report and get it to him. If that time had passed…

"You look like someone just murdered your pet cat," Fari remarked.

Lira shook off the dread and focused on the present. She wasn't going to be able to undertake any tasking for the Shadowcouncil if she didn't escape this tower. "I hate to agree with you, Mage-prince, but you might be onto something."

"It can't have been more than two weeks, or everyone would be back from mid-winter break," Lorin said, finally stopping his pacing.

Lira cast around, eyes falling on Egalion's desk. "Tarion, when was the last time you were up here? Does anything look different, out of place?"

He walked straight over to the desk without protest, eyes narrowing as he rifled through the parchment lined up in neat piles. "These are the papers Mama had on her desk. There's nothing new here, nothing moved or changed." Tarion's voice was quiet, barely audible. He stood frowning over the desk. "I remember. I talked to her up here the morning she left."

Fari went over to take a look, then dropped into Egalion's chair with a sigh. "So no matter how long we slept your mother hasn't returned."

"If Lira was right before about whatever is going on being bigger than Temari Hall, then maybe she hasn't come back for a reason. Maybe she was attacked too," Lorin said wildly.

"Ok, stop there," Lira snapped, rapidly losing patience. "Let's stick with what we know instead of making wild assumptions. Whatever is going on, this tower is a dangerous place to be right now, so we go back to the original plan of finding the others, bolstering our strength and then getting out."

"But where do we go for help?" Fari asked.

"As far as we need to—a town big enough to have an army barracks." Despite the confusion of what she saw out the windows, Lira was still confident this was a small operation. An army they'd have noticed, and they certainly wouldn't have gone undetected so long inside Temari unless there was only a small crew who'd infiltrated with at least one person controlling the creatures.

And if she had to guess, there were likely only two monsters—one patrolling the grounds outside to stop anyone escaping, and one that had been let out of the library; *probably* to help look for the apprentices that had gotten loose. Why it had been in the library in the first place was a question for another time. Which meant if they stayed where they were, they'd eventually be found. They needed to keep moving.

"Where's Lorin?" Tarion asked suddenly.

Lira looked around. The Shiven initiate had vanished. She cursed herself for not noticing him slip away. She had to be sharper than that.

"He must have gone to look for his friend," Fari said. "Haler, wasn't it?"

Tarion headed for the door.

"Where are you going?" Lira snapped.

"To make sure he's okay." He spoke as if he was confused that she'd even ask.

"We need to stick with the plan and stay together, search the floors one by one and build our strength," she said. "If Lorin wants to be an idiot and go off on his own, then that's his problem."

Tarion's mouth thinned. "He's our responsibility."

"He's not mine."

Fari sighed. "You really don't like people, do you?"

Lira rounded on her. "Survival is my priority. We need to get ourselves out. Chasing stupid initiates through the halls isn't going to accomplish that."

"No, but we need Lorin," Fari insisted, not at all bothered by Lira's snappish tone. "If he gets picked off by one of these creatures, that's one less person to help us escape."

Despite agreeing with Fari's logic, Lira hesitated, desperately wanting an excuse to break free of these apprentices. Trusting herself alone was the only way to ensure she got out of this. And for all she knew, there *were* no more students alive. The few others still here might have woken too—especially after the noise she'd made fighting the creature in the library—and found themselves at the mercy of the blood-drinking monster when they went to investigate.

"Lorin's a concussive mage, remember?" Fari added with a hint of a smug smile.

"A raw, untrained one." She huffed an impatient breath. "And magic is useless against those things. Look, you two go, start searching the second year dorm level. I'll catch up soon, I just want to check something here."

"And Lorin?" Tarion pressed.

"We'll search as fast as we can, hopefully catch up before he gets himself in trouble. And if he does get himself in trouble, by the time we get to him, we'll have collected all the students still here and have a better chance of helping him, no?" She held his gaze.

"Fine." He waved Fari out the door. "But it's not safe for you to be on your own either, so don't linger long."

She dismissed him with a scornful wave, then went over to the desk to rifle quickly through the papers there. They were all boring. Nothing in them seemed relevant to the current situation. No urgent missives warning of an army descending on Karonan. It had seemed highly unlikely anyway but was worth ruling out.

For a brief moment she wondered what had happened to Greyson and the other members of Underground in the city. The cell leader's eyes would light up at the thought of her with free reign to go through Egalion's papers like this. Were they still alive? Rotted carcasses... now she was alone, the consequences of failing in her task came rocketing to the forefront of her mind. Not that going back to the library to rifle through A'ndreas' office was an option right now.

Uneasiness and concern shafted through her then. She couldn't afford to fail in this task. Getting out of this tower alive wouldn't matter much if she didn't do it quickly enough.

An idea occurred to her.

Whirling, she left the office and padded quietly down the stairwell to the third year dormitory on the fourth floor. The entire way, her senses strained, alert for any unusual sounds that might indicate a monster creeping around nearby. But everything was still and quiet. No rattling, and the air remained cold but not freezing.

Were they alone in the tower? Or were they playing a dangerous cat and mouse game with whoever had killed the guards and was controlling the monsters? If so, the chances of being found increased the longer they stayed here. Her pace slowed as she stepped into the darkness of the hallway, hand up and gripping her staff in case she needed to draw it.

The door to her room stood ajar—exactly how she'd left it what felt like hours earlier. Cautiously, she stepped inside, casting her eyes over her rumpled bedding, the neat covers of the empty bed across from hers. Then, with a flicker of magic, she opened the lid of her storage chest.

The brief violet glow showed all her belongings exactly as she'd left them. Spare robe, shirt, breeches, socks, and underwear. The ratty bag she'd brought with her from Dirinan. Spare parchment and quill. Her copy of *History of Mages*.

Frowning, she reached in and pulled out the book, flicking through it. The corner on page fifty-six was turned over—something she'd done in class a few days prior. A brief rummage underneath everything to tug up the false bottom she'd installed showed the folded and sealed parchment with her comments on the most recent Underground meeting was still there too.

She'd written that the night before. It was untouched.

Another careful study of the floor, desk, and chest surface revealed no obvious accumulation of dust. All indications were that not much time had passed. Or at least that nobody had returned to the tower while they slept. Her mind turned it over and over, viewing the problem from all angles. But she failed to come up with a reasonable explanation. She took a few steps back, listed out what she knew for certain.

Most of the students and masters had departed Temari Hall for mid-winter break throughout the day. By nightfall it had been quiet inside the walls, but the city beyond remained well-lit. Lira had eaten dinner in her room, and had looked out her window before closing the curtains and seen nothing amiss.

Then she'd woken. Some of the students who should have been here were missing. There was a monster inside the library and at least one more creeping around outside. But someone had doused all the lamps in several sections of the tower. Her mind focused on that.

You doused lamps when you wanted darkness. When you wanted nobody to see what you were doing. All the dormitory floors had been affected... and that's where the students were located at night. And it seemed sensible to assume whoever had done that had been the ones to kill the Shiven guards.

So maybe they wanted to get to the students. The creature outside was there to stop any from fleeing if they woke up? It had certainly seemed to herd Lira back inside when she'd gone out.

Lira carefully closed the lid on the chest, then rose to her feet and headed back out the door, planning to go and find Tarion and Fari. The sooner they gathered everyone still here and got out, the better.

She'd taken one step past the threshold when she stilled, her sweeping gaze—searching for any danger in the hall—catching on something on the floor. She crouched, summoning a tiny amount of magic to provide just enough light to illuminate the small, circular-shaped spots clustered together right beside the bottom of her door.

Frowning, she reached out and tentatively touched whatever it was. Her nail scraped one of the spots off the floor and she lifted it to her nose, catching a faint sweet scent. Wax. It was scented wax.

Someone had burned a candle outside her door. Close enough that its smoke would have flowed under the crack between the bottom of the door and the floor, especially if someone were blowing on it...

The delivery she'd seen halfway through her fight with Garan, the one that had roused her old instincts. A delivery of candles.

Realisation swamped her, and with the thought of the unknown delivery person walking past the windows came the sharp memory of the first lesson of survival she'd ever learned.

Always cover your back.

Lira shot to her feet, instincts shrilling, furious at herself for the misstep. She half turned toward the movement in the shadows to her right, but it was too late. An arm wrapped around her throat, wiry and strong, and a cloth was pressed against her nose and mouth.

Lira struggled furiously, magic roaring to life and bathing the corridor in bright violet light, but whatever the cloth had been doused in was fast acting. She lost her grip on the magic as soon as she'd summoned it, and all strength left her legs. Oxygen cut off as she hung in her captor's grip.

And then everything was black.

CHAPTER 11
BEFORE

Lira moved quietly through the pitch-black crawlspace on her stomach, sweat slicking her skin, muscles already aching from the awkward movements.

There was barely an inch of space on either side of her, and if she tried to rise to her hands and knees her head bumped against the low ceiling. Dust covered the wooden surface underneath her and hung thick in the air. Several times she had to stop and bury her nose in her shoulder to stifle a sneeze. Her hands and bare feet were dark with grime, the shirt and trousers she wore now more brown than their original colour of blue.

Sound drifted up from below, a raucous hum of conversation, laughter, and mingled cries of excitement and disappointment. As she crawled a bit further, a shaft of light ahead broke the darkness; flamelight rising through the grating of an air vent.

When she reached it, Lira lay flat and took a moment to catch her breath, letting her aching arms and legs rest. Then she peered down through the grating to the scene below. She was in position—now she just had to wait for her cue.

She was excited, eager, impatient to move. If they pulled this off tonight, Ahrin would be pleased with them. It would mean extra blankets, some food, maybe even a bigger place soon. Somewhere that smelled better.

And Lira had been given the most important role.

Maybe it was just because she was the only one small enough—even at ten years old she was still smaller than most Shiven children her age or even younger—to fit in the vents, but she didn't care. Ahrin trusted her to do it. She wasn't going to let the crew down. After tonight Lira would win even more respect. And respect would keep her safe. Less hungry. Warm.

But even better than all that, pulling off jobs like this was *fun*.

In the two years since that night she'd met Ahrin in the alley, that warm thrill she'd felt walking away into the dark had grown a little with every pocket successfully picked, each small job completed without being caught, each dangerous situation her crew had slipped away from unscathed. She'd learned if she embraced that feeling, it filled the emptiness inside her, took away her despair and fear, and made her better, braver, stronger.

Tonight was the biggest job they'd ever attempted. Any other crew boss in Dirinan would scoff if Ahrin suggested it to them, casting a practised glance over the scrawny group of children and laughing at the thought of them even attempting it.

And they would be right to.

But that only made the thrill sharper, more exciting. A tremor of it rippled through Lira now, a smile curling unbidden at her mouth.

The gambling hall below her was far from the harbour streets their crew haunted—it sat miles away, in the wealthiest area of Dirinan. A place for its rich citizens to have fun, gamble away their money, and enjoy the pretty men or women of their choice. It was the only district of the city without a gang boss controlling its territory. That fact made it fair game for all crews, but there was a reason no boss had staked it out. The city's wealthiest citizens were well protected.

The city guards paid particular attention to halls like this. Its patrons made sure of it. Yet the city guards weren't her crew's most dangerous threat. Mage warriors assigned to the Shiven city governor in charge of Dirinan often moonlighted for its wealthier citizens. Their attention would be drawn if this all went wrong, and they were much harder to evade.

Getting caught would mean jail at best, execution at worst. And even if the city authorities didn't kill them, Transk, the ultimate crime boss of the harbour district, might, for failing and drawing the city's attention to him. Another thrill shivered through Lira at the reminder of the consequences they risked.

The thought of mages had Lira glancing at her hands, where the violet light still sometimes flashed unbidden. Ahrin lectured her constantly on it, pointing out it only happened when she was emotional, and that emotions were a weakness that needed to be buried.

The concept of Temari Hall had grown so distant it wasn't real to her anymore. What *was* real was the scent of salt and seaweed on the breeze, the rough language of those that lived in the Dirinan harbour district, the warm glow of pride at a successful job. The pride of being part of Ahrin's crew. The satisfaction of not just surviving day to day anymore, but starting to thrive.

Lira had finally found a place that wanted her. They were criminals, not to be trusted, as likely to put a knife in her back if she stepped wrong or messed up badly as have her back. But those were things she could control. Could make sure didn't happen. And they wanted her on their crew.

That was enough for her. It was more than she'd ever had.

A shout of triumph went up from one of the cardplaying tables directly below Lira. An older woman in a velvet blood-red dress was piling up tokens while her companions crowded around offering their congratulations. Their faces were flushed with drink and contentment, skin unlined from never having to worry about where their next meal came from.

Lira's gaze shifted to a nearby table, closer to the centre of the room, where Timin and Yanzi sat amongst several others playing one of the popular card games. Dressed in stolen linen shirts and velvet breeches, they looked older than their fifteen years. Even so, they must have done some fast talking to get inside. They didn't look quite old enough for this place yet.

Ahrin hadn't wanted to use Yanzi. There weren't many Zandians to be found in a Shiven gambling hall, which made him stand out to an uncomfortable degree, but his tongue was the smoothest Lira had ever encountered, and it was unlikely Timin would have gotten past the front door without him. As handsome as Timin was, he was blunt, rough, unable to spin a story convincingly. Unable to shed his criminal skin to fit in anywhere else.

It was just the four of them on the inside tonight. The newer members of the crew waited scattered in the streets around the hall, loitering, in case a distraction or assistance in escape was needed.

Lira intended to make sure it wasn't.

Movement at the edge of her view of the floor signalled Ahrin's arrival. She stalked through the hall, long coat swishing around her ankles—velvet cobalt tonight—looking like any noble or rich merchant's daughter. Her raven hair shone in the lights from the chandeliers hanging from the ceiling, her pale skin marking her as one of them. Her walk was purposeful, gaze searching as if she were looking for a parent, and that would be her story if anyone asked questions.

Her appearance, the single hand tucked in her left pocket, the other loose at her side, was the signal to go. Lira watched as Yanzi and Timin saw her, glanced at each other.

Moments later, Timin shouted, face suffused with anger, pointing a shaking finger at Yanzi. The Zandian stiffened with affront and shouted something back at him. The card dealer tried to get them both to calm down.

Lira waited until Timin threw a punch. Until the guards lining the walls of the hall began closing on that table, until every attendee's attention was drawn by the fight, which was rapidly turning into a brawl.

Then she started scrambling furiously along the crawlspace.

She made it the distance to the other end of the hall in a few minutes, kept crawling until she reached the next grating. This one looked down into the office of the manager who ran the business.

He sat on his chair, frowning over a ledger, chewing on a half-smoked cigar. The ruckus in the hall outside came loudly through the walls, but he clearly trusted his paid security to handle it, because he stayed where he was. Or maybe brawls were a regular occurrence here; part of the entertainment the bored rich folk liked to come for.

Lira carefully lifted the grate up and set it aside in the thick dust, moving painfully slowly so she didn't make a sound and alert him. It took a long time, too long. Timin and Yanzi couldn't keep the fight going forever.

Eventually the grate was out, and Lira positioned herself over the opening. She pushed up her sleeve, slid out the small needle strapped to her forearm and unbound the cloth wrapping it, then dropped through the opening.

She landed on the desk before the manager, filthy bare feet thudding onto the surface, dropping into a crouch to break the momentum of the fall. The man's eyes widened, but that was all he had time for before Lira reached out and buried the drug-coated needle in the fleshy skin of his neck.

Her other hand grabbed for the knife in the small of her back, just in case, but the drug was as fast-acting as Ahrin had promised. He managed a single grunt, then his widened eyes rolled back in his head and he slumped forward over the desk, scattering parchment everywhere and forcing Lira to jump back out of the way. Once she made sure he was fully unconscious, she dropped off the desk and ran for the office door.

Four different bolts were drawn across the inside, meaning nothing short of a battering ram would get through it from outside, but Lira had them drawn back in moments. As soon as she cracked the door open Ahrin slipped inside. Lira caught a glimpse of bright lights and richly dressed people brawling with each other, then closed the door again.

"Nice work," Ahrin said as she moved to the safe. "Is he out?"

"Completely."

"Did he see your face?"

Lira nodded, having to stop herself hopping from foot to foot at the rush of excitement that swept through her. It was all going so well, and it felt good. "The way the vent is positioned above the desk, I had to drop down in front of him to get a clean shot at his neck."

Ahrin said nothing more, turning to begin working on the lock of the safe. Lira moved back to the desk and picked up the small bags of coin the manager had been counting. She shoved them into her pockets, then smiled when a small click from across the room signalled Ahrin's success at opening the safe.

Lira's crew leader pulled a velvet bag from inside her coat—one wealthy ladies regularly carried around with them—and began scooping out the piles of coin into the bag. Lira crouched beside her, filling the remainder of her pockets with the contents of the safe.

Within a few minutes they were done.

Ahrin stood and walked over to where the manager still lay slumped over the desk, his steady breathing rustling the sheets of parchment near his face. Ahrin's knife was in her hand in a blur of movement, and in the next second it was sliding across the man's throat. Blood sprayed onto the parchment and began pooling under his neck.

Ahrin stepped away, straightened her coat to ensure it hid the bulging bag strapped around her waist, then met Lira's gaze. "He saw your face."

Lira accepted that without a word.

"You good to get out?"

"Easy." Lira nodded.

"See you at the rendezvous point."

Ahrin cracked the door open, slipped out. Lira closed it behind her and then slid home all the bolts. She climbed onto the desk, pausing only a moment at the sight of blood soaking through parchment and wooden surface alike, its sharp scent filling her nose. Death was a familiar and sometimes necessary part of her life. If the man described her well enough to the authorities, it would be Lira's life that was forfeit, and she would take hers over his any day.

Avoiding the blood as best she could—not out of squeamishness but because blood-spattered clothes would mark her to any city guards noticing her making her way through the streets to the rendezvous— she quickly piled several of the man's books into a small tower atop the desk. From there she could just jump high enough to reach the hole in the ceiling.

Grunting with the effort, she managed to drag herself back into the crawl space. By then she was trembling with exertion, sweat soaking through her shirt. But triumph buzzed inside her, dispelling any discomfort, giving her extra strength and energy.

The moment the grating was back in place, she was moving, crawling along on her stomach. The stentorian shouts of the city guard arriving to break up the brawl echoed through the floor. Lira hurried, having no desire to get caught by one of them.

Eventually she kicked out the grating on the opposite end and slid out into the cold autumn night. She hurriedly tugged on her worn boots, hidden in the shadows against the wall, and slipped further into the dark alley.

Ahrin, Timin, and Yanzi waited three blocks away at the rendezvous point. The two boys were play wrestling, spirits high after such a success. Ahrin didn't share in it. Her brows were drawn in thought. As if already contemplating the next score.

"You know the drill. Split up," Ahrin said as soon as Lira appeared, her midnight-blue gaze raking her from head to toe. "I had to kill the manager, so there will be extra heat. Make sure you're not followed before coming in. You lead the guards to us and I'll tear you apart before Transk can."

The threat wasn't an idle one. Ahrin killed without remorse, regret, or mercy. Somewhere she'd been taught how to use the blade she wore at her hip like it was an extension of her arm. Not to mention her ability to kill without a weapon. Lira had once wondered at who would train a child to kill so ruthlessly, but not anymore. It didn't matter.

"No coming up coppers for us tonight," Timin crowed as he tossed Lira a duffel bag. "All gold for us."

Lira took the bag and emptied her pockets into it before handing it over to Ahrin. "Want me to come with you?"

Despite Timin's gloating, all that money wasn't theirs. It was going to the leader of the Revel Kings, the biggest organised gang operating along the docks. All smaller crews on the Kings' patch paid a tithe to them, or they were wiped out. It was a simple equation. Ahrin would return with less than five percent of what they'd just stolen. If Transk didn't decide to take it all. There would be no recourse for them if he did.

"Not necessary." Ahrin made a sharp gesture. "The three of you get gone."

It didn't pay to question Ahrin, so the three of them disappeared without a word, taking separate streets to begin the long journey of winding their way home.

STILL FILLED WITH ADRENALIN-FUELLED ENERGY, Lira took a lengthy, circuitous route back to the harbour district. While part of her focused on her surroundings, automatically cataloguing and assessing potential threats as Ahrin had taught her, the rest reminisced on the past hour's activities.

It was the scent of dead flesh and blood drifting on the night breeze that slowed her footsteps, brought her focus entirely to the present. She was in an empty street far from her destination, but it looked familiar. It took a few moments for her to realise it was the same street she'd come to on the night she'd fled the orphanage and followed the man who'd wanted to buy her from the matron.

The abattoir looked as empty as it had then, but some strange curiosity had her ducking down the side of the property, pushing through the same shrubbery she had that night.

Like then, a faint light flicked through the broken glass of the cellar window, and she could hear chairs scraping and people moving about.

Unlike then, instead of fear, she only felt more curiosity. She was looping through the industrial district, run by the Coin Tossers, but their headquarters was several blocks away. Maybe one of the Coin Tosser's subservient crews used the abattoir as a base? But when Lira lingered, still and silent in the shadows as men and women filed out of the side entrance as they had that night, she frowned.

These people weren't crew. They didn't have the watchful looks, the twitch of ready fingers, the tattoos or scars. These people were poor, that was clear from their clothing, and their skin was creased with dirt. They were workers, residents.

Even more curious now, Lira waited long enough for them all to disappear, then left the place and turned in the direction of the harbour district.

Time to get back.

It was well into the early hours before Ahrin's tread sounded on the warped wooden staircase leading down into their cellar home. They'd moved into it a year earlier, after starting to earn enough to pay the owner of the inn on the floors above.

The entry was through a rusted hatch at the end of a dark alley smelling of piss and rat droppings, and the cellar was small, a single rectangular space. Ahrin slept in one corner which was curtained off from the rest for privacy. The six boys of the crew slept in a nest of worn cushions and blankets in another corner. Lira had two blankets and three cushions she slept on in the corner furthest from the door and as far from the others as she could get.

It didn't pay to trust them too much. In her first year with Ahrin's crew, one of the older boys had crept into her blankets while she slept, and had her shirt off and pants down before she woke, struggling. Ahrin hadn't been there, but the noise had been enough to wake Yanzi, who had a much healthier respect for their crew leader and her rules. He'd yanked the older boy off, made sure Lira was unharmed, then told Ahrin the moment she returned.

Ahrin had ordered them all out into the alley, made them watch while she sliced off each of the fingers on the boy's right hand, then sent him, bleeding and sobbing, into the night. The punishment had been accomplished with a ruthless efficiency that was Ahrin's hallmark. She was brutal when necessary, irresistibly charming when that worked better to accomplish her goals, and she never, *ever* flinched. Lira had stopped wondering a long time ago how a girl not much older than her managed to control a group of older boys who were bigger and stronger.

But she did make sure to learn from it.

No crew member had come near Lira since, but even so she'd learned to sleep lightly, able to come awake in a blink clutching the knife that always rested under her pillow. Next time Lira would look after herself.

The centre of the room was taken up by a low table, three tattered armchairs, and a potbelly furnace that kept them warm in winter. The room was cosy at night with the flamelight flicking against the walls, but dull and stark during the day, where the only light was that which came through a single narrow window up at street level.

But it was home.

Lira was still awake, waiting curled up in one of the chairs, the boys passed out. Yanzi snored horribly, but she'd gotten used to that, and now she found the sound comforting. The fire in the potbelly burned low. The glow of their job earlier was still with her, and she replayed it in her mind, knowing the rush would fade and wanting to prolong it as much as she could.

Ahrin's flat gaze scanned the room as she always did on arrival— anything out of place or unusual and she'd pick up on it straight away —before she walked over to drop into the chair beside Lira's. She stretched her legs out towards the warmth of the fire and dug into her coat to pull out two thin cigars. Lira watched as she leaned forward to light them in the pot belly before wordlessly passing one to her.

The cigars were the only reward Ahrin allowed herself after a successful job. But she'd never offered one to Lira before, or any of the crew. Lira fought the smile that wanted to stretch over her face.

"You did well." Ahrin's gaze was on the fire, thoughtful.

Lira nodded. That was true. A puff on the cigar had vanilla-tasting smoke filling her lungs. She coughed, once, then breathed out. Took another drag. Didn't cough the second time. Contentment settled over her.

"He took almost all of it, rotting carcass of a bastard." Ahrin shifted, reaching into her coat to pull out a single bag of coin and toss it onto the nearby table. Quiet anger coated her voice. "Once we pay this month's rent, we'll have barely enough left over for food."

It was their constant, overriding concern, overshadowing every-thing they did. Lira ate enough to survive since joining Ahrin's crew, but worrying where the next meal would come from hadn't changed. Jobs weren't just fun. They were their only means of staying alive.

"One day I'm going to be the one doing the taking," Ahrin added.

Lira smiled, inhaled again. The vanilla really was rather delicious. Smoke curled between them, hazy in the firelight. "Will you move against him soon?" Transk had ambition and his gang's territory had expanded rapidly over the past months. Once he controlled the entire dock territory, he would be amongst the most powerful gang bosses in Dirinan.

Ahrin's mouth thinned. "That would be suicide. We're too young, still children to them. No, we'll bide our time. Keep getting bigger and better scores. Until one day..."

"We own him. We own all of them." Lira looked forward to that day. To having power of her own.

Ahrin didn't say anything to that. Her gaze was distant as she took a long drag on her cigar. The sleeve of her jacket had crept down, revealing the small tattoo on the inside of her wrist. Lira had never gotten close enough to make out exactly what it was, and she'd noticed the effort Ahrin went to to keep it hidden—she'd never seen her in anything but long sleeves.

It was a curiosity that nagged at her. Ahrin didn't have a weakness, or a tell, but there was that tattoo and the way she tried so hard to keep it hidden.

A flash of midnight-blue eyes in her direction caught Lira staring at the tattoo, and that dangerous look rippled over her face.

Lira smoothly changed the subject. "Is something going on in Coin Tosser territory?"

"Why?"

"I circled through their patch on my way back tonight. There was some gathering happening in the cellar of an abattoir... it seemed odd. They were furtive, didn't look like crew."

Ahrin let out a long breath, smoke clouding. "They're not. There's some sort of group of discontented-s roaming through the city. Something about restoring the old ways and making the poor richer." Ahrin must have caught the look on Lira's face. "You don't believe me?"

"I followed a man the night I fled the orphanage. The matron got scared after I was almost killed by some of the girls there and tried to sell me to him." The remembered fear at not so much their words, but what had been in their voices, came back clear as day. Why had that man wanted her? "He went to a gathering at the same place like I saw tonight. I thought maybe I'd join them, but they felt wrong. The kind of wrong that makes you abandon a job rather than push through when you feel it. So I ran."

Ahrin huffed an impatient breath. "You were young and scared. They're nothing. Transk won't even let 'em in his patch, says they're mad and that's dangerous to business, and he's right. Coin Tossers must have had a different view, but that's their mistake. Don't spare them another thought."

Lira's curiosity faded. They did sound useless and crazy, and clearly were no threat to their crew, which had been her main interest.

Abruptly Ahrin stood. "You should be sleeping. I don't want you tired. We've got another job tomorrow."

The thrill leapt in her chest, so soon! "What is it?"

"I'll tell you when you need to know." The edge to Ahrin's voice was back. The one that warned not to push harder. So Lira didn't. Instead she stubbed out the cigar, rose from the chair and went over to her corner without a word. There, she curled up in her blankets and dreamed of the day when Ahrin's crew ruled the Dirinan docks.

It would happen. Because she was Ahrin's secret weapon. After all, mages weren't compelled to study at Temari Hall. Lira didn't have to go there when her magic broke out.

She could stay. And have a life that she controlled. A life where people feared and respected her because of who she was and what she'd done, not some long dead ancestor. Where she could dance with danger, live on the thrill of it, winning over and over again.

If Ahrin didn't give it to her, she'd take it.

But something inside her knew instinctively that Ahrin understood Lira's value. That she would respect it. That together they might be unstoppable.

One day.

One day soon.

CHAPTER 12

Lira woke to more darkness, but knew instantly she wasn't at Temari Hall anymore. She was groggy, mouth dry, her thoughts fragmentary and hard to capture.

Soon, though, the cold bit right down to her bones, slicing through the haze that hung over her and giving her enough clarity to take stock of her surroundings. She was lying on her back on a rough surface, something knobbly pressing into her spine, a thick blanket covering her. An icy draft numbed the skin of her face.

The bite of cold was familiar, like her oldest friend, allowing her to quell the urge to scramble, to fight, to flee, and instead focus on learning her situation first. When she stretched out her hands, her fingers scraped over rough wood to her immediate left, and some sort of starchy fabric barely an inch above her face. The draft was coming from behind her head, and when she concentrated, she caught the snatch of voices floating on the air. Her groping right hand found the staff lying at her side.

As far as she could tell, nobody was immediately nearby—there was no sound of breathing or movement, and the voices were at least several feet away. Painfully slowly, so as not to make a noise, she turned onto her stomach, then inched forward to the narrow rectangle of faint light where the air was drifting in. The voices grew clearer and she forced her still groggy mind to try and make out what they were saying.

"We're almost there, and that wheel is properly broken. We'll... walk the rest of the way and... for it when it's light and not so damn cold. We've already... behind and the others will..."

"You want to carry the... because... not? And what if someone comes across the cart... we get back for it. She'll have our heads."

A telling silence. Whatever it meant, that threat had struck home.

Her groggy mind tried to focus, figure out what the words meant. Whoever had taken her hadn't stopped on purpose. She was in a cart, probably covered in a canvas sheet to keep her hidden. They didn't expect her to be awake either, she guessed. Her focus sharpened—this would be her best opportunity to get free before they arrived wherever they were taking her and there were more abductors to deal with. Gently, she lifted the flap of canvas just enough to be able to peer out.

A wide road stretched behind the cart, well-worn, with enough weeds and holes in the hardpacked dirt to indicate it hadn't been kept up in a long while. That probably meant it wasn't often used. They were taking her somewhere isolated.

Trees crowded all the way up to the road's edge on either side, obscuring much of the light from the full moon above. Nothing else was visible. The voices must be coming from the front of the cart. A soft neigh from the same direction confirmed her suspicions.

Lira didn't hesitate. She wriggled out of the cart and dropped into a crouch behind it. No voices raised in alarm. She couldn't quite make out what they were saying any longer, but the murmurs had changed to a more argumentative tone.

Reaching up to brush her fingers over her staff, she edged her way to the side of the cart and peered around. Two men, tall and dressed plainly, huddled by twin horses standing patiently in the road, hitched to the cart. One man gesticulated wildly with his right hand, his left tapping impatiently against his thigh. The other kept shifting his gaze between the trees and the road stretching away ahead of them. She recognised the look on his face as fear.

Lira turned away, moved to the other side of the cart. Bracing herself, she dashed across the open space into the trees, staying as low as she could so that the cart hid her movement. Once she hit the dark space between the tree trunks, she straightened and kept moving, running several metres into cover before coming to a halt, listening.

Darkness hung thick between trees on all sides, barely illuminated by moonlight from above.

No sound of pursuit. They hadn't seen her.

Lira smiled, taking a deep, savouring breath as the caress of night and triumph of escaping her captors cleared the remaining fog from her thoughts. Whatever drug they'd given her had worn off too quickly. She wondered if she'd woken in her dormitory for the same reason. If so, that was two costly mistakes by her captors already.

Slowly, still scanning her surroundings for danger, she checked her clothes—the tunic and breeches were the same ones she'd been wearing back at Temari. A sniff at her skin had her making a face. *That* smell usually came after two or more days without a wash—a normal state of affairs back in Dirinan but not since arriving at Temari where she bathed every day to make sure she'd never have to smell it again.

Where in all magical hells was she? Better yet, how had she gotten there? She tried to search her memories for anything since being grabbed outside her dormitory room, but there was nothing there. Just emptiness.

Days... something about that nagged at her, she... *rotted carcasses!* She was supposed to be stealing a report. If she didn't show up soon with the information Underground needed... dammit dammit dammit. She'd fail at the first hurdle. They'd write her off, if not grow suspicious of why she failed, not to mention why she'd vanished. The group was suspicious, paranoid. If they set the Darkhand on her before she had a chance to get back and explain what had happened...

Lira reached for the calm objectivity she'd practiced at Temari, the collected thinking, keeping all emotion buried deep. First things first. If she was really lucky, her captors wouldn't notice she was gone until they got to wherever they were going. But there was an even chance they finished arguing and decided to abandon the cart and carry her. She had to get clear.

Then she had to figure out how to get back to Karonan and steal that report before Underground noticed she was missing.

The forest was on an incline, a relatively steep one. Staring up through the treetops, she tried to make out stars or a moon to give her a sense of direction, but she was fooling herself. She had no idea what the stars or position of the moon meant in relation to where she stood —Mapping class was far from her strongest.

She headed down.

Lira moved with all senses alert, sensitive to the slightest change in her surroundings. She'd been unconscious a couple days at least. Maybe much longer. She swallowed, corralled the fear that spiked at the thought with a well-practised ease. The key to using fear was not letting it control you.

Her boots sunk into soft earth as she moved steadily downhill. Trees clustered close together, their branches looming over her as if keeping a close eye on her progress. Mist wreathed the trunks, sliding over the ground like a funeral shroud. Lira's breath steamed in the cold air.

Abruptly she stopped.

Going down was the easiest route. Which meant if they realised she was gone and came after her, they'd likely assume she'd head down-wards. And like a fool she was doing exactly that.

Immediately she changed direction, heading across the incline instead of up or down, moving away from the direction of the road they'd been carrying her in on. She'd barely taken four steps when the trees ahead of her rustled, their branches swinging down to block her path.

Lira stopped, heart thudding. She had her staff drawn in the next second.

Nothing else moved. The night remained hauntingly still. The trees ahead of her rustled again, then grew silent, even though there was no breeze.

She closed her fingers more tightly around her staff and kept walk-ing, pushing her way through the branches in front of her. They resisted her efforts, and when she eventually broke through, the trees ahead of her did exactly the same thing.

The forest was trying to stop her forward progress.

Lira swallowed the hysterical laugh that tried to escape. Maybe Fari had been right. Maybe they were all hallucinating. Or maybe it had just been Lira hallucinating this whole time. A side effect of the drug they'd knocked her out with?

When Lira persisted moving in the same direction out of sheer bloody minded-ness, a more limber branch curled out of the darkness to wrap around her waist and physically pull her out of the tangle of branches she was fighting through.

"Hey!" Lira shouted in affront, her magic instinctively bursting out of her and ripping the branch away. Violet light flashed through the darkness.

Rotted bloody—

She dropped, panting, to the forest floor, the violet glow still lighting up her hands. She quickly extinguished it, furious at herself for the slip. The night was so dark that her light would have been visible for anyone nearby to see. She should have had better control than that.

Temari Hall had made her soft. The realisation was quick in coming. For over two years she hadn't lived on the constant edge of danger that had characterised her life in Dirinan. She'd been protected, wrapped up in safety, the worst difficulties she'd had were the unkind whispers of her fellow students. Students that would never think to harm her, not outside the duelling ring anyway.

It was coming back, though, the old skin she'd once worn, the edge, and her heartbeat quickened. She hadn't felt alive like this in years. Warning rose in the back of her mind—she'd buried all that in her past and left it there. Welcoming it back now would only make it that much harder to lock it away again. She fought to focus her mind. Keep it clear. Practical.

Her mouth curled with determination and she climbed to her feet. Whatever this was, let it try and take her down. It wouldn't find her easy prey.

The trees rustled in agitation, as if warning her not to try again.

Lira stared ahead, contemplated using her magic to force her way through the trees trying to stop her progress. Stubbornness pushed at her to attempt it. Just as she was about to draw her staff and step forward, something brushed over her right ear, an almost affectionate stroke.

She jumped, heart thudding, only barely holding back a shout, and spun to see a smaller branch full of soft leaves withdrawing. It waved slightly in the non-existent breeze.

Fine.

She turned and continued downhill. This time she held her staff ready.

Clearly someone, or *something*, wanted her to go this way.

After what felt like about an hour of walking, the incline began levelling out, but the darkness and the rapidly thickening mist hid enough of her surroundings that she had no better idea of where she was. The trees gradually thinned as the incline flattened entirely, though, and eventually she stepped out into open space.

Here she paused, eyes running over the odd shapes looming out of the mist and darkness, all in differing sizes. A quick investigation revealed the nearest one to be stone—rubble by the cracked surface and uneven edges—covered in ivy and moss. Weeds and grass grew tall around the base. Whatever they were remnants of, they'd been there long enough for the forest floor to grow over them.

Senses alert, she slowly weaved her way through the rubble. One particularly massive piece she passed looked like it had maybe once been a stone foundation block. Then she spotted a light through the mist.

Orange. Flickering. High above the ground. At a guess it was a lit window. She halted again. This had to be the place those men had been taking her to.

The obvious course of action was to turn and run in the opposite direction, find a place where she could sound the alarm. But she had no food, no water, and no idea of which direction to head to find a village or town. If she'd been taken to one of the more isolated areas of Shivasa, Tregaya, or Rionn, she could starve before getting anywhere on foot. Not to mention the apparently sentient trees.

And always nagging at the back of her mind now was her mission for Underground, Greyson's expectation she would be at their next meeting. What would happened if she failed to do either of those things? Everything she'd been building towards would collapse.

The last thing her captors would expect once they realised she'd escaped would be her coming straight to them. They'd be searching for her everywhere *but* here. She could sneak in, steal some supplies, one of their horses, and then make her escape. Thievery was one of her strengths, after all.

A shiver of anticipation rippled through her at the thought of walking right into the most dangerous place to be. They weren't an infallible enemy. After all, they'd already made mistakes with her. A smile curled at the thought of pitting herself against them.

Decision made, Lira started forward again. Soon the rubble cleared, the ground becoming easier to cross. Then the heavy cloud above cleared briefly to allow a shaft of moonlight to shine through.

A hulking mass shrouded in shadow loomed immediately ahead of her, and her footsteps slowed, anticipation increasing, heating her blood. The light she'd seen resolved into the orange flicker of lanterns lit in windows on higher levels of what looked like it might be some sort of rambling castle. Or very large house.

She squinted, trying to make out more detail, but it was too dark and foggy.

Lira glanced around. The area *seemed* deserted. She could hear the occasional hoot of an owl, a rustle in the undergrowth from a night forager, her own quick breathing.

No sign or sound of people or guards. Except for the lights.

Turning back to face the building, she hefted her staff and squared her shoulders. For a moment she thought of Fari, Tarion, and Lorin. Wondered if they'd been brought here too. She dismissed the thought as quickly as it had come. They weren't any of her concern.

She crossed the open ground between where she stood and the wall of the house at a light-footed run, gambling on not being spotted by anyone inside looking out the windows. Like the rubble on the valley floor, ivy crawled across the surface of the stone wall, and on closer inspection, many of the ground floor windows had wooden boards covering broken or missing glass. Some of the boards hung loose, ravaged by time and weather.

A single arched door sat several paces along the wall to her left, festooned with ivy and spiderwebs, that looked undisturbed, but Lira didn't want to take the most obvious entry. Instead she walked further along the outer wall until coming across a set of narrow stone steps leading up to a door set into the first floor level.

She placed her feet carefully, using the silent tread of her days in Dirinan. Her fingers closed tight around the wood of her staff, and her breaths came fast while she fought to maintain a steady, objective calm.

The mist had grown so thick that even when the clouds shifted away again, she could see only a short distance in any direction. Even the bottom of the stairs she'd just climbed had vanished beneath a shroud of fog.

The handle of the door was rusted, spiderwebs clinging to the corners. She reached out, the metal icy against her palm, and turned the knob. It stuck, and she had to make more noise than she liked to force it to turn, but eventually the door swung inward with a soft creak.

Darkness beckoned.

Lira stepped cautiously inside, closed the door, and stood still, waiting for her eyes to adjust to the dimness. Squatting, she reached out to run her fingers over the floor. No dust, no dirt, no musty smell. It had been swept clean.

Interesting. That didn't fit with the obviously abandoned nature of the exterior of the house. She filed that away, then rose to get a better look around her.

It was hard to see much in the darkness, but the corridor yawned in each direction to her left and right. Swinging her staff to let out some of her restless energy, she turned right, where there seemed to be the faintest glow at the end of the hall—perhaps signalling the presence of people. If she wanted supplies, she was going to have to get closer to the area inhabited by whoever was here.

She'd barely covered half the distance when a figure emerged from the dim light, moving towards her at a quick walk. Her adrenalin, along with a fierce surge of anticipation, came rushing to the surface and she dropped into a combat stance, staff ready, magic pushing at the limits of her control.

If this was the person who grabbed her from Temari, she was going to make them sorry they'd ever laid a hand on her.

"Lira, is that you?" The voice was scared, but familiar.

"Fari?"

CHAPTER 13

Lira blinked as Fari ran towards her. "What are you doing here?"

Fari sagged in relief and came to a stop. "Thank magic I'm not the only one here. I literally just woke up, and I'm sure I was given some kind of drug, because my head is all groggy and—"

"Woke up where?"

Fari pointed back the way she'd come. "In a room downstairs. When I woke up, I was alone and the door was unlocked, so I came this way because it was dark up here, so I figured I'd be less likely to run into whoever kidnapped me, and I wanted to try and escape before—"

"Wait." Lira once again interrupted the rambling tirade. "The door was unlocked?"

"Yes."

"And nobody was guarding it?"

"I haven't seen a single person."

"Odd behaviour for kidnappers, don't you think, if that's really what's going on?" Lira spoke mostly to herself, taking another glance around the empty hallway. Unease rippled down her spine.

"I can't think why else we'd have been taken from—" Fari began, but froze when a shout sounded in the distance. The cry was filled with fear. For a moment they stared at each other through the gloom. Fari swallowed. "I think that was Lorin's voice."

"He's here too," Lira murmured, frowning. So it wasn't just her. They'd all been taken from Temari and brought to this place.

"What should we do? He sounds like he needs help." Fari was already turning back in the direction she'd come.

Lira barely heard the words, her thoughts racing to figure out the best course of action. She should ignore Lorin, continue with her plan of finding supplies and a horse. But he was a concussive mage, a potential asset. And that shout... whoever or whatever had caused that note of fear in Lorin's voice, she might need help if she encountered it herself.

She hesitated a moment further, torn, before cursing at herself and moving in the direction of the shout. "What's this way?" she asked Fari.

Fari heaved a sigh, then came running after Lira. "An open space with lots of broken furniture, then stairs down to the ground level. That's where I woke up. I thought it best not to venture around any further down there as it seems well-lit and I thought hiding might be the better..." She trailed off when it became apparent Lira had stopped paying attention.

Silence had returned after the echoes of the cry died away. Lira reached the end of the hall and turned left into the open space Fari had described. Arched windows set into the stone on one side of the room probably let in a lot of light during the day, but on such a cloudy night they barely let in enough to make out the desks and chairs scattered over the floor, most broken.

She weaved through the furniture to the wide stone staircase on the opposite side of the room. The light was coming from somewhere at the bottom, but it wasn't much, just a faint wavering glow. Lira started down, staff ready, and came to a stop just before the bottom step, in the shadows where she would remain invisible to anyone below.

Before her stretched what looked like an entrance hall with a high roof. On the other side of the entrance foyer, faint orange flamelight spilled into the space from somewhere around to the left.

More dim light from outside shone through windows set above two massive entrance doors leading outside. Straight across from them were more, equally impressively sized, doors. Her gaze narrowed— both sets looked new, polished, the chains looped through the handles shining in the faint light.

Before she could follow that thought to discern its meaning, movement blurred in her peripheral vision and Tarion appeared, running out of a corridor to the left of the stairs and heading across the foyer.

A boom roared out then, tearing the silence to shreds—the distinctive sound of a concussive burst ripping through the stillness. Even at a distance, Lira felt the pressure of it closing like a vice around her chest before letting go just as quickly. Tarion slid to a halt, clearly startled.

"Must be Lorin," Fari said in relief, clattering to the bottom of the steps and stopping beside Lira. She hunched over her knees to catch her breath. "Let's go—"

"Wait." Lira held up a hand to stop Fari as she registered the sudden ice-cold of the air shivering over her skin. A fierce thrill pooled in her belly at the sensation, entwining with the instinctive jolt of fear that wanted to surge through her. "I think those rotted things are here too." She unthinkingly slipped into old street slang.

Just as Fari opened her mouth to reply, Lorin sprinted into sight from the direction of the light, fists glowing with the pearlescent blue of his magic, another tall boy in brown robes close behind him.

What she could only describe as *darkness* came questing after them, multiple writhing tendrils of shadow. They spread over the floor, along the walls, up toward the roof, dwarfing the running boys. A tell-tale rattle followed the fading echoes of the concussive boom. Whatever it was, the creature was fast, its looming form closing the distance on Lorin and his companion at a breathtaking rate despite their desperate long-legged strides.

"You have to help them," Fari urged, pushing Lira forward. Her breath frosted as the temperature continued to plummet.

Lira rounded on her with a furious scowl. "Don't touch me. Ever."

Fari's mouth pursed. "Fine, but go. You can do something to help."

Lira calculated the situation in a heartbeat—the creature was going to catch Lorin and the boy in seconds, and Tarion was only halfway there. Her magic was ineffective against this creature, which meant she'd be left with her staff and her quickness against something more than triple her size and at least that many times faster.

A smile curled at her mouth, the headiness of imminent peril rushing through her veins like wildfire.

Lira wanted another chance at this thing more than she wanted to take another breath.

"Stay back here in case someone gets hurt," she snapped at Fari. "We might need your healing magic."

Then she started running, boots pounding over hard stone.

Tarion had almost reached Lorin and the other boy but the monster was closing the distance rapidly. Two of its shadowy legs arched down from the roof in front of them, almost entirely enclosing the two boys within its embrace. Lira could just make out the flash of silver eyes from the thing's angular head.

The closer Lira got, the darker the entrance hall became, the air so cold it was like blades of ice on her skin now. She glanced back to check on Fari, only to see the inky darkness had shrouded the stairs from view.

"Lorin, run faster!" Tarion bellowed, his voice loud and deep and clear.

His form blurred. He vanished from sight.

Then reappeared inside the cage of limbs right beside the two boys' running figures. Shadow blurred and the tendrils coalesced into scaled limbs, one stabbing at Tarion.

He lifted his staff, swept it at the leg. The monster reared up to avoid the blow and lashed out with a second scaled limb at Tarion's head. Tarion shifted aside with all the grace and speed of a Shiven warrior, his staff already moving to block then lash out with another blow.

Lira was only paces away from the monster now, and she swore as she glimpsed one of the shadowy limbs wrap itself around the unfamiliar boy's neck. His eyes bulged and he writhed helplessly as the limb yanked him to the floor and dragged him towards an angular, scaled head shaped around those three liquid-silver eyes. Wisps of darkness leaked from it every time the head moved.

Lorin cried out in mixed fury and fear.

A triumphant rattle rang in Lira's ears, and she swore again as a scaled limb flashed by her head and she had to drop low to avoid it.

Then, with two sliding steps, she was inside the cage of writhing limbs, some still in deep shadow, others materialised into hard scaled carapace. The boy began screaming, the sounds high-pitched and panicked as he was inexorably dragged along the floor. Both Tarion and Lorin were trying to fight through to him, but there were too many limbs, and they were barely avoiding being ensnared themselves.

Swinging her staff furiously merely just to keep from getting grabbed, Lira tried to make her way towards Lorin and Tarion without much luck. As she fought, part of her focus stayed on the thing's head, her sole determination to get to it and kill it somehow.

The initiate let out another scream. Lira danced aside from a sweeping limb and glanced over at the boy as the curved fangs she'd seen in the library, at least twice as long as her arm, flashed down and buried themselves in his chest. His entire body arched and then he slumped, head falling listlessly to the side.

For a moment the tendrils stopped trying to attack them, instead waving around as if in some kind of ecstasy, moving in eerie rhythm with the sound of sucking as it fed from the initiate. She stared in horror, the sight making her hesitate.

The thrill of walking so closely to death was still there, still feeding her strength and speed, but the objective thinking she'd forced herself to cultivate over the past years was also warning her how dire a situation this was.

"My magic doesn't work," Lorin said, voice unbelieving. For a moment he looked completely lost, young and scared, but it only lasted a heartbeat. Before Lira could say anything, he shook himself, and his Shiven features closed over in determination. He swung his staff and continued trying to fight through to the initiate's body. "We have to kill it."

Lorin at least seemed to have basic knowledge of how to use his staff in combat, but he was a raw first year. He lunged straight at the monster, swinging fiercely. Its head lifted abruptly, blood dripping from its fangs, and it gave a furious rattle.

A leg whipped down from somewhere to the left, almost slicing Lorin's chest open. Tarion slid in to take the hit on his staff, grunting with the force of the blow, swinging away just in time to keep from losing his fingers.

Lorin's attack had broken the lull of the monster feeding and it roared back to life, darkness creeping across the floor and walls, keeping them entirely surrounded. Lira ducked and swayed, trying to figure out where best to attack before one of the limbs inevitably caught her. She was skilled with a staff, mostly unbeaten at Temari Hall, but these creatures moved faster than any opponent she'd ever faced before.

"It's too quick," Tarion shouted, echoing her thoughts as he and Lorin were forced apart, dodging. "We have to attack simultaneously, try and distract it long enough to hit somewhere vulnerable. The eyes, I think. The rest of it is either shadow or tough scales. It looks like it can only materialise a few limbs at a time, too, so we can use that to our advantage."

Lira nodded. The plan was a good one, and she caught Lorin's gaze. "You follow our lead. You attack when we do, you duck when we do. No solo heroics, because that will get us all killed. Clear?"

"Clear," he confirmed, dark Shiven eyes glittering.

At first it was clumsy. The creature moved so fast, and their reactions were so desperate, that it was hard to coordinate anything. None of them had ever fought together before, and Tarion was too fast and too skilled for either Lira or Lorin to keep up with—a surprising revelation for her to ruminate on later—so they were constantly a step behind where he needed them to be.

Lira didn't trust either of them to have her back so she fought conservatively, refusing to leave herself open despite the frustrated glances Tarion threw her way. Lorin was reckless, upset about his friend, heedless of the danger he was in, caught up in the bloodlust of battle. It made for a chaotic and dangerous fight.

However, inch by slow inch, they worked their way closer to the monster's centre of mass, to where Lira could see the flash of its fangs as it moved, the flame-like flicker of its silver eyes.

On the first occasion they managed to coordinate their blows, the creature wasn't fast enough to react to all three of them at once. It let out an angry rattle when Lira landed a hard blow on its left eye. She made it count, shoving her wooden staff deep into the luminous orb as hard as she could before dancing away.

The silver light in the eye faded to dullness and a sticky substance trickled out of the socket, splattering over her hands. The nauseating scent of rotten eggs filled the air. The creature's rattling turned into a high-pitched squeal. She stifled a wince as the noise tore through her eardrums, then a wide smile of pure satisfaction spread across her face.

This thing was going down.

"Attack from the left side where it's blinded," Tarion bellowed over the screeching.

Lira gave a brief thought to the fact that the uproar they were making must surely be drawing their kidnappers like flies to honey, before following Tarion's orders. One danger to face down at a time. The thrill rose back up through her, stronger and more powerful than before. Everything slowed down: the rasp of her breathing echoing in her ears. The sweat on her skin turning to ice from the intense cold.

The loss of an eye seemed to hamper the monster's quickness, and another hit from Tarion had it seething back towards the wall, lashing out wildly with its limbs in a desperate attempt to keep them from closing on it.

One leg materialised behind Lorin's foot, grabbing firm hold of his ankle. He bellowed in anger as he hit the ground. It dragged him mercilessly towards those fangs.

"Ignore him and get to another eye," Lira shouted at Tarion, who was already turning to try and help the initiate. "We can't afford to let it distract us."

The battle grew even harder then, as they were forced to spend most of their concentration and effort dancing away from the lashing limbs. Her breathing started to burn in her chest, and her legs trembled with exertion. She was going to start slowing down as her body tired, and she couldn't afford that or one of those legs would get her. They had to end this quickly.

"Lira, we have to help Lorin!" Tarion shouted, gaze on Lorin as he fought bitterly, clawing at the floor as he was dragged along it.

"We can't afford to," she snapped back. "We have to—"

"It's keeping its head too high for us to reach the eyes." A frantic note entered Tarion's voice.

"Lira!" Fari suddenly called out.

Lira ducked a wild swing, then backed up a few paces, turning to see Fari had left the safety of the stairs and come close enough to watch the fight. She'd lined up a series of objects a short distance away —a number of rusted iron wall brackets, some large pieces of broken glass, and a marble vase. The girl put her hands on her hips and lifted her eyebrows as if to say, 'well, be useful.'

Lira risked a look at Tarion. He'd seen the same thing, and he gave her a little nod before diving into a tiny gap between two swinging legs. She lowered her staff and took a steadying breath as she continued dancing around writhing darkness. Once she had the focus she needed, she summoned her magic. Violet light flared through the hall as it rose up in her, lifting the pressure from her chest and dispelling all fear and physical weariness.

She sank into the thrill of it. Of knowing nothing but surging strength and power.

Her fingers flicked and she lifted one of the stone vases Fari had found.

The magic leapt through her veins, and she sent the vase flying straight at the creature's other eye. It sensed the attack coming and shifted away just in time so that the vase shattered against the wall.

But Lira didn't stop. Didn't pause.

One after the other, she picked up the objects and flung them with as much strength and accuracy as she possessed. Her heart thudded in time with each throw. Her breathing eased. Magic surged in her body, a steady rhythm.

She might not be a mage of the higher order like the Darkmage, but she'd honed her telekinetic skill to make it strong, skilled, better than that of any mage she'd yet faced. She ignored the part of her that still wanted more, that felt limited with only this, and dived completely into what she had.

Coppers, it felt amazing.

Rattling in thwarted fury, the creature dodged and ducked, growing more and more desperate as the speed and accuracy of Lira's attacks increased. Eventually it was forced to lower its head enough that Tarion was able to leap forward and bury his staff in the second of its three eyes. The rattling sound turned into a loud, high-pitched shriek that spread outwards. Lira winced, forced to cover her ears, but she kept her gaze moving, watching out for flailing limbs. Then the creature stilled, before collapsing ungracefully to the floor.

For a moment all Lira could hear was the panting of her breath, the heavy thudding of her heart. Adrenalin and magic flooding through her all at once. The grin on her face was back, triumph surging through her.

She'd defeated it.

Tarion stood with his staff still raised, chest heaving, eyes wide at the dead creature before them. Then Lorin scrambled to his feet and ran over to drop beside the boy's body. "Haler!"

Fari was there moments later, but she was already shaking her head as she placed a palm on the boy's forehead. Tears glistened in her eyes. "I'm so sorry, Lorin. There's too much blood loss, even if the fangs hadn't punctured his heart."

Lorin flinched and stood up. His face hardened, and he took a breath before dispelling all emotion from his expression. Tarion's gaze was on the body, sadness written all over his face. Lira breathed in the rush still swirling through her. It had been so long, and she yearned for more of it.

The moment lasted a handful of heartbeats. Maybe seven breaths.

And then the silence was broken by a series of simultaneous, high-pitched screams, echoing from a good distance away. They sounded like they were coming from all different directions.

Silence fell again.

Lira looked at Tarion, instinctively re-drew her staff, then shifted her gaze to Fari and Lorin. They looked as apprehensive as she felt.

The silence held for another handful of seconds before rattling echoed through the halls. Chains creaking together. Unhappy and angry. And unmistakably heading in their direction.

"Any chance that thing has friends, and they know we just killed it?" Fari asked, her voice rising to a higher pitch.

The rattling grew louder, closing quickly on them, signalling the approach of more than just one monster. It sounded like a horde of them, the sharp pitch of the noise making Lira want to cover her ears.

"We can fight them," Lorin said, stubbornly standing his ground, staff raised.

Fari was already backing away. "No we can't. If we want to stay alive, we run."

"What about Haler's body?" Tarion looked torn. "We should take it with us, bury it properly. His family would want that."

Lira hesitated. She wanted to keep fighting, to take on multiple monsters if that's what they wanted to throw at her. "You take the body and I'll cover you."

"Lira, don't be an idiot. We barely survived one of them," Fari shouted, already turning to run. "Tarion, you know better too. Haler's body isn't worth our lives."

The girl's insult stung, but it brought Lira crashing back to reality. The healer was right. She was letting her hunger for the thrill overtake common sense. The situation had changed, and now survival meant running instead of fighting.

"We'll come back for him," Tarion muttered to himself, then let out a breath before running after Fari.

Lorin was still refusing to move, so Lira grabbed the initiate's arm and dragged him after her as she broke into a run after Tarion and Fari back towards the stairs, wondering why she was bothering. She should just let the idiot get himself killed.

Tarion's long legs quickly outpaced them. A glance behind revealed a writhing mass of darkness spreading through the hallway after them, completely blocking any light. It made no sound but that infernal rattling that had shifted to an unsettling mix of anticipatory and angry. The cold was so deep it burned her lungs when she breathed.

They scrambled up the stairs towards the first floor landing. Lira ploughed straight into the back of Tarion when he slid to an abrupt halt ahead of her. Swearing, she regained her balance, only for Lorin to collide with her from behind.

"We can't outrun them. We have to try and lose them!" Tarion said as he broke into a run across the furniture-strewn room rather than continuing up the stairs.

Lira took one look at the writhing tendrils of inky darkness already sliding up the stairs towards them, and followed. This time Lorin came after without complaint, Fari bringing up the rear.

"How many of them are there?" Fari asked breathlessly, and uselessly.

"What about ducking into one of these rooms?" Lorin suggested as they returned to the dark corridor Lira had first entered from outside. He waved at the closed doors on their right.

"Without knowing what's beyond them, we could find ourselves trapped inside a room without a way out," Tarion said. "Better we try and lose the monsters completely and then find a safe place to bunker down."

"They're getting closer!" Fari shouted in panic.

Lira didn't need to look back to realise the same thing. A shadow crept along the wall to her left, stretching down towards the floor and her ankle. The light grew dimmer and dimmer, the deepening cold like ice against her sweaty skin. She swerved away from the questing limb.

The rattling grew more high-pitched, as if in excitement. Her hands flared violet as her magic tried to come to her aid, but there was nothing it could do.

All of them increased their pace, but it didn't last long, as growing weariness sucked at the strength in their legs. Three classes a week of sparring drills hadn't prepared any of them for this kind of physical exertion. Anger at herself surged. She was a rotted fool for allowing that to happen. Allowing herself to be lulled by the safety and softness of Temari Hall. It might cost her life.

Even if they made it to the end of the corridor, at the speed they were moving the creatures would catch them before they made it much further beyond. Tarion's plan to lose them was doomed to fail. Worse, they had no idea what was around the corner. What if it was nothing but a dead end? They'd have trapped themselves with nowhere to go.

Her mind raced, searching for alternatives, refusing to give up.

Then, unbelievably, a doorway further down the hall on their right swung open. A tall, broad-shouldered figure in a grey apprentice robe burst out of it. "This way!" he bellowed, waving them towards the open door while he stepped clear. Lira stared.

It was Garan Egalion.

CHAPTER 14
BEFORE

Ahrin dropped down on the ragged couch beside Lira, sending a cloud of dust billowing into the air, and let out a satisfied sigh. "Want a drag?"

Lira took the thin cigar she offered with a smile of thanks, sucking in a deep breath of the spiced smoke before handing it back. Ahrin usually preferred vanilla but this one tasted like cinnamon. It prickled on her tongue in a pleasant way and she breathed out the smoke slowly, savouring it.

The warehouse loft they'd recently moved into was hazy with cigar smoke and the soft glow of firelight from the pot oven in front of them—much larger than their previous one. Dark sheets they used as curtains were drawn firmly over the square windows along one wall to keep the light and heat from escaping.

Chatter drifted down from the opposite end of the loft, where the rest of the crew—thirteen strong now—slept in a nest of blankets and mattresses covering the floor. Only the four original members were allowed at this end of the loft, where Ahrin still had a curtained-off corner to herself.

The space in the middle, dividing the two ends of their home, was cluttered—stuff they'd stolen in a pile in one area, broken shelves crammed with books that Yanzi and Picker liked to read right beside it. There was a table and chairs large enough to fit them all where they ate their meals. A larder used to store what food they could get sat along the wall by the entry door.

It was cluttered and broken and nothing matched, but it was home. Every time Lira stepped foot inside she never wanted to leave again. She smiled up at the rafters, head leaning back on the sofa, basking in the glow of another successful robbery. Tonight's had been the most dangerous so far, and she had a stinging knife wound along her ribs to show for it. But she savoured the pain too. Because once again she'd come out on top. *They'd* come out on top.

"Why is she your favourite?" Timin complained. He sprawled on a pile of cushions by the potbelly, the firelight flickering on his handsome face. "You never share your cigars with us."

Ahrin smiled lazily. Tonight she was at her charming best, most of the sharp edge that characterised her usual interactions with them softened by the glow of satisfaction. She'd just returned from a meeting with Transk—passing on the proceeds from the job—to announce that he'd gifted them the four-block territory around their loft.

They had a patch of their own now. Still under Transk's ultimate control, but otherwise theirs. The protection money from the inns and shops inside the four blocks would come to Ahrin directly, with only a percentage off the top going to the Revel Kings. Their larder wasn't going to be mostly empty much longer.

"Who said she was my favourite?"

Not long after turning thirteen, Lira had finally started growing, so that now when Ahrin shifted beside her, lifting the cigar to take another long drag, their shoulders pressed warmly together.

"She's the youngest crew member, still a kid, and yet she gets your cigars, the top cut of every job we pull, and she's the only one you let plan jobs with you."

"I'm younger than you, Timin. You saying you should be leader?" Ahrin's voice turned cold in a heartbeat, the tone that signalled danger for those who knew her. Lira smiled inwardly. Timin's constant whining about his place in the crew irritated her to no end, and she enjoyed those times when it grew strident enough that Ahrin was required to put him in his place. The flat look she delivered the words with always did the trick. It was the same look she wore whenever she killed.

"Dig yourself out of that one, Tim." Yanzi laughed softly from where he lay sprawled beside Timin, head in the other boy's lap, staring up at the ceiling.

"I'm not challenging." Timin sounded surly. "You know I'd never do that."

"I do. Because you're too cowardly." Ahrin mocked, mouth curled in a smile. "That's why I trust you."

His jaw tightened and he looked away. Lira smirked.

"Right again!" Yanzi whooped. A grudging smile flitted over Timin's face, and his hand idly ran through Yanzi's short hair. Yanzi beamed adoringly up at him, pupils wide and glassy.

"What's he been smoking?" Lira asked Ahrin in a murmur.

"Cloudweed." Ahrin shifted again, stretching out her legs. Lira did the same, trying to work out the kinks. Growing so rapidly left her with aching joints some days. While Timin and Yanzi looked more like men than boys now, she and Ahrin were transitioning through the awkward phase between scrawny child and gangly teen. Only Ahrin had managed to develop curves, while Lira was all narrow limbs and bony knees. "I keep a strict eye on how often he smokes, but he pulled that job well today, and that's the reason Transk gave us a patch, so he's allowed a reward."

"You never give me cloudweed."

Ahrin's blue eyes shifted to her. "Cloudweed messes with your head. I need you sharp, Lira. You're my number two."

Lira already knew that. Would never willingly compromise her instincts or clear thinking by taking a drug, but she liked to test the boundaries with Ahrin, see how far she could push. She smiled at Ahrin's words.

"Besides, you don't need it," Ahrin murmured, voice pitched only for Lira's hearing. "These boys do what we do because they have to survive, because they want a hint of power, and Timin likes his violence. But you're addicted to the thrill of the chase, the win, don't think I haven't noticed."

"Is that a problem?" Lira lifted an eyebrow.

"No." Ahrin took a long drag, then leaned in closer, one arm stretched along the back of the couch. "Unless you allow it to make you reckless and put us all at risk. Have you dealt with that properly?"

She was pointing to Lira's ribs, where spots of fresh blood had soaked through her shirt. Lira shifted away, hiding her wince at the movement. "I cleaned it, it's fine."

"It better be." Ahrin let those words linger a moment, then sat back and pulled a folded sheaf of parchment from inside her jacket pocket. With quick movements she unfolded it on the table before the couch.

"Next job?" Lira scrambled forward eagerly.

Ahrin nodded. "These are the plans for Hester Milenar's residence. He's a merchant, lives in Karonan, makes his fortune from the fleet of trading ships he owns."

Lira ran her eyes over the parchment, a little thrill echoing through her. They hadn't hit a private home before. The lines and markings didn't make a whole lot of sense to her, but they didn't need to. Once Ahrin explained it, the details would stick in her memory. "A man that wealthy will have private guards."

"Right. You and Picker are going to spend the next week watching the place. Count the guards, when they change shift, where they eat."

"Where they eat?" Lira lifted an eyebrow.

"Quickest and easiest way to knock out the guards at once is to put something in their food. Otherwise we risk not killing one quick enough and them calling for help." Ahrin frowned over the map, smoke curling into the air from her cigar. "His neighbourhood will be impossible to get out of if the alarm is raised. Mage warriors and Shiven soldiers will swarm the streets in minutes."

"Those are walls, right?" Lira pointed at a line on the map. When Ahrin nodded, she continued. "If we can take out the guards like you say, then this is a two man job—you and me. Over the walls, inside the back door. We'll be in and out before the guards are awake. Rest of the crew can linger around in case the alarm goes up to cause a distraction while we get clear."

"You have to get the guard numbers and rotations right, or this could go bad quickly," Ahrin warned. "Especially if he's paying for a mage amongst his private security."

"I won't get them wrong." Lira scoffed.

"I should be your number two," Timin grunted, breaking into their murmured planning. He and Yanzi had been quietly listening—understanding their job would be managing the distraction.

Ahrin leaned back into the couch and smiled lazily at him. "When Lira's magic breaks out and she abandons us all for that fancy mage school in Karonan, you can be number two."

"That's never going to happen." Lira laughed, reaching out to snatch the cigar Ahrin was holding and take a drag. The spiced smoke filled her lungs and calmed her even further. She relaxed into the couch, enjoying the warmth of Ahrin next to her and the comfort of having a place where she felt mostly safe.

They were criminals. Increasingly daring ones. Well-known ones now too, despite their youth. The city guard might come bursting in any day. Or a rival gang might decide they were too dangerous and stage a hit. All were constant possibilities. But Lira had learned and grown in five years. She knew herself. Knew Ahrin and their crew.

One day, one of those things might happen. But when it did, they would deal with it.

"Give that back!" Ahrin snatched the cigar from her fingers with an uncharacteristic smile. Lira wondered briefly if she'd had some of the cloudweed—their cold-as-ice, ruthlessly practical crew leader had never relaxed like this before. "If I had magic I'd be gone faster than Timin can complain about not getting enough food."

"Yeah, well, I'm part of your crew. This is my home. I don't need to learn magic at Temari Hall. When it breaks out, I'll teach myself, here." Here where nobody looked at her like she was a monster about to unleash terror on the world. Here where she had a place. Where she fit.

Ahrin took a deep drag, then rested her head back against the couch, eyes sliding closed. "You're meant for better things than this, Lira."

There is nothing better than this, Lira wanted to say. But she didn't. She'd never heard Ahrin say anything like that before, wasn't sure she wasn't being set up for some sort of mockery. So instead she joked, "Did you take some of Yanzi's cloudweed?"

Ahrin's eyes opened and stared straight into hers, the familiar coldness back. "This life is going to screw you in the end. You'll eventually see that it's no different to the orphanage or the village that didn't want you. Get out as soon as you can, that's my advice."

Lira frowned. "I'm not leaving you, Ahrin."

Ahrin smiled then, in a blink the good mood returning, and she reached out to sling her arm around Lira's shoulder. "I hope not."

Lira shoved at her, made another grab for the cigar. Ahrin held it higher than she could reach, and soon they were wrestling for it, laughing and scratching and hair-pulling, Lira completely heedless of the wound in her side. Ahrin won, of course, and smoked the last few puffs with a smug air.

"See, favourite," Timin muttered. "She'd murder any of the rest of us that tried to steal her cigar."

"Here, have a drag of this," Yanzi offered. "It'll make you feel better."

"Not tonight," Ahrin said sharply, rising to her feet. "He hasn't earned it."

Timin accepted that with a roll of his eyes. "You off to check on Boya?"

"She and Ternal should be finishing up their job about now. I want to make sure they haven't screwed anything up." The fun persona of moments earlier had been replaced with the cool and dangerous haughtiness of Ahrin the gang leader.

"Ahrin?" Lira's gaze was on the map of the merchant's residence, something occurring to her.

She stopped at the door, eyebrow raised.

"The next job. How are you going to get to the guards' food to drug it?"

A smile curled at Ahrin's mouth. "While you're watching for the guards' rotations, Yanzi's going to have a chat with the house's cook when he just happens to run into him in the markets. We're going to deliver the doctored food right into their kitchen."

Lira settled back against the couch, watched her go, then sent a smug smile Timin's way after the door had closed behind her.

He scowled, looked away.

Her grin widened and she closed her eyes, content and warm.

CHAPTER 15

Lira ignored her astonishment at Garan Egalion, of all people, showing up in the corridor ahead of them and focused on pushing her tired body to keep running. The hallway had grown incredibly dark, the cold biting, the infernal rattling of the monster growing in pitch and intensity as its prey continued to evade it.

A scaled limb swung down from above, too fast for Lira to react, and slammed into her shoulder. She flew sideways, hit the opposite wall hard, and pain bloomed through her side. Swearing, she ignored the pain, pushing off the wall and twisting aside as another tendril writhed toward her leg.

"Lira, duck!" Tarion's voice shouted.

Her heart pounded as another limb swept out to try and wrap around her throat. She lunged backwards, falling to the floor to avoid it. She was almost entirely surrounded now, the darkness sinking down around her. Tarion, Fari, and Lorin were almost at the doorway where Garan stood. She could just make out another grey-robed apprentice hovering behind Garan, reaching up to lay her hand on his shoulder. He closed his eyes in concentration then lifted his arms. "Tarion, get inside. I've got this!"

His magic swept out just as Tarion reached him.

Tarion didn't hesitate. He dove through the doorway. A step behind him, Lorin paused as if wanting to stay and fight, but Fari gave him a good shove, pushing him through ahead of her. Lira scrambled off the floor, stumbling, dancing aside from two waving limbs, as Garan used his magic to tear doors off hinges and hurl them at the writhing darkness between Lira and where he stood.

The shadowy tendrils waved around frighteningly fast, and the doors seemed to fly into a vortex of inky blackness with absolutely no effect. But it slowed them fractionally, enough for Lira to stumble the final few steps and duck through the doorway, for Garan and the female apprentice to follow after and slam the door closed.

Lira's gaze was already scanning the room as she entered it, drawing on magic to wrap around the nearest piece of heavy furniture—a chest. Without any finesse at all she dragged it across the room and dropped it in front of the door. Garan followed suit, stacking two chairs and a desk on top of it.

By the time they finished, the female apprentice had crossed the small room and was opening a door on the opposite side to usher the others through. She was vaguely familiar, but Lira couldn't place her name.

Rattling hissed through the doorway, infuriated, and seconds later something slammed into it, shaking the door on the hinges. One of the chairs from their barricade crashed to the floor.

"Quick, this way!" Garan ran for the door the girl was still holding open.

Lira swallowed her questions and followed. The door opened into another corridor, this one narrower, but just as dark. Garan turned left, everyone falling in behind him. They ran, making an effort to be quiet despite their rasping breathing and exhausted legs. After fifty metres or so, Garan skidded right around a corner, ran almost the entire length of another hallway, then slid to a halt outside another door. This one was small, unobtrusive. Garan yanked it open, then stepped back to wave them all through.

It was a small room, no windows, faint light from the hall outside showing what looked like a desk and single chair, plus a row of what

138

might be cupboards. Another door stood ajar, revealing a set of narrow stone steps lit by wavering torchlight coming up from whatever was below. Garan headed straight for it, waving them after him.

The scent of spices hit Lira's senses and moments later they emerged into what looked like a kitchen storeroom. It was a large space, half-filled with sacks of unknown supplies, with stone walls and floor. A quick glance around revealed only one other entrance, and that had been barricaded by a haphazard stack of crates. Drag marks in the dust on the floor indicated this was probably Garan and his friend's work.

Putting this room together with the smaller room upstairs and the furniture she'd seen in it—she hadn't cased a place with a single glance in a few years but the instinct had never left her—she figured that it was the kitchen manager's, or head cook's, office. It fitted well with her earlier guess they were at some abandoned lord's estate. An isolated one.

The kitchen... She frowned, chasing that thought, trying to—

"Are you all okay?" Garan's voice broke into her focus. His green eyes were studying them all in concern.

"We're fine," Lira snapped, his concern irritatingly cloying. "How did you know we were out there? Scratch that. What in all rotted hells is going on?"

The female apprentice answered coolly, her perfectly manicured eyebrows raised in distaste at Lira's cursing. "We thought we were the only ones here. Then we heard the unbearable screeching and a concussion burst go off, and rapidly re-evaluated that theory."

"After some debate we decided to go and check it out." Garan shot a smile in the girl's direction that indicated she'd vigorously disagreed with that plan. The smile faded quickly though, a shudder rippling through him. "We saw you coming, and that... *thing* chasing you, and thought fast."

"Thanks," Tarion said, his voice sincere but not overly warm, or filled with the relief Lira would have expected at seeing his cousin alive and well. She frowned—she'd imagined the sons of Alyx and Ladan Egalion would be as close as their parents were.

"Who are you?" The haughty girl pointed at Lorin, her blond curls swinging as she shifted her gaze between them.

Lorin straightened his shoulders, neatened his robe. "Initiate Lorin Hester."

"And he just watched his friend die, so maybe you could lay off the interrogation for a few seconds," Fari said, hands firmly on hips again.

Garan whitened, and even the girl fell silent. "Someone died?"

"Two people. Haler and... my friend, Derna." Fari bit her lip, tears making her eyes sheen.

A brief silence fell, but Lira scowled when the blond apprentice looked at her next, eyebrows raised. "Don't pretend you don't know me. The granddaughter of Shakar. Just as evil as he is. Likely to murder you all in your beds someday. That's me."

"We don't all think that, you know?" Garan said with a smile.

"Yeah? You could have fooled me." Lira's scowl deepened as she looked at the unfamiliar apprentice. "Who are you?"

"Athira Walden." The voice was as cool as the eyes. "Third year apprentice. We're in staff combat class together—you beat me in a sparring match last week. Nice of you to remember me."

Ah. That was why she looked familiar. Now Lira put the name together with the face. Athira Walden was Tregayan mage royalty, born of successive Mage Council members. Destined to sit on the council herself one day. "What can you do?" Lira asked her, looking to judge how useful she might be.

Athira clearly didn't appreciate her tone, and simply settled a cool glare on Lira.

"Athira's an amplifier," Garan explained, mouth twitching. "She makes the magic of those she touches more powerful."

"You!" Lira pointed at Lorin. "Where'd you find your friend? Before he was killed by that thing, I mean."

Both Garan and Fari shot Lira a scowl at her insensitivity, but Lorin straightened his shoulders. "Back at Temari, just before we got knocked out and brought here. Haler was—"

"That's fascinating," Fari broke in. "What I'd prefer to talk about is Lira's initial question—what in the name of magic is GOING ON HERE!"

"Keep your voice down." Lira rounded on her furiously. "Unless you want all the creatures out there converging on us. Not to mention whoever brought us here."

"There's at least one outside prowling the grounds too," Lorin offered. "I crept past it on my way in here."

"You were *outside*?" Fari frowned.

"You weren't?" Lorin matched her frown.

Fari shook her head. "No, I woke up in here—the last thing I remember was heading down the stairs of the tower at Temari Hall looking for you, and then bang, I woke up flat on my back in a dark room in a strange building. I waited for my eyes to adjust to the dark and the complete and utter panic to subside, and then—"

"Wait, hold up." Garan lifted his hands. "Why were you looking for Lorin at the tower?"

A moment's confused silence, then...

"Garan, did you wake in the middle of the night at Temari Hall?" Tarion spoke into the tense silence, looking uncomfortable when everyone's gaze shifted to him.

"No. The last thing I remember is hanging out in the third-year common room and making plans for the next day. It was just after dinner." Garan shrugged. "Then I woke up here."

"The last thing *I* remember was being in the fourth-year common room, with Censa. He was doing his level best to get his hands inside my shirt. Unsuccessfully, I might add," Athira said, then her eyes narrowed as they all stared at her. "What? Something different happened to you three?"

Tarion seemed to have clammed up, and Lira was already turning away, having no patience for explanations, so Fari heaved a sigh and began giving Garan and Athira a quick rundown of what had happened to them.

While she spoke, Lira searched the room, in particular confirming where the exits were—there was one apart from the stairs they'd come down—and checking whether there were any weapons lying around that might be more effective than their mage staffs, preferably something with a blade. There weren't. Although she'd come to the right place for her original plan. She could load up on food supplies here,

sneak out to find horses. Get away. Except that might prove more difficult now if Lorin was right about a monster lurking outside... damn,
damn, damn.

Next she moved to the nearest shelf lined with sacks. They weren't
dusty, and no smell of rot or mildew came from them. These hadn't
been here long.

More sacks were piled in the corner, and when she went closer to
investigate, her searching gaze landed on a trapdoor set into the floor.
The area around it was uneven, broken, as if the stone floor had been
dug up to install the trapdoor. She knelt, frowning at the reinforce-
ment of bars in the wood of the trapdoor and the thick padlock on the
opening.

She cast a speculative glance at the barricaded doorway. It had to
lead to a kitchen. And if these supplies were new, then *somebody* was
probably using the kitchen. If they tried to come in here for supplies
and found the door blocked...

"We should leave this room." Lira spoke at exactly the same time
Athira did, her voice drowned out by the other girl's much louder
exclamation.

"What do you mean, Karonan was deserted? Were you smoking
cloudweed?"

"We all saw it," Fari said. "From Councillor Egalion's office on the
top floor. Dark and empty city in all directions."

Lira didn't miss the hopeful glance between Garan and Tarion at
the mention of Tarion's mother. Did they think she was coming to save
them? Irritation bubbled in her at that thought. Depending on what
had happened in Karonan, she might not even know they were missing
yet, especially if they'd been taken somewhere close to the city and
only a few days had passed.

"I don't understand how that's possible," Garan said patiently.

Fari threw her hands in the air. "Welcome to my world."

"We both woke up here." Athira cast a glance at Garan. "In a room
downstairs."

Lira rubbed two fingers at her temple as she glanced warily at the
kitchen door again. The whole situation was off, and right now
anything out of place was sending her instincts prickling down the

back of her neck. Seven apprentices, all snatched up from Temari Hall, and dumped in... wait.

She looked up, glancing between Garan and Tarion. "What are you even doing here?"

Garan turned to her. "What? Athira just explained—"

"I don't care coppers for what Athira said. You and Tarion. Why aren't you both with your parents in Alistriem for mid-winter?"

"Feel free to un-twist that look of deep suspicion on your face, Lira. I wasn't planning to go home for mid-winter. Some friends were going camping out of the city and I didn't want to miss out," Garan said easily.

She did *not* remove the look of suspicion from her face. "Camping? In the middle of winter?"

"Sure. Haven't you ever skated on the lake?" he asked defensively. "It's fun."

Athira snorted. "Spider, doing something fun? Have you met her?"

Resentment rose, and she fought it down as she rounded on Tarion. "What about you?"

"I was planning on leaving a day late after I finished..." He trailed to an inaudible halt, eyes on the floor.

"Where are your friends, Garan, the ones you were going camping with?" Fari asked before Lira could push Tarion further.

"Yeah, it was Rodick and..." Garan's handsome face paled. "I don't know."

Fari pressed. "Do you share a room with them, or were you with them in the common room before all this happened?"

Lira glanced at the healer, confused by Fari's quick shifts from almost completely panicked to sound, rational thinker. The girl claimed to be terrible at learning, but she didn't seem stupid to Lira. Quite the opposite. Lira had told her to hang back during the fight with the creature before, but she'd still found a way to make herself useful. Another oddity. Oddities made Lira uncomfortable.

"That scowling look on your face is priceless, Spider." Athira rolled her eyes skyward. "I hate to break it to you, but we didn't kidnap ourselves."

Lira ignored her, instead waiting for Garan to respond to Fari's question. He let out a sigh, then shrugged. "I was with them in the common room. We were planning our departure for today, making sure we had everything we needed." He pushed off the wall, running a hand through his hair. "I woke up here. I ran into Athira while I was walking around. We heard you and went to find out what was happening. I don't know anything else, I swear it."

"Haler woke with me here, outside near a door. It was unlocked," Lorin said before Lira could ask. "We came inside and almost ran straight into the creature you saw chasing us."

"To be clear," Athira spoke up, incredulity written all over her face. "Someone kidnapped us out of Temari Hall and brought us to an old, abandoned estate where they've dropped us with a bunch of vicious, blood-drinking monsters. But before they took you—Garan and me too while we apparently slept through it—they somehow completely emptied Karonan?"

"It's not possible." Garan shook his head. "Not in the space of a few hours. An entire city that size, people and all? It would be impossible for even a group of powerful mages."

Athira turned a speculative glance on Lira.

Anger surged, and she met the girl's look with a scowl. "No, not even the granddaughter of the evil Shakar could shut down an entire city by herself," she snapped. Part of her fury stemmed from bitterness. Shakar probably *had* been powerful enough to do such a thing. She never would be. That disappointment was never far from the surface. Especially now.

"Master Egalion probably could," Fari pointed out.

"That seems like an unlikely scenario." Athira huffed. "Are you listening to yourselves?"

Silence fell, gazes dropping to the floor. Lira went back to casing the room to make sure she hadn't missed anything useful. It *was* insane and completely illogical. There had to be another explanation they just hadn't thought of.

Kitchens... deliveries... The thought caught and held again. She frowned.

Garan shook himself. "Either way, we know we were drugged, and we know we were taken from Temari Hall. We know we're in an isolated location surrounded by thick forest, and that we're sharing that location with multiple creatures who are immune to magic and seem bent on killing us."

"Drugged!" Lira cut over them, realisation flooding through her. "They were drugged candles, probably lit outside our doors to put us to sleep. They were delivered to the kitchens the day before—the servant said it was the usual delivery, but someone must have replaced the normal candles with drugged ones."

"And you know that *how?*" Athira asked.

"Doesn't matter." Lira spoke as Fari opened her mouth. All that realisation told her was that those who had taken them were professional, and had done this before, despite their mistakes. But no matter who they were, Lira's only goal was getting back to Karonan as fast as possible. "We need a plan to get out, and we should start with leaving this room. Those supplies look new, which means someone is probably using the kitchen and could wander in here and find us at any time."

All sets of eyes widened as they turned to the kitchen door.

"Lira's right. If Karonan has been taken, or attacked in some way, then we need to warn the council. I say we sneak out of the building while avoiding the creatures, take some supplies with us, and hike out of here as fast as we possibly can before they realise we've gone. We make for Carhall." Garan stepped forward, naturally taking charge. Lira had seen his father once, on one of the times he'd visited his son at Temari Hall, and in that moment Garan looked very much like Ladan Egalion, with his gravity and air of reassurance.

It irked her.

The others seemed to respond to it, however, and everyone started nodding along with his words. Lira fought not to roll her eyes. She couldn't help poking at his bubble of unwarranted confidence. The appearance of the monsters had ruined her original plan. The odds of successfully stealing horses and getting out via the road had dropped dramatically—those things moved faster than a horse, and there was no way of knowing whether more guarded the road itself.

"First, if something *has* happened to Karonan, you can't tell me nobody has noticed and sent a message to the council by now. Going to Carhall doesn't help anything. Second, getting out of this house, or estate, or whatever it is, is all well and good, but what do we do if those things come after us? You saw how fast they are. Not to mention the grounds are surrounded by thick forest that doesn't like to cooperate." She filled them in on what had happened to her.

Fari looked thoroughly spooked at the announcement, Athira disbelieving, Tarion intrigued.

"Why didn't you say that straight up, Lira?" Garan said in frustration. "What can you tell us about the two men? Were they mages, armed, how were they dressed?"

Lira's mouth tightened. "I'm not continuing to have this damn conversation standing in this room where we could be stumbled upon at any moment."

At that, she turned on her heel and marched up the stairs to the manager's office. After a few moments, they followed. She wasn't sure if she was relieved or annoyed by that. She really just wanted to break free of them and their damn talking and get herself out of this place.

"Well?" Athira prompted once they were all gathered. It was much dimmer up here, and Lira could barely make out their faces.

"I can't tell you much. It was dark. I was focused on getting away before they noticed I was awake."

"So you got nothing." Athira tossed her hands in the air.

"Not entirely," Tarion murmured.

They all swung to him.

He blinked, his features tightening with discomfort. "Well, they can make mistakes. Lira woke too early from the drug, and they weren't paying close enough attention to her in the cart. I'm also willing to bet that the four of us woke too early at Temari Hall too. I expect we were supposed to remain unconscious until they removed us from the tower and got us here—like Garan and Athira."

He was right. But Lira was careful not to underestimate whoever was behind this. They'd managed to steal seven magically trained apprentices away from a well-protected mage school without detection. If they were good enough to do that, they were good enough to learn fast from their mistakes.

A silence fell. Nobody seemed to have any other ideas.

"Lira has another good point too." Tarion forged ahead, staring at the floor. "If something has happened to Karonan, then going to Carhall won't help. What *will* help is learning more about what happened and who was behind it—information that will help the council deal with the situation. And since our kidnap happened at the same time as whatever happened to the city, then our kidnappers must be linked to it somehow, so we're in a good position to find out what's going on."

Fari gave him a disbelieving look. "Your definition of 'good position' and mine differ considerably, Caverlock."

Athira huffed an irritated sigh. "The likelihood of Karonan being invaded, or emptied, or whatever, in the space of hours is frankly slim, and I really think we just need to—"

"Even if it's a hallucination or there's another explanation, seven students were kidnapped from Temari Hall," Garan said grimly. "Tarion's right. We need to make sure that can never happen again, and that means finding out as much information on our captors as possible to take with us. We need to make sure the Mage Council can wipe them out completely. That's our duty."

Lira didn't even try to hold back her hard eye roll, but only Tarion caught it.

"Do you think the Shadowcouncil could be behind it?" Lorin asked unexpectedly.

Athira snorted. "Trust the Shiven amongst us to ask that question. Know all about Underground, do you, Initiate?"

"Being Shiven doesn't automatically make him an Underground member," Lira said irritably. "Maybe you could try not labelling every Shiven person you ever meet with the same motives."

"Astonishingly, I find myself agreeing with Spider," Fari said.

"Lorin's question is a reasonable one though," Garan said. "Underground do want the removal of the new Mage Council, right?"

Underground were a half-baked rabble. But Lira couldn't say that. Couldn't admit she'd attended one of their meetings only a handful of days previously. If she did that, they'd probably tie her up and leave her for the creatures to eat. The mention of Underground brought back the nagging urgency of her situation though. She needed to get back to Karonan.

"I think a mage has to be behind this." Tarion's face was deep in thought. "The logistics of kidnapping seven mage students, moving us here, not to mention whatever happened in Karonan? I doubt it could be done successfully without magic."

"Six mage students," Lorin corrected.

They all turned to him, frowning.

"Haler was a Taliath initiate," he explained, jaw set.

Lira cursed herself for missing that. She should have noticed the boy wasn't carrying a mage staff. *And he's the one who was killed.* That thought stuck with her.

"Maybe those creatures were created by magic too?" Athira suggested.

Garan frowned. "I'm not aware of any mage alive with that power."

"You know them all, do you?" Lira snapped, her patience fraying again. "As much as your aunt likes to think otherwise, plenty of mage potentials still prefer not to be trained by the Mage Council. Who knows what kind of powers those people have?"

"They're Shiven, mostly," Athira added, sending a dark look at Lorin.

"By all means, let's blame all this on the Shiven initiate," Lira snapped. She'd had about enough of standing around *talking* with these fools. It wasn't getting them anywhere and they could be discovered at any moment.

"Enough!" Garan's voice wasn't overly loud but it was granite, bringing everyone's attention back to him. "Bickering is not going to get us out of here alive."

Athira crossed her arms over her chest and leaned against the wall. Fari sat down, looking lost. Tarion's gaze was focused inward, like he was still thinking. Lorin's gaze shifted constantly between all of them like a soldier waiting for orders.

Garan spoke again. "Whoever kidnapped us, whoever is controlling the creatures, they'll be searching for us. I think—"

"Are you sure about that?" Lira asked, her suspicions crystallising as she spoke them aloud. "Doesn't it seem odd that you were all apparently left to wake up in different rooms with unlocked doors and no guards and free to wander around until we ran into their pet monsters?

Why not lock us all in a dungeon before letting us wake up, if kidnapping was the plan?"

"What if they're watching us somehow?" Tarion spoke into the silence that followed her words.

"Thanks for making me even more creeped out than I was," Fari muttered.

"For what possible purpose?" Athira stared at Tarion and Lira. "Look at who is in this room—the ransom we'll command is substantial. That's why we've been kidnapped."

Lira's mouth tightened. "Nobody is getting paid a ransom if we're torn apart by those creatures. I didn't see anyone holding them off us earlier."

Athira shrugged. "Maybe it was another mistake. Maybe they didn't have the creatures under control properly—they might just be here to guard the exterior of the grounds to prevent us escaping."

"Then why are they inside and why aren't we locked up somewhere?" Fari said reluctantly. "Lira is right, it doesn't make sense."

"It doesn't," Lira repeated flatly as she saw Garan opening his mouth to speak again. "We're currently running around blind being herded by those creatures, and the forest outside, like rats in a trap. We need to re-take the advantage if we want a chance at survival."

"All right, then we have two goals." Garan's green eyes settled on Lira. "First, find out everything we can on who's holding us and why, so we can report it back to the council. Two, work out how to kill or disable the creatures so they can't chase us if we flee via the road."

"Three, find where the horses are kept, how many guards and/or monsters are watching the horses and the exits, and grab some supplies to take with us," Tarion added, barely audible.

"No, survival is our only goal," Lira said flatly. "We're at a significant disadvantage, and lingering here to hunt clues only reduces our chances of getting out. The council can take care of themselves."

"As much as you pretend disdain, you are a council mage apprentice, Lira," Garan said mildly. "You know as well as I do that this is what they'd expect of us."

His words brought her up short. She'd forgotten, for a crucial instant, what she was supposed to be. A loyal, hard-working apprentice. Garan was right... their kidnap was a significant blow to the council. Temari Hall was supposed to be safe, its students were supposed to be safe, protected until they graduated as mages.

Yet someone had just proved that it wasn't safe. Not even close.

It would serve her purpose nicely if she were to not only help get these precious purebloods back to their families, but also deliver enough information about their captors to help the Mage Council remove all threats to Temari Hall.

Her survival instinct warred with her ambition, and quickly lost. She could do this... she'd just have to find out what they needed quickly, then get back to Karonan and report to Greyson. She'd fail in the task they'd set her, but she could hope that extenuating circumstances might convince them to give her another chance.

And as long as she *did* get back, and not disappear on them completely, she should be able to avoid them setting the Darkhand on her. She had no doubt the Darkhand could ferret out her secrets. And then she'd be far worse than out of the group.

"You're right." She lifted her hands in capitulation. "I'll take spying on our captors. The rest of you figure out the horses, guards, and a way of disabling the creatures."

"You can't go alone." Garan's voice stopped her.

She whirled, annoyed. "Says who? You're not in charge here."

"I know you like working alone, Spider, but in this situation it's not the smart thing to do."

Tarion moved away from the shadows of the wall. "I'll come with you."

"Trust me, I'll work better if I don't have to babysit," she said evenly.

"I'm going to ignore that very rude comment and volunteer to come along too." Fari rose to her feet, brushing imaginary dust from her robe, then glanced at Garan. "I won't be of much help if you're trying to figure out how to kill those things."

"Right. That leaves Athira, Lorin, and me together." Garan nodded as if it were decided. "We meet back in this room in two hours, no matter what. We'll go down and clear the crates away from the kitchen door before we follow you, hide any trace we were here in case someone goes into the kitchen. Clear?"

Lira bristled again. She didn't take orders, not from anyone, not anymore. "I told you, I don't want to—"

"His plan makes sense." Athira cut over her. "Let's just get to it."

Lira scowled, resentment at the girl's tone surging. But before she could argue further, or decide to go it on her own, Fari pushed past Lira and headed to the door. "I promise to do my best not to be a complete liability."

"Me too." Tarion gave her a little smile as he followed.

Lira stared after them, then cursed viciously under her breath and followed. Stupid. This whole thing was stupid. They were going to get her killed. She was going to get *herself* killed trying to juggle far too many balls.

"Two hours!" Garan called out.

Lira resisted the urge to tell him to shove his two hours into a dark orifice, and settled for sending him a filthy look instead. Stupid pure-blood mage scions and their infuriating air of superiority. One day she'd show them.

She'd show them all.

CHAPTER 16

Tarion cracked open the door from the office cautiously, staring out into the dim corridor beyond for several long moments before waving them out after him. Lira conducted her own careful visual search before following.

They went left, walking all the way down to the hallway's end. Here they arrived at a junction with a single option—another corridor lined with windows to their left. After a quick mental arrangement of the map she was building in her head... Lira placed them at the opposite end of the same hallway she'd first arrived in.

She stilled, raising a finger to her mouth for quiet, and squinted down into the gloom. There was no sign of the monsters that had chased them up from the ground floor, and the air was cold but not biting. The creatures had gone somewhere else.

"Where to next?" Tarion murmured.

Lira stepped up to one of the windows, staring out into the night. The fog had lifted just enough to see a little more of the grounds, though it was hard to make out anything specific. The shadowy outline of another building was visible a short distance away, too large to be a barn or stables, with a couple of flickering lights in lower level windows. "Over there," she murmured, pointing.

"Why there? Why not search here first?" Fari asked.

"Do either of you get the distinct impression we're being toyed with in some way?" Lira murmured. "You were all placed in this building with the monsters and left to roam for some reason. How about we get out of the cage they've put us in, take the advantage back?" When they didn't look convinced, she added, "You can do as you like. I'm going over there."

Tarion's expression cleared. "We know those monsters are creeping around in this building. Hard to creep up on our captors and spy when their creatures are tailing us around forcing us to hide."

"What if there are monsters out there to keep us inside? Lorin said he saw one on the grounds," Fari countered.

"Then go back to Garan and leave me alone like I wanted," Lira muttered.

She paced cautiously along the corridor, the other two following after a brief hesitation. Her irritation faded in a warm glow of satisfaction when she arrived at the door she'd entered through earlier; it still stood slightly ajar. Her mental map was accurate.

A shiver rippled down her spine and she glanced toward the open office area, where not so long ago dark tendrils of hungry shadow had filled the space. But nothing stirred now and the darkness was normal.

She pressed her hand against the door and pushed. It stuck, but she gave it a harder shove and it opened with a creak.

All three of them froze.

But the shadows remained still. No rattling sounded.

Tarion and Lira followed Fari out onto the exterior stone steps leading to ground level, then quickly pushed the door closed behind them.

Fari gave them both a wide-eyed glance at the sight of the mist-wreathed grounds spread out beyond the steps, where there was plenty of dark shadow for monsters to be lurking, but said nothing.

"We're not here alone," Tarion murmured, as if sensing her fear. "That's something. We have each other."

Lira gave him a scornful glance, but Fari's shoulders noticeably relaxed.

Nothing loomed out of the darkness as they crept through overgrown grass to the hulking building Lira had seen through the window. By tacit agreement they moved quickly, not liking the idea of being visible to anyone looking out of the higher level windows in either building.

This one was almost completely dark. Apart from a couple of flickering lights in the ground level windows, there were no other obvious signs of habitation. Two wide steps led up to an arched entrance. One of the double doors that had once stood there was shattered and charred, pieces of it strewn over the steps, while the other door hung, cracked and broken, loose from its frame.

For a moment, Lira felt the weight of the multiple balls she was trying to keep afloat, and considered turning and leaving the others, melting into the shadows to slip away and make her escape, ensuring she kept herself alive. But she forced herself to patience. There would be no point getting back to assure her place with the Shadowcouncil if she made the Mage Council suspicious of her in doing so—like Garan said, they'd expect her to help her fellow students and try to figure out what was going on, not abandon them and save herself. And if she could arrive back with information in hand, then all the better.

"This area of the building seems pretty dark," Fari murmured. "Should we risk it?"

"Better than risking being in the open much longer where anyone looking out a window could see us," Tarion murmured. "Or a monster patrolling the grounds."

Lira's grip on her staff tightened as they moved into the yawning black interior, finding themselves in a cavernous foyer, open doors to left and right. A wide stairwell was immediately ahead.

The corridor stretching away to their right was lit by several flickering torches sunk into brackets in the wall—the source of the light they'd seen from outside. But it looked empty and still.

Lira moved towards the lit corridor, relief and anticipation both rippling through her. Signs of habitation were where they'd find the information Garan and Tarion wanted; answers weren't going to be lying around in dark unused rooms. Maybe this would be faster than she'd thought—even if there was nothing there, maybe she could lose the other two, pretend to find something, then insist they all get out.

Tarion reached out to try and stop her, but she shook him off. He and Fari were smart enough not to call out, and she sensed as they reluctantly fell in behind her.

This building was in far more disrepair than the bits Lira had seen so far. Sections of the stone wall had crumbled away and rotting boards covered broken windows. Dirt and debris littered the ground.

It looked like nobody had been through here in a long time, decades even. Yet someone had lit these torches.

"Look at how badly in need of repair this part of the building is. Why keep it lit?"

"Because they're using it for something?" Fari guessed.

"Or they're trying to draw us here?" Tarion looked grim.

The hall ended in a narrow set of steps leading up to a higher level. It was impossible to tell where it led in the darkness, so Lira shrugged and started up it. There was no door at the top, only another long corridor stretching away into darkness. Doors lined the walls on each side.

"It's odd we've never heard of those monsters, right?" Fari murmured suddenly. "You'd think such large and vicious creatures, completely impervious to magic, would be pretty well known to the Mage Council."

Something cold settled in Lira's chest. She hadn't thought of that. Taliath were the only known living creatures with an immunity to magic. During the war, her grandfather had recruited a mage who could repel magic, used her to create medallions that his soldiers could wear to make them immune to magic. He'd called them Hunters, used them to track and kill mages. But Alyx Egalion had killed that mage near the end of the war. There were no Hunters left—and surely the Mage Council would know about anything else that had the ability to repel magic.

"Could someone have created them?" Fari speculated. "With magic, maybe?"

"Will you shush!" Lira hissed, cursing inwardly as the girl's words echoed uncomfortably in the dead silence. Tarion appeared to be the only one capable of being quiet. Astonishing given who his parents were, not to mention his elder sister. Caria Caverlock had been the most popular student at Temari Hall even though she was a Taliath, not a mage. And...

Lira straightened, stopping mid-stride, and kept her voice to a barely audible whisper. "Hold up, why just mages apart from Haler?"

Tarion and Fari stopped too, their puzzled expressions barely visible.

"Taliath and mages train together at Temari Hall." She spelled it out for them. "Where are the kidnapped Taliath students? Haler was the first one the monster went for earlier, the only one it killed... what if he wasn't even meant to be taken with us?"

"Whoever it was wanted mages," Tarion murmured, quick to follow her train of thought.

Fari kept her voice low, stepping closer so they could hear. "Not necessarily. How do you *accidentally* kidnap someone? Not to mention... magical hells..." She trailed to a halt, misery crossing her face. "Derna was a Taliath student too."

"Taliath swords would be a lot more effective against those creatures than mage staffs." Tarion met Lira's gaze.

"That's a really good point," she said. Maybe whoever was behind this hadn't wanted Taliath students. Surely it couldn't *just* be because the monsters wouldn't be able to contain them as easily, though?

She shook herself. Curiosity about their captors wasn't helping her get back to Karonan and Underground or impress the council. She started moving again, the others falling in with her.

"Have you noticed this floor is laid out like a grid?" Tarion gestured in a circle around them. "A square of corridors with rooms at regular intervals. Not dissimilar to the dorms at Temari Hall."

"Maybe it's just because I haven't been chased by a monster for a good half an hour now, but I'm starting to veer from terrified to annoyed. Let's see what's in one of these rooms." Fari turned the handle to open one of the doors. It stuck halfway, and she gave it a good shove to push it all the way open.

Lira, having learned from experience that barging into dark, unknown spaces was never a good idea, lingered in the hall outside, poised to draw her staff. Tarion did the same.

Fari's dark head reappeared around the doorframe a few moments later. "It looks like a dormitory room to me."

Lira ducked her head in, checking for herself. Like Fari had described, it held two narrow beds, a window, and a chest for storing clothes. The fabrics inside were so rotted it was impossible to tell what colour, or even shape, they'd once been. The faint stench of mould hung on the air. A quick look into more rooms as they passed revealed the same. The only differences between them were the personal touches of whoever had once lived in them. A hand drawing tacked to one wall. A colourful scarf on the bed of another. A boot with a hole in the toe.

Curiosity nagged at her again—why had the residents abandoned this place so quickly they'd left their possessions behind? She quelled it with an irritated huff. Whatever had happened was long ago and of no relevance now.

"So maybe this used to be some kind of barracks... maybe it isn't a lord's estate, but an old army base?" Tarion hazarded a guess.

"Maybe." Lira kept walking. Her orphanage in Dirinan had been laid out in a similar way, not to mention Tarion's earlier point about Temari Hall. Searching bedrooms wasn't going reveal any information that would help them.

After another turn, the corridor opened into a landing at the top of a wide set of steps leading down into the main entrance foyer. Here they paused.

"I think we should consider splitting up," Lira said, turning to look at the other two. Time to hurry this along. The sense of urgency was back, nagging constantly at her. "We can cover ground more quickly that way."

"We can also get eaten more quickly that way," Fari said.

"If you really want to go it alone, Lira, we're not stopping you." Tarion passed her and stared down into the foyer, neck craning as he took in the wide space before letting out a sigh and rubbing a hand over his face. He looked tired. And lost.

"Your parents are probably already looking for us." Fari laid a comforting hand on his arm. Then she made a face. "Not sure about mine."

"They won't even know where to start looking. We could be anywhere," he said quietly.

"Garan's mother is an extremely powerful telepath mage, right?" Fari shook her head. "They'll find us, Tarion."

"We have no way of knowing how far we've been taken. If we're close to Karonan, they might not even know we're missing yet," Lira's sharp voice broke their little bubble of optimism. Relying on *anyone*—let alone parents—coming to save her wasn't an option. Not since... She shoved that memory ruthlessly away and made her voice sharper. "Which is why we need to get ourselves out of this and not wait to be rescued. You two search the upper floors for secret clues to report to the Mage Council so that we can actually move on to escaping."

"While you do what exactly?" Fari put her hands on her hips, eyebrows lifted.

"There are torches lit in that corridor down there for a reason. I'm going to go and take a closer look."

"And what if you run into a blood-sucking monster while you're investigating the only sign of life we've seen in this building?" Fari hissed. "Or *we* do upstairs?"

"We run. If that's not possible, we fight it. Obviously." Lira was truly irritated now.

Tarion and Fari shared a look that only served to rile Lira further before Fari sighed. "All right, Spider. If you run into trouble and need help, yell out. We'll do the same."

"Sure." Lira intended no such thing, but didn't want to stay and debate the point. "See you soon."

She crept down the stairs, back pressed against the wall in an effort to stay hidden from anything waiting below. Lira reached the bottom and peered around the open space. It was dark, lit only by faint moonlight spilling in through the front entrance. There was no sign of anyone having followed them into the building.

Nothing moved. No rattling sounds emerged.

She glanced down the corridor behind the main stairwell. Quick investigation revealed that it led to a back door into the garden she'd seen on the western side of the building. Opposite the door was a spiral stone stairwell, its base festooned in cobwebs.

Her eyes had long since adjusted to the darkness, and she moved quickly back to the main foyer, padding lightly across it to her goal. This time she paid closer attention, noting that despite the cracked boards on the windows, the floor appeared swept clean of dust. Instinct tickled at the back of her mind—there was something to find here, she was sure of it.

Tarion might be onto something with his barracks theory—there would be no need for so many rooms on a noble's estate, and the grounds weren't big enough for it to be a monarch's residence, especially given the lack of protective walls around the place and its apparently isolated location.

Not that narrowing it down to an army base helped much. Since the war had ended after Shakar's death, most countries had reduced the size of their armies and no longer needed all their bases. While she could safely rule out Zandia, the land of deserts, the thick forest and cold air of her current location could be in parts of Tregaya, Rionn, or Shivasa.

Musing endlessly on the possibilities wasn't helping. She was getting tired, her mind starting to drift. She shook herself, taking a moment to focus herself, push away the weariness.

This time she tried the closed doors lining the corridor. Every single one was locked.

She moved all the way down to the end, reaching the stairs going upwards again, but this time she paused. Instead of going up, she rounded the side of the stairwell, finding another door hidden by the shadows. This one opened silently—no rusting or creaking here—into a hall that was a mirror of the ones they'd been searching above.

More rooms.

The first one she tried was locked, but that presented no obstacle. Lira had learned the mechanics of lock-picking at seven years old from... Her mind shied away from that thought, and she focused resolutely on the present. The breakout of her magic had only made picking locks easier—she no longer needed tools for it. This door was well-oiled too, and it opened into a very lived-in room.

A smile of triumph curled at her mouth. She'd found them.

The covers on the bed were thick and piled together under

multiple pillows. There was no fireplace, but several half-melted candles were strewn around the room. Clothes sat in a messy pile on the top of a chest.

She searched the room with a well-practised speed, but apart from learning that its occupant wasn't a fan of neatness, she found nothing to tell her about who they were. Nothing to fill the pieces of the puzzle in to help make sense of what was going on.

The only vaguely logical thing she could come up with that fit the situation was that someone wanted to test how they responded to being kidnapped, set loose, hunted. Like this was all some kind of horrible experiment. But for what purpose?

Maybe Tarion was right that magic was somehow behind all of this. Magic *not* under the control of the Mage Council. Her mind drifted to the Shadowcouncil, the only entity she knew of that might have something approaching a motivation for doing this. But they certainly didn't have the resources. And how did kidnapping apprentices help them take down the council?

Lira began moving methodically through every room in the hall. Two more were obviously lived in, while another three were empty and smelled of must. One of the occupants was most definitely a woman.

But that was all she learned. No sign of who they were or why they were living in this place. No helpful kidnap plans written out on parchment... no parchment at all in any of the rooms.

And then she heard the rattle.

She was finishing up searching the third occupied room when the sound drifted in from the darkened hall outside. Lira froze, one hand reaching for her staff, ears straining. It sounded again. Coming her way.

Her heart thudded and she warred with herself, teeth baring with the instinct to fight. But this time she checked the thrill that wanted to go rushing through her before it destroyed all common sense. The fight earlier had taught her that her chances of facing one of those things alone and surviving were minimal.

She had to move. Get out. Now.

She took two steps to the door, where she froze at the sight of dark tendrils creeping along the hall outside.

It was too late to run.

Her heartbeat quickened, mouth turning dry, and she turned, her frantically searching gaze landing on the two beds. In seconds she'd dropped to the ground and scrambled as quietly as she could underneath one of them. She pushed herself back against the wall and curled up into as small a size as she could manage.

She lay in the darkness, eyes trained on the open doorway.

There, in the place Lira had never, *ever* wanted to be again, where she couldn't do anything but hide in the dark, the fear came creeping back in. It slid through the chinks in her armour, too strong to be pushed down any longer, trapping her in position.

And when the cold deepened, like a layer of ice along her skin, the memories of that night came flooding out of the box she'd buried them in. The night when her mother never returned. The morning her head had been held in that basin of icy water with no escape.

Just like then, she had no way out. She was completely vulnerable. If the creature saw her under the bed... Panic took over, shoulders turning rigid, stomach so tight she couldn't breathe properly. It clawed through her middle and she closed her eyes, fighting with everything she had to hold onto herself. She curled her hands into fists, digging her nails into her palms and using the pain to help anchor her to the present.

She had to wrestle with herself for a long moment to force her eyes back open, make herself watch the door. Even then she couldn't stop the frantic beating of her heart, the dry terror in her throat. Her too-quick pants sent frosted clouds into the air around her face.

The rattling came again, sending a chill of fresh horror through her bones despite how deeply she despised herself for the weakness. She thought she'd gotten past this, grown stronger. And she *had*. In Dirinan she'd found the thrill of facing death and fear and *winning*. She'd embraced that rush, let it scour her of any weakness, let it blot out the memories and the terror.

But Temari Hall had forced her to let go of the thrill, push it away, pretend it wasn't part of her anymore. Life at the academy had merely papered over the cracks, the weakness that was there without the rush of winning to hide it. A pretence just waiting to crumble apart.

Then the flash of silvery eyes loomed out of the darkness beyond the door, the faint outline of a many-limbed shadow moved slowly along the corridor, and all other thoughts flew out of her mind. Its head moved from side to side as if searching for something, and it let out the occasional rattle, inquisitive, seeking.

Darkness spilled over the floor of the room, curled around the doorframe. Lira made her breathing as shallow as possible and held herself rigidly still. Time slowed. The air was so thick with tension she felt she might be able to touch it. Her chest was a vice, drawing tighter and tighter with every moment that passed.

The monster paused at the doorway. It gave a confused rattle. Sweat prickled her skin. She'd bitten so hard through her lip that blood trickled down to her chin.

And then it moved on.

The inky black shadow withdrew from the door and continued along the hallway outside, another rattle drifting back to her.

Lira waited several minutes, until she could hear nothing, until the temperature warmed, and even then, she had to fight with herself for several moments before she was able to uncurl and crawl out from underneath the bed. There she hunched on her knees, tears pricking at her eyes and her chest heaving in deep, gasping breaths. She lifted a palm and brought it slamming down furiously against the hard stone. The pain was welcome.

Whoever was behind this, she was going to make them *burn* for doing this to her. For exposing her weakness so brutally. For making her afraid again.

She took a deep, shuddering breath, difficult given her chest was still tight and closed. Then another one. If she wanted to survive, she had to get past this, find her strength again. Survival was what she did. Who she was.

So, once again, like she had that morning in the hut, she buried the memories away, piece by shaking piece. The remembered fear and horror. The trembling and the uselessness. Back in a box that wasn't as strong as it had been. One with cracks and thin walls.

Then she forced herself to stand up. To unclench her shoulders. Her palms were sweaty and residual terror made her jittery, her heart still beating too fast. She stood in the centre of the floor and took deep, steadying breaths, until she had herself under control and the tightness in her chest loosened.

By the time she stepped out of the room, the fear still lingered, and now she was beginning to tire, too, muscles and mind weary. But she was all right. She was up and thinking straight again.

She made sure the hall was empty before purposely moving to unlock the next door and start searching that room. It was empty, and she was halfway through checking the second-to-last room in the hall when a disembodied rattling came from the direction the monster had disappeared in.

It was back.

Her heart leapt into her throat with panic, until she gritted her teeth and forced the fear away with a sheer effort of will. She was *not* going to let fear of these things rule her. She wouldn't. She wouldn't. She repeated that over and over to herself until the panic subsided.

Instead of hiding this time, she moved swiftly but quietly in the opposite direction down the hall. Ducking around the corner, she dropped to a crouch and peered around, then waited.

The creature came into sight moments later, moving slowly, silvery eyes once again searching. Her heart pounded, mouth going dry.

It was looking for her.

Surely it was too much of a coincidence that the thing had come to this corridor not long after she'd arrived and started searching it? Lira glanced at her hands. Thought about how she'd used small bursts of magic to unlock the doors and search the rooms. How she'd just used it to light her way. Laziness that came with the territory of being a telekinetic mage.

The creature was impervious to magic, but could it also sense it? Smell it out somehow?

She risked another glance around the corner. The creature was creeping ever closer, darkening everything to an inky blankness, the temperature turning to ice. Lira had a quick choice to make. Run before it spotted her. Or...

Swearing under her breath, she summoned magic and used it to gently nudge one of the nearby rooms' doors open. She did it so carefully it didn't make a sound, and so slowly that in the darkness its movement wasn't noticeable. The finesse it took to do it without allowing her violet light to break free drained her, leaving her trembling.

The monster rattled, glowing silver eyes sweeping in her direction. Its rattle came again, sounding triumphant, predatory. It had found its prey.

Lira scrambled to her feet and ran.

They could sense magic.

CHAPTER 17
BEFORE

S houts sounded behind her, too close, and Lira pushed herself to run even faster through the crowded streets after the others. Timin was in the lead, clutching the silver statue they'd just stolen. She couldn't help the fierce smile spreading over her face at the sight of it despite the serious trouble they were in, and how badly it had all gone wrong.

Standing at roughly the length of her forearm, their prize was a detailed sculpture of a man wearing a jacket and tall hat, his hand resting on a cane—a marvellous likeness of the Silver Lords' leader—and they'd stolen it straight from his office in the middle of the rival gang's warehouse base in the merchant district of Dirinan.

The evening was busy, people spilling in and out of the storefronts crowded together, most seeking a bargain before the shops closed for the day. It was a far cry from the inns, whorehouses, and gambling dens of the harbour district where Transk ruled. The people here weren't flushed with drink and cloudweed and ignorant of the biting cold or the snow drifting through the air. Here they wore coats and scarves against the weather.

Though she ran as fast as she could, lithe and agile on her feet as she danced through the thronged streets, Lira struggled to keep up with the others, steadily falling further and further behind as they approached the edge of Silver Lords territory and burst into another street.

The whole way she berated herself internally. She'd been too reckless, too confident, and she'd screwed up. The job—her idea and one it had taken almost a month to convince Timin, Picker, and Boya to help her with—had gone without a hitch until right at the end.

She hadn't calculated on the Silver Lords having a mage working for them. The man was young, and didn't wear the blue cloak of a council mage who'd been trained at Temari Hall, but he had enough self-taught telepathic ability to pick up their thoughts as they crept out the side door.

He'd raised the alarm instantly and Silver Lords had poured out of the warehouse after them, bellowing challenges and brandishing weapons. Fury over the incursion into the heart of their territory had laced their yelling with a dangerous edge. A city guard standing on a nearby corner saw the four ragged youths running away from the Silver Lords' base and a larger group of armed men and women pursuing them, and shouted an order for them all to stop.

Nobody listened, of course. He shouted again, then started in pursuit.

Now an all-out foot chase barrelled out of the merchant district and straight through into the main shopping area of Dirinan, moving steadily towards Revel Kings territory. The chaos and speed of it made Lira's blood sing.

But seconds later, the guard chasing them blew three sharp blasts on his whistle. The shrill sound cut over the noise of the crowds milling around the shopfronts, designed to draw the attention of any other city guards within range. A glance over her shoulder caught more guards already starting to move in pursuit of both gangs.

Rotted carcasses. Now she'd drawn in the city guard. She had screwed up majorly. Ahrin was going to be furious. Worse than furious. *If* they managed to get away.

Fear tried to rise in her chest, but she ignored it, holding onto her earlier confidence and focusing her efforts on running faster. On ignoring the burning of her lungs and trembling legs. Picker and Boya were well ahead, Timin bringing up the rear. Boots pounded relentlessly behind them, Silver Lords and city guards both. They moved steadily away from the merchant area, the streets thinning rapidly, sky growing darker. The scent of salt and seaweed filled her senses as an easterly wind gusted off the ocean.

Lira followed the others around a sharp turn, scrambling over a half-fallen fence and sprinting to the end of the alley beyond before taking another sharp right. They weren't far from the Revel Kings' patch now—where they had multiple routes to their hideout, routes that would lose their pursuers easily. The Silver Lords would think twice about following them in there, but Transk would be livid at city guards combing through his streets, and he'd quickly find out who was to blame for it.

Damn. Damn. Damn. Rotted fish carcasses, she'd completely screwed this up.

"Come on, Lira!" Timin shouted back at her, finally noticing that she was lagging.

She redoubled her efforts, but she could only run so fast on shorter legs, and the others kept moving further ahead. The distance between her and the closest Silver Lords shrank rapidly. She'd had the advantage in busy streets where her quickness at weaving around people kept her ahead, but now the longer legs of her pursuers were inevitably going to close the distance.

"Hey, stop!" a city guard shouted from behind. Ahead of him, one of the Silver Lords whooped, a dark edge of violence in his yell, sensing victory. Everybody ignored the guards.

Relief gave Lira an extra burst of speed as up ahead, Timin turned into a familiar alleyway. She half turned-half slid around the corner, almost falling and losing a few precious seconds of her lead. The closest Silver Lord reached out to try and grab her jacket, but she swung away just in time. A knife flashed in his other hand.

Down the other end of the alley, where the territory officially became that of the Revel Kings, Timin was waving Picker and Boya through a door set into the wall. He motioned at her impatiently, but she still had a good distance to go. Boots pounded behind her, closer, ever closer. She didn't dare look back in case it cost her the scarce lead she had.

But then Timin gave her an apologetic shake of his head.

"No!" she shouted. "Wait for me, you rotted bastard!"

But he didn't. He didn't even hesitate at her shout. He stepped inside and slammed the door shut, no doubt dropping the bars on the inside to keep the gang members and guards from following them through.

She reached the door in time to hear the last bar dropping into its socket and Timin's receding footsteps. "Timin, let me in!" she roared, pounding on the door once in frustration. "LET ME IN!"

But it was too late. Her pursuers had her.

She turned, backing slowly away towards the dead end of the alley, panting breath steaming in the bitter air. The faster Silver Lords had come to a halt, fanning out across the alley to prevent her escaping, their eyes gleaming as they watched her.

Two guards arrived seconds later, blowing their whistles, and one of the gang members turned to them. "We just havin' a little fun 'ere, sirs. No harm meant."

Lira's heart dropped. If the guards left her here with the Lords, they'd kill her. That was what happened when you tilted at a rival gang and failed. A rule she'd known before stealing the statue.

She'd gone too far this time. Her mind raced, trying to figure out an escape, something, *anything*.

"You clear out before we arrest you all," the guard said, voice firm and unyielding. A second guard moved up behind him, hand on the hilt of his sword. A sharp whistle from close by announced the approach of more guards.

The Silver Lord that had spoken lifted his hands in mock surrender and backed away. The rest of them melted into the darkness, but not without looks shot in Lira's direction which told her she would die in a horribly uncomfortable way if she stepped foot in their territory again.

She straightened her shoulders and winked at them, refusing to show fear. The thrill surged at once again avoiding death. City guards were a far easier challenge to face than rival gang members.

"What did you steal?" The second guard spoke, the two of them pacing closer. Their cheeks were flushed, chests heaving from the chase.

"Nothing." Lira lifted open palms to show them, insolence in her voice. "Don't know why they started chasing me. Maybe they didn't like the look of my face."

"We'll see about that."

His fist cracked into her jaw, sending her staggering back, unable to avoid the second blow to her stomach that had her doubling up and collapsing to the ice-cold ground. Stars blinked in her vision and pain spiked hot and agonising through her face.

She hadn't expected this. Had thought the guards would let her go when they saw how young she was and she showed them she had nothing of value on her. A boot slammed into her ribs.

"Teach you for making me run halfway round the city." Another boot to the ribs. "Next time you stop when I tell you to stop."

She curled up on the ground, choking on the fire in her chest, doing her best to protect her head from their blows. Trying not to grunt in pain with each hit, and mostly succeeding. While they beat her, they spent a good deal of time debating whether to arrest her and take her to the city jail.

Eventually they ransacked her clothes, hands grabbing and sliding everywhere despite her bitter struggles, before leaving her bleeding in the snow when they found no stolen material.

Alone.

BY THE TIME Lira managed to drag herself to her feet, the evening was deepening towards midnight, and bringing the temperature down with it. A grunt escaped her as she forced herself to her knees, then braced herself, palms in the icy snow, until the pain faded enough that she could stagger upright.

Once up, she swayed, almost going down again. It felt like every single muscle in her body stabbed in pain with each movement, and she was certain something in her face and several ribs were broken. Blood trickling from her nose and mouth had frozen to the skin on her face. One eye was so swollen she could barely see out of it.

The first step was an exercise in swallowing down agony. As was the next, the one after only worse. Even so, she took a long, convoluted route back to their warehouse loft, careful to make sure she wasn't seen or followed by any Silver Lords that might have risked the guards and lingered. Her anger at herself kept her going despite the cold, pain, and exhaustion. How could she have messed up so badly? It galled her beyond measure.

Eventually, confident nobody was trailing her, Lira turned a corner and began limping down the street to their loft entrance. Ahrin came out of their doorway as Lira was halfway there, a long grey coat swirling around her ankles.

Lira paused, debating whether it might be smarter to let Ahrin walk away before getting any closer—she wasn't sure how much more punishment her body could endure tonight—but it was a foolish thought. Ahrin spotted her the instant she stepped out into the street.

Her blue eyes went dark with cold fury, so much that Lira's heart thudded in fear and she almost came to a halt in the snow. Ahrin's rules were clear and Lira had broken them. She forced herself to limp the rest of the distance, inwardly bracing herself for the consequences that would come.

"Timin will be punished." Ahrin's voice was as cold as her gaze.

Lira blinked, taken aback. She'd expected that fury to be directed at her. Had Timin not told Ahrin what happened? "Did he tell you why he left me?" Her voice rasped, the effort of speaking making her face and chest start throbbing all over again. Everything in her just wanted to lie down and rest and she fought not to sway on her feet. Best to get this over with. Then she could rest and recover.

"Yes. That's one of the reasons he's not dead right now." Irritation rippled over Ahrin's face and she stepped forward to slide an arm around Lira's waist. "You're going to need help getting upstairs."

"Don't... I'm fine." Lira tried not to wince at the pressure of Ahrin's hand on her ribs but failed miserably. "You were heading out somewhere. Don't let me stop you. I can take care of myself."

"I can do it later." Ahrin's clipped tone warned her not to argue further.

Lira bit her lip with a combination of pain and dread. "I screwed up," she muttered. "He left me out in the cold because he's jealous of me, but it wasn't the wrong call to make. If he'd waited they could all have gotten caught. This was my fault."

"That's what he said." Ahrin's voice was flat, no inflection in it to give Lira an indication of what she was thinking. The fingers of her free hand were tapping against her long jacket, though, a rare tic. Lira had once thought Ahrin had no tells—she rarely felt *any* emotions, as far as Lira could see—but after years together in the same crew, she'd noticed there were rare times when something inside her crew leader fought to rise to the surface. Tapping her fingers was the single tell she had.

Seeing it now made Lira wary of how deep her fury with Lira's actions ran.

With Ahrin's help, Lira managed to make it into the loft, though getting up the narrow stairs was an agonising endeavour and she let out several embarrassing grunts of pain before they reached the top. The area near the stairs where the crew slept was dark, their snores and rustling blankets the only sounds in the cavernous space.

Lira limped slowly after Ahrin to the opposite end of the loft and into the curtained-off corner that was hers—the privacy afforded a crew leader.

"Sit." Ahrin pointed to the rickety table by a pot belly fire much smaller than the one they shared in the main room. The flames inside it flickered, dancing orange shadows against the dark curtains.

"I didn't see Timin out there," Lira ventured, doing as instructed and gingerly lifting herself to sit on the edge of the table, boots resting on the chair below it. She hunched over the stabbing pain in her ribs and tried to breathe through it.

"He's on watch duty on the roof. And will be for the rest of winter," Ahrin answered her unspoken question.

Ahrin carried two small pots, a basin of water, and bandages to the table beside Lira. She briskly took Lira's chin in her hand and inspected her face. "Want me to try and set your nose? It's definitely broken, but I can't promise to make it any straighter."

Lira shook her head. She didn't care about how her nose looked, and it was hurting enough already without someone messing about with it. "It's fine."

"What happened?"

"Silver Lords and City Guard caught up. The Lords ran, but the guards beat me." Lira let out a slow breath. "They were mad I'd made them chase me across the city."

"Beat you where?"

Lira huffed a pained laugh. "Everywhere."

"Specifics, please," Ahrin snapped.

"Face, chest, stomach," Lira rapped out, responding instantly to the command in Ahrin's voice, despite her grogginess.

"I need you to sit up straighter so I can get a proper look at you."

Lira swallowed the stab of agony as she cautiously straightened her shoulders, a strangled gasp escaping her despite her best efforts to hold it in. Ahrin was uncharacteristically gentle as she eased her jacket off, but Lira still hissed in pain when Ahrin unbuttoned her shirt with deft fingers and gently palpated her ribs. "Just one broken rib, I think. Lucky you, the rest are probably just badly bruised." She glanced up. "I'm surprised your magic didn't break out during such a bad beating. You're nearly fifteen, no?"

"Maybe. I'm not entirely certain of my birthday." Lira swore. "That hurts!"

"Deal with it. I need to make sure there are no further breaks," Ahrin said briskly. "A shard of bone in your lungs could kill you."

Lira bit her lip and endured, maintaining a stony silence until Ahrin had palpated and prodded to her satisfaction. Black and purple bruising was already spreading across her stomach and crawling over her left side.

"You tilted at the Silver Lords?" Seemingly satisfied with her inspection of Lira's ribs, Ahrin set to cleaning the blood off her face. Her touch was sure but gentle, surprising Lira. She hadn't thought her crew leader capable of gentleness.

"Almost got clean away too. Didn't account for them having a half-assed telepath mage on the payroll, though. Damn fool I am." Her anger rose again at the senseless mistake she'd made. How could she have been so stupid?

"I warned you about this, Lira." The edge was back in Ahrin's voice, sharp and coiled like a spring ready to explode.

"I know."

Ahrin's fingers tightened on her chin, forcing Lira to meet her gaze. "That thrill you feel, the headiness, I understand it more than you realise. But *you* have to control *it*, not the other way around. Am I clear?"

"Very." She meant it. She *could* control it, she'd make sure of it. She wouldn't do anything to compromise Ahrin's crew, never again.

Ahrin's fingers tightened, almost bruising, then she let go and went back to her work. "Good. Now tell me, what exactly were you seeking to achieve?"

Lira glanced at her, trying to judge how furious she still was, but her face was narrowed in concentration as she cleaned a cut on Lira's jaw. "I figured it would come to Transk's attention, make him notice you more. He has to see you and your crew as worthy of respect before you can go at him, right?"

Ahrin paused what she was doing to lean back and catch Lira's gaze. "Are you planning to supplant me one of these days, Lira?"

Her answer was firm and unhesitating. "No."

"Why not?" Ahrin sounded curious rather than threatening.

"I don't want to be the leader. I just want respect. For people to look at me and see me, not the fact I'm Shakar's relative or that I'm not Shiven." Lira paused a moment, then took a shallow breath. "You were right about my magic breaking out sooner rather than later. When it does, we can go at Transk. No mage on anyone's payroll will be as strong as me."

"You don't know that," Ahrin murmured.

"Being the Darkmage's granddaughter has to be good for something." She winced as Ahrin applied paste to one of her cuts. "I'm going to be a mage of the higher order like him. Nobody in Dirinan will be able to stop us, not even Transk."

Ahrin didn't say anything to that, and silence fell as she finished up cleaning and dressing the cuts and bruises. Once she was done, she rubbed some stolen herbal ointment over the worst of the bruises on Lira's chest and ribs, then re-buttoned her shirt. By then Lira was only half-awake, lulled by the contentment of being in her home and the soft touch of Ahrin's hands on her skin.

"Hey!" Ahrin's hand cupped her cheek. "How many times did you get hit in the head?"

Lira blinked her eyes open. "Not sure."

"You need to stay awake. You hear me?"

She swallowed, nodded. Her gaze slid to Ahrin's tattoo, and still a little dazed, she reached out and closed her fingers around her wrist, turning it so she could see the ink better. "When did you get that?"

Ahrin stiffened, but didn't move away. "When I was a child."

"What does it mean?" She slid her thumb slowly over the marking on Ahrin's skin, three jagged lines, almost like claws, or talons.

Silence held for a moment, thick and dangerous, then Ahrin yanked her hand from Lira's grip and stepped back, her sleeve falling to cover the tattoo. "It represents a very dark hole I clawed my way out of. Don't ever ask me about it again."

"All right," Lira said softly.

Ahrin moved the bowl of bloodied water and spare wrappings to the side and then helped her down from the table. Gingerly, Lira limped out of the curtained area and over to her pile of cushions and blankets in the nearest corner.

She blinked in surprise when Ahrin slid down the wall to sit beside her. "I'll sit with you, make sure you stay awake."

"You have a job with Eser tonight. That's where you were going, wasn't it?"

"He's a big boy. He'll be fine." Ahrin's voice hardened. "And we'll discuss how you monumentally screwed up tomorrow, when you're not half dazed from a concussion."

She accepted that, settling against the cushions, trying to keep her eyes open. "Roof watch duty. Timin's going to hate me even more after this."

"Timin is all bluster." Ahrin nudged her with a shoulder. "You know I'll look out for you."

"Why?"

"What do you mean?"

"Why am I your second? I joined the crew after Timin and Yanzi and I'm the youngest. You should have left me out on the street tonight," Lira murmured sleepily. "I screwed up."

"Timin screwed up too. We're a crew, and that means we look out for each other. He abandoned you."

"You didn't answer my question."

"A leader has to have some secrets," Ahrin said softly, then her whole demeanour shifted, quick as a blink, businesslike again. "Are you certain it wasn't a council mage that caught you?"

Lira didn't reply instantly, instead going back over her memory to make sure she had all the details right. Ahrin didn't accept mistakes. "Close to. He didn't wear a blue cloak, and while he might have just been off-duty, he was unkempt, tattoos on his neck. When he found us and was calling out for help, he wasn't composed, or clear... he was urgent. Council mages are trained better than that."

"Interesting."

"Why?"

"You haven't noticed the lack of mages in the crews these days? I figured that's why you made the mistake of assuming the Lords didn't have one."

Lira blinked. She was still groggy, not at her best. "You saying there aren't as many mages around? Or just that they're all joining the council?"

"I'm not sure. Could be nothing." Ahrin's gaze was distant, thoughtful. "One of Transk's runners found a dead one washed up on the shore last week. No obvious sign of death—no stabbing or bruises around the neck like you'd see in an inter-crew killing. Two more washed up a couple months back, similarly without obvious signs of injury... I don't think anyone else made the connection they were also mages. All three were from different crews and patches."

"You're keeping track of the crew mages?"

"Of course. I need to understand what we're facing once you break out and we make our move against Transk. Such a move needs to be planned very carefully." Ahrin looked away.

"Ahrin, you didn't abandon me tonight, and I'm not abandoning you," Lira said stubbornly. Her crew leader had stopped talking about Lira going to Temari Hall as the years passed, but there was still something in her voice when she talked about Lira's magic that made her doubt Ahrin was completely convinced. "Not ever."

"I didn't say you would." Excitement flashed in Ahrin's eyes. "Which is why I'm planning for when our crew has a mage amongst us."

Answering excitement surged in Lira, dispelling some of her grogginess. "I told you, I'm going to be a mage of the higher order, just like the Darkmage."

Anticipation lit Ahrin's eyes. "We'd be unstoppable."

"Better. I'm going to make you invincible."

CHAPTER 18

They could sense magic.

The knowledge only added to Lira's sense of vulnerability. She couldn't use magic to defend herself against the monsters hunting her though the darkness, and now she couldn't use magic at all for fear of drawing them to her. Not to mention hours had passed and she was still no closer to figuring out how to get herself out of this and back to Karonan.

Returning to the main foyer, Lira pressed herself into the shadows along the wall and turned utterly still. The urge to simply get out, get away, was rising in her like a tide and Lira had learned not to ignore instincts like that.

She might have to contend with an adversarial forest and getting lost before finding a village and help, but the deep unease in her bones warned her that was a better prospect than remaining in this place any longer. The Mage Council would surely understand her making that decision. After all, she had *tried* to find more information to take back to them.

But the others didn't know the monsters could sense their magic.

She swore inwardly. They weren't her problem or her responsibility. *Her* survival was what counted. Lira had survived for years without magic in a world just as dangerous as this one. She would adjust, and do it faster without them nagging at her heels.

Yet... she'd needed Tarion's help to defeat that monster. And if she wanted to get off the grounds, she doubted she'd be able to do it without having to get past at least one of the things. Plus... she *hated* it, but that fear from moments earlier was still churning in her gut, making her more hesitant. The thought of help was an annoyingly strong reassurance.

She didn't need to trust them. Or save them. She just needed to use them to get herself out.

Decision made, Lira sent one final, lingering stare around the shadowed foyer to ensure the space was empty, before dashing over to the main stairs across from the entrance. She'd find Tarion and Fari first, then they could all go and warn the others in the main building. There was nothing more to learn in this one. She pushed herself to climb the stairs at a light-footed run, despite the weariness pressing down on her.

The stairs went up four levels before ending, and Lira figured she'd start there and work her way down till she found them. Some of the doors here stood open, track marks in the dust indicating Fari and Tarion had already searched them. Lira's pace increased despite knowing a monster could be lurking anywhere.

She turned left, then left again. There was no sign of either apprentice, but halfway down the corridor running along the western wall of the building, Lira paused outside a larger door. It stood open like many others, markings in the dust indicating it had been opened recently.

The space within was much larger than the rooms she'd seen so far —perhaps three or four of those could fit inside it. Some sort of common area, maybe, a shared space for soldiers in the barracks to spend their free time? Whatever it had been, it now oozed desolate emptiness from the unlit and spider-webbed fireplace to the rotting furniture and shadows in the corners.

A faint gust of air whispered over her cheeks. For a moment she panicked, thinking it was a monster moving out of the darkness. She'd half drawn her staff when she realised the air hadn't grown cold enough and there was no movement in the shadows. This whisper of air was just a draft coming from an open doorway near the far corner of the common room. Her searching gaze hadn't caught it in the dim light through the single arched window.

The door stood ajar, beckoning.

Glancing behind to make sure nothing was creeping up behind her, Lira crossed to it in quick, silent strides, peering into whatever was beyond: service stairs, by the look. Narrow, unadorned, spiralling up and down into darkness. She wondered if Tarion and Fari had chosen to travel that way to lessen their chances of running into the monsters —the space was far too narrow for them to fit inside.

Even if not, she'd searched this floor, and these stairs were a safer way of getting to the next floor. She stepped into the stairwell and was immediately enclosed in complete darkness.

Step by careful step she inched downwards, palms pressed against the rough stone on either side for balance, foot testing each step for damage. At one point her right palm slid over wood instead of stone— a door into another room. Presumably it was an entry into the next floor down.

Pressing her ear to the wood, she heard only silence beyond it. It was too dark in the stairwell to tell whether the door had been opened recently, and there was no light coming from under the crack below the frame. Satisfied the room beyond was empty, she was just about to turn the handle when the faint murmur of voices drifted up from around a curve in the stairwell below.

Lira froze, ready to turn in an instant and flee back up the stairs, but the voices didn't appear to be coming any closer. And they were too distant to make out what they were saying, or even tell whether the speakers were male or female.

Pressed against the wall, she took two more cautious steps down so that she could peer around. A faint light glimmered just beyond the bend, causing Lira to freeze again.

Anticipation uncurled in her chest and she grabbed hold of it tightly, using it to ward off the fear and lingering panic that also wanted to rise. Tarion and Fari surely wouldn't be walking around with a torch or lantern, which meant whoever was talking must be their captors, the people living in the rooms on the ground floor.

And now Lira had the element of surprise.

Exactly how she liked it. She felt steadier, suddenly, more in control. The churn of her stomach eased.

The voices were still indistinct, muffled. She listened for a moment longer, then when she grew confident enough that the sounds weren't coming from within the stairwell itself, she kept inching down.

Then stopped again as she rounded the curve. The light was brighter here, enough that she could make out Tarion and Fari's indistinct forms, still as statues, pressed against the wall a step below another door. The voices sounded like they were coming from somewhere on the other side of it. The light spilled from the crack underneath.

She must have made a sound, because Tarion turned suddenly to stare up at her, panic flaring on his face before he recognised her. He pressed a finger to his lips. She scowled—what did he think, that she was going to start throwing a party to announce their presence?—and crept down to join them. Fari lifted her hand in a wave. The moment Lira was standing beside him, Tarion leaned down to murmur in her ear, breath tickling her skin. She fought the urge to shove him away.

"We heard faint footsteps and then a cough, so we lingered. A few moments later it sounded like a door opened somewhere inside and then we heard voices."

Lira nodded to show she understood.

"The words are mostly indistinct, so it's hard to tell what they're saying. It's definitely not Garan or the others, though."

"I found living quarters being used on the ground floor. Three rooms," Lira risked replying in a murmur.

Though they appeared calm, Tarion's shoulders were as rigid as a statue and Fari's brown skin was positively bloodless, her hands trembling at her sides. They were under significant stress. Lira couldn't blame them, especially after she hadn't been able to stop herself falling apart earlier. Even Transk would probably be requesting new underwear if he found himself being kidnapped and hunted by blood-sucking shadowy monsters and invisible captors.

Not Ahrin though, she would... Lira cut that thought off ruthlessly, swallowing a small protest as Fari suddenly shifted closer, pressing into

Lira and Tarion so she could murmur, "I thought you'd take longer to search. Or leave us completely. Is something wrong?"

"I ran into another one of those monsters. I got suspicious of how it found me, so I tried a little experiment. They can sense our magic. Came to warn you," Lira breathed, intensely uncomfortable at the close press of bodies in the confined space, and fighting the constant urge to push them away. The stairwell was so silent she was reluctant to make any noise whatsoever, but it couldn't be helped. They needed to know.

Fari gulped, one hand unconsciously grabbing Lira's arm. Tarion turned to press his forehead against the stone, eyes closing. His pulse beat frantically in his throat.

Lira gave them a moment. For the very first time, she was glad she hadn't abandoned them. It might be a weakness, but right now, she was just glad that she would have some help to get out of this.

Seconds later, the voices started up on the other side of the wall again. One was female, authoritative, and the other a male, his voice almost entirely indistinct. What Lira wouldn't give for telepathic magic at this moment. Bitterness surged at the reminder she was no special mage. Her fists curled at her sides.

"Where... go to... not good enough. I..." the woman's voice said. The tenor of it sent an icy prickle of unease down Lira's spine. Her street instincts roused again. She hadn't heard that tone in a long time. It was a tone you learned to be afraid of, learned to respect, learned to avoid at all costs.

"Can't..."

"Just... if we don't... now."

"What if they're other apprentices like us? Kidnapped and brought here." Fari pressed even closer, making Lira's discomfort skyrocket. Too close. Too confined. Her shoulders turned rigid and she pressed a palm against the rough stone, focusing on the cold sensation of it against her skin rather than the stifling presence of Tarion and Fari.

"No."

Tarion and Lira whispered at the same time, then looked at each other in surprise. His tall form crouched awkwardly as he tried to lean close enough so they could hear him murmur. "They sound like adults to me. And they don't sound scared."

Lira wasn't sure about that. But every bone in her body sensed something in that woman's voice that made her shiver from head to toe. "What's on the other side of the wall?" she breathed. "Same as the one we entered the stairs from, looked like a common room?"

Tarion nodded. "Think so."

Lira curled her hand into a fist in frustration when the voices started up again, but were still too muffled to make out. She turned to lean up and murmur in Tarion's ear. "I'm going to go back up, circle around and see if I can get an idea of who they are and what they're saying. You two should go back to the meeting point and warn Garan and the others about the monsters sensing our magic."

Fari brightened. "That's actually a good plan, Spider."

Tarion's hand settled on her shoulder. Her first instinct was to shrug it off, but there was no threat in the gesture, and his touch was warm and solid. "Don't risk yourself. If you can't get close enough without exposure, then let it go. If you're not back at the meeting place within a half hour, we'll come looking for you."

"That's not necessary," she muttered, made uncomfortable by his words. She couldn't trust them—she was Spider after all. They would save themselves ahead of her. But that was okay. For now their goals aligned, and she could trust that.

Tarion and Fari crept down the stairs, and Lira waited until they were out of sight around the corner before turning to head back upwards.

She hadn't even taken a step when the door opened unexpectedly, flooding the stairwell with orange flamelight. A tall woman stepped into sight. Her eyes went straight to Lira, and a little smile curved over her austere features. There was no warmth in that smile. "Well, this isn't quite where I expected to find you."

Lira's first instinct was to turn and run. But if she did that, they would chase her. Tarion and Fari were still in the stairwell—if she ran towards the ground floor and the only way out, it would risk all three of them being captured. And that wouldn't serve any good purpose.

"I wouldn't. You won't get far." The woman seemed to read her instinct to run. "There's no need for dramatics. Why don't you come in here and we'll just have a little chat?"

Lira bolted *up* instead of down, her intent to force the woman aside and escape into the corridors upstairs where there would be more space to lose pursuers. She got one step before the woman barked an order and two men stepped out of the room from behind her, blocking Lira's escape entirely.

Even so, she threw herself at them, jabbing her staff hard and fast at the stomach of the closest man—there was no room to swing it. He jerked back to avoid her blow, stumbling on the step behind him and falling into the wall.

But that was the only move she had room enough to make in the cramped confines of the stairwell. Quick as a spider, she dashed into the gap made by the fallen man, her body swinging sideways to avoid the lunging grasp of the second man.

But the first recovered faster than she'd expected, blocking her exit before she made it through the gap. She pivoted, throwing her shoulder into his chest, hoping to force him off balance again. Her moves were blunt and ruthless, maneuvers she'd learned in Dirinan when her small size and relative lack of strength meant her greatest chance of survival lay in escaping the fight rather than staying in it. Taught to her by—

The air rushed from his chest in a grunt, but as she stepped past him, the first man grabbed her arm, yanking her towards him. Violet light flared from her forearms and for a moment she considered unleashing her magic. But if she did that, the creatures would come and she'd be trapped in this stairwell—men inside, creatures waiting without.

So she stifled her magic with an effort and kicked out instead, slamming her boot into his shin. He swore, loosened his grip on her. She yanked free only to find herself wrapped in the burly arms of the second man.

"Let go of me!" she bellowed, kicking and shouting as they dragged her into the room. Her magic surged, but she fought it down and used fists and feet instead, mouth curling in a snarl. Humans were a beatable foe. Numerous monsters were not. None of her opponents had tried to use magic on her. Maybe they weren't mages.

Or they knew it would draw the creatures too.

Kicking, biting, struggling the entire way, Lira found herself being unceremoniously dumped into a chair. Her wrists were dragged behind her back before being tied together with rope. Her ankles received the same treatment and then the men stepped back. They hadn't said a word the entire time.

Abruptly she stopped fighting. No amount of brute strength would free her now. Better conserve her energy for when she figured out a way to get free of the ropes.

She hung there, panting, gaze flicking between the woman and two men, sizing them up in seconds the way she'd learned to assess marks years ago. Her confidence surged again at being faced with a threat she understood, assuredness in her ability to defeat it rising like a tide to drown the uncertainty and residual panic from earlier, washing all traces of it away.

She breathed in, then out, relief filling her. And she started planning.

All three looked over thirty years old and probably closer to forty. The two men were dressed in plain clothing with no obvious insignia. No mage staffs hung down their backs. No other weapons she could see either, which struck her as odd. Both had fair skin, so not Zandian, and neither were pale enough to be Shiven. Clean shaven. Well groomed. So not poor either, and they didn't have the furtive, watchful air of the street criminals.

The woman was a different story. What was starkly clear, the very first thing Lira picked up on, was that she was indisputably in charge. Her air of authority was absolute, the deference of the other two marked whenever they glanced in her direction, in how they stood back to cede her the room.

More, everything about her screamed control, precision—from the tailored cut of her expensive but unadorned jacket and skirt, to the neat arrangement of her dark hair, the way her hands clasped loosely at her front, the unmarked shine of her leather boots and her perfect posture. Not a single tendril of hair escaped her braid.

Then Lira's gaze snagged on a fourth person in the room. He or she stood in the far corner, deliberately out of Lira's line of sight. They wore a loose cloak, hood drawn down to completely case their face in shadow... but there was *something*... an odd type of energy that drew Lira's attention.

Even though she couldn't see beneath the hood, she got the distinct sense that the person was staring right back at her. The intensity of their attention was palpable.

Annoyed, she dismissed the hooded figure and turned back to the woman, giving her attention to the leader of the group. She was watching Lira with a faint smile on her face, seemingly content to wait for her to say something. Lira was happy to oblige.

"What in rotted hells is going on?" she seethed, yanking at her bonds. It was mostly for show—without magic she wasn't getting out of them. But she didn't want them thinking for a second that she was going to be easy prey.

The smile widened slightly, but there was only coolness in her eyes. "You haven't completely lost the gutter language of your youth, I see."

Lira stilled, gaze narrowing. This woman knew at least a little of her past.

When Lira stayed silent, the woman continued, "You didn't try and use magic to fight your way out. And you're not using it now, even though I know you could rip those ropes off in a heartbeat. Interesting." She moved then, her strides steady, even, as perfectly controlled as the rest of her, and crouched in front of Lira. "Don't tell me you've already worked out that the razak can sense it? That was quick. Far quicker than we expected."

"Who are you and what do you want?" Lira spoke slowly and clearly, holding the woman's gaze the entire time, mouth curled in quiet fury. It was no longer an act. Anger was easier than fear. It made her stronger.

"My name is Lucinda." She reached out, gripped Lira's chin with long, cool fingers. "And I already know who you are, Lira Astor."

Lira rolled her eyes and sat back, ripping her face out of the woman's hold in the process. "That's your big reveal to try and scare me? I already figured you know who I am—people rarely go about kidnapping random people they don't know. Also, I hate to burst your bubble, but pretty much *everyone* knows who I am."

"How about this." Lucinda leaned forward, right into Lira's personal space, those fingers curling around her jaw again, her hold tightening until it was painful. "I know who you are, and I know that you—unbeknownst to the Mage Council or anyone at Temari Hall—are a member of Underground."

CHAPTER 19

Lucinda's words echoed through the room, but Lira didn't allow her expression to change, even though those cold eyes were still looking directly into hers as if they could read everything she was thinking.

"That's quite an imagination you have." Lira smiled a little, enjoying this battle of wits. Whoever this woman was, she was in charge, which meant she'd orchestrated everything that had happened to Lira.

She was the one Lira was going to destroy.

The one she would make pay for her breakdown earlier. The anticipation of that burned through her, dimming the pain of her bound wrists and masking her weariness. A prickle on the back of her neck reminded her of the figure across the room, the intensity of the gaze which she knew without looking was focused entirely on her.

Lucinda eventually let go of her chin and moved to sit in the chair opposite Lira, crossing her legs languidly. Her attitude was one of someone who'd taken Lira's measure and discounted it as any kind of threat. Someone who was used to being in complete control of every situation. "There's no need to do this little dance. I know everything about you."

Lira's glance flicked between the entrance door—it was closed—to the two men standing silently, one behind Lucinda, the other to Lira's immediate right. She calculated her odds. The men were close enough to each door to cut off both potential exits even if she managed to get out of the ropes and run. They weren't good odds, but that was how Lira liked it.

She reached for the thrill, the seductive pull of pushing at the boundaries of danger and threat until she defeated them. She needed it to ensure she survived this. It trickled through her, and she took hold of it, demolished the self-imposed barriers holding it back.

And for the first time in years she let the heady rush have her.

A smile had curled at her mouth without her even realising. She'd missed this feeling desperately, no matter how much she'd tried to forget, to pretend she was perfectly content at Temari. She finally felt alive again.

Lucinda gave a little shake of her head at the smile, as if speaking to a wayward child. "If you'd just stayed in the cart, none of this would have been necessary. You'd be resting in a comfortable room right now."

Lira's smile widened. "Would that be before or after one of your pet monsters tried to eat me?"

Lucinda's posture hadn't changed, not once, her hands neatly folded in her lap, legs crossed. "You're the Shadowcouncil's greatest hope, their symbol for the future."

Inwardly, Lira stilled. Either Lucinda was making some oddly accurate guesses, or she *did* know about Lira's involvement with Underground. She'd have to play this very carefully. She shrugged in as nonchalant a manner as she could manage. "That's very poetic. I've no idea what it means, but it's lovely."

"And you are admirably discreet. You're a member of Greyson's cell in Karonan. Would you like me to list out the names of the other members of the cell? The name of the tailor's cellar where you meet every few weeks?"

Lira eyed her, settling into the enjoyment of wordplay with this woman. "Who are you, exactly?"

"Isn't it obvious by now? I'm a member of the Shadowcouncil."

Silence fell like a thick, heavy blanket over the room. Lira carefully schooled her features to blankness even as her thoughts turned over furiously. She'd been arguing with Greyson for access to the Shadow-council for months, but he'd continually refused, claiming it was too dangerous. He hadn't even been willing to tell her anything about their identities, which meant she had no way of verifying whether Lucinda was telling the truth.

Still... maybe she could use this conversation to learn something. "Then to be absolutely clear, *you're* the one who kidnapped all of us?" she pressed. "Underground is behind this?"

Lucinda merely smiled. "Yes."

"*If* that's true—which I'm far from convinced is the case—and *if* you really think I'm a member of Underground, then why am I amongst the kidnapped students?" Lira enquired.

Lucinda picked a piece of invisible lint from her skirt and flicked it away. "I had a few reasons, actually, but the main one was to keep up appearances. We have big plans for you, Lira, and for those to come to fruition, they need to completely and utterly believe you're one of them."

"They?" she asked, even though she knew the answer.

"The other students, of course. And by extension, the Mage Council."

Lira savoured the small thrill that Lucinda's talk of the group having plans for her summoned, and narrowed her eyes. "A plausible story doesn't prove anything. They're just words."

Lucinda's predator-like gaze held hers. "Greyson has already reported that you've missed the deadline to get him the report we were after. The one sent to Finn A'ndreas by Councillor Duneskal? He seemed almost concerned about you, though he hid it well. I assured him you were required unexpectedly on another assignment and to give someone else the task."

Lira tried to keep her reaction to that from showing, but wasn't sure she'd succeeded.

A little smile crossed the woman's face. "Like I said, while we kidnapped you for appearances' sake, you would have been a lot more comfortable during your stay here if you'd just stayed with the cart."

Danger whispered through Lira, the peril of making a single misstep with this woman. If the wrong people found out Lira was a member of Underground, all her plans would come tumbling down. But it seemed increasingly likely that Lucinda was who she said she was. And *if* she was ... well, that would be an opportunity indeed. Excitement warmed her from the inside out.

"If we really are on the same side, then how about explaining yourself. If stealing that report was so critical, why kidnap me before I had a chance to steal it?" Lira glanced at the door again. Three long steps from her chair, turning the handle, pushing it open. Too much to accomplish before one of the men would be on her, even if she did get free of the ropes without magic. "What are those creatures? Where are we? *Why* are we here?"

Lucinda's gaze flicked briefly to one of the men. He was the shortest of the three, with short-cropped dark hair and trimmed beard.

"We're not going to hurt you any more than is necessary." Lucinda stood, a simple, graceful movement, answering none of Lira's questions. "Though we will have to make it look realistic, so I apologise in advance."

The cold look that slithered over the woman's face told Lira that she wasn't sorry for anything. Anger flared and she yanked discreetly at her bonds. "What happened to me being comfortable?"

"I'm afraid your actions have complicated the situation."

Without thinking, Lira turned and glanced over her shoulder at the hooded figure in the corner, eyes narrowed. The energy hanging around the person, it was almost familiar, like... "You have magic. Is it you controlling the forest?"

Whoever it was said nothing. Lucinda glanced between them. "You're a quick one. A definite asset for the future. I'm pleased, Lira."

"I don't believe a word you say." Lira flung the words at her, trying to taunt Lucinda into staying, talking more. Telling her *something*. "Who's controlling the monsters? Was it *razak* you called them? You know one of them tried to kill me—was that part of your grand plan too?"

But her words fell on deaf ears. Lucinda hadn't even blinked. Her control was a formidable thing. "You'll wait here for now. I'll be back."

Lucinda had only taken a single step when the door from the back stairwell slammed open. Tarion swept inside, staff raised. After a moment's shock that he'd be so foolish, Lira bellowed at him. "What the hell are you doing? Get out of here!"

He ignored her, instead going straight for the nearest guard, mage staff slashing through the air. He managed to cross half the distance before he froze into stillness.

Lira glanced straight at Lucinda. That predatory little smile was back on the woman's face, and she had one finger of her left hand raised. A panicked breath escaped Tarion, his hazel eyes dark with shock and fear. He clearly couldn't move.

"You're a mage too," Lira said blankly. Her shock was deeper than the realisation this woman had just frozen Tarion in his tracks. As far as she knew, Underground didn't have any mage members apart from Lira and those on the Shadowcouncil. Not yet. Controlling a forest, forcing people into paralysis... Lira didn't know of any Mage Council mages with those abilities either. And she'd made it her business to learn about the strength of the council mages.

Lucinda was telling the truth about being a member of the Shadow-council.

Not to mention that the fact she was using magic without blinking an eye meant they weren't afraid of the razak. So one of them had to be controlling the creatures.

Lira's initial ire at Tarion's appearance switched abruptly to delight. She could have kissed him for bursting in like he had. She'd learned more in the last minute than she had after going several rounds trying to force something useful out of Lucinda. The idiot had inadvertently proved himself useful.

"Why didn't you just use that trick on me earlier?" Lira asked, genuinely curious.

Lucinda's gaze flicked between Tarion and Lira. "I prefer to watch people squirm, it's a useful way of getting their measure."

"Did I pass the test?"

"I'll let you know." She turned to the two men. "Jora, Dasta, you know what to do. Take them both to a cell after."

Lucinda turned her back, opened the door, and stalked out with quick, precise strides. The hooded figure remained in the corner, still and silent. A look of focused concentration fell across the short man's face as Lucinda left, one of his fingers flickering. Lira caught a glimpse of rippling darkness outside, felt the slither of ice-cold air in the room, before the door closed.

Then they were alone with Jora and Dasta. Both men moved towards her, filling her vision. The taller one lifted a hand, slammed it across Lira's face. Agonising pain exploded through her left cheekbone and jaw. Spots blurred her vision, and for a moment she hung in the chair, her thoughts sent flying into a hundred scattered pieces by pain and grogginess. Another thudding impact, another line of fire, this time her nose.

And then blackness took her down.

CHAPTER 20

L ira woke to throbbing pain in her face. When she tried to lift her head, the throbbing exploded into a fiery agony encompassing her entire skull, and a grunt escaped her. She went still. Rotted carcasses. Shadowcouncil or not, she was going to *bury* Lucinda and her henchmen. Once she got what she needed from them, of course.

"Lira?"

Groaning, she moved more slowly this time, painfully dragging herself into a half-sitting position. The vision in her left eye was blurry, and a sticky substance covered her face under her nose and on her cheek. She rubbed at it, hissed at the pain that caused, then stared at her fingers.

Red.

She blinked. Blood. She was bleeding.

"Hey, Lira? Can you hear me?"

The voice was coming from somewhere nearby. She turned too quickly, cursing in agony at the movement. Ugh, she had to stop doing that. Once the pain had dulled again, she shifted her head much more slowly, squinting to try and see better.

Tarion's face swam into her vision, though she had to blink a few more times before the image was clear enough to recognise him.

"What in rotted hells were you thinking?" she muttered.

"They've locked us in a cell. With bars."

"Wow, what a clever deduction. You worked that out from opening your eyes and looking at our surroundings, I take it?" The snappish response was instinctive, a way to hold him off while her groggy mind swung back into use and she could process her situation.

"Foul mood fully intact then. Good, I was worried a head injury might have made you nicer." He sounded genuinely reassured. Her thoughts stuck on that for a moment, trying to process the oddity. Maybe he had a head injury too?

Lira took several deep, slow breaths to try and pull together all her scattered thoughts. Clarity of thinking slowly returned, and if she didn't move too much or too quickly, the pain in her head remained on the bearable side of agony.

"Are you all right?" he asked after a short time had passed, clearly having waited patiently for her to collect herself.

"Do I *look* all right?" She stared at him, still blinking. He didn't seem to have any apparent injuries. "They broke my rotted nose. Why is your face still as pretty as ever?"

"Whatever magic that woman has, I was completely frozen. They didn't need to beat me into submission." He looked around, a little frown creasing his forehead. "And my face is not pretty."

"It's prettier than mine." She bit her lip as more pain throbbed through her jaw and cheekbones, a terrible idea since she'd bitten through her lip earlier, and the movement just caused the scabbing to break open. She tried to focus on something to distract her from the stinging pain. "Could you tell where they brought us?"

"No. They blindfolded me. I counted a lot of stairs though, going down, I think. I reckon we might be underground. She did mention a cell—the paralysis didn't prevent me hearing or seeing or smelling—so I'm guessing that's where we are."

She squinted at him to try and be sure it actually was Tarion she was looking at. "You're awfully chatty all of a sudden."

"Talking's easier when a group of people aren't staring at me," he said, glancing away in discomfort.

When people weren't staring at him? Maybe her brain was temporarily broken. "Were you adopted or something?"

A bitter laugh escaped him. "Don't think I haven't asked myself that question a thousand times. But no."

"What, growing up at court in Karonan and Alistriem didn't prepare you for talking in front of people?" Lira wasn't sure why she was so fixated on that point—maybe it was something to do with her head injury. Or maybe it was just that there were so many dissonances, so many confusing things, in her situation she wanted to at least make sense of *something*.

He didn't say anything to that, so she pushed. "You're the son of two war heroes, Tarion Caverlock. Younger brother to the best Taliath the world has seen since your father. Nephew of more heroes. Everyone looks at you and thinks you're wonderful, perfect, just like your parents. You've had your entire comfortable life handed to you. How can it be difficult for you to *talk*?"

"It just is," he said quietly.

"Is it because of your magic? Don't try and tell me those perfect parents of yours don't adore you no matter what magic you have." She paused. "Or *don't* have."

He flinched. "You like making a point of my less than amazing magical ability, don't you?"

She huffed a laugh. As if. "I don't care about your magic."

"So why keep bringing it up?"

"Because it's obviously a sore point for you—not that I have any idea why—and it keeps you at bay." Lira risked moving, but did it slowly, rising to her knees first. "How many guards are out there?"

"You're good at keeping people at bay."

"It helps with survival." She shifted from knees to feet next, swaying and almost falling in the process. She did *not* feel good. But she was up, and determined to stay up. She re-focused her attention on Tarion. "Guards?"

He frowned, then shook his head a little. "Not sure how many there are. The two men who carried us down here disappeared out that door. I didn't see anyone else."

Lira waited for the wave of dizziness to disappear, then took two unsteady steps towards the bars of the cell and peered out into a short, empty corridor. Lit torches made the space bright. At one end was a hardpacked dirt wall. At the other sat a closed wooden door.

The cells were lined with bars, and there was an empty cell on either side of the one where she and Tarion were. The floor was covered with straw. The ceiling was more hardpacked dirt. In the corner of the cell to their left, the straw was dark with spatters of old blood. "Why did you burst in like that? Don't get me wrong, it actually helped me work some stuff out, but you were supposed to go and warn the others."

"We heard you get caught. Fari went to warn the others. I came to help you," he said simply. "I listened at the door to try and figure out what was going on, but couldn't hear well enough, so I just figured I'd burst in and take them by surprise."

She barked a laugh, then winced as the movement sent pain stabbing through her face. "What's the real reason?"

"I don't know what you mean." He looked confused.

"Yes you do," she said. "I'm Lira Astor. You didn't come to help me, Tarion. What was it, you think I'm more useful to you free because of my scary Shakar magic?"

"Think whatever you want." He waved that off. "You said you learned something?"

"First..." Lira hesitated. "Lucinda claimed to be a member of the Shadowcouncil."

A thoughtful looked narrowed his face at that revelation, but he didn't say anything, merely waited for her to keep going.

"Also, you bursting in showed us that Lucinda has magic, that it's powerful. That she wasn't afraid of using it and drawing the monsters, meaning she has a way of controlling them. Probably one of the men in the room with us. Should I go on?"

He shifted closer, concern on his face. "You keep blinking... is your eyesight blurry? Maybe I should look at your face, make sure nothing is broken."

"And what are you going to do if it is?"

"I'm the son of war heroes whose closest friends include a war hero healer mage, remember?" He threw her words from earlier back at her. "Uncle Finn taught me a thing or two about healing."

"Fine." She faced him, forcing herself to stand still as he came closer, hazel eyes narrowing in focus as he lifted a hand to trace over her cheekbone. A memory of the last time she'd had her nose broken flashed through her head, vivid and bright, bringing with it an ache of warmth and grief and.... She jerked away from Tarion, the air sucked from her chest in a blink. She shoved those memories away as quickly and ruthlessly as she could.

"Did I hurt you?"

"No." She forced herself to shift back towards him, to keep her mind blank and still while he looked at her. Until the bitter, clawing ache of memories and associated feelings faded.

Despite Tarion's light touch, his exploration hurt, and she bit the inside of her cheek to hold back a cry of pain. He persevered, gently palpating her cheekbones and jaw. Eventually he reached down, tore a long strip from the hem of his tunic, then lifted it.

"What are you doing?" She flinched back.

"I want to clean some of the blood away so I can see the damage properly," he said patiently. "Okay?"

She hesitated. Nodded. Then closed her eyes tight, fiercely warding off the memories that wanted to rush back. Cool fingers pressing lightly over her ribs, dark blue eyes narrowed in concern... No! The ache was suddenly so fierce that tears pressed at the backs of her eyelids and she had to force them away.

Tarion clearly made an effort to be gentle, even though each swipe of the cloth sent sharp flashes of pain through her face. She welcomed it though. Throwing herself into the pain kept the memories at bay. It took three strips of his tunic before he was satisfied and stepped away.

"It's already swelling up," he murmured. "But I don't think your cheekbone is broken. Your nose is another story. Want me to set it for you?"

"No." She stepped away, at her absolute limit. "It's fine."

"It's going to heal crooked if I don't."

"Then let it. I don't want you messing about with my nose." She honestly didn't care two figs if her nose healed crooked or not, and the last thing she wanted was more pain to interfere with thinking clearly. She needed to be able to focus if she wanted to get out.

"You've been beaten like this before."

"Have I?" She dismissed him and turned back to study the corridor beyond the cell, looking for any possible exit. Her roving—admittedly still blurry—gaze saw no obvious options.

"If I'd taken a beating like that I would still be curled up in the straw moaning in pain," he said. "But not you."

"Is there a point to your observations?" She turned to stare at him. The last thing she was going to do was tell him that yes, she had been beaten multiple times before, and dragged herself up off the ground each time. She hadn't needed help those times, despite having fooled herself into thinking she'd had a family and a home in Dirinan, and she certainly didn't need anyone's help now.

"Not big on trust, are you?" He let it go and moved away, studying the bars. "Is your magic strong enough to tear these out?"

"Maybe. If we want to call every razak in the place down on us." She gave one of the bars a hard yank, ignoring the agony that stabbed through her face at the movement. It seemed firmly embedded in the stone. "Maybe not." Her eyes shifted to the locking mechanism, and she bent down to study it, closing her eyes briefly at the rush of dizziness that swept through her head. "This I could unlock if I used magic."

"Razak?"

"It's what she called the creatures."

He nodded as if something had been accomplished. "So if we figure out a way to deal with the razak, we can get out?"

Lira frowned, turning to look at him. "You seem awfully calm about all of this."

He lifted an eyebrow. "You expected me to be screaming in panic? The son of two war heroes?"

She rolled her eyes. "You did just admit to the fact you'd be moaning in pain in the straw if someone broke your nose."

His mouth quirked in amusement. Another oddity. What young

man wasn't bothered by admitting weakness? The smile faded quickly though. "I *am* scared. That Fari might be caught by one of those creatures before she can reach the others. That they won't be warned in time and accidentally draw the razak to them. That more of us will be killed. That we'll never get home. That if something *has* happened to Karonan people I love might be hurt or dead." He spoke quickly, jaw tight. "But terror isn't going to help prevent any of those things."

Interesting. He hadn't mentioned being afraid for himself once during that long run-on sentence.

"You do get chatty when you're alone," she remarked.

"Let me guess, you're not afraid at all?"

"Relatives of evil all-powerful mages don't get scared," she murmured, bending to look at the lock again. Maybe if she planned out exactly how to break it before summoning her magic, limiting the length of time she needed to use it, the razak wouldn't sense it.

"I bet. Especially when most people assume those relatives are just as evil and powerful," Tarion said. "You like trading on that, don't you?"

She spun, sudden fury filling her so strongly that she spat the words. "*Like?* You think I *like* it when every single person I ever meet assumes I'm just as bad as my dead grandfather who wasn't even alive when I was born?"

"I..." He froze, mouth open, eyes going wide. "I did, yeah."

She turned back to the lock, mortified at the tears that flooded her eyes. Her rotted broken nose was making her weepy. "Then you're as big of an idiot as the rest of them."

"The rest of them? You mean everyone at Temari Hall?"

"I mean everyone I've ever met. People are either terrified of me or think they can use me. It's just how it goes."

Carcasses, now she was the one spilling out words everywhere. She was clearly exhausted and losing her focus. She needed to get a hold of herself.

There was a brief silence. Her shoulders loosened as it appeared like he was going to let it go and forget her outburst had ever happened. But then he started speaking.

"I hate it. The dinners and the gatherings and the balls. The constant spotlight. My parents were born for it... the attention, the regard. My sister too. But it makes me freeze, makes me want to run and hide, and no matter how hard I try, I can't control it. I'm the son of Alyx Egalion and Dashan Caverlock, and all I want is to have my own space. I love them all, more than anything, but I don't want to *be* them."

Lira's hand curled over the lock. She didn't want to empathise with Tarion Caverlock, didn't want to start *liking* him. She was never going to survive this if she did something as stupid as that.

He hadn't come for her because he wanted to help her. He'd come because they needed her help to survive. She had to keep reminding herself of that. "This is not a sharing session, Caverlock. I don't care about your insecurities. Not sure if you noticed, but we've been kidnapped and are being held prisoner. How about we focus our thoughts on that situation?"

Astonishingly, he smiled. And when he did, the closed expression he wore all the time faded, replaced by what looked like it might be a piece of the real him. It wasn't a handsome smile full of roguish charm like his father's, or Garan's. Tarion's smile was simple. Sincere.

"I can do that, Spider."

She rolled her eyes, ignoring how, once again, he'd completely disarmed her irritation.

"I have an idea," he said, the smile fading, the thoughtful look returning.

She abandoned studying the lock. Turned to look at him. Tarion had a brain, and he wasn't panicking. She didn't need to trust him to let him help them both. "Wow me."

He pointed to the back of the cell, where a steel grating sat high in the dirt wall. There was no trace of rust on its surface. It looked big enough that Lira could wriggle through on hands and knees, though Tarion would be a tight squeeze.

She gave him a dubious look. "Even if we wanted to climb into that comfortable looking space, we're not getting that grating off without magic," she said. "Not even you are tall enough to reach it to manually pull it out."

"Who said anything about climbing?" That smile was back. "I can transport us both into the space on the other side of the grating.

Doesn't matter if a hundred razak sense my magic and come piling into this cell. They're not going to be able to chase us inside—they're too big."

She stared at him. "And what if there's nothing back there? We'd be trapped inside a tiny space in the wall with a bunch of slavering razak below. Then the delightful Lucinda and her cavalry will arrive and promptly yank us back out."

Tarion shook his head. "Look around you. I would bet everything I own that this cellar wasn't part of the original building. There's no sign of the age or disrepair we saw upstairs. It's been dug out more recently. That grating is there for a reason. My guess is as a way of bringing fresh air down here from outside. You don't want your prisoners expiring from stale air before you do what you need to with them."

A smile curled at her mouth. He was right... but still... "What if the size of that grating is misleading and the air shaft is too small for both of us, what happens then?"

"Then we get crushed to death." He shrugged. "I'm more than willing to hear your better idea, Spider."

She didn't have one. And he knew it. The smile came back. "They might not know what my magic is," he continued. "If you pop that lock on our cell the moment before I transport us, then they'll assume we escaped that way. Which means they'll have no idea where we are or where we escaped to."

A big part of her thrilled at the idea of confounding that smug look right off Lucinda's face, but trusting a boy she barely knew made her deeply uneasy. "*If* we escaped. As opposed to simply trapping ourselves in a hole neither of us fits in." She pegged him with a look. "Have you ever transported another person before? I've never seen you do it in class." Tarion usually sat at the back of their classes, refusing to do any magic unless specifically called upon. She hadn't realised before that it was because he was *shy*. What an idiot.

"I did it with Caria. Once."

"Once?" She couldn't help but grin through her aching face. "So you're telling me I have to choose between sitting here and waiting for that irritatingly superior woman and her goons to come back, or getting transported into a tiny shaft I might not fit in by an apprentice mage who's only ever successfully transported someone *once*."

"You have an excellent knack for concisely summarising a bad situation."

"I have many knacks." She strode over to the wall. "Let's do it."

He blinked. "Just like that?"

"I'm aware you don't know me at all, Tarion Caverlock, but I am not the type to sit around waiting for a bad situation to get worse. I prefer to re-take the advantage where possible. I also feel fairly safe in assuming you'd never willingly risk your sister's life, so you must be confident in your magic."

He stared at her. "You realise that I'm not the only suddenly chatty one, don't you? Three years at Temari Hall and I've never heard you speak as many words together as you have since we got locked in this cell."

She opened her mouth, a retort ready, but closed it abruptly as a high-pitched screaming sounded in the distance. It was faint. Barely there. But she'd heard it before. Another sounded on its heels, a little closer, then another, barely audible. Then a whole cacophony of them echoing through the air above their heads until slowly fading away.

"They killed another razak." Tarion's excitement was tangible and she felt it leaping through her chest too. The rush was there, providing the helping hand she needed.

Her smiled widened. "Come on, Caverlock, let's go now, while they're distracted."

Not giving Tarion a chance to protest or respond, she lifted a hand and sent a tendril of telekinetic magic snaking through the lock on their cell door. It was a simple device and she had it in seconds. The lock popped open and she gave the door a nudge for good measure. It swung open silently on well-oiled hinges. He was right about this cellar being new.

The next thing she knew, Tarion's arm was wrapping around her middle and her vision suddenly became intensely blurry. Her stomach heaved with nausea, she felt a forceful tugging on her muscles, and then her surroundings vanished.

The disorientation lasted several moments. When she could think again through the throbbing in her face and the remnants of Tarion's disorienting magic, she found her left side pressed against cold, hard-packed dirt. She was on her knees and surrounded by darkness broken only by the light through a grating to her right. It was just enough to make clear that they weren't trapped—the narrow crawlspace stretched away in both directions. "You did it!"

"I find the surprise in your voice offensive," Tarion said good-naturedly. He was hunched over far more than she was, but at least he seemed to fit inside the space. "Come on, let's move before the razak show up."

"I don't care what anyone says, mage-prince, you are no lesser mage," she muttered as they began crawling.

"Nobody uses that term anymore."

"But they all still think it, don't they?"

"Yes." There was a moment's silence, then, "I'm only just starting to realise it, but... you don't, do you?"

No, she didn't. But that wasn't something she was going to admit to Tarion Caverlock. So she stayed silent.

And they crawled on.

CHAPTER 21
BEFORE

Her magic finally broke out when she was fifteen.

For a period of several months the flashes of violet light that surrounded her hands when her emotions became volatile had been happening more frequently, and become harder to subdue.

The hard-won control that she'd learned over the mage light vanished, and she'd had to stop participating in jobs on Ahrin's orders, unable to afford one of the city guards, a rival gang, or even one of the residents of Dirinan to see it.

Ahrin knew well what would happen if her identity was known to the crime gangs. Lira would become hot property, and none of the bosses would ask nicely or offer a choice about becoming theirs. So Ahrin had kept her secret all these years, and since those at the orphanage had no idea where Lira had gone, or even if she was still alive, her identity as the Darkmage's granddaughter remained hidden.

Once she broke out, of course, that would be an entirely different matter. Any crew boss would be wary of trying to take her by force then. And her name would only give Ahrin more prestige. But until she did, she was virtually locked up as a prisoner.

The forced inactivity only made her emotions more inclined to spill over into irritated anger, frustrated taunts, or snapped responses to even the mildest questions from her fellow crew. It was a vicious cycle she couldn't break no matter how hard she tried to control herself.

It wasn't just her. Ahrin grew edgier and colder the less Lira was involved in the crew's jobs. They took less. Yanzi got caught and arrested and they had to use most of what they'd saved up for emergencies to bail him out.

Lira hated it. Ahrin wanted more; more territory, more power, a bigger crew. And all Lira wanted was to help her, be a part of it, but her stupid uncontrolled magic meant she couldn't. Worst of all, she hated the look of impatience and irritation she saw on Ahrin's face when the crew leader didn't realise Lira was looking.

"I'm sorry." Lira said it a hundred times.

Each time she said it, Ahrin flashed that charming smile of hers and told her not to worry. "It'll break out properly soon, and then you'll learn to control it. Everything will be fine."

It was like she didn't know Lira could tell the difference between the charming smile Ahrin wore as a mask, to manipulate and control, and her genuine smiles, which were rare as waterholes in a desert.

"Hey!"

Lira snapped back to the present, managing to give Yanzi a distracted smile as he dropped into the chair beside her, his deep voice breaking through her maudlin thoughts. His dark skin gleamed with sweat, and a wide grin stretched across his face. In the hall around them the night's revelry had already grown raucous.

Transk threw this party once a year—he liked to say he did it as a gesture of appreciation to his crews and their leaders. Lira figured he just liked to showcase his wealth and status. Make sure nobody got any ideas about challenging him.

It was the first year Ahrin's crew had been invited, having finally achieved enough status to warrant it. Lira's theft of the Silver Lords' statue months earlier had made sure of it. Still, status could vanish in a blink in the ever-shifting sands of power on the streets, and Lira moved anxiously at the thought. Her inability to do anything rose in a familiar tide of frustration. She just wanted to break out already so she could dedicate herself to learning to use and control the magic simmering inside her.

The entire warehouse floor was full of tables and dancing bodies. The lowest level crews were co-opted to ferry drink and food around all night, and the local city guard detachment were bribed handsomely to ensure they didn't come anywhere near the block.

It was a night of freedom, debauchery, entertainment. Lira sat there, watching it all, and brooding. She couldn't settle enough to enjoy herself, couldn't seem to settle at all these days, feeling constantly on edge and moody.

"Why are you not having fun?" Yanzi peered at her. "It's the first time you've been out of the loft in days."

"I am," she snapped.

He laughed at the absurdity of her words, almost falling off the chair with the force of it. Lira glowered at him.

"Lira!" Yanzi leaned forward and slapped her knee. "Let's at least get you bedded tonight, it's well past time for you. Boy or girl?"

She ignored the question. "Where's Tomin?"

"Fetching drinks." Yanzi beamed. "Poor boy needed a break from my glorious dancing. No distracting me now... there are plenty of handsome lads and ladies here tonight that would be happy to introduce you to the delights of bedding. Apart from the crooked nose, you're not entirely bad to look at. It would have been nice if you'd made an effort with that crow's nest you call hair, though."

She fixed him with another scowl. The *last* thing she cared about at this moment was how her hair looked. Nice hair wasn't going to help her get back into running jobs and making sure the crew stayed afloat.

"Come on," he wheedled, leaning closer. "Let me do this for you. I'll make sure it's someone who'll treat you well."

Lira's gaze drifted to where Ahrin stood by the wall talking to one of Transk's runners. Even with the tables and dancing bodies between them, Lira read the stiffness in her shoulders that indicated she was angry. Her chest ached with something she couldn't name, leaving her confused and anxious.

Yanzi snorted. "She's unattainable, Lira. Pick someone else, *anyone* else. She'll have her pick tonight, and it won't be you."

"What?" Lira turned her attention back to him, kicked at the legs of his chair. "You idiot."

He half-fell to the floor, breaking out in another laugh. He must be smoking cloudweed again. "Fine. Sit there and be sour then. Don't say I didn't try."

"Drinks for everyone!" Timin appeared then in a cloud of uncharacteristic exuberance, dropping four glasses of amber liquid on the table so hard a good portion of the drink sloshed over the sides.

"Thanks, Timin." She took the glass he offered, and they shared a brief smile. The drink was bitter, but it loosened some of the tight ball of anxiousness in her chest, so she drank down a few more mouthfuls.

Yanzi and Timin drank theirs in the space of about five minutes before Yanzi dragged his boy back out to join the dancing bodies. Lira watched them for a bit, wondering how they managed to find such simple happiness. Eventually she grew bored and began searching the room for where Ahrin had gone. She wasn't in the mood for this, and maybe she'd be allowed to leave early if she promised to take Picker's watch shift back at their loft.

"You could try dancing, you know." Ahrin dropped into the chair beside her. Her coat of choice tonight was a deep red, fitting her form perfectly, and she lifted a booted foot to rest on the table. The necklace around her neck glinted in the flamelight where it disappeared under her shirt. "You're allowed to have some fun, Lira."

"Sure." Lira rolled her eyes, forcing her gaze away from Ahrin's neck. "I will when you do."

Midnight eyes shifted to her, a smile curling at her mouth. "Fair."

"Who were you talking to? You looked upset."

Ahrin leaned forward, grabbed the fourth cup off the table and drained it in three long swallows. "Nobody."

Lira's eyes narrowed. It wasn't like Ahrin to drink at all, let alone do it so eagerly.

"Look at him," she murmured before Lira could say anything. Her gaze was focused on Transk. The most powerful organised crime boss in Dirinan sat at the top of the room, sprawled in a massive chair on a raised section of floor that allowed him to look down over the entire party.

"What's he done to earn your ire tonight?"

Ahrin shrugged. "What makes you think I'm angry at him?"

There was that edge again. The one that warned not to push any further or you'd see the dangerous side of Ahrin Vensis. But Lira had blurred that line a long time ago, and it had been even longer since she'd been afraid of her crew leader. She opened her mouth to push, but surprisingly Ahrin continued.

"He has everything. Wealth. Power. That seat up there. I want all of it."

There was an odd mix of hunger and bitterness and danger in her voice as she spoke, and Lira wasn't sure how to respond to her words. She wondered briefly if there was going to be blood tonight. If Ahrin had decided to make a move without telling her. But before she could think of anything to say, Ahrin stood abruptly.

"I need to talk to someone. I'll be back."

Lira lasted until Ahrin was halfway across the hall, weaving gracefully through packed dancers, before her patience ran out and she rose to follow. Ahrin pushed through a side door at the edge of the room and disappeared. Moments later Lira got there and went after her.

Ahrin waited in the dimly lit hall beyond, expression cold, voice even more wintry. "You know better than to follow me without invitation."

"I want you to tell me what's wrong." Tired, stressed, Lira was sick of trying to figure it out. She just wanted to know what she could do to fix it. "If it's not my magic failing to break out yet, then what's bothering you?"

"It's nothing."

"It's not. You're hiding something from me."

Danger flashed in Ahrin's blue eyes then. "Careful, Lira."

"I'm your second. You know I'll do whatever you need." Lira stepped closer. "This is my home. I want to build our territory too. I want to grow stronger so that we can stay safe, so that we can keep each other safe, so that we never feel hunger or cold ever again."

"You're a mage, Lira!" Ahrin had snapped. "Pureblood no less, no matter how evil your grandfather. It's different for us."

Lira recoiled. Ahrin had never drawn a barrier like this between them before. "I'm not any different to you."

"Yes, you are. You just haven't realised it yet."

The words rang through the hallway, clear and stark despite the racket coming through the thin walls from the party.

Stung, Lira shook her head. "Why would you say that?"

"You should be thinking about going to Temari Hall, that's all." The edge was still in Ahrin's voice but the coldness had gone. She sounded almost unhappy. But that was impossible. Ahrin didn't get unhappy. Lira was missing something.

"I don't want to go there. How many times do I have to say that to you before you'll believe me?" It was true. The last thing she ever wanted was to leave Dirinan, to leave Ahrin's crew. "I'm *staying*, Ahrin."

Ahrin's hard expression softened, and she moved closer, one hand lifting to tuck a strand of hair behind Lira's ear before trailing her fingers along her jaw. "I want more, Lira, more of what I can never have. But the moment your magic breaks out, you're going to be given more. And that's where we're different."

Lira's hand lifted of its own accord, hovered close to Ahrin's, *so* close but not quite touching. She wasn't brave enough for that, even though her heart was thudding and she had no idea what this sudden warmth spreading through her meant except that she craved more of it. "Whatever is given to me, I will share with you. I'm not going to leave you. I swear it."

Something unnameable flashed over Ahrin's face, and she moved, shifting almost impossibly closer. Then her eyes slid closed.

"We can have it," Lira murmured, breath catching, the ache in her chest so fierce it hurt. "The money. The power. I just need time. It won't be long."

The moment held, so fragile Lira didn't dare move or breathe for fear of breaking it. But then Ahrin's eyes opened again, and as they did, her face hardened. She stepped away, her voice harsh. "That's not the problem, Lira. You'll never understand."

"Then explain it to me."

"I don't want to." She cut Lira off, cool, dismissive. "Go back to the party. If you follow me, you're out, am I clear?"

Lira stiffened. "Very."

Ahrin turned and strode away without another word.

AND THEN HER magic had broken out.

She should never have left the loft that day. But Ahrin had been edgier than usual all morning, snapping at all of them, before disappearing around midday. Lira had wanted to do something to improve her mood, to make her feel better, to fix whatever was wrong. They'd barely spoken since the party, and when they had Ahrin had been distant, cold.

Dirinan town square was firmly inside the territory of Transk's biggest rival, the Coin Tossers. You only crossed into their territory to work if you were stupid, had a death wish, or wanted to display your lack of fear of one of the scariest gang leaders in the city.

If Lira spent an hour pickpocketing there, it would get back to Transk. If she spent an hour there without getting caught and came back with full pockets, it would gain his attention.

The familiar thrill rose up to claim her as she began working, the first part of her plan going off without a hitch. Despite being a little rusty from months of inaction, she managed to fill her pockets and the inside of her waistcoat with several small bags of coin.

She was strolling away, headed back to her patch, smiling a little smile of triumph, when a group of Silver Lords happened by. She'd been marked by them ever since the theft of their leader's statue and it took only a second for them to recognise her.

They were surprisingly quick in coming after her, despite the fact they were all on rival territory. The fastest of them, a boy a couple of years older than her, lean with long limbs, closed the distance uncomfortably quickly.

Lira ducked down a narrow alley, using the sharp turn to try and slow his pursuit even a fraction, but he was still too close. He would catch up before she could scramble over the locked gate cutting the alley in half.

In desperation—if they caught her they would kill her— and not even thinking about what she was doing, she willed the gate in front of her to open before she got to it.

Unfocused, untrained, and raw, her magic sent the gate flying from its hinges and slamming into the stone wall on the side of the alley. Gasping, exhausted from the drain on her energy, she'd forced herself to keep running. When she glanced back, it was to find all three of her pursuers stopped dead, eyes wide with terror.

Slowing, she looked down at the bright violet light shrouding her hands.

She huffed a bitter breath.

Everyone feared her. Eventually.

Fine. That fear would only help her crew now that she'd broken out. Lira reinforced their terror by fixing a determined expression on her face and waving an arm in their direction. They'd scattered, one of them even letting out a scream.

Then she turned and dragged herself away, taking a convoluted series of streets back to Revel Kings territory in case the Silver Lords were brave enough to get reinforcements and come after her again. Instead of going to the loft she climbed up to her old bolt hole under the eaves of the gambling den. Over the years she'd still gone there occasionally when she needed time to herself, but it had been months since she'd visited, and a faint mouldy air hung over everything.

She barely noticed, though, because once she was safe and could marshal her thoughts, the joy and relief of her magic breaking out rushed through her like a snow-melt flood.

Her magic was out.

To make sure, she lifted a hand and willed the empty sack by the pile of straw she'd used as a bed rise into the air. Something inside her shifted, stuck, then came free, like a loosened bolt. The sack lifted into the air, violet light flashing from her skin as it did. Weariness crashed through her a moment later and it fell back to the ground.

Telekinesis, that was her first ability. Surely now there'd be more coming, too, if she was like Shakar. She could start trailing other mages in the city, absorb their abilities from them. She'd become more and more powerful.

Tears threatened to fall and a trembling smile of relief crossed her face.

She could help Ahrin now.

SHE WAS GLOWING with triumph and the heady thrill of winning as she made her way up the rickety staircase into their loft, only to stop dead at the top of the stairs in confusion. The area of the space that held all their stash was cleared out, every penny and jewel they'd saved gone. Ahrin's corner was utterly empty too—the curtains gone, her bedding, her little stove.

Timin stood in the middle of the floor, glaring at a torn piece of parchment in his hands.

"What's going on?" Lira asked. "I've got news, I—"

"Ahrin's gone."

The words hit her like a punch to the jaw. "What?"

"Something about those words don't make sense to you?" Timin snarled, walking over to shove the parchment into her hands. "She's found something bigger and better than us, and she's gone."

Lira took the parchment, gaze running over it. A short note was etched in Ahrin's familiar scrawl. It was blunt, concise, and simply said that she'd identified a better opportunity. She warned them not to look for her.

And that was it.

She hadn't said goodbye. Wished them luck. Nothing.

Timin's laugh barked out as the realisation of what had happened showed on Lira's face. "And here I was thinking you were her favourite. But in the end she abandoned you too, huh?"

Lira swallowed, tried to make sense of what was happening. "My magic broke out today. I can fix this. We'll go and find her, then we'll put things back together."

"Maybe you need to re-read her note." Timin's voice was harsh, ugly. "I stuck around because she was a harsh but fair crew leader and she made sure we were comfortable. But she's gone, Lira, and I don't want you, or anyone else."

"What about Yanzi?"

"He'll figure it out when he gets back. The rest are all gone, off to find other crews with warm beds."

Timin's boots thudded on the stairs as he left too.

None of them came back, not once in the long night that followed as Lira sat there, back pressed against the wall. Waiting. Night fell, the temperature dropped, and darkness filled the loft.

It was her mother never coming home all over again.

Ahrin's note sat on the floor beside her, and Lira read it a hundred times over, certain there was some sort of code or underlying message. Something to reassure Lira that Ahrin hadn't really walked out on them, on *her*. But there wasn't.

Ahrin was gone. Their crew was gone.

Her life was gone.

CHAPTER 22

The shaft was barely big enough to fit them even scrambling along on their stomachs. Lira had no idea how Tarion was managing given how uncomfortable she was, yet he hadn't made a murmur of complaint. The mage-prince had more grit than she'd given him credit for.

It was pitch dark. There was no way to see what was ahead or behind. She knew where Tarion was only by the sounds of him breathing in front of her. Both of them were trying to move as quietly as possible but that wasn't easy in the cramped space.

With every slithering movement forward, memories of the night she and Ahrin's crew had robbed the gambling hall in Dirinan kept flashing through her mind. The narrow shaft, just like this one, the thrill of anticipation, the sight of Ahrin striding through the hall below her. She couldn't stop them.

Lira had spent the past two years living with that old life buried away, never to be taken out again. She'd thought she'd been successful, that it was gone for good—she'd fought hard to do it, forcing herself to look only at the future and what she needed to do.

She thought she'd been changing, making herself into what the council wanted. What she needed to be to claim her place in the world. The model mage apprentice. But it hadn't been changing. It had been *pretending*.

The bitter truth was that since finding the monster in the library at Temari she'd felt more alive, and engaged, and *awake* than she had since leaving Dirinan. The old Lira was still very much there and battering at the walls that the new Lira had unconsciously built up to keep her locked away. She'd let her out back in that room with Lucinda and it was slowly dawning on her that it might not be possible to put her back away.

Worse, that terrifying emptiness was closer to the surface than it had ever been—she hadn't broken down like earlier since before meeting Ahrin.

She felt so... chaotic inside. Like she couldn't keep proper hold of her emotions, swinging wildly from one to the other as she tried to grasp the one she *should* be feeling rather than what was truly hers.

"You all right?" Tarion murmured from ahead, as if sensing the quality of her silence had changed. Or maybe he'd noticed the quickening of her breathing as panic threatened to descend once again.

She nodded, realised he couldn't see that, then cleared her throat. "Fine. Keep moving."

She'd been kidnapped, chased by monsters, tied to a chair, and questioned by a Shadowcouncil member. That was why she was so unsettled. She repeated that to herself a few times, ignored the dark whispers at the back of her mind that told her she was glad to have been kidnapped and chased by monsters, then finally shoved the entire topic out of her thoughts and focused on the details of her surroundings instead.

After a short distance the shaft turned into a steady upward incline. It grew so steep at one point that moving forward became more like climbing than crawling. She slipped once, her boot sliding on loose dirt, and almost went tumbling down.

Soon the throbbing in her head intensified, responding to the burning ache of muscles in her hunched shoulders and back and bruised knees. Her heartrate began to increase, sweat breaking out on her skin. The tops of her shoulders grew so tense they began to ache in rhythm with her face.

She and Tarion stopped moving when light appeared ahead of them. It was dim, watery, but in the utter darkness of the shaft it was almost too bright. Tarion continued on, more cautiously this time, his bulk blocking Lira from being able to see ahead.

When he stopped suddenly and she ran into the back of him, her heart thudded in shock and she almost swore aloud. A faint scuffing sounded, then he scrambled forward and disappeared entirely. Lira blinked, eyes watering at the sudden light ahead. She crawled after him, finding herself above a stone floor in a room larger than any she'd seen yet, long and rectangular, with large windows set into the wall down one side of it.

Below, Tarion put a finger to his lips and remained still. Lira nodded and studied the rest of the room. A table sat by one of the windows, chairs surrounding it, a handful of mugs scattered across its surface. The rest of the room was empty, despite its size.

She listened carefully but heard no sounds indicating anyone was nearby. She silently swung herself down, gaze taking in a half-open door three paces to the right of the vent—the source of the light. Otherwise there were two other visible exits.

As soon as she was down, Tarion lifted the grating up and placed it carefully back into the shaft opening. Then he turned to her, voice a barely audible murmur. "Now what?"

Weariness tugged at her focus, making it harder to think. But she'd been weary before, and she knew how to keep it at bay.

"I'm exhausted," Tarion said softly, before she could answer. He leaned against the wall by the vent, shoulders bowed, hair hanging over his face. Dark stubble had started growing on his jaw.

A shaft of energy bolted through her and she straightened. "Did they shave you, or have we really only been gone from Temari a day or so?"

His right hand went instantly to his jaw. "They shaved me. They must have. You can't tell me they transported us just a few hours from Karonan and neither my aunt nor my mother have managed to find us yet."

She frowned in thought. "When I escaped the cart, I smelled like I hadn't bathed in a few days at least. Still do. Why would they bother *shaving* you though?"

"They want us to question how long we were unconscious." He met her gaze.

Excitement crept through her. "They're playing mind games. For some reason they want us sneaking around, hunted by their monsters, scared and wondering what's going on. There *has* to be a purpose to it." A shiver went down Lira's neck at the memory of the look in Lucinda's eyes. Could she just be having a bit of sadistic fun with them? No, Lucinda didn't strike Lira as the type of person who did anything without a reason. Everything about her had screamed control and purpose. Whatever was happening here had been planned meticulously.

She straightened, the weariness draining away as purpose gripped her. "We should find Garan and the others. We have to assume the razak we heard dying back there was them. Maybe they've learned how to kill them. Even if not, I think we need to re-visit our game plan."

"Why?" His eyes narrowed. "Do you know more about what's going on? What did that woman say to you before I showed up?"

"Nothing useful, but if you're happy to stick around and be toyed with, then go for it. I want out." Lira crossed to the half-open door and peered through the gap. Her heart leapt at their first bit of luck. It was the kitchen. "We made an attempt to find information to take back to the council, but don't tell me your parents would prefer you stay here and risk your life further rather than escaping while you can."

His mouth tightened but he didn't argue. "There's something else you're not saying, about why you're so desperate to leave."

"Instinct," she said tersely. "There's something going on here that we don't understand. And that means we're vulnerable. I don't like feeling like a rat in a trap, Tarion."

Not interested in talking further, Lira pointed through the kitchen door and gave him a questioning look. Nobody appeared to be inside, but the cooking hearth was lit and a pan sat over the low flames, steam rising from its surface. Tarion pressed beside her, eyes widening at the sight. He gestured to a door on the opposite side of the room, and she nodded. It was probably the entrance to the storeroom they'd been in earlier. A direct route to where they were supposed to meet Garan and the others.

Lira slid through the gap in the door, Tarion after her, her gaze scanning the room to make sure—

A man stood at a cookfire that hadn't been visible before, his back to them, idly stirring a pot of something that smelled delicious. She didn't recognise him as either of the two men that had been with Lucinda before—Jora or Dasta.

She froze, Tarion going just as still at her side, and glanced back out the door. She tried to calculate which were the better odds: returning the way they'd come or forging onwards. In the kitchen there was only one man, and his attention was focused away from them, but finding another way to the meeting point meant traversing halls potentially full of razak.

She glanced up at Tarion, tilted her head towards the storeroom door.

He nodded.

Lira began inching along the wall behind him, step by step, quiet as she could. Tarion followed without protest. Her body was poised, ready to attack and silence the man the second he caught sight of them.

They both froze again when he turned to his left. He reached for a small jar, unscrewed the lid, then scattered some contents into whatever he was making. Once his attention was back on the pot, they kept moving.

Eventually they hit the storeroom door. Lira's hand closed over the handle and she moved it painfully slowly, pressing her weight against the door incrementally so that it made no noise as it opened.

Tarion slipped in behind her and she closed it just as quietly.

Backing away from the door, hope unfolding as no alarm sounded and nobody followed them through, Lira came to a halt. They waited another few heartbeats, staring at each other, but nothing happened.

Shoulders relaxing, she turned and headed for the narrow steps leading up to the kitchen manager's office. It was empty, the door out into the corridor closed.

"How long do you think it's been since we separated from the others?" Tarion asked in a low voice. Worry made his features grim.

"You said I wasn't unconscious long, but even so I think we're well past two hours."

"Let me guess, you're not the type to wait here and do nothing?" He sighed. "So we're going to go and look for them instead."

Lira didn't reply immediately. Now that she was clear of the cells and momentarily safe, she wasn't sure what was the best course of action. She believed Lucinda was who she said she was, but she didn't trust the woman an inch. And while she hadn't been willing to sit locked in a dungeon, she had to be careful about outright challenging Lucinda and her people.

If Lira threatened them, they'd kill her without a thought, but that wasn't her only concern. She needed them. Needed to be a trusted member of Underground's ranks.

At least her immediate need to get back to Karonan had vanished. That meant she had time... time to learn more about what was actually going on here, and hedge her bets. Keep the apprentices alive and earn the gratitude of the council, while simultaneously worming her way deeper into Underground. *And* planning how best to destroy Lucinda and her minions.

"Lira?" Tarion pushed.

Lira nodded, regretted it as soon as fresh throbbing set off in her face. "Yes, I think we should go and look for them, for one key reason. If they've been caught and compromised, it's too dangerous to stay here in case they tell our captors about the meeting spot."

Ire flashed in his eyes. "In addition to the most important reason, of course, which is helping them if they're in trouble."

She rolled her eyes. Chatty *and* argumentative in the absence of others. Or maybe she just brought out the worst in him. "Really? Because you and Garan don't seem all that close to me."

"He's family." Tarion's jaw clenched, shoulders turning rigid. He didn't like this, didn't like asserting his will or having a confrontation with her, but the fact he cared enough to do it anyway left Lira at a loss. She didn't understand that type of caring. It had never led to anything but pain or betrayal for her.

She let out a breath, in annoyance as much as capitulation. "Fine. Let's go."

"In what direction?" he asked. "The less aimless wandering we do around dark halls potentially infested with razak, the better, no?"

"I don't think we have much of a choice. We'll go level by level, and maybe learn something along the way." Preferably something she could use to her advantage next time she ran into Lucinda. She didn't like how thoroughly in control the woman had been during their last encounter, and didn't want to face her again until she was on more solid ground. She needed Underground, but always in the back of her mind was how dangerous they were, that she might need to cut and run one day. Survival would always be her first priority.

His shoulders straightened at that. "We still haven't got anything useful to take back to the council except that Underground are the ones behind our kidnapping."

Lira opened the door, made sure no razak were lurking, and headed out. "In that case, off we go to play cat and mouse with Lucinda and her razak."

A smile curled at her mouth at the thought.

By now Lira had a fairly good mental map of the layout of the main building, and it didn't take long to circle around to the sweeping stairs leading down to the entrance hall, finding no trace of the others on the way.

Motioning for Tarion to wait, Lira crept down the steps far enough to get a view into the hall. It was dark, but the faint light was enough to see that Haler's body had been moved, leaving behind dark smears of his blood on the floor.

Even though it looked empty, she doubted the main entrance—those doors so solid and new in contrast to everything else here—was unguarded. No, they'd be watching it somehow.

She rejoined Tarion and they headed up the stairs to the second floor, which opened into an empty square space. While Lira stared down a torchlit corridor to their immediate right, Tarion padded over to a set of double doors with light spilling out from underneath it.

Stifling the urge to move out of the light, Lira ran her gaze over the several lit torches hanging on the walls, indicating it was a well-used area. Unlike much of the building she'd travelled through so far, it was also in much better repair. The walls were solid and dry, the floor covered in soft rugs, no trace of dust or cobwebs anywhere.

Underground were working in this section.

"Lira!" Tarion hissed, almost making her jump.

She was already a few steps down the corridor but went back at the odd note in his voice. He was peering through a square of glass set into the wood. Cursing inwardly, she ran over, reaching up on tiptoe to look through. "What are you..."

A long, rectangular room lay beyond. It was filled with beds just like those in the rooms they'd searched earlier. Only these had fresh sheets and blankets on them, the floor was clean, and each bed had a small table sitting beside it.

"Those are basic healing ointments and supplies." Tarion pointed to the items sitting on each table.

"So it's a healing ward of some sort?" she asked.

Tarion shook his head, leaning away from the glass to point at the steel lock on the door. Lira glanced from the lock to the brackets on either side of the door. For bars.

Another shiver crawled down the back of her neck. Lucinda claimed to be a member of the Shadowcouncil. Maybe that fit with kidnapping mage students. But nothing else that was happening did. Including the razak. Or this strange place, half in disrepair, half clearly lived and worked in.

Underground were up to far more than she'd ever realised. She wondered if even Greyson knew about this place or what was happening here.

Tarion shifted restlessly from foot to foot, hazel eyes fixing on hers. "We need to get out of here and warn my parents, Uncle Tarrick, all of them. Something bad is happening—"

"I thought getting out of here already was our primary plan," she said lightly, trying to dispel the bone-deep fear rising in his eyes. "And you're a middling excuse for a mage, remember, not a telepath. I'm sure that once we figure all this out, it won't be as bad as it seems."

"Are you trying to make me mad so I won't be scared?" he murmured as they moved away from the door and headed down the lit hallway.

"I'm trying to make sure you stay useful to me," she countered. "Panic is not useful."

"I'll take that under advisement. Next time panic sweeps through me I'll tell it to make itself useful."

She rolled her eyes at him, but couldn't entirely hide the little smile that wanted to break free.

The lit torches ended where the corridor turned right to follow the northern side of the building. Lira and Tarion sped up once they were around the corner, glad to be away from the light. Eventually they ended up before a pair of arched double doors. They were broken, collapsed in on each other, and the stone on either side was charred.

Puzzlement stirred again. What they'd seen wasn't just evidence of simple disrepair. A battle had happened here; a long time ago judging from the overgrown gardens outside and the empty air about the place. But people hadn't left in an orderly fashion. They'd fled. The abandoned military base theory seemed less likely—unless the soldiers had fled during an attack and never come back.

Tarion's glance communicated unease, but he said nothing as he stepped over the broken doors. She followed, and they stood there in complete stillness for several moments. There were no sounds. No rattling. No voices. No footsteps echoing. Nothing.

"This looks like it was a library," Tarion murmured.

Her gaze narrowed, taking in the cracked and broken shelving scattered across the floor, more charring on the wood. Any whole books must have been taken away years earlier, but hundreds of damaged ones remained, mostly beyond repair if the charring and size of the remaining pieces was anything to go by. "Army barracks don't have libraries this big."

"No," he said. "They don't."

"Either way, they're not here." She turned to leave, but Tarion was already moving further inside. He walked swiftly, staff ready, seeming to know exactly where he was going. Lira frowned but followed. The musty scent in the air grew thicker and the space between bookcases even narrower. Some towards the back were still standing, though the books had long been emptied from their shelves.

Tarion's steps slowed as they reached the end of a long shelf running along the northern edge of the library. A narrow corridor branched off at the end, a series of closed doors set into either side.

"Private study rooms." Lira jumped when Tarion leaned down to murmur in her ear.

"What?" she hissed.

"Libraries usually have them," he explained. "The ones at the Alistriem palace library look out over the... anyway, at Temari Hall, Garan likes to bring girls to them. Hardly anyone uses them, so they're a good place to find some privacy."

Her eyebrows shot upwards. "And you think he's hiding out in one here?"

Tarion shrugged. "If they ran into a razak, he might have come here looking for a place to hide. It's worth checking before we move on."

Lira shrugged. "He's your cousin."

She idly wondered whether Tarion had ever brought any girls or boys to the study rooms at Temari Hall. Somehow she doubted it. She'd certainly never been invited to one by an apprentice with amorous intentions. An amused smile twisted her face at the thought. None of them dared come near her, let alone invite her for a tryst.

Which was exactly what she wanted.

They both froze when they spotted a faint orange light flickering under the door at the far end. Glancing at each other, they crept forward, magic ready. While Tarion reached out to open the door handle, Lira lifted her fists and shifted from foot to foot, ready to strike. She wished she had her staff, but that was in the possession of Lucinda and her delightful crew.

Tarion turned the handle and pulled it open in one quick movement. A single candle flickered on a table in the middle of the tiny room, and then a lot of hissing protests hit her ears.

"Get in here and shut the door!" Garan's voice was the loudest.

Lira found herself being yanked into the room by Tarion, who let her arm go the moment she was inside before he closed the door as quickly as he'd opened it.

For a long moment they all stared at each other in the dimness. Lira felt some of that tightness return to her chest, along with a stir of irritation. She'd felt much better operating alone, or with the quiet Tarion. Now she had to deal with people again.

"You got free!" Fari's face brightened. "Did Tarion rescue you?"

"Tarion got himself caught along with me. We escaped together." Lira brushed over the details. "Where did you get a candle?"

"Took one from the kitchen storeroom earlier," Garan said.

"You okay?" Lorin asked, stepping forward, his dark Shiven eyes running over her face.

She scowled. "Broken nose and a bruised cheekbone. I'll live."

"It doesn't look good." Concern filled Garan's face, and he glanced over at his cousin. "You okay, Tar?"

He gave a single nod.

"I can take a look at your nose if you like, Spider?" Fari offered. "I won't promise to be able to set it successfully, but I can definitely bring down some of that swelling and maybe reduce the pain a little."

Discomfort crawled through Lira. "Thanks, but I'm fine. What are you all doing in here?"

Garan straightened. "Fari found us outside, it must have been a library once, and warned us about the monsters sensing magic—"

"They're called razak, apparently," Tarion said quietly.

"Oh, okay, well the warning was a bit too late because I'd been using magic to move stuff around, hoping one of the readable bits of the books out there would give us some clue about killing those things. One—"

"You actually thought you'd find something about monsters nobody has ever heard of in one of the thousands of charred bits of parchment out there?" Lira stared at him incredulously.

"It seemed worth a shot... at the time." He shifted uncomfortably, and Athira shot him a glance. "None of us knew what else to do. Plus, I thought there might at least be something that might tell us where we are."

"Horses? Supplies?" she asked. "Did you at least—"

"Will you please let Garan finish?" Athira cut over her. "Then you can go back to treating us all like useless fools to make yourself feel better."

Her mouth thinned, and Garan spoke quickly. "Anyway, one of those creatures came creeping in just after Fari. We managed to get one of its eyes, but its shrieking drew others, and the injury made it angrier, so we had to run. We lost it in the stacks, but by then the entrance was blocked off by more razak, so we came here to hide until they left."

"They've gone," Lira said impatiently. "So we should get moving before they come back."

"Yes, but we figured out something even better, Spider." Garan flashed her a grin. "We learned how to kill them all."

CHAPTER 23

"What he means is that we've come up with a theory that *might* be a way to kill them all," Athira clarified, eyes shooting skyward.

"Yes, yes, Miss Naysayer, but that's still better than what we had," Fari said, then turned to Lira. "It was Lorin that figured it out."

The initiate's shoulders straightened with pride. "I merely recalled one of Master Rayer's lessons," Lorin said.

Lira gave him a sharp glance. Rayer taught agriculture to the mage apprentices with abilities that would one day have them involved in large-scale farming or similar roles. Lorin was never going to be anything but a warrior mage. "You took Rayer's class?"

His jaw tightened slightly. "I found it... comforting in its familiarity."

"Lorin's family works a farm." Athira waved an impatient hand.

Abruptly Lira understood, and wished she hadn't said anything. Lorin hadn't come from a well-off family and probably hadn't had a much better education than she had. Rayer's class was likely the one place he felt he was doing well. She met his dark eyes, haughty and challenging her to think him weak. She knew that behaviour all too well and had to stifle the jolt of empathy she felt for the young man.

"What was so important about Rayer's lesson?" she asked, switching her gaze back to the others and aiming to move their attention away from his discomfort.

"Think about the behaviour we've seen those monsters display." Garan spoke. "Twice when we've killed or injured one, the others have known instantly and come running."

"Which indicates they're connected somehow," Fari added.

"Like hive animals," Lorin said with a flourish.

A moment's silence fell.

"Before you turn that disbelieving glare on the rest of us, Lira, think about it a second," Garan chimed in before she could open her mouth.

Lira glanced at Tarion, who hadn't yet said a word. "So your theory is that the creatures are like bees. Part of a colony controlled by a queen razak, like bees are controlled by a queen?"

"Actually, queens don't control a hive. It's the other way around, sort of, but yes, they're all connected," Lorin said.

Garan nodded. "Precisely. Therefore, we kill the queen and all the members of her hive will die."

"Theoretically." Athira cleared her throat.

"Well, actually, no, bees don't necessarily die, not unless they can't find another queen," Lorin said. "The bees of a hive will swarm after a queen's death, their primary focus to find a new queen to make sure the colony survives."

"Fine." Garan rubbed at his face. "We kill the queen and all the razak are distracted by finding a new queen—probably not an easy job in the middle of nowhere—giving us time to escape."

"If the queen razak is here, of course," Fari added. "And assuming razak operate the same way bees do."

At this point, Lira's head began to ache. Was this really all they had? The fools should have been finding a way to get out, not theorising about bees and hives.

Lorin nodded agreement. "We know very little about these particular creatures. The fact they are impervious to magic, and can sense it, sets them apart from any other documented animal."

"Even if your guess is accurate about them being hive animals, I think it's more complicated than killing a queen." Tarion finally spoke, that little frown back on his face. "Lira and I are pretty sure one of our captors, a man working for Lucinda, is controlling them."

"Doesn't matter," Garan cut in as everyone seemed about to pile in with their own thoughts. "We kill the mage controlling them, *and* the queen monster if it exists. Same outcome, no?"

Fari put her hand up. "Who's Lucinda?"

Lira shook her head in dismissal. "Not important. I—"

"Going to stop you right there, Spider," Athira said coolly. "At this point, we have literally no idea why we're all here or why any of this is happening. Answer Ari's question."

"Who in rotted hells is Ari?" she asked, mystified.

"Delightful language," Athira muttered, rolling her eyes. Lira made a rude gesture in her direction.

"It's what my friends call me," Fari piped up. "Not you, of course."

Lira's scowl deepened. "I don't—"

"Athira is right, Spider," Garan said, again accurately judging that the attention of the room was splintering and jumping in to bring their focus back. "Please tell us what you know—maybe together we can work out what's going on."

She took a breath to stall for time so that she could bury the frustration rising to the surface and figure out exactly what to say—in particular parsing her conversation with Lucinda to remove any mention of Lira being a member of Underground. Jaw clenching at their attentive gazes, she told them what she could, impatience making her brusque.

The longer she talked, the more impatient she became—she didn't want to be standing around *talking*. She wanted to be away from this room and getting herself out of this damn place, preferably after burning it down with Lucinda and her monsters inside it. Not to mention they were going to eventually be found in the library if they lingered too long.

"So Underground *is* behind this." Garan looked stunned.

"I'm not surprised. Underground wants to unseat the Mage Council and return to the rule of a single Magor-lier over everyone," Lorin said.

"They believe the power of the Magor-lier trumps that of any single king. But—"

Athira rolled her eyes hard. "We may not all be Shiven but we do know what your subversive rebel group wants. It's *us* they want to unseat, after all."

Lorin stiffened, pale skin flushing red.

"Leave him alone. It's worth talking through," Fari defended the initiate. "Maybe it will help us understand why we're here. Underground believe the Magor-lier should rule over kings, and should be the most powerful mage alive. They certainly don't think Tarrick Tylender should be Magor-lier, or that he should share power with the council."

No. If Lira had things her way, *she* would be Magor-lier. She was the Shadowcouncil's biggest drawcard. The reason they'd come looking for her. With her they had not only a powerful mage to put in the position of Magor-lier, but Shakar's direct heir. A persuasive recruitment tool for an organisation that needed an army if they ever wanted to see their ambitions realised.

"Not the time to air your family grievances with the Tylenders, Ari." Athira crossed her arms over her chest. "But to humour you, what makes you think Underground is actually capable of pulling off something like this? Getting scowled at by surly Shiven every time I go out in the city isn't my idea of a fun time, but as far as I'm aware Underground is a rabble."

"Try getting scowled at by *everyone* you ever meet because of a long dead ancestor," Lira snapped, unable to help herself. Athira's rotted *entitlement* was irritating her beyond measure, and her usual controls over her emotions were faded by exhaustion and the fear of the past few days. "Try almost getting drowned at seven years old because of it. I'm sorry a few dark looks spoil your fun, Athira, but maybe you should count yourself fortunate that you've got the opportunity in your life to *have* fun. I hate to break it to you, but not everyone does."

"Oh please." Athira snorted. "You're no victim, Lira Astor. You play on your grandfather's name because it makes you feel powerful, like you're better than the rest of us."

She was momentarily speechless. *"I'm* not the one who thinks she's better than everyone, Miss pureblood mage royalty."

"You know what?" Athira stepped forward, fury snapping in her eyes. "I never stole things from people, I never hurt people. I'm not a criminal who preys on others to survive. Don't blame me because I had an easier life than you did. You still had choices."

Lira took a step towards her, literally vibrating with her fury. "And what choices do you think I had? The choice between stealing or starving? Between stealing or freezing to death? Between hurting people and *living?* Which would you have chosen?"

"You could have found honest work to survive." She scoffed.

"Could I?" Lira's voice had gone up an octave. She couldn't believe this girl's ignorance. "And what do you know of being homeless and penniless and a child in Dirinan? What work exactly was anyone going to give a scrawny seven-year-old girl?"

"You—"

"Enough!" Garan wasn't foolish enough to yell the words, but the iron in his voice was enough to cut through Lira's anger and jolt her back to sense. No matter how infuriating Athira was, now wasn't the time for fighting amongst themselves, nor was the girl worth her anger. The depth of her ignorance though, it shook Lira to the core, her fury at it still vibrating through her.

"Did you really almost get drowned?" Tarion asked quietly, horror on his face.

"Yes, but that's not relevant to our current situation." Lira pushed her anger away and kept her voice cool.

Lorin persevered into the silence that followed. "Leader Astohar and Lord Caverlock have been working to uproot Underground with the help of Magor-lier Tylender and the council."

"What are you trying to say, Lorin?" Garan asked as Athira opened her mouth to make what would no doubt be another cutting comment. Lira found herself siding with Garan. She didn't enjoy taking orders from him, but he admittedly had a natural instinct for managing a room. It was a rare quality—in her experience it was what separated the successful gang leaders from those that followed them. These sons of Alyx and Ladan Egalion were not what she'd imagined them to be.

"I was *trying* to agree with Athira. They don't have the strength or the resources for this," he finished, snappy with irritation.

Lira looked at Lorin, her gaze speculative. She'd been a member of Underground for several months and fully concurred with the initiate's assessment. She wondered what his knowledge was based on. Was the group spread more widely across the country than she'd thought?

"We don't actually know what 'this' is." Fari spoke up. "Six mage students and a Taliath were kidnapped by Underground. Rather than tie us all up in a dungeon together, they placed us separately throughout a mostly falling apart estate and left us to wander amongst their pet razak. When they did capture two of us..." A glance at Lira and Tarion. "They didn't try to kill you. But apparently it's fine if the razak kill us."

Lira wasn't so sure about that, but she stayed quiet, tired of talking. Her mind was toying at the beginnings of a plan.

"You counted at least one mage with Lucinda?" Garan glanced between Lira and Tarion. "And three men overall?"

Lira stayed silent, forcing Tarion to respond. He gave her a look, then mumbled, gaze on the floor, "Yes. Lucinda is definitely a mage, and I'm sure one of her men in the room with us was controlling the razak. I didn't see the other one use magic. We saw a third man in the kitchen on our way here. None were visibly armed."

"Did either of you get the impression there are more people here than the ones you've seen?" Fari asked.

Lira shrugged—it was impossible to tell given how big the place was. Tarion said nothing.

"I really don't think any of this is that important." Athira's voice vibrated with the same frustration Lira felt. "No matter what their purpose is, it won't help us get out. And the fact a Shadowcouncil member revealed herself to Lira probably means they're not intending to let us leave alive."

"Then we defy them. We've already talked about this. Master Egalion is going to want to know everything we can tell her about our captors," Lorin said gravely. "So she and her husband can tear them limb from limb and feed them to a pack of hungry wolves."

Garan grinned. Fari chuckled. Lira almost smiled too—in such dire circumstances a moment of levity was welcome. Lorin hadn't meant to joke, but his words were true.

"I like your positivity." Fari reached out to squeeze Lorin's shoulder. "Great attitude for a mage initiate. You're going to do well."

Lorin frowned, as if he weren't sure whether Fari was making fun of him or not.

"At this point, I think we need to prioritise escape over everything else," Garan said steadily. "We can at least name our captors now, and I'm starting to agree with Lira that the longer we remain, the more danger we'll be in. If we learn more to take to the council on our way out, great, but if not, we forget it. I want us all back home safe and alive."

Nobody disagreed with that.

"It seems to me that if we can destroy the razak by killing their queen—and/or the mage controlling them—then all we have to deal with, at worst, is two to four mages," Tarion said quietly. "Lucinda will be the hardest to deal with, but if we took her out first, the others might be easier for us to take together."

"Three big assumptions there." Lira couldn't help herself. "That the queen creature is somewhere here where we can get to it, that there are only four captors here, and that the mages other than Lucinda don't also have a powerful mage ability."

"Agreed." Tarion turned to her. "But—"

"There's no better plan on the table, so I say we go for it," Athira interrupted. Beside her, Garan and Fari nodded.

After a brief hesitation, Lorin did the same. Relief spread through Lira. This was her opportunity to get free of them, and she took it without hesitation. "I'll go and look for the queen while the rest of you stay hidden. Once I've located her, we'll come up with a plan to kill the thing."

They all stared at her.

She scowled. "Like any of you want to risk your lives creeping around out there to find the queen. Don't pretend like you're not happy I'm the one volunteering to do it."

"And you'd like us to do what in the meantime?" Garan asked. "Paint our nails?"

"Keep yourselves alive. Get some food so that when we flee we won't die of hunger before reaching help. Maybe try and figure out where the horses are kept, like you were supposed to before. Come up with a plan on how we can take out four potential warrior mages." She glanced around. "And get out of this library. It's a dead end with only a single way out. I'll meet you back at the office above the storeroom."

"I'll come with you—"

Lira waved Garan's words away. "I'm not trying to be a hero, but I spent my life sneaking through the dark streets of a city far more dangerous than the one you grew up in. I can do this more successfully on my own."

Fari let out a breath, then stepped around the table. "Will you at least let me look at your nose before you go?"

The throbbing had mostly faded by now, and Lira didn't trust the barely-trained second year not to make it worse. "It's fine. Save your strength—we might need it later."

"You take care, Spider. We'll be waiting on you," Garan said.

"Don't screw it up," Athira said far less pleasantly.

Lorin lifted a hand in farewell. She fought the urge to wave back—ugh, weariness and stress were beginning to make her sentimental.

Tarion tried to follow her out the door. "I'll come with you, I can be quiet."

"I'm going alone. It's non-negotiable." Lira shoved the door closed in his face, then set off down the hall before he could come after her.

The initial beginnings of a plan that had come to her while talking with the others turned over and over in her thoughts as she crept through the empty library, ensuring it was clear of razak before moving into the open. While killing the queen razak was a simple plan, it was also based on a lot of shaky foundations. They could be searching the grounds of this very large compound for a long time and never find the creature.

And they couldn't afford that kind of time.

The urgency was back, clawing at her. They'd been set free for a purpose, allowed to roam and hide, but whatever this was—some kind of test or experiment, maybe—it would end sooner rather than later.

Lira was far from convinced Lucinda wouldn't have her killed too.

She might be useful to Underground as a symbol, and she was banking on that, but if her value to them ever faded, they wouldn't think twice about killing her.

And even if Underground were planning on keeping her alive while killing the others when they'd served whatever purpose they'd been brought here for... Lucinda had been right about Lira needing to maintain her cover. If Lira was the only one to survive this mess, the council would be suspicious.

Either way, she needed to have a plan to get herself out if it all went to hell. And that meant keeping at least one of the apprentices alive—Tarion was the most useful—to help her in that eventuality, and knowing where to find the razak queen. There was only one way she could think of to learn about the existence of such a creature quickly and painlessly.

Once she was clear of the library, she headed back towards the first floor hallway with the outside exit she'd used earlier, fortunately not running into any razak on the way. Though the absence of them made her uneasy... where had they gone?

The grounds were wreathed with mist, and it was still dark. Lira didn't dwell on that, on wondering how much time had passed, instead focusing on getting to the dormitory style building unseen. The foyer remained dark and empty. When it was clear there were no monsters lurking, Lira abandoned stealth and headed straight up the main stairs.

On the second floor, she circled around to the common room she'd been held in earlier. Orange flamelight spilled out from underneath its door.

When she knocked on it, it was opened a few seconds later by Lucinda. She smiled without warmth and stepped back to wave Lira in. "We've been waiting for you."

Lira shrugged, calm and at ease, thoughts carefully locked down behind her mental shield, just in case. "Sorry it took me so long. I had to lose the others first."

CHAPTER 24
BEFORE

It took Lira a month to make the journey from Dirinan to Temari Hall in Karonan. With the coin she'd pick-pocketed in the days before leaving—Ahrin had cleaned out the crew's stash when she'd vanished—she'd had enough to pay a merchant to carry her in his cart nearly half the distance southeast. From there she'd had to walk the rest of the way, trudging along increasingly busy roads the closer she came to the capital.

Winter was approaching and the air was bitterly cold. She spent most of the walk shivering, her fingers, nose, and toes numb—forced to rest during the day so she didn't accidentally freeze to death while sleeping at night. Her food supplies ran low, then were gone completely, and she had to resort to stealing from the occasional farm or village store.

It didn't matter.

All she had to do was keep putting one foot in front of the other. Get to Karonan, to Temari Hall, and everything would be fine. Ahrin's betrayal wouldn't matter then. The loss of her crew wouldn't matter. She'd deluded herself into thinking those things were home, that Dirinan was home, but she'd been a stupid fool.

She would never be a stupid fool again.

She had magic. Alyx Egalion had told her she would be welcome. She would make a new life at Temari Hall with the mages. That's where she would find her place in the world. Not on the streets of Dirinan. The harsh, unforgiving life she'd known was soon to be over.

It became a mantra in her head as she took one step after the other. A mantra that allowed her to bury her memories of the last few years deep down where she'd never have to think of them ever again. That allowed her to keep forcing her exhausted and freezing body onwards.

And eventually she made it.

On a grey day she approached Karonan from the north along the main road. When the tower of Temari Hall appeared on the horizon she almost wept with relief. The bone-deep exhaustion seemed to slough away and her steps moved faster.

The gates of the mage academy stood open, and Lira approached slowly, wide eyes taking in the high walls, the tower beyond, the sight of Karonan across the causeway. She'd never seen anything so big and sprawling in her life. Dirinan had been a big city, but this... it was overwhelming.

The first worm of doubt coiled through her then; that she could ever belong somewhere like this. She was a criminal, the dirt of Dirinan still under her nails, the scent of fish and days of not having had a wash hovering thick around her.

She brushed the doubts away. She was the granddaughter of Shakar. She belonged here. Alyx Egalion had said she would be welcome.

A young woman wearing a grey robe with a sword hanging at her hip stepped forward when Lira approached the gates. She had green eyes, dark brown hair, and a friendly smile. "Can we help you?"

"My name is Lira," she said, making sure she spoke clearly and didn't shorten her words in street slang like she was accustomed to. "Councillor Egalion told me to come here when my magic broke out and I'd be welcome."

The girl's smile widened, eyes twinkling at the sound of Egalion's name, as if she were amused by some secret joke. "In that case, you're very welcome, Lira. I'm Caria. Will you wait here while I go and fetch one of the masters?"

Lira nodded and the girl disappeared inside the gates, her stride long and graceful. A Taliath trainee, probably, given the sword at her hip. The boy who'd been on guard with her had a staff hanging down his back. He'd been watching her carefully since she first came into sight. Soon though, his gaze grew bored and drifted away.

For fun, Lira calculated how much she could slip from his pockets before he realised. The moment she took a step towards him, though, his gaze was back on her, wary.

She offered a smile. His suspicion faded. Her smile widened—such an easy mark. She bet no student at this fancy place had ever been pick-pocketed. They wouldn't even know what hit them. With a little shake, she put those thoughts aside. They didn't belong here and they weren't her anymore.

Two mages in royal blue cloaks, a leaping flame etched in scarlet on their chests, came out a short time later. The Taliath trainee wasn't with them, and at a word from one of them, the boy mage walked away too.

"You're Lira?" The tallest of the two—a man with pale Shiven skin and greying brown hair—spoke. "Shakar's granddaughter?"

They'd figured it out from her name, which meant they *had* been expecting her. The relief bubbled back up. "Yes, I am."

"Will you demonstrate your magic for us please?"

Happy to oblige, Lira dropped her bag to the ground, then called upon her still-raw magic to lift it into the air. Violet light sparked and shimmered around her hands. The second mage gasped. The first's expression closed over.

And Lira saw it.

The fear in both their eyes.

And not just fear, but worry. About her. About having her amongst them. In that moment all her remaining hopes crashed to the ground and the yawning chasm in her chest opened wide enough to swallow her whole. A gasping breath escaped her.

This wasn't going to be any different to the village, or the orphanage. She'd been an idiot to ever think it would. It was just going to be the same thing all over again. Mages were as afraid of her as everyone else was. There wasn't going to be any welcome or acceptance for her here. She was never going to have those things.

The bitter injustice of it had tears springing to her eyes—how was what Shakar had done her fault?

"Thank you, Lira." The Shiven mage spoke carefully. "I am Master Cogen. This is Master Ettern. We'll show you inside where you can fill out your admission paperwork. Councillor Egalion would like to speak with you as well. Could we start with your full name?"

Lira looked between them. Forced down the despair and the tears that wanted to cascade down her cheeks. Straightened her shoulders. She might not have acceptance, but she'd figure out a way to win their respect. One day they would look at her and see Lira, not Shakar.

And if they wanted to be scared of her, treat her like she was just like her grandfather, then fine. She would use it to her advantage.

"Astor. Lira Astor." She chose the name her grandfather had used to infiltrate the Rionnan court as part of his war to bring the Mage Council down. It was a name that would always remind those around her of who she was.

They both flinched. Satisfaction filled her, making her suddenly, fiercely glad to have caused that reaction. She hefted her bag and levelled a haughty look at them. "Are we going inside?"

THE GROUNDS inside Temari Hall were sprawling; gardens, training courts, stables, and other outbuildings all surrounding the centre tower. Lira caught only a glimpse of them all as she was escorted down the circular drive and into the tower.

The two mages flanked her up seven flights of stairs to the top, not saying a word the entire way. Lira kept her shoulders straight, her chin up, forcing her legs to keep climbing even though they burned with exhaustion and her stomach ached with hunger. At least it was warm inside. For the first time in over a week her body had stopped shivering.

Brown and grey-robed students passed them occasionally, heading up or down, each with a curious look in Lira's direction. When they saw the expressions of the mages with her, those curious looks turned to puzzlement, but none of them stopped to ask questions.

Cogen rapped on the closed double doors at the top of the stairs, and immediately a voice called out asking him to enter. He opened one of the doors and waited, clearly expecting Lira to walk through.

She did, deliberately not looking at him as she passed him and stepped inside the room beyond. He closed the door behind her, leaving her alone with Alyx Egalion, head of Temari Hall.

Lira remembered her, vaguely, from the time they'd met at the orphanage. She certainly hadn't forgotten the tangible aura of assured power that cloaked the woman like a glove. Egalion sat behind her desk, green eyes calm and curious as they regarded Lira.

"Long trip?" she asked, raising an eyebrow. She spoke in Shiven, just like those on the gates had, though from her accent it was clear it wasn't her first language.

"Long walk." Lira dropped her bag and went to sit in one of the chairs in front of the desk without waiting for an invitation. Egalion's mage staff rested against the wall behind her, and Lira's gaze lingered on it, intrigued, something about it drawing her attention.

"I'm glad you're here, Lira." Alyx's voice jerked Lira's attention back to her.

"They didn't seem to be." Lira jerked a thumb at the door. "You said I'd be welcome here."

"And you are."

"So when you tell everyone here who I am, they're not going to look at me like I'm about to eat their children or blow up the school with my scary magic?" Lira challenged.

Alyx hesitated, clearly trying to craft a diplomatic answer, but was saved from replying by a quick knock at the door. Whoever it was didn't wait for approval to enter. The door opened and clicked shut. A small, wiry man crossed to the desk. He had too-long curls of dark hair and inquisitive green eyes several shades darker than Alyx's.

"You must be Lira?" He offered a hand. "I'm Master Finn A'ndreas, one of the teachers here."

She stared at his outstretched hand for a long, considering

moment, then dismissed it and turned back to Alyx. Instead of looking annoyed, he shrugged and perched on the edge of Alyx's desk. The glance they exchanged revealed a comfort and familiarity years in the making. One Lira couldn't interpret.

"What happened to you?" Alyx broke the silence, eyes narrowing. "After we met at your orphanage, I asked council mages travelling through Dirinan to keep an eye on you, make sure you were okay. But you vanished years ago. The matron told us she had no idea where you went."

Lira shrugged. "I left the orphanage after they tried to drown me. Figured I'd have a better chance of surviving on my own."

"At seven years old?" Alyx asked incredulously at the same time Finn spoke, his jaw tightening.

"Who tried to drown you? The matron?"

Lira glanced between them, decided to answer Finn. "The other girls there."

"We asked around about you, tried to find you, to make sure you were okay," Alyx said. "Where did you go?"

"I lived on the streets."

Another unreadable glance between the two. It was starting to really irritate Lira. "Look, can I stay here or not? If you'd rather I leave, that's fine. I'll find somewhere else to go." There was no way she was going to beg these people to keep her.

"Lira, you're a mage. You are welcome and wanted here," Alyx said firmly, then paused. "If here is where you want to be."

Lira shrugged. Truth was, she had nowhere else to go. This was her only remaining option—she had no choice but to stay and try to force them to at least respect her, if not welcome her. At least it was warm here, and they would teach her how to use her magic properly.

"That was a genuine question." Alyx's voice didn't change, but something about her manner did. It became watchful, the air in the room carrying a razor-fine thread of tension. "How do you feel about the Mage Council, Lira?"

Lira didn't look away from her gaze. Didn't hesitate or shift in her chair. Didn't respond too quickly either. "I wouldn't have come if I didn't want to be here. I want to learn my magic."

"And if your grandfather were alive today?"

She'd never thought about that. What her life would have been like if she'd grown up with the Darkmage as her grandfather, teaching her magic, sharing his power with her. It was a tantalising thought, but she pushed it away before it could take hold. She knew the right answer here, and besides, hankering after something she'd never have wouldn't suit any good purpose. "I wouldn't be out there at his side killing mages and innocents if that's what you're asking me."

A silence fell while both mages studied her, seemingly trying to detect how sincere she was being. Lira hid away her despair, her exhaustion, her desire just to curl up in a ball and hide from the world, and showed them her best Dirinan poker face. Egalion was a mage of the higher order, meaning she had multiple mage abilities, and Lira was certain telepathy was one of them. She couldn't stop the woman rifling through her thoughts, but could at least try to keep them deliberately blank.

"Do you mind if we ask a few questions?" Finn spoke eventually. "You'll start as an initiate, with the other first year students, but I'd like to know more about you so that I can place you in the right classes."

Lira relaxed at the change of subject. They either hadn't noticed she hadn't answered their question about her thoughts on the Mage Council, or they'd let it go deliberately, satisfied with her answers. "Ask away."

"Can you read and write?" he asked, but in Tregayan, not Shiven. Lira had picked up enough of the Tregayan language—also the main language spoken in Rionn—on the streets to understand it, but couldn't speak it herself.

"I learned to read and write Shiven in the orphanage. I can understand Tregayan and snatches of Zandian but not speak, read, or write either." It galled her to admit weakness in anything and she hated them for making her say it out loud.

"And what other studies have you had?"

She fixed them both with an incredulous glare. Were they *serious*? "How to steal enough food to keep from starving. How to steal enough money to stay warm in winter. How to escape, or fight back, when people bigger and stronger than you want to hurt you. Mastering those things left very little time for studying Languages."

"You're a thief?" Alyx asked carefully.

"How exactly do you think I survived after running away from the orphanage? I was seven years old!" Lira snapped.

Silence settled over the room.

"Your magic?" Finn cleared his throat, shifted on the desk.

"Shakar was a mage of the higher order, so I probably am too." She was sullen now, exhausted and upset by their carefully concealed horror at her upbringing. "But telekinesis was the first ability to break out."

"No indications of anything else?" Alyx asked.

"Not yet."

"Mages of the higher order are extremely rare," Finn said gently. "There's a very good chance you're not one of them."

Lira said nothing. Her only remaining hope was that she could be like Shakar. How else to make them all forget him and see her instead? What else could fill this void inside her?

Alyx seemed to sense this, because her expression softened. "How old are you, Lira?"

"Fifteen, I think."

Another shared glance between the two masters. "I'm surprised it took you so long to break out, given how young you first displayed your mage light," Alyx said. "I honestly expected you here well before now. Do you have any idea why that might be?"

"No," she said.

Finn turned to Alyx, dropping his voice to a murmur. "Malnutrition and... might have..."

Alyx frowned at him. "Maybe, but that was the case when she was a child too, and the light still emerged."

Finn shrugged and slid off the desk, friendly gaze turning back to Lira. "As a start, how about I take you down for a hot bath, clean clothes, and a meal. Then I'll show you around, take you to your assigned room to rest. Tomorrow morning you and I will talk through the classes you'll need to attend. You'll have some catching up to do, unfortunately."

Lira stood, picked up her bag. "What happens if I can't catch up?"

"Something tells me you'll be just fine," Alyx said dryly. "I'll see you later. Welcome to Temari Hall."

"You were right earlier, you know," Master A'ndreas said abruptly as they were halfway down the tower stairs. "The war with Shakar scarred a lot of people, and they carry long memories. The reaction is almost instinctive. Here at Temari Hall, with mages, it will be even more pronounced."

"So they're all going to hate me too." She was quickly becoming resigned to it. "It's not like that will be any different to how my entire life has been."

"It doesn't help that there are those out there trying to rekindle his cause, keeping his memory fresh in all our minds," Finn mused, almost to himself.

"What?" Lira asked sharply. "Who?"

But A'ndreas continued smoothly, ignoring her question completely. "Maybe you could try putting yourself in people's shoes, understanding why they might react the way they do?" he suggested. "Then try to make them see that you're nothing like him."

"You don't know that," she said coolly.

He smiled, unbothered by her comment. "I suppose we'll see."

Yes, they would all see. Eventually.

The master kept talking as they walked, pointing out things along the way, not stopping even when she made no reply to any of it. She barely listened, cataloguing his words for later consideration.

This was her last chance. If she didn't make it work here, she'd have nowhere else to go. No home, no family, no crew in Dirinan. Her survival instinct kicked in. She was going to have to make herself into one of them. Put away the street slang, the thieving, and most importantly that addictive thrill. The hunger for danger and risk. None of those things had any place here.

She was going to have to show these educated, well-fed, sheltered mages what they wanted to see. A dutiful mage student. She would give them what they wanted, she would work hard, and eventually she'd be better than all of them.

'*Those out there trying to rekindle his cause*'. The words stuck with her in the days and weeks that came, nagging in the back of her mind.

Maybe there might be another option, if necessary.

Maybe she could force them to accept her.

CHAPTER 25

Lira swept into the room, shoulders straight, expression as imperious as she could make it. There were no ropes or men grabbing at her this time. Nobody else was in the room. Lucinda closed the door behind them and waved Lira to the chair by the fire.

Her eyes narrowed at the idea that Lucinda might literally have been sitting there waiting for her... that she'd been *that* confident Lira would come. Something akin to glee rippled through her as she dropped into one of the chairs with a faintly irritated sigh. "I didn't appreciate being locked in a dungeon and having my nose re-broken."

"None of that would have been necessary if your friend hadn't swept in here trying to rescue you. I'm sure we can agree that it is imperative nobody learn of your membership in Underground."

"Friend!" Lira snorted in disgust. "Go on, there's nobody watching now. I've demonstrated my loyalty by returning of my own volition. It's time to tell me what's going on."

Lucinda cocked her head, her features carefully arranged into an expression of cool interest. She was just as perfectly attired as the last time Lira had seen her, not a single hair or stitch of clothing out of place. "One might argue that fleeing your cell wasn't much of a show of loyalty."

Lira smiled. "I know we've only just met, but something tells me you wouldn't have sat idly in a cell, no matter who put you in there, either."

"You are quick," Lucinda murmured.

"Quick *and* good at paying attention. You just said how crucial maintaining my cover is. Me helping Tarion escape has made them trust me. I'm in the position you *said* you wanted." Lira was careful to emphasise that word. She wasn't putting any weight on anything Lucinda claimed.

Lucinda considered that a moment, her expression revealing nothing, before coming to sit in the chair opposite. "That looks painful." She gestured at Lira's face. "I'm sorry that it was necessary."

"No you're not."

Lucinda smoothed her skirts. "Is that so?"

"You don't care about me beyond my usefulness to you as a living symbol of Shakar's mission. That's fine. I joined Underground because I want the same things as you do, so feel free to stop faking care and concern and just be honest with me." A smile curled at her mouth, the moment poised rocking on a knife's edge, where Lira most liked to be. "We'll get along much better that way."

Lucinda regarded her, unblinking, before she leaned forward slightly, her gaze catching Lira's. "So if I were to ask you to kill those students, that their deaths would advance our goals?"

"I'd ask how necessary their deaths were," Lira answered without hesitation. "I'm not going to insult your intelligence by asking if you know who they are. You know the consequences if they were murdered. I wouldn't recommend risking those consequences without a very good reason. Unless Underground is *far* stronger than I've been led to believe." She added that on the end deliberately, hoping it would elicit some more information about the Shadowcouncil's resources.

"And if there *was* a very good reason?"

Again, she didn't allow herself to hesitate. "Then I'd do it."

Lucinda's gaze held hers for another long moment, a viper sizing up its prey. The longer it went on, the wider Lira's smile became. It wasn't the first time she'd been studied like this by someone who could kill her in a blink, and she'd yet to come out the loser in any of those exchanges. Ahrin Vensis included.

Lira had realised within moments of engaging with Lucinda that the woman wasn't ever going to be fooled by a pretend act of obedience and loyalty. Those things were too anathema to Lira for her to pull off well enough for someone of Lucinda's clear sharpness. So she'd have to toe the line of confidence and submission instead and hope she didn't push the woman too far.

"Let's be clear on something, Lira Astor," Lucinda said, voice so cold it scraped along Lira's nerves, pushing her ability to hold still and seem unbothered. "I could squash you like a bug, and I would have no hesitation in doing so."

Danger and fear shivered through her, perfectly entwined. "You've made that very clear," she murmured.

"I know you think you have the measure of me, that you've dealt with dangerous people before." Lucinda leaned closer, her hand lifting to capture Lira's chin in a vice-like grip once again. "But you're wrong. You challenge me, and I'll come out on top, time and time again."

Part of Lira warned her Lucinda was likely right, at least for now, until Lira understood her better. Still, Lucinda was wrong in thinking that fact scared her... quite the opposite actually. But fear was what Lucinda wanted, and Lira was here to ingratiate herself, so she allowed unease to flash in her eyes, her shoulders to stiffen.

Eventually Lucinda gave a little nod and broke her gaze, letting go of Lira's face and settling back in the chair. The sense of danger didn't evaporate, the imprint of her fingers still pressing into her skin.

Freed, Lira's gaze shifted around the room, ensuring they were alone, confirming the two exits were unblocked. She wondered where the other men were. And the hooded person. Whoever it was had been itching at the back of her mind. "I noticed none of your pets were guarding the door out there. One of your men controls them, yes?"

"Before I answer your questions, I have one for you." Lucinda's expression didn't change. "Where are the other students?"

"What do you need them for? I suspect it's not just to run around this place being chased by your monsters. And don't tell me you couldn't have caught them all by now if you'd wanted to. You're playing some sort of twisted game with them."

Nothing changed in Lucinda's face or voice to indicate whether Lira hit the mark. "They're here for a purpose. I need to locate them," she said simply.

Lira stared at her for a moment, weighing up the best course of action. If Lira wanted to know more about the razak, where the queen might be, not to mention embed herself deeper inside Underground, she was going to have to earn some trust. But giving up the others was proving surprisingly difficult. She bristled at her own foolishness.

"Your hesitation bothers me, Lira."

"I'm trying to figure out whether I should keep telling you things without getting anything in return. That's not how I generally operate," Lira said coolly. "We're both working toward the same goal. A little trust would be nice."

"Dasta controls the razak, as you assumed. He's out with them now, looking for your friends."

Lira couldn't hesitate now, and she didn't, even though the reluctance that tugged at her was unexpected and annoying. "I left them hiding at the back of a rather large area that looks like it used to be a library. They think I'm out scouting for the location of your beasties so we can plan an escape."

Lucinda rose without another word and left the room. Lira sat by the fire for a few moments, finding herself knotting her fingers in anxiety—she hoped Garan and the others had listened to her and left the library.

Cursing at herself, she stilled her hands. If they hadn't followed her advice, they were fools, and being captured would be their own fault. And if they were killed, well, she'd just have to rely on herself to get out. The thought of Tarion or Lorin—or even Garan or Fari—being torn apart by razak was oddly upsetting, though, and it was hard to push that worry from her mind. It was a weakness that Lucinda would prey upon if she learned it.

Eventually, the door opened again and Lucinda returned to sit in the same chair. This time, however, the man Lucinda had called Jora followed her in and hovered by the door.

"What does he do?" She gestured at him. He returned her look, unblinking.

Lucinda ignored the question, smoothly crossing her legs. "I have to admit, despite what Greyson said about you, I'm surprised at how easily you just gave up your fellow students."

Lira's gaze narrowed. She could play this game. "If you really did listen to what Greyson said about me, you wouldn't be surprised."

Lucinda relaxed back in her chair, a genuine smile on her face this time. "You have me there. You're everything that was reported to me, and not just by Greyson."

"So you've been spying on me inside Temari Hall too?" Lira fought not to betray how unsettling that realisation was. She'd been wrong, deadly wrong, about Underground's reach and influence if Lucinda was telling the truth. It meant the situation wasn't under Lira's control as much as she'd thought it was... which meant she'd made a potentially critical mistake.

"The less you know the better." A note of earnestness filled Lucinda's voice; Lira didn't trust it for a second. All she saw in the woman's gaze was a calculated purpose. "Not because we want to hide things from you, but because it's safer that way. You live amongst mages, some of whom have telepathic ability. Alyx Egalion counts telepathy amongst one of her many powerful mage abilities. She'll be our most formidable adversary."

Again, Lira didn't believe Lucinda was afraid of anyone, Egalion included. Still, she played along. "I guess I should be relieved that you're intending for me to go back there, then," she said dryly.

"I told you before, Lira, you won't be harmed here more than what is required to maintain your cover."

Lira's mouth curled in a smile, though inwardly, frustration built. "If you want me as your shining symbol of hope, I need to know more than nothing. I can shield my thoughts as well as any fully trained mage." Since being taught how, she'd practiced it every single day. The thought of anyone being inside her head was terrifying, for many reasons.

Lucinda met her gaze. "We want to continue what your grandfather started. The Mage Council is standing in the way of that."

Unhelpful. Lira already knew the Underground manifesto by heart. She let that irritation leak into her voice. "Thanks for clearing that one up for me. And how exactly does kidnapping a handful of mage students and putting them in a half-destroyed building of some kind to be chased around by razak further that cause?"

"What is happening here is a crucial piece of our overall plan. That's all I can safely tell you for now."

"Not good enough," Lira said flatly, trying to make her voice and bearing resolute. "Why'd you take me too?"

"I told you. For your cover." Lucinda pierced her with a look, annoyance edging her voice, the first time some of that perfect composure had frayed even if it was only barely perceptible. "We're aware that you are not well-liked at Temari Hall. Your value to us goes beyond your bloodline. We need them to trust you, respect you. By taking you along with the others, we've made sure you'll never come under suspicion."

"Except if you kill them all and Shakar's heir is the only one to survive, they'll be even more suspicious of me than they were already," Lira countered. "So either you're telling the truth now, and were just testing me before to see if I'd give them up, or you're lying about wanting to maintain my cover."

Lucinda said nothing, the little smile on her face giving nothing away.

Lira matched the smirk with her own. "Fine. Why didn't you have Greyson tell me this from the start? I could have spent the past year making friends. It would have been a far easier way of gaining deeper access to the council than being kidnapped."

"You were being evaluated. Greyson was instructed not to breathe a word to you of our plans until the Shadowcouncil agreed you could be trusted." Lucinda cocked her head. "We don't make a practice of trusting arrogant children with our secrets. Especially criminal ones with no loyalty to anyone but themselves."

Lira swore inwardly. Talking with this woman was like playing mental chess, and Lira was slowly realising that she was out of her depth. Everything Lucinda said made sense but some deep instinct told Lira there was a whole lot she wasn't saying.

"What about your pets? I've never heard of an animal that is impervious to magic. They can sense it too, right?" Lira tried to circle around to her original reason for coming.

"You are correct on both counts." Something dark flashed in Lucinda's eyes, as if she were remembering something, something awful. Odd. It was as close to real emotion as Lira had seen in the woman. Maybe there was something there Lira could use. "And as such, they are hard to control. Dasta is with us for that purpose."

"And what happens if something happens to Dasta? How do you control your murderous pets then?"

"There's a failsafe in place for controlling them in that eventuality."

"They all screamed when we killed one before." She tried to sound casually curious, unbothered by whether Lucinda answered or not. "Almost blew my eardrums. It wasn't a pleasant experience."

"Yes, they—" The door opened, cutting off Lucinda's response. Lira could have cheerfully murdered the man who entered. It was Dasta, the razak mage. He gave Lucinda a little shake of his head.

Lucinda frowned slightly then spun on Lira, eyes narrowed. That unspoken threat leapt across the room between them, making Lira's heart thud. "They weren't there. Did you lie to us?"

"I did not. Bring a telepath mage in here if you like and I'll prove it. Last place I saw them was hiding in the back of the library."

Lucinda glanced at Dasta, gave him a nod. He spoke. "There were the remains of a burned-out candle in one of the small rooms at the back, Seventh."

Seventh? And had Lucinda just had to give him permission to speak? Lira tried to keep the curiosity from her face. These people were causing an odd note to chime in the back of her mind. There was something off here.

"I think we've let them run enough. Jora?"

The man nodded. "It's been several hours. I think it's sufficient for what we need, Seventh."

"Good. Dasta, you know what to do."

The mage bowed his head and left. Lucinda turned back to Lira. "Those students were brought here for a purpose that hasn't been fulfilled yet, but once they've served it, I don't intend for them to return home alive. Your return will be above suspicion, that has been well planned for, so don't concern yourself with it."

Deeper. The hole she was in was growing deeper and deeper. And darker. There was nothing for it but to hold on until the end. Either that or give up now. And Lira didn't give up on things, so she sank further into the thrill of danger, let it consume her. Then she smiled, anticipatory. "What do you want me to do?"

"We'll deal with the children. But we have another purpose for you while you're here." Lucinda rose from her chair, and the look she directed at Jora sent ice cold slivers creeping down Lira's spine. Her eyes literally gleamed with excitement. It was only there for half a heartbeat, but Lira didn't miss it.

Lira's smile vanished. The rush of danger pulsed through her in a spike of adrenalin so strong she almost gasped. Pure instinct—born of surviving amongst hardened criminals since young childhood when almost anything could kill her—responded to that look on such a fundamental level that she could not control or fight it.

She was on her feet, ready to flee, hands curling into fists at her sides before her brain could tell her body to stop. She wanted to maintain her position with Underground, but her instincts warned her this situation was more dangerous than she understood.

And she *always* trusted those instincts.

"I said I'll help, but I need to understand what I'm doing first." Lira's gaze shifted between Lucinda and Jora. Both were in the space between her and the main door.

"You don't. And while I admire your spirit, there are reasons you can't be told anything further," Lucinda said, mouth thinning. "I don't like to repeat myself."

Lira held her gaze. "Neither do I."

Lucinda took a single step towards her. Lira braced herself, fingers curling and uncurling at her sides.

"Be careful not to confuse me with Greyson, Lira. I'm prepared to humour you for the benefit you bring our cause, but I won't let you stand in the way of achieving it. Do I make myself clear?"

She wanted to say yes.

Wanted to follow Lucinda's orders and cement her membership with Underground.

Wanted to throw away the lives of Garan and the others like they would no doubt throw away hers if given the opportunity.

But that look in Lucinda's eyes... no, conceding like this simply wasn't in her. She couldn't submit to being used as a puppet without any knowledge of why she was doing what she was doing, not for any cause. Not even to achieve what she wanted more than anything else— erasing Shakar's name and replacing it with her own.

Lira couldn't entirely hide her reluctance, and Lucinda caught it. Danger pressed down on her at the change in the woman's expression. But Lira was quick, a quickness born of a keen survival instinct, and she was a heartbeat faster in drawing on her magic.

Violet light lit up the room and a chair lifted from the floor and flew at Lucinda's head. The woman ducked, temporarily distracted from using her own magic, and Lira dived for the side door leading into the spiral stairwell. Jora lurched after her, but magic surged through Lira's veins and she ripped the main door from its hinges in a single, brutal move, slamming it into Jora with enough force to send him crashing to the floor and Lucinda stumbling out of its way.

And then she was in the dark stairwell. Sacrificing safety for speed, she pressed her palm against the rough stone and headed down as fast as she could. Her heart thudded, expecting Lucinda's mage power to close over her at any moment, terrified that it would. That terror gave her an extra burst of reckless speed. At least any nearby razak wouldn't be able to follow her in here.

Behind her, a door slammed open and Lucinda's voice shouted. Lira dug deep and forced herself to run faster. She had no idea how far the woman's magic extended.

She stumbled on the final step, righted herself before hitting the ground, then shoved open the door at the bottom. A dark corridor loomed ahead and Lira's boots echoed as she sprinted down it before emerging into the entrance foyer. In another twenty strides she was across and out the main doors into the garden.

She had no plan, no specific idea of where to go, she just knew she had to get away from Lucinda and her magic. It pounded through her brain over and over. Once she was clear she could stop and figure out how to rectify the situation. But for now a single word pounded through her brain. Away. Away. Away.

Her legs burned as she ran across the still mist-wreathed garden towards the main building and wrenched open the door she'd seen earlier. Despite the adrenalin, the rush of danger, her body was reaching the edge of its limits. She'd been going for hours now, without food or water, and it was beginning to take a toll.

She got inside, pulled the door shut, then peered out the nearest window. She couldn't see anything moving in the garden, no sign of Lucinda or Jora following her. Eyes still on the garden, she tried to push away the exhaustion and think through what to do next.

The urge to flee was so strong she had to constantly fight it back to allow rational thought. Even the thrill of danger was fading with her weariness.

She took a breath. Focused on a simple goal. Meet the others in the agreed place before Dasta and his monsters found them. Then get out together, whatever it took. She'd deal with Underground once she was safely back in Karonan.

Steadied by the plan, Lira moved away from the window and quickly reviewed her mental map. She wasn't too far from the meeting place. All she had to do was head up one level, then—

The hungry rattle had her freezing to the spot, then swearing at herself for not realising amongst all her frantic planning that the temperature had dropped.

Darkness spilled around the corner to her left, tendrils of shadow curling along the walls and floor, seeking its prey. In seconds the razak had fully appeared, a flash of flickering silver eyes, another triumphant rattle.

Lira turned and ran.

Breath rasping, face throbbing, she sprinted down the corridor with the monster coming after her. Its rattle was angry, challenging, and it rapidly closed the distance. She wasn't going to make it to the stairs, the distance was too far. It would catch her well before she—

The sound of a concussive burst exploded somewhere above her, loud and electric. The razak in pursuit paused as the use of magic washed over its senses... paused long enough for Lira to reach the main stairs leading up.

Violet light flared even brighter around her forearms as she called upon every bit of magical strength she had left to try something she hadn't quite mastered in class yet.

Using her telekinetic magic on herself.

She *leapt* upwards from the bottom step, wrapping her magic around herself, giving her lift as she flew up towards the next landing. Her magic drained rapidly, and her body skewed wildly in mid-air. She was barely able to correct herself in time. She hit the landing beyond the top step hard, the impact thudding painfully through her hip and shoulder, before sliding across the floor and into the wall. The breath whooshed out of her.

She glanced down, wheezing. The razak was already sliding up the stairs after her, long spider-like limbs crawling towards the top step, scales scraping on stone. Its rattle echoed more loudly, reverberating through her bones, hungry. The cold buried deep into her and the darkness deepened to inky blackness.

Swearing, Lira scrambled to her feet just as another concussion burst went off—this one closer, on this level. It had to be Lorin. Dasta must have found them already.

After a brief hesitation, Lira ran in the direction of their meeting place. She yanked the doors off walls with magic as she ran and sent them flying back at the creature. It won her an extra second of space when the razak was forced to dodge aside before continuing to come after her. But that was all. Her magic flickered out then, almost entirely gone.

She reached the end of the hall, somehow still upright, and forced her body to keep running. The thing was almost on her as she skidded around the corner.

"Lira! This way," Garan's voice shouted.

She turned from looking back at the razak pursuing her to see Garan and the others ahead—they were hovering at the doorway of the small office that was their meeting place. At the sight of her, Lorin and Fari ducked inside, then Garan shoved Tarion in before following at a shout from Athira, who was holding the door open.

The razak was almost on Lira. It was moving too fast and she was slowing from exhaustion, legs trembling, magic drain sucking at what remained of her strength.

For a moment memory blurred. The razak became a city guard. The dusty floor under her feet turned into melting snow over cobblestones. Timin stood ahead, yelling at her to hurry, already preparing to close the door in her face, though at the time she hadn't realised it.

It was too far. She wasn't going to make it. They were going to shut her out, leave her to the razak. She was going to have to fight it off somehow, despite being exhausted and drained of magic.

But her vision cleared. It was Athira standing at the end of the hall, not Timin. The third-year apprentice lifted her hands, and a second later Lira felt raw magical strength flood through her. Gasping with the force of it, not questioning it, she lifted her hands and reached out for anything nearby that could be lifted, torn off walls, or thrown.

It didn't slow the creature enough. It dodged too fast, still closing the distance, its hungry rattling drowning her senses and making her want to scream. Lira tried to run faster, tried to ignore the pain throbbing in her face and the burning exhaustion in her muscles, but it was a losing battle.

Athira continued to stand there, holding the door open, unflinching as the razak bore down on them both. She could have ducked inside to safety. Barred the door. If she stayed and Lira didn't make it the creature would get Athira too.

But she didn't move. Her face was bloodless but determined.

Lira reached the door a heartbeat ahead of the creature and dove inside. Using the reserves of magic she had left, she yanked the door shut behind her and Athira. One of the creature's legs missed being crushed by a second. The door thudded as the creature slammed against it. Lira groaned, then forced the fading remnants of her magic to drag the heavy chest across the door. Once that was done, she bent over her knees, gasping, utterly done in.

"Can't stay, have to head down," Athira said breathlessly, sounding as drained as Lira felt.

Lira nodded. "Go," she panted. "Just a second and I'll be right behind you."

Athira started down the stairs into the kitchen storeroom and Lira straightened, swaying on her feet. Once she had some control over her breathing, she forced her leaden legs into movement and went after Athira.

Her breathing was still coming in pants as she tried not to fall on the narrow stairs, legs rubbery under her. She reached the bottom step to find the others standing strangely still in the centre of the storeroom floor.

Standing between them and the exit was Lucinda—a razak hovering just outside the open door into the kitchens behind them.

Lira's magic was almost completely depleted, her body exhausted. But she had the advantage. Lucinda hadn't seen Lira yet. Lira was exposed at the bottom of the stairs, had foolishly come into the open without thinking, but she had a second before they spotted her. Lira could take Lucinda down first and as a group they could take the razak, and Dasta too if he was nearby.

Her hands twitched, she dug deeper than she ever had before for what was left of her magic, gritting her teeth with effort. She prepared to reach out for Garan's staff to bring it slamming down on Lucinda's head. And she breathed easier, because she knew she was going to succeed, that it was going to work, that she could...

Then someone else walked through the kitchen door, long coat swishing around her ankles, stride graceful and confident. Her dark hair was loose around her shoulders, midnight-blue gaze as cool as Lira remembered.

And Lira froze.

Ahrin Vensis smiled, her gaze instantly landing on Lira in the shadows. And Lira couldn't do anything. Her magic drained away. Her emotional shields shattered.

She took a single, heaving breath before a fierce ache closed over her chest and her world broke.

Lucinda saw her in the next second. Bands of steel closed around her body, freezing her in place. Panic flooded her, raw and powerful. But she couldn't move, couldn't blink, couldn't *think*.

She was frozen.

Now Lucinda had them all.

CHAPTER 26
BEFORE

Lira failed her classes over and over again. The masters made allowances for her complete lack of education beyond the basics of reading and writing in Shiven, but almost without exception the other students at Temari had come to the academy after several years of formal education. Even the poorer students, who were most definitely in the minority, had more learning than Lira.

When she arrived at Temari, she could write Shiven painfully slowly, as well as read and speak it fluently, but anything written in Tregayan or Zandian was completely foreign to her. On top of that, she had no familiarity or understanding of mapping, politics and strategy, or mathematics. Yet she had to try and start learning all of it all at once. It was an impossible task.

Still, she had a warm bed every night. Three large meals a day. Guards and apprentices patrolling the gates and walls to keep everyone inside safe. Students and masters inside who steered clear of her but never thought about trying to hurt her in any way. When those realisations began to sink in within her first few weeks at Temari Hall, Lira's constant watchfulness—learned since first arriving at the orphanage—began to relax.

It wouldn't ever vanish completely, though, and she wouldn't allow herself to trust her new safety. Always foremost in her mind was that she had to succeed here, had to figure out *how* to succeed despite how foreign it all was, because there were no other options remaining.

So she attacked her education like she'd attacked everything else in her life. She did whatever she needed to survive.

She was old enough now to understand that not every student at Temari was scared of her because of Shakar. They were all too young to have any personal memory of him, of the damage he'd wrought, outside the stories their parents had told them.

But other things about her kept them away. They knew she'd come from the streets, realised quickly she didn't know anything worthwhile, and guessed at her criminal background. They didn't like her aloof demeanour or constant suspicion as to their motives. She knew nothing of their world, and they nothing of hers.

She didn't know how to bridge that gap. Nor did she particularly want to—why should she feel bad that she'd done what she needed to do to survive? What did these pampered boys and girls know about having no safety, no stability? Of being always hungry and cold?

Even if she had wanted to try to make friends, there was no time for it, because Lira spent literally every waking moment outside classes in the library trying to catch up on her lessons. Used to not eating much, she skipped lunch every day to study. She stayed up well beyond curfew every night reading. The task of catching up remained impossible, but at least she felt as if she were doing everything she could to achieve it.

Six months in, she passed her first Languages test. Barely.

Seven months in and she was reading, writing, and conversing almost fluently in Tregayan, the language used by everyone at Temari Hall—despite how much the Shiven students and staff clearly hated that fact.

"Lira?"

She looked up from the parchment in front of her, blinking. It was late, and her eyes were tired. "Master A'ndreas."

He peered over her shoulder. "Mapping homework?"

"No." She couldn't *do* her Mapping homework because she didn't understand what Master Eren had been droning on about for the entirety of that day's class. She'd noted down the key phrases he'd used and now was reading up on them, hoping it would make the homework clearer. So far she wasn't having a lot of luck. But she certainly wasn't going to admit that to Master A'ndreas. She'd had quite enough of the pitying looks whenever her complete lack of education became obvious. They were much worse than the scornful or wary ones.

He shot her a bemused glance, but didn't press. Instead curiosity crept over his expression. "You're looking at a world map that includes Rotherburn, I see. Fascinating mystery, what happened to that place. It's my current research project, actually."

She gave him a blank look.

He pointed to one of the maps she was poring over, where neatly drawn lines showed a landmass to the west of Shivasa. "They all just vanished, about fifty years or so ago." When Lira merely shrugged, utterly uninterested in his pet project while she was drowning in learning, he sighed in disappointment. "Do you have a moment?"

She nodded and rose, following him across the atrium and down a short corridor to the left of the main doors where his office sat. Once inside, he waved her to a chair. "You're up late studying."

"Yes, sir."

He gave her a knowing look, indicating she wasn't hiding her struggles from him in any way, but he didn't make her uncomfortable by saying it aloud. "I wanted to talk to you about your magic."

She tensed. "Yes, sir."

"You've been here just over nine months now, Lira."

"I do actually know how to count the passage of time," she snapped, irritated by the forced politeness of this interaction while he danced around the real reason for the conversation.

"You're not a mage of the higher order." He delivered the words gently but bluntly. "I assume you've already worked that out for yourself?"

"It hasn't been that long, sir, and it took longer than expected for my magic to break out, so maybe..." She trailed off, hating the begging tone of her voice. That wasn't her.

"You're a telekinetic mage, Lira, and that's all. Nine months of close association with so many mages would have seen another ability break out before now. I'm sorry."

His words were enough to break the bubble of denial she'd been hiding in for weeks. Something in her chest squeezed so tightly that she couldn't move or breathe for a long moment. And he sat there with a *sympathetic* look on his face that just made the whole thing worse. "Was there anything else, or can I go now, sir?" she asked when she was able to speak again.

"Yes."

She was at the door when his voice stopped her. "At the risk of getting more attitude for telling you things you already know, the initiate exam is next month. You have to pass that or you don't get to continue here." Her hands curled white-knuckled around the door frame as he continued. "I suggest you forget about Mapping and concentrate on your *History of Mages* book. The exam content is drawn entirely from there."

She spun, eyes widening in surprise. Nobody had told them what was going to be in the initiate exam, which she assumed was a deliberate tactic to make sure they didn't slack off in any of their lessons.

"You never heard that from me." He smiled. "Now go."

The squeezing sensation in her chest was back as she trudged to the table she'd been using to study. It was so late the atrium was empty, which was how she preferred it. The sight of the scattered parchment and quill only served to deepen her despair.

Tears pricked at her eyes as all the denial finally drained away and she allowed herself to acknowledge the truth. She hated everything about this place. Classes bored her, forcing herself to study was a constant battle, and now she wasn't going to be a mage of the higher order. She was just an ordinary telekinetic mage, one of many.

In a moment of despairing temper, she sent the pages and books flying off the table, then slumped in the chair and covered her face with her hands. After a few moments, galvanised by worry that Master A'ndreas would come out and see her like this, she bent and collected her studies, stood up, and left the library.

In her dark room, she dumped the pile on the desk, then undressed and crawled into bed.

She cried herself to sleep that night for the first time since before her mother had died. As she lay there, curled in a ball, the only thing she wanted was to be back in that loft in Dirinan, covered in the pile of blankets, not safe, and not warm, and hungry... but content. Happy. She wanted it so badly her chest literally ached. But that had all been an illusion.

There was no home for her. Nowhere else to go. Nothing to return to.

She had to make this work. She had to forget about all of that.

The next morning she got out of bed dry-eyed and pushed away the despair, replacing it with a new determination. She would be the most powerful telekinetic mage in the council.

Two weeks later she beat her sparring partner in staff combat lessons for the first time.

Three weeks later she passed her first test in Mapping class.

Five weeks later she passed her first-year exam by scant inches. But she passed it.

One day at a time. She would best them all.

CHAPTER 27

Lira blinked awake into complete darkness. For a moment she wasn't sure she *was* awake, it was so dark. But then she heard breathing; quick, rasping breaths nearby. And rustling, as if someone were shifting.

"Who's there?" she demanded, hating that fear made her voice tremble just the slightest bit.

"Spider's awake." Fari's voice. Sounding relieved?

Lira tried to sit up, but instantly slammed into a thick metal bar across her chest. Her ankles were similarly restrained. There was no space between the metal and her clothing. She couldn't move properly, couldn't sit up, couldn't... She let out an incoherent sound of panic.

"You okay over there?" Tarion asked.

His voice was warm. Familiar. Solid. She grabbed hold of it, the voice that had never held fear, wariness, or mockery in it when talking to her. Then she tried to calm her breathing, but it was a losing battle. She couldn't move. Couldn't even wriggle, she—

"We're trussed up too." Garan's voice then. More familiarity, that easy charm she usually found so annoying. She allowed herself to lean on it, even as she hated herself for the weakness.

She eventually steadied her breathing. Tried to ignore the fact she couldn't move. Failed. Tried to breathe through it and focus on some-thing else, at least briefly. "Where are we?" she managed, voice terse, her entire body rigid with holding back panic. If this was Lucinda's idea of bolstering her cover, she was going to murder the woman. With her bare hands. Lira didn't care how dangerous she was.

"We don't know. You're the last one to wake up," Fari said. "We were concerned about you."

They were? Maybe she was delirious. "What about Lorin and Athira?"

"Here," Athira called out. Her voice was smaller than usual, breathy, like she was holding back the same panic bubbling in Lira's chest.

"Me too." Lorin. He sounded grim. Haughty. *Offended* that he was being held in restraints.

Lira pressed her eyes closed, biting down on her cut lip so hard it started bleeding again, still struggling to calm herself. She tried to focus on her anger at Lucinda for doing this to her, but she couldn't grab hold of it well enough. The thrill of danger was long gone, failing her, buried by the dark and the bars holding her down. And every time she began to steady herself, she remembered, and it all went to pieces.

Ahrin.

Ahrin Vensis was here. She'd kidnapped Lira. *She'd* done this to her, Ahrin and Lucinda and those rotted mages. Her breath gasped. She wanted to be angry, tried again to use it to fuel her, but the anger was gone, and she just felt devastated. Lost. Broken.

Lucinda needed Lira. Her bloodline, her magic. Without her Underground were nothing but a ragged group of misfits. Lira kept telling herself that, trying to use the refrain to calm her mind. Bring back her focus.

Athira suddenly gave an inarticulate cry of distress, and her boots drummed on what sounded like wood. For the first time Lira realised she was lying on a hard surface. No padding underneath her.

"Athira—" Garan started.

"Let me out of here!" she screamed. "What the hell is going on?"

"Athira, you need to stop that." Fari's voice was calm, steady. "I know enough healing to know wrenching yourself against these bars is going to cause you serious injury. We need you strong."

"Can't one of you telekinetics rip these things off us?" Athira panted, desperation trembling in her voice. Lira felt her own panic surge in concert, and she was too overwhelmed to respond. The trapped feeling was unbearable. It caught in her chest, burned through her blood, made her breathing shallow. Dots danced in her vision.

"I can't. Something in the metal is blocking my magic. I can't even feel it." Garan spoke quietly. There was barely-repressed panic in his voice too, now.

Lira sucked in a horrified gasp, silently trying to access her own magic.

It wasn't there. An inarticulate scream built up in her throat. She writhed on the table, swallowing it down over and over again until she almost passed out from lack of air. Sweat slicked her skin. Her heart beat too hard, too fast.

"Lira?" Lorin called out. "You all right?"

"Fine," she managed, only her fear of the others knowing how panicked she was giving her enough focus to speak. "I can't access my magic either."

The silence that settled over the dark room then was thick with rising terror. Pushing it back was one of the hardest things she'd ever had to do. It was just like being back in the orphanage, being held down by the bigger girls, her face thrust into icy water that burned her eyes and nose, water trickling down her throat, into her lungs...

"This is absolutely the worst day of my life," Fari said suddenly. Her voice was forced but bright, mostly hiding the tremor underlying it. "Here I was looking forward to mid-winter break, an hour or two in the stacks with Derna before she left, *maybe* even the opportunity to get her up to my room to spend the night. Yet the next thing I know I'm kidnapped and trapped in a weird nightmare at some half-falling down estate in the middle of nowhere being hunted by monsters right out of a fairy tale book."

There was a moment's silence, then, "Second worst day for me." Garan's voice came through the darkness, stronger now. "Worst was the day Pa caught me messing around with *Mageson*. He grabbed the

sword from me just before I almost took my arm off with its edge—
I've never seen him so angry and disappointed."

Fari chuckled. "I can see Lord Egalion being scarier than a razak."

"*Mageson* is his Taliath sword. It is a thing precious beyond
measure," Lorin said quietly.

"Okay Shiven-boy, what was the worst day of your life?" Athira's
snotty tone was back, though her voice was strained, as if she was
exerting the same effort Lira was not to lose her mind.

"When I was eight years old I broke my leg falling out of a tree on
the farm. The bone was fractured in three places—for a whole week
until a healer mage could come to our village I was terrified that it
wouldn't heal right and I'd never be able to become a warrior mage,"
Lorin said. "You can't imagine what it was like... to have your whole life
ripped away before it even started."

"A broken leg was worse than being kidnapped, chased by razak,
then bound to a table in a dark room?" Garan asked sceptically. The
panic was entirely gone from his voice, the jocular, bantering tone
back. Fari had managed to break the escalating fear in the room and
now Garan was driving them firmly away from it.

"Much worse." Lorin's voice rang with certainty.

"This is the worst for me." Athira spoke quickly, her breathing still
coming in short pants. "I can't... I can't be held down like this."

"How about you, Lira?" Garan asked. "Care to contribute to this
cheerful conversation?"

"Not really." Even though the talking, the rhythm of speech, was
helping distract her just enough to keep her mind functioning, she
didn't want to share anything personal, didn't even want to think about
her worst day. She had to hold onto herself. If she gave in she'd be lost.
But it was hard, her mind teetering constantly on the edge, exhausting
her.

"My worst day was the day my magic broke out and everyone
learned what it was," Tarion said. "I felt like the biggest failure. Still
do. And the worst thing is, Caria and my parents don't think of me
that way at all. It's just every other mage or Taliath who looks at the
son of Alyx Egalion and Dashan Caverlock and sees a disappointment.
They all expected so much more."

267

Lira shifted her head toward him, even though she could see nothing in the darkness. From the direction of the voices, it sounded like Fari was immediately to her right, with Garan beyond her, then Athira. Tarion and Lorin were on Lira's other side.

"She certainly succeeded in making a better, less corrupt mage order, but she hasn't changed much of the old thinking, your mother," Fari said thoughtfully.

"Or done much for those with mage power who aren't pureblood or nobility," Lira couldn't help saying.

"She wants to, so do Mama and Uncle Tarrick, but I think something like that takes more than a single generation," Garan said. "I'm sorry you feel that way, Tar. I didn't know."

"I didn't want you to. How could you understand? You're everything that's expected of the son of Ladan Egalion and Dawn A'ndreas."

Garan didn't argue. Silence fell again. Across the room, Athira's breathing grew more laboured. The darkness didn't lift, the silence growing thicker and thicker.

"I'd really like to hear your answer, Lira," Lorin said unexpectedly. "Something tells me this isn't the worst day of your life."

"What about almost drowning at age seven?" Garan asked with a smile in his voice.

"No, not that," she said without thinking.

"Something worse happened to you than that?" Fari's voice was small, stunned.

A silence fell. They were clearly waiting. So she gave them an answer—maybe not the real answer, because she couldn't find the words to say that aloud, not ever, but close enough—because it was growing harder and harder to control the panic. And because the image of Athira holding that door was still bright in her mind. It wouldn't let go, like a nagging itch. "The worst day of my life was the day I first arrived at Temari Hall."

There was a brief, puzzled silence, but before anyone could say anything the door opened and bright light flooded the room. Lira squinted, but it took several seconds before her eyes adjusted enough to make out anything useful.

In that time all she could hear was booted feet and two indistinct male voices. She struggled against the bars holding her down, desperate to escape them despite knowing it was no use, temporarily giving into the fear. Her chest ached from pressing so hard against the metal, and her ankles were sore and probably bleeding, but she couldn't stop herself. Panicked air rasped in and out of her lungs.

By the time she could see, one of the tables was being wheeled out of the door. Lira blinked, trying to make out who it was, but tears from the sudden light blurred her vision.

"Hey! Stop! Where are you taking her?" Garan's voice bellowed, full of fury. It was an intimidating sound, nothing like she'd ever heard from the amiable apprentice. But the two men paid no heed to Garan's demands and the door swung shut, completely cutting off the light again.

"Who was it? Who did they take?" Lira demanded, fruitlessly making another attempt to free herself from her bonds. All she managed to succeed in doing was drenching herself in sweat and creating some new cuts and bruises. Across the room, Garan was clearly doing the same, grunts of effort and anger echoing through the room. The scream rose up in her throat again, begging to be let out.

"Athira," Lorin said.

"This is insane!" Fari sounded a terrifying combination of angry and hysterical. "What in all magical hells is going on?"

Lira felt stirrings of anger return, and focused on it, stoking it, allowing it to spread through her and push out the fear. She hated that she felt this way, that Underground had found a weakness they could exploit.

Her anger built, hot and cleansing, taking some of the edge away from her panic.

She no longer cared that she was supposed to be a member of Underground. Once she got herself out of here—and she would—she was going to hunt them all down, Lucinda included. And if the Mage Council didn't want to help they could get out of her way.

They would pay for doing this to her. Ahrin too, if it came to that.

And that's when she smelled it.

The faint scent of vanilla wax. Lira frowned, trying to figure out why it was such a familiar scent. Garan's struggles made concentrating impossible. "Stop!" she snapped at him. "Can't you smell that?"

To her surprise, he stopped immediately, and the room subsided into stillness. As soon as it did, the scent grew stronger.

"It's a drug," Tarion said quietly. "Drugged smoke, I'd guess. You said that's what they used on us back at Temari, Lira?"

Lira arched her neck to look in his direction, even though it was useless. Her heart thudded in her chest. She wanted to tell them to breath shallowly, turn their heads away from the scent, but the words proved hard to grasp. She shook her head, tried again, but failed.

"Poison?" Lorin's voice shook.

Lira heard someone begin to reply to that—Fari, maybe?—but her eyes were sliding shut and she couldn't make her brain work.

And then she was out.

CHAPTER 28
BEFORE

Three days before mid-winter break during Lira's second year at Temari Hall, she received an unexpected summons in the middle of Languages class instructing her to go back to her dormitory room and wait there for a visitor.

Her initial response was relief at the idea of a break in the tedium of sitting in the classroom. But that quickly faded, irritation rising in its place. She was only just starting to grasp Zandian verbs, and leaving the class meant hours of studying later to try and catch up on what Master Kalia was teaching.

Kalia took exception to the irritation on her face, misunderstanding the reason for it, and refused to tell her anything other than that the note wanted her to leave class and go to her room. "Come and see me later for your homework," he added.

Every other student sitting at the desks turned to stare at her as she collected her parchment and books, then rose and walked the distance to the door—all except for Tarion Caverlock, whose gaze was very firmly focused on the books in front of him as he scribbled notes.

She shoved open the door to her room, books balanced precariously in her other hand, only to stop dead at the sight of a woman sitting on the unused second bed. Lira's eyes widened before she could stop herself—she was beautiful, with long dark hair and striking blue eyes enhanced by the royal blue of the mage cloak she wore. She rose at Lira's entrance, giving her a warm smile that struck Lira as sincere, not just something pasted on her face to be polite.

Lira lurched away from the sense of comfort and safety she instantly felt in the stranger's presence and closed the door. After dropping her books on her bed, she remained standing, keeping a good distance away. "Who are you?"

"Dawn A'ndreas." The woman offered a hand. "Technically it's Lord-Mage A'ndreas, but I hate the title. It's lovely to meet you, Lira."

Lira stared at the hand, the woman's title reverberating through her mind. The Rionnan king's most senior mage advisor was standing in Lira's dormitory room. Uncomfortable being on the back foot, Lira shifted quickly to the offensive. "My grandfather was your predecessor."

Shakar had spent years playing the role of Lord-Mage Astor, Alyx Egalion's godfather, all the while secretly building his army and preparing to bring down the Mage Council. Lira envied the masterful way in which he'd fooled everyone for decades.

"He was. Hence hating the title." Dawn smiled again, unoffended, hand still outstretched.

Lira stared at the hand. Not only was Dawn A'ndreas Rionn's lord-mage, she was also Alyx Egalion's closest friend, wife of Rionn's most powerful lord, Ladan Egalion, and—most importantly—reputed to be the most powerful telepath mage alive. Their only son was an insufferable brat who also attended Temari. Lira didn't take the hand, instead moving a step further back and carefully reinforcing her mental shield. "What do you want?"

Dawn still didn't seem to be bothered by Lira's rudeness. "A conversation, to start with. Is that okay?"

"Yes." Lira perched on the edge of her bed, curious despite herself and welcoming the break in the endless tedium of classes and study that weighed on her. She felt no threat from Dawn, and her shoulders relaxed a little. It was getting easier to do that inside these walls. Easier to stop worrying about danger coming in the night, or every time she turned a corner. Easier to stop thinking constantly about where her next meal was coming from. She kept telling herself that was a good thing.

Dawn sighed, her magic likely picking up Lira's suspicion even if it wasn't obvious from how she was holding herself. "Your wariness is understandable, but I'm very sorry that it's necessary."

"It's not your fault." She rolled out the expected answer, what they always wanted to hear.

"Maybe not. The world can be an unforgiving place, can't it?"

What did this woman know about an unforgiving world? Lira scoffed inwardly, but said nothing.

Dawn smiled a little, but sobered quickly. "Lira, I won't insult your intelligence by dwelling on pleasantries. What do you know about Underground?"

Startled by the question, it took Lira a moment to gather her thoughts. "They're some kind of rebel group who hate the Mage Council. They think..." Her grandfather's name about to come rolling off her tongue, Lira stiffened and cut herself off. This conversation had just turned dangerous.

"They think Shakar had it right," Dawn finished for her. "That mages should be sitting above the kingdoms, ruling them all, that they're superior to people without magic."

"Maybe their leaders do, but most of them just want food to eat and clothes on their backs," Lira said without thinking. In the months before leaving Dirinan, the name Underground had started whispering through the streets. She'd stayed well clear of them, as had the crews, but the things she'd heard had rarely been about insurrection. Their discontented mutterings had more to do with the misery of their lives and wanting to change that. It wasn't until she'd gotten to Temari that she'd heard how strong the group's connection to Shakar and his goals was.

"Shivasa suffered during the decades of war in ways that Rionn didn't." Dawn nodded, accepting Lira's words. "Leader Astohar is trying, but it will take decades more for this country to recover, and it doesn't help that he doesn't hold the absolute power of a king. But those who suffer most blame him, and the council. They think a return to a world like Shakar wanted would make things better for them. Or at least, Underground's leaders make them believe it would."

"A world where the Mage Council gave a toss about them might help with making Underground less appealing."

"They do, Lira," Dawn said gently.

Maybe they did. Lira was in no real position to know. She'd seen no evidence of it, though. "That's not what Underground thinks, and it's not what they tell people. *That's* what matters."

"I agree."

Lira's gaze narrowed. "Why are you talking to me about this?"

"You are Shakar's last remaining heir," Dawn said carefully. "You would be a very powerful symbol for Underground."

Lira leapt to her feet before she realised what she was doing, furious. "Are you suggesting I'm one of them? It's not enough to hate me or fear me because of him, now you assume I *am* him and that I'm what? Plotting to bring down the council from within?"

"No, I don't think that for a second. Nobody does." Dawn's expression remained calm. "But I think the Shadowcouncil might approach you, Lira. In fact, I'd be extremely surprised if they didn't."

She wavered, anger disarmed by Dawn's sincerity. "What is this conversation about?"

"If Underground approach you, I'd like you to consider agreeing to join them, and then gathering information on our behalf."

"Our behalf. Do you mean the king of Rionn or the Mage Council?"

"Both. The kingdoms and council are allies, Lira."

"You want me to be a spy?" Lira wanted to make sure she'd heard right. Could Dawn A'ndreas really be considering trusting her with something like this? A second-year apprentice who hadn't passed her trials and was barely scraping by in most classes? Excitement tingled deep in her belly, and she lurched toward it hungrily before pulling herself up. That wasn't her anymore.

"Yes," Dawn said.

It was too simple. Surely they were trying to set her up in some way. And if so, Lira wanted none of it. So she challenged Dawn, trying to get at what was really going on. "Why do you care so much about Underground?"

"Dashan's soldiers caught one of their members yesterday. Since Ladan and I are here to join Garan for mid-winter, Dashan asked me to sit in on the interrogation."

Lira blinked at such casual references to General Caverlock and Lord-Taliath Egalion, but forged ahead. "And?"

Dawn's eyes darkened briefly. "He didn't say anything particularly revealing, and his thoughts didn't tell me much, but..."

"But what?"

Dawn didn't react to Lira's sharp tone. "The tone of his thoughts... the darkness in them. It scared me."

Dawn A'ndreas scared. How was that possible from a single foray into a man's mind where she'd learned nothing specific? Something else was going on.

"There had to be more than that to bring you here to me." Lira glanced around. The possibility of this being a trap reared its head again. "And for us to be meeting so secretly. Nobody knows you're in here, do they? Not even the clerk that brought me the note in class?"

"Have you heard the term 'Darkhand' before, Lira?"

She shook her head, her confusion deepening.

"That name was the one clear thing I got from the man's thoughts. He kept repeating the word over and over as if saying it in his mind kept him safe somehow. It did make reading him more difficult." Dawn rose suddenly, walked over to the small window. "Dashan said he's heard the name once or twice now. It's what Underground call the right hand of the Shadowcouncil, apparently. Whoever it is appeared a few months ago. They're rumoured to be frighteningly effective at carrying out Underground tasks."

"The Darkhand." Lira turned the name over on her tongue. It wasn't radically different from some of the names criminals took. It helped their reputations, inspired fear. A useful tool.

"This man was terrified of him, but at the same time spoke his name as a talisman against my power. It scared me."

Lira's eyes narrowed at the second mention of her being afraid. Dawn A'ndreas was the most powerful telepath mage in existence, why was she admitting to fear in front of her? "Fine. Tell me why you're really asking me to help."

"I know what it's been like for you here," Dawn said. "But—"

"No, you don't."

"Believe me, I didn't have much of a good time at DarkSkull Hall either." A dry smile crossed the telepath's face. "Count yourself lucky you don't have a violent and powerful apprentice mage of the higher order trying to kill you every second day."

Lira stiffened. "Nobody here would touch me. They wouldn't dare."

Dawn turned towards her in a single, graceful movement. "I'm asking you because Underground idolise your grandfather and word of your existence has spread since you arrived at Temari Hall. They no doubt have also heard that you're an outcast here. You're the ideal recruit for them."

"You're not worried I'd truly join them?"

"No." Dawn had said it without hesitation.

Her certainty had taken Lira aback. "How can you be so confident?"

"Because you've dealt with the effects of being his granddaughter your entire life. You have no desire to be like him."

Heat flooded Lira's cheeks in realisation, and she instantly reinforced her mental shields, but it was too late. "Get out of my head," she snarled.

"I've been reading you since you walked in this room. Your shielding is good, but not good enough to defeat me. Not yet, anyway." Dawn had moved closer. "I had to be sure, you understand?"

Humiliation flooded Lira, and she said nothing. She abruptly wanted this conversation over and the mage gone from her room.

"If they come to you, all I'm asking is that you agree to join. Go to whatever meetings they have. Learn what you can by listening and paying attention. I don't want you to put yourself at risk any more than that."

"What do I get in return?"

"My gratitude. A safer world for mages."

Lira cared nothing for either of those things. She'd never lived in a safe world. But she quickly realised what else this would bring her, if she carried out the mission successfully. The council would know her name. They would begin to respect her. Start to see her as someone separate from Shakar. And she had little doubt she could do what Dawn was asking. The people who made up Underground were the same people she'd lived most of her life amongst.

"Why all the secrecy? Why isn't Councillor Egalion asking this of me?" Lira couldn't avoid the nagging feeling that this was some kind of setup, and she wanted to be sure.

"We know the Shadowcouncil are mages, but none of us know what sort of reach, if any, they have into Temari Hall or the council, nor what abilities they have. The fewer people who know, the safer you'll be, and that is my main priority." Dawn sounded genuinely worried about her.

"You're telling me only you and I know about this?" Lira's wariness increased. If Dawn hadn't been so warm, so genuine, she'd have been certain this was a trap.

"For now. Next time I'm in Carhall I intend to talk to the Magorlier in private so that he's aware of it," Dawn said. "And if you are approached and join the group, we'll see how it progresses. If at any point your safety requires others being brought in, I'll do it without hesitation."

Lira studied her for a moment, trying to see if she could detect any evasion in Dawn's words. But all she could read was sincerity.

"I'll give you some time to think about it." Dawn moved for the door.

Lira wavered. She *wanted* to do this. Despite her wariness of a trap, everything inside her was leaping at this opportunity to break from the confines of her studies and her constant, unrelenting struggle with them. But that was the problem... she'd sworn to push away that part of herself so that she'd fit in here. Doing this, putting herself back into dangerous situations, it risked all of that.

"I'll do it." The words came out in a rush, before she could stop herself. "If they come to me, I'll join."

"Thank you." Dawn took a breath. "If you're approached, I ask that you write me regular reports. For your protection, this assignment stays between us. You tell nobody else at Temari Hall." Dawn smiled suddenly. "And before I leave for mid winter, I'm going to teach you how to shield so well that even I won't be able to read your thoughts."

Lira nodded, and the woman left. Slowly, she turned and collected her books, prepared herself to go back to class. She'd made the right choice. This was a much faster way of making them all accept her, and she could manage that old part of herself, keep it at bay. She'd deal with the temptation, and eventually it would fade away like it had never been.

A MONTH after Dawn left to return to Alistriem, Greyson reached out to Lira, discreetly, and asked her to consider joining their cause.

She'd left them hanging for a week, not wanting to appear too eager.

Then she'd gone to her first meeting. She'd ignored the excitement in her bones, refused to acknowledge it, and kept her thoughts strictly focused. She didn't care a toss for Underground and their goals, or for helping the Mage Council get rid of them. She cared only about one thing.

Shakar would be forgotten, and they would remember her instead.

CHAPTER 29

Lira woke in a soft bed, warmed through, no restraints holding her down. Her eyes blinked open to welcome daylight falling across the covers of the bed. For a moment she was content. Until she remembered.

Panic swept through her veins and she shoved off the blankets, scrambling for the edge of the bed and getting to her feet. Her heart raced and her gaze swept the room, looking for...

Lira froze, a cage closing in around her chest so tightly she stopped breathing for a moment. After waking in the dark room with the others, part of her had been hoping that she'd been seeing things, that exhaustion and magic drain had distorted her vision down in the kitchen somehow. That it hadn't been Ahrin but just someone who looked like her.

But she'd been a fool to hope.

Ahrin sat by the crackling fire, before a small table covered with steaming food. A second chair sat opposite her. But Lira didn't see any of that. All she saw was Ahrin. Her long legs were stretched out and crossed at the ankles. Smoke curled into the air from a narrow cigar held loosely in her right hand. Vanilla teased Lira's senses.

It couldn't be...

Something unfolded in Lira's chest, equally agonising and warm, clear and confusing, fury and joy, all combined into something she couldn't recognise and couldn't fight down. Like in the kitchen, she was completely untethered, the ache of all those things so fierce that for a moment it brought tears welling to her eyes.

Ahrin smiled at her before rising gracefully to her feet. She wore the same tailored, long coat she'd always favoured, though this one was black velvet, and Ahrin had always worn colours before. "It's really good to see you, Lira. And no, you're not hallucinating. It's me. I'm actually here."

A thousand possible responses flickered through Lira's mind but they all slid away as quickly as they'd come. All she could do was stare.

Almost three years and Ahrin looked completely different and no different at all. Taller, definitely. Harder, a little. But stunning, with the same long dark hair and midnight-blue eyes and the dangerous air that warned you not to get too close or you might get burned.

Lira swallowed. Tried to suck in a steadying breath. Memories unfolded from the box she'd buried so deeply she hadn't once gone near it since leaving Dirinan. And the first thing that spilled out of her was, "*You* did this to me?"

"That's a much longer conversation," Ahrin said, lifting her cigar to take a long drag before gesturing to the table. "I'm betting you're hungry—you haven't eaten in hours. Unless you'd like a bath first? There's one just through the door there."

It took another few heartbeats for Lira to orient herself, to ride out the wave of shock that was still resounding through her, and roughly shove as many of those memories as she could back away into their box. They wouldn't help her here.

Because along with everything else she remembered how formidable an adversary Ahrin was. She kept hold of that knowledge, used it to try and rebuild her shattered walls.

Then she straightened her shoulders and firmed her voice. She was Lira Astor now, and she was nothing like the girl that had once run the streets of Dirinan with Ahrin and pretended it was home. To Lira Astor, by standing in this room, Ahrin Vensis had become an enemy. "Are you with Lucinda?"

"Yes."

"Why isn't she here?"

"She acknowledges that her approach was not the ideal way to deal with you." Ahrin shrugged, languid, the gesture so familiar that it made Lira's chest hurt. "So I'm here instead."

Anger uncurled. "I'm not a prized horse to be managed."

"No, you're much more than that." Ahrin drew on the cigar again, gaze contemplative as she studied Lira. It was the same look she always wore when planning a score. "Did you know that a large percentage of non-council mages are eager to join our cause when they hear that the Darkmage has a living heir?"

She didn't. Lira only knew what Greyson had told her, over and over by rote, that she was the symbol they needed. But never any specifics. The knowledge elated her, but the feeling was fleeting, one of several that had been tumbling uncontrolled through her since she'd seen Ahrin sitting in that chair. She couldn't hold onto any of them, could barely keep her thoughts straight enough to conceal how utterly thrown she was.

Ahrin continued when Lira said nothing. "Lucinda is used to getting her own way. Most of the Shadowcouncil are. But they understand how necessary you are to their cause, so Lucinda has agreed to a change of approach."

"And this is what, some attempt at an apology?" Lira snapped, finding enough anger to line her voice. It didn't go anywhere near explaining what Ahrin was doing here, but it was a start.

"Oh, I'm sure you remember me well enough not to mistake this for softness, or caving to your pride," Ahrin said, that edge returning. Her midnight-blue eyes glittered with warning. "But you should be treated with respect, and that's what we intend to do. We put you in that room so the brats would know you were held with them, but we got you out as soon as we could."

"We?" Lira froze as the realisation finally settled in, too long in coming. "You're a member of Underground."

Ahrin's eyes darkened even further, the flat look she got in her eyes when she killed. "I'm no mere member, Lira."

Lira stilled, shock and realisation combining to make her stomach curl in on itself so tightly she had to fight not to empty its contents over the floor. "You're the Darkhand."

A smile flickered across Ahrin's face, the anger vanishing as quickly as it had come. "Coppers, I've missed that quick mind of yours."

Lira steeled herself against the warm familiarity in Ahrin's voice. "Lucinda wants something from me, and that's the only reason she's agreed to a change of approach, but I'm no longer interested in what *she* wants. So what I'd like instead of breakfast or a hot bath is to leave this place and go back to Temari Hall."

Ahrin cocked her head. "Is that really what you want?" she asked. "I remember a time when the last thing you wanted was to go to Temari Hall. You insisted on it, over and over."

"You think you know me?" she said flatly. "You don't. Not anymore."

"Unfortunately, I can't allow you to leave just yet." Ahrin sounded genuinely apologetic. "But I'd like you to be as comfortable as possible while you're here, so if there's anything you need, just ask."

"I'm not your crew anymore, Ahrin, not your pet to be looked after. I don't want anything from you." Ahrin's refusal to let her go was to be expected, but she'd wanted to push anyway, just to see how far she could get with this 'new approach'.

Ahrin shrugged, dug in her jacket pocket, pulled out a fresh cigar. She offered it to Lira. "This one's cinnamon. I remember those were your favourite."

Lira ignored the proffered cigar and kept her voice cool, face expressionless. "So your idea of moving up in the world was to join Underground? You abandoned us to be a pawn for the Shadowcouncil?"

"In a manner of speaking."

Her mouth thinned. "Why are the other apprentices here? What does Lucinda want from me?"

Ahrin tucked the cigar back into her pocket. "How about we make a deal? You sit down and eat something with me, and I'll answer a question."

"Fine." Lira crossed to the table, sat down, and began spooning oatmeal into an empty bowl. The first mouthful proved to be delicious —milky oats seasoned with apple and cinnamon. Shrugging, she kept eating. Survival was the priority, and her body needed sustenance. There was no reason to let pride get in the way of a good meal. Once the edge of hunger had worn off, she looked at Ahrin. "Go ahead."

"You already know that Underground has big plans." Ahrin waited for her nod. "What you're doing here has to do with one of the ways in which we will achieve those plans."

Lira couldn't help herself. "There's that 'we' again. How long have you been Underground?"

"A while."

"That's not cryptic at all." Lira spooned up more oatmeal. Her mind turned Ahrin's sudden appearance over and over, a way to distract herself from how floored she was by it. Did Underground know that she and Lira had once known each other? Had Ahrin told them? "Where are the others?"

"Where you left them," Ahrin said simply.

Lira's mind flashed back to that dark room. The restraints. The terror she'd sensed from all of them. "What is she doing to them?"

Ahrin smiled faintly. "I know you, Lira. You don't actually care about them. They'll cut you loose as soon as you're no longer useful to them. Ask me a question you actually want the answer to."

Lira took a breath, thought about the door and the razak bearing down on her. About Athira holding it open. "Careful, Ahrin, you're describing how I feel about *you* there, not them."

Ahrin's face tightened, anger flashing bright in those midnight-blue eyes. The quiet menace she carried with her, always simmering just under the surface, flashed from beneath her masterful control. Ahrin only let it out when she wanted to intimidate, to frighten, a deliberate instinct.

Not for the first time, Lira wondered where she'd learned it. What had happened to the eight-year-old child she'd met on the streets of Dirinan that had made her a ruthless killer even then?

A moment later she shook herself. She was allowing herself to get distracted by the warm room and tasty food. "Another question then. What purpose do they serve?"

"There are reasons I can't tell you everything just yet, but I promise in time you will know everything." She leaned forward, sincere, an unusual look for Ahrin. "We're going to be partners, you and I. We're going to rule them all, like we talked about back in Dirinan. Only on a much grander scale."

Lira laughed, a sound rich with scorn. "You forget I know you too. You don't care about me, or anyone else. You *abandoned* us. All you care about is gaining power or wealth—preferably both—for yourself."

Ahrin didn't flinch. Didn't protest. She held Lira's gaze. "Forget about the past. Think about what's possible for the future."

Lira's gaze narrowed. Ahrin had only ever worked for herself. She accepted no master. "Oh, I understand. Joining Underground has made you delusional. What exactly have they promised you that has you bowing to their commands?"

"I imagine it's the same thing that has *you* bowing to their commands," Ahrin murmured, holding her gaze.

"*I* didn't check my pride at the door. You saw how things went with Lucinda when she tried to control me. Now I'm here in this nice room."

"You came within seconds of death for that little rebellion. Try it again and Lucinda's reason might not win out." Ahrin's voice was blunt, cold.

"Maybe, maybe not," Lira murmured. "But who was the one sent here to make nice with *me*?"

Ahrin's mouth curled. "I'm the Shadowcouncil's right hand. At this moment, you're nothing more than their symbol."

Tension built in the silence that followed. But then Ahrin flashed her a quick, charming smile and sat back in her chair. "How's this for some specific information? Lucinda found me in Dirinan and offered me a position in the group." The grin faded and a loneliness Lira was all too familiar with flickered in Ahrin's midnight blue eyes. "You know as well as I do what life on the streets there is like. Uncompromising. It gives people like us few real choices."

Lira refused to look away, did everything she could to keep her expression impassive. "I'm marked forever by who my grandfather is. You had more options than I ever did."

"You have no idea what you're talking about." Lira's gaze caught Ahrin's fingers unconsciously tracing over the tattoo at her wrist as she spoke. "I had even fewer choices than you. Having nobody to rely on, nobody that's truly yours. You remember. We were always cold, always hungry, always having to plan the next score to keep in Transk's good graces."

"Always looking over our shoulders," Lira finished.

She nodded.

Lira's mouth thinned and she sat back. "That's a clever manipulation. You almost had me. Except you loved that life, Ahrin. And so did I. The only difference between us is that I believed it was real, that it meant something."

The truth hung thick in the air before them, Ahrin's miniscule flinch telling Lira she'd scored another hit, so she pressed her advantage. "We're not the same, remember? I'm at that fancy mage school now, and instead of running your own crew, you're scurrying around at the beck and call of the Shadowcouncil. I'm their symbol for the future —you're their maid."

"I'm their blade." Ahrin's voice was tight, cold. "And don't think I don't know you're manipulating me too."

"Since when have you ever cared about the mission of Underground?"

"Since they gave me power." Ahrin shrugged, the anger gone as quick as it had come. "I'd be thinking the same if I were in your shoes, but what I said was all truth, Lira. I swear now that I will never lie to you. Not about anything."

Lira didn't want to play games, not with Ahrin. It was exhausting. She just wanted to figure out what was going on and then get herself out. "What do you want from me?"

"For now, to stay here and talk with me. I'll tell you what I can."

"And then?"

That intensity came back to Ahrin's face, the kind that had always drawn Lira in like a moth to flame. It did again now, like no time had passed, despite how she fought against it. "Then I want you and I to take on the world together."

"Why me?"

"Because, like me, you're extraordinary."

A knock came before she could manage a response to that, and

Ahrin rose to walk over to the door. It was made from thick wood, and when she pulled it open, Lira spotted the brackets for bars on the other side. Definitely still a prisoner then.

There was a murmured conversation she couldn't hear, then Ahrin turned her way. "Think about what I said. I'll be back soon."

Lira settled into her chair, staring at nothing.

"You're extraordinary. Like me."

Lira's eyes closed, head tipping all the way back in a useless attempt to stop the tears welling behind her eyelids from falling. For the first time, she felt a hint of doubt about what she'd agreed to do for the Mage Council, and about her ability to succeed.

Being a member of Underground had just become *a lot* more complicated.

CHAPTER 30

E ven after the door closed behind Ahrin and the sound of her footsteps had faded from hearing, Lira sat and stared.

Ahrin was here.

She was a member of Underground. Lira leaned forward in her chair, pressing a hand against her eyes and trying to recover some focus. Despite the fact she'd slept, she felt wrung out and hollow. No matter who Ahrin had once been to her, no matter *how* it had happened, she was now the Darkhand of the Shadowcouncil.

Lucinda was a foe Lira didn't fool herself into thinking she could easily outmanoeuvre. But with Ahrin at her side... even though Lira's fear of the girl had long since gone, she knew how ruthless, how capable, how clever she was.

Her hands were still shaking. She clasped them together, trying to stop it. The experience back in that room, strapped to the table, had left her raw. And Ahrin's appearance... she took a deep breath. She just had to centre herself again, find that thrill, the love of danger that had kept her alive so far. Use it to paint over the fear and vulnerability like she used to.

Survival was the priority. Always.

Lira leapt to her feet and began a meticulous search of the room for any potential weapons or an escape route. She quickly found her mage staff lying neatly at the end of the bed she'd been in, but no other obvious weapons had been left lying around.

Next she studied the windows. They were locked, but even if she used her magic to unlock them and risked drawing the attention of any razak outside, there was no way to get through the bars on the other side. She lingered there anyway, staring out into overgrown grass.

Mist still wreathed the grounds beyond the windows, making the light dim and murky. She narrowed her eyes at that. Natural mist usually didn't linger this thick for so long, at least not in her experience.

A mage must be behind it. Probably one of the men dogging Lucinda's heels in that oddly reverential manner. It was a useful skill to keep a place hidden, both for those inside and out. That meant at the very least, they were facing Lucinda's paralysis ability, a mage who could control the razak, and a mage with the ability to affect weather.

And Ahrin's elite killing skills.

She huffed a breath at a sudden realisation—they no longer had to wonder who'd killed those Shiven guards on the front gate of Temari Hall. Ahrin had been part of the kidnapping crew. She'd probably led it. The ache in Lira's chest intensified at the thought, and she was helpless against the force of it as it washed through her.

A deep breath, and she let it fade, instead focusing her thoughts. She'd been lazy in her spying, taking one look at the people gathered in the tailor's cellar in Karonan and deciding they were a ragged group of hopeless types from the fringes of society. She hadn't bothered to look deeper and see what was really going on. She'd assumed if the Shadowcouncil were any more organised or capable, their members wouldn't be growing so restless at the lack of action. That they'd be doing more. She'd been wrong.

She wouldn't make any more mistakes like that.

Returning to the bed, she buckled on her staff's harness and slid her staff into it, feeling instantly more comfortable at its reassuring weight settling down her back. Then she paced the room, thinking over her conversation with Ahrin, trying to find some advantage she could use. She had to admit Ahrin's words had had a ring of truth about them...and it didn't hurt that Lira had long since learned to tell when Ahrin was lying. Still, something about it didn't feel right.

Ahrin was an orphan like Lira. She might have been a crew leader in Dirinan, but theirs had been unimportant in comparison to the numbers and wealth Transk and the Revel Kings commanded, even though their ambitions had been big. There'd been nothing notable or special about them. Ahrin had wanted more territory, more numbers, more wealth, but she'd always, *always*, insisted on her independence. She'd refused multiple offers to be subsumed into larger, more successful crews.

Why had Underground picked Ahrin, of all people? She didn't have any... a cold sensation settled in Lira's chest as realisation snapped through her. The hooded figure in the corner watching while Lucinda questioned her. Lira had been certain that whoever it was had magic. They'd vibrated with intensity that spoke of power. She'd seen it a hundred times in the more powerful students at Temari Hall who hadn't yet learned how to control their raw magic.

It had been Ahrin. That was why Lira's mind had kept returning to the hooded figure. She'd known deep down who had been standing in that corner staring at her.

Is that why she'd left Lira and the crew? Because her own magic had broken out and she didn't need Lira anymore? Had Underground learned of it somehow and recruited her with promises of power?

Bitterness burned in her chest at the thought of Ahrin abandoning them for Underground. She was still standing in the middle of the floor, wrestling with the ache in her chest, when the door opened to admit Ahrin.

Lira waited only until she had closed it behind her before she challenged, "You have magic."

"Yes." Ahrin didn't seem bothered or taken aback. "But I'm a little different to you and your council mages."

Lira flinched, stung and unable to hide it. For years she'd told Ahrin that she didn't want to be a mage, that she had no desire to go to Temari and join the council, despite Ahrin's constant urging. And yet now Ahrin threw those words at her like they were something lesser, something contemptable.

Ahrin caught the look on her face and her jaw tightened. "Don't pretend they didn't welcome the scion of Shakar with open arms at Temari Hall, Lira. That you didn't fit in there instantly, that you haven't even thought about me or Dirinan or our crew once since you first stepped foot in there."

"You're right," she said coldly, the words coming out before she could stop them, aiming to wound as Ahrin had wounded her. "I haven't. I should have gone earlier instead of wasting my time with you."

It was Ahrin's turn to flinch, but her response was so quickly hidden by a casual shrug that Lira wasn't sure if she'd really seen it. "I told you the mage world was where you belonged, didn't I? You should have listened to me all along."

"Were you hiding your magic from me?" Lira was rapidly losing all the focus she'd regained in Ahrin's absence, but some stubborn part of her needed to know this. "You're a year older than me, you should have broken out before I did. Is that why you left? You didn't need us."

Another shrug. "You saw what I did with the forest?"

Ahrin had been the one using the trees against her in the forest. Lira refused to dwell on the shock that rippled through her at that revelation, she needed all of her wits about her for this conversation. "So you won't lie to me but you'll completely avoid answering my questions?"

"You're quick." A wicked smile replaced the anger, reminding Lira that Ahrin didn't feel things like she did. She could fake emotions impeccably, but they didn't knock her off course like they did most people. Lira had fought hard during her time at Temari to learn that level of control but now it was nowhere to be found. She hurt too much.

Lira took a breath. She was allowing Ahrin to distract her. Her focus had to be on getting to the others, killing the razak, escaping this rotted place. "Your magic can what, affect plants and trees?"

"I can control living vegetation, yes. My range extends to every plant and tree and bush in roughly a mile wide radius around this place."

Lira hid her surprise. If Ahrin was telling the truth, she had a significant amount of power. "Interesting. And what exactly is different about you from us council mages?"

Ahrin's smirk returned, her eyes lighting up. "I can also do this."

Lira's gaze went to the table by the fire as several of the plates and dishes lifted into the air. Her chest tightened with a tangled mix of envy and bitterness and shock that was impossible to push away. When she spoke, her voice was strangled. "You're a mage of the higher order."

"No. I told you, I'm different."

Lira's gaze shifted from the table back to Ahrin. "Mages either have one ability, or they're a mage of the higher order." In her shock, she was parroting what she'd learned at Temari. Taliath were the only exception to that rule, but then there was considerable debate over whether Taliath were actually mages or something different entirely.

"Ah." Ahrin winked. "But I was born with no mage power."

The questions wanted to pour out of her, but she held herself back and summoned a snappish tone. "If you think I'm going to stand here and fight to pry answers out of you just to make you feel like you're in control, then you're sorely mistaken. I'm not your second anymore, Ahrin."

Surprisingly, Ahrin laughed, blue eyes turning bright, the sound genuine and unforced. "Fair enough. Have a seat, and I'll tell you all about it."

Ahrin took her hand before Lira could stop her, tangling their fingers and leading her to the table by the fire. While Lira sat, she crouched down to toss a few more logs on it, then busied herself tidying the breakfast dishes. Then, with a touch of magic, she sent the neat pile floating over to land on the ground by the door.

"Quit trying to impress me," Lira said, surly now. "It's not working."

"You sure about that?" Ahrin smirked and pulled the second chair closer to Lira, *too* close, then sat down. "In short, the Shadowcouncil have discovered a way to give someone mage power. In some instances, more than one ability."

"You're saying they *gave* you magic?" Lira asked slowly, not sure she'd heard correctly. It was insane... but it would partly explain why Ahrin was with Underground. After all, she'd always wanted power. And magic was a heady form of it.

"Exactly. They gave me the ability over vegetation first. Then the telekinesis." Ahrin smiled. "My body apparently takes very well to the process."

The process. Something about the way she said it sent shivers down Lira's spine. "And what did you have to do in return for the magic they gave you? I doubt it came free."

"Nothing does," Ahrin agreed. "I agreed to be a test subject. There was no guarantee it would work when they first started testing on humans. It could have killed me."

Lira couldn't stop her indrawn breath of shock. "Ahrin, why would you risk that?"

She shrugged. "Was it any less risky being a crew leader in Dirinan? Especially a crew leader with aspirations to take down Transk."

It was a fair point, but still... Lira's foreboding deepened. "And what exactly is the process?"

"That's something I can't tell you yet, I'm sorry. And to be honest, I don't quite understand the ins and outs of it." Some of the edge came back to her voice. "I haven't had your fancy Temari education after all."

She forced herself not to bite at the taunt and concentrated on what she'd just heard instead. "That's why the others were taken and brought here, isn't it?" she said. "They're being experimented on in some way?"

"Yes."

"Why them? They already have magic." Lira's mind raced. "Do subjects with existing mage ability help somehow? But why take such high profile mage students? Why not the poorer ones, the ones without powerful families who will tear apart the world looking for them?"

Ahrin leaned closer. "I love your mind," she murmured. "I can't believe what a tool the council has in you, and they haven't even bothered to notice. You should be a warrior mage already, Lira. I've heard about how skilled at combat you are. How you've bested every student at Temari."

Lira tried not to let the heartfelt words in. To let them *draw* her in. Even though it was the first time anyone had said anything like that to her. Despite herself, Lira's voice was just as low. "You threw me away too, Ahrin."

"You weren't a tool to me." Ahrin's breath was warm on her face, her blue eyes gone so dark they were almost black.

"Yes, I was," Lira hissed, pulling away and ignoring the effort it took. "And had you waited, like, a whole extra day, I could have been an even more powerful tool. But you decided that your own power was worth more than me, than your crew. So don't talk to me about how the Mage Council treats me. You don't get a say."

"Forget about the Mage Council, Lira—"

"And join Underground instead? I've already done that. I'm not a fool. I know how the council thinks of me—why do you think I let the Shadowcouncil recruit me?" Lira snapped, desperately trying to regather her poise and move into the offensive. "Tell me, do they know about us?"

A wicked, knowing smile spread over Ahrin's face. "What about us?"

"That we know each other." Lira held her look without flinching. "Is that why they recruited you? Because of me? That's it, isn't it? You're not special to them, Ahrin. *I* am."

A cold shutter came down over Ahrin's face and she sat back, causing a ripple of triumph to go through Lira. "They know nothing about our past. And if they learned of it, they'd kill me."

Lira froze. "Are you serious?"

"The Shadowcouncil, Lucinda, they're powerful and well-resourced," she said. "Their methods are harsh and ruthless. But that doesn't matter. Because all you and I have to do is use them to achieve what we want."

"Which is what, exactly?"

"No more stares, no more disrespect, just because we're poor or because we fight to survive by whatever means necessary. No assumptions about who we are because of who our relatives are. Underground can give us the power that we deserve."

"You sound like my grandfather," Lira said drily. "No wonder they recruited you."

Something unnameable rippled over Ahrin's face, and again her fingers brushed absently over her tattoo. Then the look vanished and she smiled. "Tell me this, Lira, am I wrong to say that you're bitterly disappointed you're not a mage of the higher order like him, that all you'll ever be is a telekinetic mage? I remember how badly you wanted that."

As well as Lira knew Ahrin, could read when she was lying, so Ahrin knew Lira. She saw the answer written all over Lira's face. She couldn't hide it quickly enough. The yearning was too much a part of who she was.

Ahrin's hand reached out to take hers, her thumb sliding back and forth over her knuckles. "I can give you that power. Extra abilities. As many as you want."

Lira's heart leapt with hope. She tried to shove it back down, to tell herself that she couldn't trust Ahrin or Underground, that they certainly had ulterior motives.

But did that matter? With the type of power Ahrin was talking about she didn't need Underground. She could destroy them without having to waste time creeping about to secret meetings and writing reports to Dawn A'ndreas. She could be done with it all and move on. Get her revenge on Lucinda by destroying Underground and rise rapidly up the ranks of the council as a result.

Ahrin pressed. "The Mage Council would never give you more power. You know that. Even if the Shadowcouncil handed over the secret to it, they would deny it to you, Lira, because of who you are."

Lira smiled wryly, trying to pretend she was unaffected, trying to remember she was supposed to be a member of Underground. "Save the recruitment pitch. I already signed up, remember?"

"Then why hesitate?" Ahrin's intensity was back. "Why mouth off to Lucinda instead of just accepting she's in charge for now? Take what they're offering you. Use it to be great."

"You said it could have killed you. I'm not quite stupid enough to offer my neck up to Lucinda like you did." Lira cleared her throat, fighting a losing battle to stay clear-headed.

"Really?" A smile teased at Ahrin's mouth. "Because I remember how much you loved danger, how you got off on the thrill of risking your life. We both know that's exactly how this makes you feel."

"And you told me I had to control it." Lira tried to sound firm, but it came out as more of a whisper.

"I'm not telling you that anymore. I'm telling you to embrace it. Let it make you powerful." Ahrin held her gaze.

Lira wavered, and looked away. She wanted it badly, more than she would admit to herself. But if the council found out she had more mage abilities... they probably wouldn't harm her, but they'd be deeply suspicious of her. Could she argue that she'd been forced into it to maintain her cover as a spy?

Did it *matter* what the council thought?

No, it didn't.

"Say yes, Lira. I won't force it on you. This is your choice."

She met Ahrin's eyes. Nodded. "Yes."

Intensity lit up Ahrin's face, and her fingers tightened around Lira's. Lira started; she hadn't even realised she was still holding her hand. "Good," the Darkhand murmured.

She cleared her throat. "What comes next?"

Ahrin reached into her pocket. "This will sting, but then you won't feel a thing."

Lira held that gaze, refusing to look away as Ahrin lifted a hand to slide around Lira's neck, drawing her closer, ever closer. Then she paused. "We'll have to put you back in that room with the others when we're done, so you're there when they wake up. But it won't be too long, and you won't come to any further harm, I promise you."

"Do it," Lira said, the excitement uncurling in her stomach and spreading out through muscle and bone, hot and seductive and *alive*. She was going to be more powerful than all of them.

"See you on the other side," Ahrin breathed. Her mouth was so close to Lira's she could feel her warm breath on her cheek. Her heart kicked hard against her ribs. In that same moment, Lira felt a sharp sting in her neck. Seconds later, she swayed forward, dizzy.

The last thing she remembered was Ahrin catching her and holding her close.

CHAPTER 31

When Lira woke next, her eyes were closed, and she wasn't quite... *awake*... but she was conscious enough to hear voices. They were oddly dissonant, both close and far away at the same time, but recognisable.

"Well done, Darkhand." Lucinda's voice, controlled and even.

"I told you I could deliver her without protest."

"I didn't think you'd succeed. She's more stubborn than I'd expected."

"Lira is on your side, but she won't tolerate disrespect. All you need to do is appeal to what she really wants and she'll follow you anywhere." Ahrin's voice was lazy, cool. Oozing with confidence.

"It's interesting that you've learned so much about her in so short a time."

Ahrin scoffed. "I'm your Darkhand for a reason. I deliver results. Have I failed you yet?"

"No, not yet." A pause then. "She has no idea of the potential consequences?"

"You told me to convince her to submit willingly to this, not to tell her the truth." Ahrin sounded almost bored. "She knows it's risky, but not the extent of what you're trying to do here."

Lira shifted, the words and voices processing too slowly through her thoughts for her to really follow them, understand them properly. Whatever drug they'd given her was clinging too strongly to her mind. But unease spread through her anyway, strong and viscous, setting her heart thudding. Whatever was happening was wrong, bad. The strength of her dread was enough that she was able to momentarily force her eyes open.

Her vision was blurry, but Lucinda's face was surprisingly close, leaning over Lira on the table, studying her. There was triumph in that gaze, the emotion so strong it leaked through her perfectly controlled exterior. Triumph and satisfaction.

The dread clamped down tightly over Lira, sucking her breath away.

No. This was all wrong. Whatever this was, it wasn't about giving her magic. Lucinda had lied… Ahrin had lied… There was another purpose to having her on this table. It was clear in the triumph glittering in Lucinda's eyes. She'd wanted something from Lira, and now she felt she'd gotten it.

Lira fought, but her limbs were sluggish, slow to respond. Lucinda's face moved away from her field of vision. "She needs another dose, I think she's waking up."

A prick in her arm and the sluggishness got worse, her limbs heavier. Her eyes slid closed.

Blackness returned.

No, no, no, no.

SHE THOUGHT there might have been pain, later; burning, fiery pain that seared every muscle in her body. She thought she might have screamed. Screamed until her voice turned hoarse and then died altogether.

But maybe she was dreaming. Everything was so unclear. Hazy. Doused in orange and fiery heat.

She thought it might have gone on for hours. The pain and the screaming. The furnace burning in her muscles and tearing through her body. Sweat slicking her skin. More agonising pain. Her body thrashing on the table.

But maybe it never happened at all.

When Lira woke again, she was back in that room. The bars held her down, pressed her firmly against the wood of the table beneath her, draining her magic. Like before, she couldn't move an inch.

And everything was dark, pure blackness.

Ahrin.

Had she really seen Ahrin, talked to her? Had she ever been in that warm room with the comfortable bed? What about the other room, the drugs, the pain? Lira blinked, trying to work out whether those memories had been real, or a hallucination brought on by the drugged smoke. It was all so faint, like wisps of mist that disappeared when you tried to grab hold of them.

The panic descended again.

She'd fought for what felt like days now. Thrown herself without hesitation at every obstacle that had come up, determined to fight her way through, even though she had no real idea what was happening. Had refused to back down. But now she was exhausted, drugged, emotionally wrung out. Bound to a table and unable to move, her magic inaccessible.

She didn't know how much fight she had left.

Deep down, she just wanted the nightmare to be over.

She wanted to be back in her bed at Temari Hall. Where she'd felt properly safe after years of not knowing safety. Where she'd been warm after years of not knowing warmth. Where she'd refused to acknowledge either of those things because deep down she hadn't wanted to give in. She had tied herself into knots to become one of them, but at the same time had been too *stubborn* to let them accept her, welcome her as one of their own. Too stubborn because she hadn't known how to do otherwise.

She just wanted *something* to ease the constant aching loneliness inside that had been there since the night her mother died. She'd filled the void with the thrilling danger of her life in Dirinan, then ignored it by training and studying incessantly at Temari Hall despite how bored and restless she was.

But no matter what she did it had never gone away and now it rose to swallow her whole. Because she didn't have the strength left to bury it or ignore it. Ahrin's calculated betrayal had torn away every last shred of resilience she had. And now there was nothing but emptiness.

Then Garan's furious voice tore through the darkness in an angry bellow, and she started, breaking momentarily free of the sinking blackness of despair. Her head ached, a sharp throbbing. Was it just her broken nose causing it, or had that room really happened... or...

Wait, Garan's voice. She wasn't alone in here. She—

"You awake over there, Lira?" Fari's voice asked.

"Yeah." Her voice was raspy, and it hurt to talk. *The memory of screaming in agony until her voice turned hoarse.* "How long have I been out?"

"Not sure. I only just woke up," the girl responded.

"We all did," Garan answered, voice thick with fury.

"Is everyone here?" Lira shifted, trying to get comfortable under the restraints. It was an impossible endeavour. Tears spilled silently down her cheeks.

"All but Athira," Lorin said quietly. He sounded beaten down too, like whatever had happened had worn out his haughtiness, his proud dignity.

"Has everyone been taken out of the room?" Lira asked.

"I don't think so." Tarion's voice was soft but warm, as if he could sense the ragged edge underlying her words. "It's hard to tell because they keep putting us to sleep, but so far I think it's only been Athira."

Relief tried to shiver through her. Maybe that room hadn't happened. Maybe she hadn't seen that look of triumph on Lucinda's face, hadn't felt the sickening realisation that she'd allowed Ahrin to manipulate her into doing what Underground wanted.

No. Lira took a long, deep breath and concentrated on the details. The hooded mage standing in the corner when she'd first spoken to Lucinda, the forest trying to stop her going the wrong way after she escaped the cart, and most damningly to Lira... the dead Shiven guards back at Temari. The efficient way they'd been taken down was Ahrin's hallmark.

Ahrin was here, with Underground, and she was the Darkhand.

Ahrin had manipulated Lira into handing herself willingly over to Lucinda. Something had been done to her and she couldn't remember it. Her breathing grew short, and the panic was about to win when Garan spoke again, almost making her cry out with relief.

"We need a new plan, I think." Garan tried to sound strong, but his voice wavered too.

"The only time we're free of these restraints is when they take one of us," Tarion said. "That's our only play."

Lira fought for control. Even if she felt hopeless, despairing, she wouldn't give in to it. Not Lira Astor. That would never be her... *that* was something she could hold onto, no matter what. "They haven't always been accurate with their doses, either that or the drug has inconsistent results," she said. "We wait for the moment one of us wakes early outside this room, we break free, then come back here to let the others out."

"That could be a long time coming, Spider." Fari's voice trembled.

"Then we hold on, we stay strong, and we wait however long it takes," Lorin insisted. "We are mages. We can do that."

Fari sucked in a breath. "My family does insist on calling me ridiculously stubborn."

"My father is known for his stubbornness," Garan added.

"As is mine." Tarion actually sounded like he was smiling. "Mama yells it at him *all* the time."

"And you've been stubbornly refusing to melt under my dazzlingly charming offers of friendship for years, Lira, so I think you win the stubborn prize in this room," Garan joked.

Lira relaxed at the warmth in his tone, the teasing that didn't have an edge. "That's the plan, then."

In the following silence, a slightly lighter one now, Lira made a promise to herself. Despite their differences, despite who her grandfather was, it had become clear that amidst the worst thing that had ever happened to them in their lives, these mage students considered her one of them. And she was. She was a mage. Born with magic, just like them.

So if she was the one to wake first, she would fight, and she would come back for them. And they would leave this place together. She would make sure they got out safely. And then she would tell Underground she'd done it to maintain her cover, just like Lucinda claimed she wanted.

Even if Lira now knew differently. That they wanted far more from her.

She would tell them whatever they needed to hear so she could remain with the group, continue to spy and feed information to the Mage Council, as long as she needed to in order to gather enough to bring them down. They'd used monsters to hunt her and strapped her to a table, making her weak again in a way she hadn't been since she was a small child.

She would destroy them for it. No matter who was part of the group.

As the new plan solidified in her head, Lira's breathing calmed and her panic eased. It was an aspirational plan, the chances of success slim, but those had always been her favourite types of plans.

But all thoughts of escaping vanished from her head when the door swung open and light flooded the room. She blinked, eyes watering at the sudden brightness, but she forced herself to look towards it anyway, to try and make out any detail of who was coming in. She told herself it was to learn more about her captors. Not to see if Ahrin was amongst them.

By the time she'd blinked the blurriness away, she could make out a table being wheeled in. Athira lay on it. Her skin was pale, and purple shadows filled the space under her eyes, but her chest moved. Shallowly.

How long had Lira been gone? Panic clawed back up through her chest, merciless. She couldn't bear the not knowing. By the time she had herself under a modicum of control, the door had slammed closed, leaving them in darkness.

"Athira?" Garan called out. "Athira, can you hear me?"

Nothing.

"Fari, can you tell if she's okay?" Worry poured from his words.

Lira twisted, trying to turn towards them, not that there was any point in this darkness. She bit down hard on her bleeding lip again, the sharp pain halting the panic and despair.

"I... I can't access my magic." A grunt of pain sounded as Fari tried to move. "I don't know. I don't know."

"She was breathing!" Lira shouted, seeking to calm the panic in the room before it got out of control. Before it sent hers spiralling back out of control too. "I saw her chest moving when she was brought in."

"So did I," Tarion added. "She's okay."

For now. The words glimmered in the air. Unsaid but there nonetheless.

"To be clear." Lira's mind couldn't stop worrying on this point. "Nobody else remembers being wheeled out of here? Nobody saw... me... or anyone else being taken?"

"Just Athira," Garan confirmed. The others chimed in agreement.

"It's probably deliberate." In the darkness, where nobody could seem him, Tarion's voice was stronger, more confident. "To keep us afraid, on edge. There's a purpose to all of this, even if we can't see it."

Fear... that word played on her mind, nagging at her. While they'd made mistakes with their drug dosage, Lucinda had clearly been in control of the situation this entire time. "What if fear is the point?" She spoke aloud without meaning to.

"What do you mean?" Garan asked instantly.

Lira hesitated, debating whether to tell them what she'd learned from Ahrin. "This is all some kind of experiment, right? It has to be," she said eventually. Of that much she was sure. "They're testing something."

"Did Lucinda tell you that?" Fari asked.

"Not directly, but it fits with what's happening." She hesitated again. "Why the razak and the mind games? I think maybe they wanted us afraid, *really* afraid, and uncertain, lost, confused. Maybe that's part of the experiment."

A moment's silence, then, "My healing ability is strongest with blood," Fari said. "I knew I'd broken out when I sensed my little brother almost slice his finger off cleaning Da's sword without permis-

302

sion. I'm not great with much else, and although Master A'ndreas has endless patience, I'm really close to failing—"

"Fari," Garan interrupted gently.

"Right, sorry. My point is... and I'm a bit hazy on the details... emotions can affect our bodies, the makeup of our blood, particularly when we're under high levels of stress. If Lira is right, then these crazy nuts holding us might need that stress response as a variable in their experiments."

"There's a not-at-all terrifying thought." Garan groaned.

Lira thought it made a lot of sense... *if* Ahrin had been telling the truth, then maybe the process of 'giving' people magic was more successful when the subjects were afraid? Or Underground was testing to see if that was the case. "I think we should also assume that once they're finished experimenting on us they probably won't let us leave here alive."

Nobody replied to that, but the fear in the room spiked.

Garan said determinedly, "Let's think of a better plan. I won't let them keep doing this to us."

Lira found herself nodding. "To do that, we first need to figure out how to get out of these metal bars that drain our magic," she said.

"Drain our magic?" Lorin asked, sounding puzzled.

"I think Lira's right. Don't you feel tireder than usual, weaker?" Fari asked. "I started suspecting it before they put us to sleep."

"If we got free of the bars, we could rush them next time they open the door." Lorin spoke, fierceness edging his voice. "I could melt them all with a single burst—I've been practicing larger concussion balls."

Maybe she was delirious from her head injury. Maybe she was just exhausted and unable to raise her defences. But Lira found herself *liking* Lorin. Liking how unwavering his voice was, how unhesitating his offer to fight for them was. He was fifteen years old, a raw initiate with barely any training, and he wasn't letting his fear defeat him. It impressed her more than she wanted to admit.

So did the others, if she was being brutally honest with herself. Ugh, she must still be under the influence of the drugs they'd given her.

"But then we'd have to deal with the razak no doubt lurking

outside, plus the ones that would come rushing the moment we used magic," Lira pointed out.

"Such a naysayer, Spider," Garan said, but there was a smile in his voice.

"Just covering all the bases," she countered.

"So we get out of these bars, fight the razak and somehow get clear, and then what?" Fari asked.

There was a moment's silence. "Tarion, what do you think?" Lira asked. If nothing else, she'd learned Tarion had a sharp mind despite his reluctance to speak up.

"Garan was right before. If we can kill or slip past the razak outside, the mages become a manageable problem, especially if there are only five of them," he said in his quiet way. "But the larger issue is getting out of the forest surrounding this place. We don't know where it is or how far from a main town we are. And using the road would mean we'd have to make sure *all* the razak were dead, because they'd catch us far too quickly."

"It has to be a mage controlling the forest," Lira said, skirting as close to the truth as she was willing to go. "The primary goal should be to take out that mage, as well as the mage controlling the razak, during our escape." She forced the words out, ignored the fact she was talking about killing Ahrin, and ploughed on. "But that doesn't guarantee the monsters won't still chase us."

The relief that shimmered through the darkness at Lira's words was almost palpable.

"Okay, then we go back to our earlier plan and send Lira at the queen monster then?" Fari joked.

They all chuckled. But it wasn't a resentful, uneasy chuckle, a way of staving off fear. It was a teasing laugh, like Lira had heard a hundred times over in the rooms and corridors of Temari Hall. Just never directed at her. She wasn't sure how to feel about that. Before she could work it out, figure out how to respond, they'd moved on.

"Lorin, tell us more about bee colonies," Tarion asked once the laughter died away. "Can they go for long periods without water?"

"No. They're built underground, or in trees. The queens are buried the deepest inside the hive, in a warm, safe location."

Another brief silence, and then, "Lira, Tarion, you said you were held in an underground dungeon?" Garan's commanding voice was back.

Lira took pity on Tarion this time. "The air shaft we escaped out of had a steady upward incline and we emerged on the ground floor, so yes, the cells must have been underground. We both thought they'd been recently dug out, not part of the original structure."

"Maybe they weren't just dug out for cells." Hope leapt in Fari's voice. "Maybe they needed to dig out a home for a razak queen."

"If she's here at all," Lira cautioned. "I think we're relying too heavily on the bee analogy."

"Even so, it's our best option," Garan said firmly. "We manage to get out of these bars and this room? We head underground and hunt the queen."

"To join Lira on the naysayer team, a queen is likely to be bigger and nastier than its hive workers, and we'd have to kill it fast, before the hive senses danger and rushes to protect her." Tarion spoke quietly. "Not to mention Dasta figuring out what's going on and bringing Lucinda."

Even Lira shuddered at that thought.

"Then we kill it quickly. Once the razak are gone, we take out whatever mage gets in our path on our way back up," Lorin added fiercely. "We take horses from the stables, ride out via the road. And we don't look back."

They would also have to hope Lucinda didn't have more mages stationed around the place. That they weren't more powerful and skilled than five mage apprentices and an initiate. Lira counted off the potential issues instinctively. "Yes," she said, biting her tongue instead of saying any of it aloud. It was the best plan they had.

The hopeful words, a detailed plan of action, sustained them for a few moments. But then the darkness began to creep back in, along with the quiet. Lira's panic, temporarily at bay, began forcing its way into her consciousness again. She pressed her eyes closed, all muscles tensing as she fought it.

She might have to kill Ahrin. The knowledge was a dead weight in her chest. She didn't shy from it, understood it to be necessary. Ahrin had placed herself in Lira's way. And Ahrin knew better than anyone that Lira would always fight to survive. But killing Ahrin... despite everything... it might break her.

When the door opened again, sending more light shafting into the room, they all jumped. This time Fari was taken out. No words were spoken by their captors. No response to any of their entreaties. The scent of vanilla smoke seeped through the room a few moments later.

And then she was asleep.

CHAPTER 32

Lira was still blinking back to alertness when the door opened. Only this time it was opened quietly, and a blurry figure stood framed in the light from the corridor beyond. She blinked again, trying to clear her vision as the figure entered the room, closing the door just enough to let a bit of light through.

"Who's there?" Garan demanded blearily.

"Shush!" Fari's voice quieted him. Lira's heart leapt when she recognised the girl's voice. "We don't have much time. I used magic and the razak are probably already on their way."

Lira lurched upwards, forgetting in her relief about the bars. The breath whooshed out of her when her chest slammed against them and she swore in pain. Fari made straight for Garan, quick fingers unlatching the bars. No panic. No fear. Just steady movements. "How did you get free?" he asked her, his whole body rigid with anticipation as she worked.

"Explanations later."

Garan let out a soft groan of relief as he rolled off the table, almost falling when his legs buckled. Then he was up and making straight for the door to keep watch. After Garan, Fari made a beeline for Lira.

Freeing the strongest mages first—it showed impressive presence of mind. "What did you do?" Lira demanded.

"Knocked out the two men in the room with me. It's a basic healing technique, one of the first things I learned." Fari squinted at the catch of her bars, then started to work. "I'm not great with skill or book learning, but I do have a lot of raw power. I think that's the only reason Master A'ndreas hasn't given up on me."

Lira had gone rigid, the desperate desire to be free roping through her. If Fari didn't hurry she was going to scream with the strength of it. She needed to be out, out, out. Seconds later, a clicking noise sounded and then Fari was heaving the bar across Lira's chest upwards.

The moment the pressure lifted Lira gave a sobbing gasp of relief and rolled off the table, like Garan almost falling when her legs buckled under her. Her magic surged back through her and she had to close her eyes with the force of it.

It spread through her, heady and strong and soothing every rigid muscle. She breathed it in, revelled in the sensation. Let it drown the despair and fear. No matter what, she would always have this, her magic.

Fari moved to free Lorin and Tarion, while Lira joined Garan in his watchful position. From the door, one dark corridor stretched directly ahead, while a second—this one lit with torches—headed away to the right. Both were empty. It had been daylight when Lira had spoken to Ahrin... and though it was hard to tell as no windows were immediately visible, it *felt* like night had fallen again. Had just the single day passed, or more? A shiver trembled down her spine.

"Were they far from here, the men you knocked out?" Lira asked Fari. She needed to know what the situation was before they did anything. Fari had used magic against her captors, which meant the razak could be already on their way.

"No, the second door on the right down the lit hall." Fari seemed to understand what Lira was getting at. "We should hurry—razak aside, I don't know how long they'll be out."

Another click sounded and Lorin was free. Waving Fari to Athira's table, he moved to Tarion's and began working on the bars. Fari paused at Athira's table. The apprentice had yet to regain consciousness. "What should I do?" she asked.

"Can you wake her?" Garan asked.

Fari nodded, placed a palm over the girl's forehead. But seconds later she removed it. "Something other than a drug is keeping her under, and I can't tell what. I'm sorry."

"We'll carry her then." Garan spoke as Tarion was already heading for the table. Tarion lifted Athira with ease once Fari had unlocked the bars, gently slinging her over his shoulder. Lorin hovered nearby, his frequent glances indicating he was ready to step in and help Tarion if needed.

"You saw nobody else while you were in the room?" Lira pressed, thinking of Ahrin and Lucinda. "Were the men Lucinda's mages, the ones we've already dealt with?"

"Nobody else, and I don't know, I haven't seen them like you and Tarion. I woke up, saw them hovering over me, and lashed out before I could even think what I was doing. Can we go now please?" Fari was on edge, hopping from foot to foot. Her urgency was infectious.

Lorin straightened his shoulders. "We're heading down, right, follow the plan to find the queen razak?"

Tarion glanced at Lira. "The kitchen storeroom?"

So he'd seen the trapdoor in the floor too. The reinforced wood and sturdy lock suddenly made a lot more sense. She nodded. She'd yet to see any other obvious way underground during all her creeping about.

"You lead the way, Spider." Garan gestured. "We're right behind you."

They slipped out the door, quiet as possible, ears straining for any rattling sounds. Lira glanced left and right, hesitating before starting down the dark corridor and away from the unconscious mages. They needed to clear the area before the razak inevitably showed up, which could be seconds away.

Yet...

She thought over what Fari had said about not knowing how long her captors would be out. It was clear what needed to be done, a simple matter of survival. "You all head away from the light, and I'll follow in a bit." Lira shifted her gaze to Garan. "If we make sure those men *stay* incapacitated, then that's two less to deal with once we kill the razak queen and make our escape."

A beat of silence filled the torchlit hall as the meaning of Lira's words sunk in.

"You're going to kill them." Lorin was the one to say it aloud.

"Yes." It was the best way to improve their chances of survival. "Go," she urged. "I'll follow as quickly I can."

"You don't have to do this just because you're Lira Astor," Tarion said unexpectedly.

"Yes, I do," she said simply, mouth twisting. "Best the grand-daughter of Shakar do the cold-blooded murdering, right?"

Lorin stepped forward. "I will help you."

Fari let out a breath, dark eyes full of concern. "Maybe nobody has to do it. We can just leave them there. We've got a good head start."

"And what if one of them has an ability like Lucinda's? If we take them out now, then we only have her and one other to deal with. One might even be Dasta. Those odds are survivable," Lira snapped. "There's no time to argue this. Go, find the queen. I'll follow. Lorin, you too. This doesn't need two people."

"Lira..." Garan was clearly torn. He knew it was necessary, but he couldn't make himself volunteer for it. "I... thank you."

She turned and walked away before there could be any more ridiculous sentiment, moving into a swift jog down the lit corridor. She didn't have far to go before she reached the open doorway on the right that Fari had mentioned.

She inched carefully inside. The space was large, long, and rectangular. Warm, too, and more brightly lit than any room she'd seen so far. Lira noted all those details almost instantaneously, her practiced gaze landing next on the table Fari must have been lying on. It stood near the centre of the room, a single bar hanging down one side, covered in a dark sheet.

The two mages—Jora and another man she didn't recognise—lay sprawled on the floor near the table, eyes closed, chests rising and falling slowly. A curtain hung across the middle of the space, opaque enough she couldn't see what was beyond it.

Memory flashed, hazy with drugs... writing on a table... someone removing her restraints because she was thrashing too wildly. Lira blinked, forced the images away before they could distract her.

Beside the table was a chest with a wooden tray sitting atop it. A knife, a small vial of dark purple liquid, and three pots of ointment sat in a neat row on the tray. Cabinets lined the far side of the room between arched windows. To the right a banked fire crackled, and another lantern hung down from the ceiling directly over the table, presumably to provide extra light as the healers—experimenters—worked.

Experiments. The thought made her stomach churn unexpectedly with nausea.

What had they done to her in here? She had no idea how long she'd been out. No idea how long any of them had been in this place, whether her memories were of nightmares or reality. The nausea deepened into a bone-deep fear of the unknown.

She took a shuddering breath, summoning the white heat of her anger and resolve as a way to dispel the sense of fear. No matter what had happened, she would burn Underground to the ground.

As Lira hesitated at the entrance, Jora twitched. His head moved slightly.

Rotted carcasses. He was about to wake up.

Lira cast her gaze around until it landed on the healer's knife sitting amongst the other implements on the small table. She walked over to pick it up. Forced herself to turn, to kneel beside the stirring man.

She swallowed. Ignored how her stomach twisted as she placed the knife at his throat. She'd paid attention in healing class, knew exactly where to cut to cleanly bisect the artery and ensure he bled to death in seconds. Better, she'd seen throats cut more than once while growing up. Fast, and he wouldn't know what hit him. He wouldn't feel any pain. His life would just bleed away on the floor in a matter of seconds.

Her hand trembled and she pressed deeper. A bead of blood formed around the edge of the knife as she broke skin.

Sweat beaded on her forehead. The aching pressure in her broken nose made her head throb. She could do this. She just had to cut once.

Deep and swift. She would take Jora out of the equation so that *she* could survive.

Lira shifted, gathered her focus, and pressed again with the knife. Jora muttered, twitching slightly. Across the room, the other man stirred too. That snapped her resolve back into place, but just as she dug the knife in with purpose, a shiver of awareness brushed over her senses.

She spun, palming the knife and summoning her magic simultaneously, then froze at the sight of Ahrin leaning in the doorway, frowning. "What happened to them?"

Lira rose to her feet. It looked like Ahrin was alone, the corridor empty behind her. Her arms were crossed loosely over her chest, long coat falling to her ankles, head cocked to the side as she leaned against the doorframe. Lira's brain raced for a plausible lie. "I found them like this. Fari said she'd knocked them out, so I came to make sure they were okay."

"Oh?" Ahrin lifted an eyebrow. "Is that why you had a knife to Jora's throat?"

"Don't even think about it," she warned before Ahrin could use her magic, giving up all pretence as useless. Ahrin had figured out what was going on the moment she'd appeared in the doorway. "You've seen how quick I am. Do you really want to risk that I can have this knife flying at your throat in the instant before you attack me?"

"Why would you want to attack me, or poor Jora or Timor?" Ahrin asked, voice casual, as if asking whether Lira was cold. "We're on the same team, remember?"

"Oh, we are, are we?" Anger unfurled, bitterness leeching into her voice.

Another lifted eyebrow. "Whatever do you mean?"

"I know what happened." Lira's voice was flat, empty, but despite herself she couldn't keep the betrayal out of it. "I know you manipulated me into doing what Lucinda wanted."

"What do you—"

"I woke up." Lira cut over her. "In the middle of whatever you all were doing to me in here. I heard you and Lucinda talking, saw that look of triumph on her face. You sold me out to her."

"I told you, I'm the Darkhand of the Shadowcouncil. What part of that didn't you understand?" Ahrin's gaze locked on hers, intense, unyielding. "Underground's goals are your goals, remember? I just made it so that you and Lucinda both got what you wanted."

"Yeah, well, your approach isn't working for me." Lira tightened her grip on the knife.

"You're exhausted. Stressed. Those drugs have side effects." Ahrin glanced at the knife in her hand and back up to Lira's face, then took a step into the room. "Besides, you know I've never been scared of you, Lira. And we both know what I'm capable of."

"You also know that being exhausted and stressed only makes me more effective."

"But you hesitated to kill Jora just now, and that mistake has cost you." Contempt was cold and dark in Ahrin's voice. "What do you think's going to happen when my mages wake up? That's three against one, not good odds."

"*Your* mages? They don't belong to you. They belong to Lucinda, just like you do. You're a pawn in whatever game she's playing." Lira wondered if she could sway Ahrin temporarily to her side, use her to get out... play on her ambition, her need for power, to turn her against Lucinda.

Ahrin merely smiled, her stance loose and relaxed. "That's what Lucinda thinks. I thought you knew me better than that."

"I know you're not as perfect as you pretend." Lira spoke to stall for time, time to work out how best to play this. She needed to get out of this room without dying or completely blowing her cover. If Ahrin figured out she was a spy for the Mage Council... "You didn't prepare for Fari using her magic on *your* mages."

"No." Ahrin conceded that. "Our reports indicated she was fairly useless at healing magic. We won't make that mistake again."

"The Ahrin I knew didn't make mistakes." Lira stepped closer, hand twitching for her missing staff. "Where is Lucinda, anyway?"

Something flickered over the Ahrin's face. "She has other matters to deal with."

Lira's gaze narrowed. What *was* Lucinda up to here? It couldn't just be a base for experimenting on kidnapped mage apprentices. All the work that had been put into the place... they'd been here a long time.

She took a breath, tried another tack. Ahrin hadn't shifted an inch away from the door, and despite Lira's taunts so far, she'd barely scored a hit. But that wasn't surprising. Ahrin had never flinched. Never looked worried or scared. She'd only ever been in complete and utter control of whatever situation she'd found herself in.

Lira had never once imagined she'd find herself on the opposing end of that. That Ahrin would one day be her enemy. An enemy she'd have to destroy to survive. It tore something inside her, but she pushed that away, hardened herself against it. "What's *your* goal here? Take over Underground, take over the world?"

Ahrin took a step closer. "I want power. Influence. I want to determine my life, not have someone else determine it for me. You already know that."

"So being Underground's lackey isn't your end game? You want to use them for your own ends," Lira murmured. "Even you have to see how insane that is. Lucinda isn't Transk—she'll kill you in a blink if she figures out what you're up to."

Lira glanced down as Jora groaned, his eyes blinking open before sliding closed again. She had to make a move quickly or the mages would wake and the odds would be completely against her. Time to end this conversation and find the others.

She loosened her control, let her magic stir inside her, and with it, that heady thrill. Of danger. Of pitting herself against impossible odds. A smile curled at her face as she welcomed it back, that powerful rush of invincibility.

She lifted her boot and slammed it down on Jora's face. The crunch of his nose breaking echoed through the room. He went still.

"Not a nice way to treat a comrade." Ahrin's gaze shifted down, then back to Lira, calculating and cold. "He'd have had less of a headache if you'd just run the knife across his throat. I know you're mad, but I'm also starting to wonder about your loyalty."

"Like I said, this isn't working for me. I don't take well to being hunted, kidnapped, tortured. Underground will have to re-adjust its approach if it wants to keep me winning mages to their side. Until then, I don't have any compunctions about killing or hurting *comrades* who try to hurt me." She cocked her head. "I'll have power, Ahrin, but it will be on my terms. Not yours or Lucinda's."

"I'm nobody's pawn either, if that's what you're suggesting. We could help each other, Lira. We could be great, together."

"No," she said flatly.

Ahrin's eyebrows went up. "Just like that?"

Lira stepped forward until she and Ahrin were bare inches apart, not shying from the implicit threat in that midnight blue gaze. "You walked away from me without a second thought. If you think I hold on to *any* part of the friendship we once had, then you're fooling yourself." Lira paused. "I am Lira Astor, granddaughter of the Darkmage. I will one day be the *leader* of the Shadowcouncil. You are nothing but a trained killer. I don't need *you* to be great."

Ahrin's eyes narrowed. "Back in the room, you said—"

"I said what you wanted to hear so that I'd get what *I* wanted." Lira smiled coldly. "Just like you taught me."

Silence hung between them, the tension so thick it was palpable. It vibrated with danger and malice. When she spoke, Ahrin's voice was low and cold. "If you get in my way, I won't hesitate to destroy you."

In that moment, Lira didn't care about razak or Lucinda or Jora waking up on the floor. All she wanted was to show Ahrin that she was no second anymore. That she was stronger and better and more capable, and she certainly didn't *need* her. "I feel the same way. Underground is going to be *my* puppet, Ahrin Vensis, not yours."

Violet light flashed as Lira summoned magic and sent it slamming into Ahrin. The girl flew backwards, barely catching herself before crashing into the wall. Lira ran across the room, the hilt of the knife hot in her fingers as she raised it. But she was still a step away from Ahrin when it was torn from her hand with magic.

Snarling, Lira reached out with her telekinetic power and the knife hovered in the air between them as they battled. Power surged through her and Lira won, the knife veering back towards her and sliding into her palm.

"Not bad." Ahrin flicked a hand, sent the chest beside the bed flying at Lira's head. She ducked, wrenching her magic away from the knife to slam into the chest and divert it away. It crashed against the wall nearest her. The wooden tray and all its implements clattered to the ground.

Sense slammed back into her at the noise it made. Dammit. The ruckus was enough to alert Lucinda, the razak, and anyone else nearby. Lira didn't have time to linger or they'd all be on her. She couldn't let this become a standing fight.

She started moving even as she was still straightening up, quick as lightning, launching herself straight at Ahrin.

Ahrin's eyes widened in surprise, and a second later her fingers flicked. Telekinetic magic tried to hold Lira back, but her momentum was too great. She collided with Ahrin and they flew backwards before crashing to the floor in a tangle of limbs. Before Ahrin realised what she was doing, Lira wrapped her magic around her own hand and used the force of it to drive the knife into Ahrin's body.

Blood sprayed, warm droplets splattering onto the bare skin of Lira's hand and collarbone. Ahrin gave a grunt of pain. For a moment, a single heartbeat, they stared at each other, horror and anger and resignation all tangled up together.

She'd buried a knife in Ahrin's shoulder. She'd—

Ahrin moved, slammed her knee in Lira's stomach in a move Lira had seen her use multiple times before. The air whooshed from her lungs in a gasp and she fell sideways, curling in agony around her stomach.

"Forgotten the streets in all your fancy mage staff training, I see," Ahrin spat as she slammed her fist into Lira's jaw, then rose to her feet and delivered a hefty kick with her boot into Lira's ribs. But it wasn't contempt Lira read in her eyes, blurred as her vision was from agony, it was shock. Dismay. Ahrin reached up and pulled the knife from her body, letting out a painful hiss as she did.

Violet light flashed, and Lira used magic to drag the table between them and give her enough time to stagger to her feet, still bent over with pain and desperately trying to suck in air. Ahrin vaulted the table in a single graceful move and Lira backed up towards the wall, feigning retreat.

The moment Ahrin got close enough, Lira changed direction and dived forward, driving her shoulder into Ahrin's knife wound and sending them crashing back to the ground. There they wrestled, clawing, elbowing, punching, each trying to get the upper hand.

But Ahrin was relentless. Determined. A far better fighter than Lira—taught to be elite as a child before they'd ever met. And now she had magic too. Realising she was losing, Lira scrambled out from under her, trying to suck in enough breath but dizzied from the lack of it. She tried to get to her feet. Get to the door and run.

But Ahrin gave her no space or time to get clear. She reached Lira before she could get to the exit and slammed her against the wall, pressing her left forearm into Lira's throat.

Her free hand lifted, hovering by Lira's face. With a click of her fingers a scarlet concussion ball blinked into existence, perilously close to Lira's cheek, its heat threatening to scorch her skin. Confusion and shock writhed in her chest. Ahrin hadn't told her about this ability. She'd lied.

Ahrin was stronger than her.

The helpless fury that realisation brought was burning hot. She refused to be weaker than any other mage. She had to be better than all of them. Ahrin especially. Her lip curled in helpless fury.

"Quit letting your pride get in the way and stop fighting me." Ahrin's chest heaved with exertion, sweat beading on her forehead. Lira's eyes were drawn to the black tattoo on the inside of her right wrist before she flicked back to meet Ahrin's gaze. "You're one of us. You don't need to do this. If you don't back down they'll have to terminate you. They can't afford a rogue operative, no matter how important."

Lira writhed, chest heaving as her lungs struggled to get enough air through Ahrin's hold. "Don't pretend like you care, I don't believe it. I'll discuss my own terms with Lucinda and the Shadowcouncil, not with their pet killer. Let me go."

Unexpectedly, Ahrin smiled. "I've got a concussive burst hovering inches from your face, and you're angry, not scared."

"You don't scare me," Lira spat.

"I don't want to scare you, I—"

"Well done, Ahrin."

Both girls shifted their attention to the doorway, where Lucinda had appeared, her cool gaze taking in the waking mages on the floor and the state of the room.

"I told you I could contain her." Ahrin stepped away from Lira. The concussive ball vanished, and Ahrin pressed her hand to her bleeding shoulder, not even wincing at the pressure.

Lira instantly leapt forward, summoning a burst of magic to send the knife—lying forgotten on the floor—at Lucinda while shoving Ahrin as hard as she could in her injured shoulder.

Then she ran for the door.

Lucinda's magic caught her before she got two steps, freezing her to stone.

CHAPTER 33

When she woke, Lira was slumped in a chair, her arms drawn around the back of it, wrists bound tightly in rope. Voices were the first thing she registered, and so she kept her eyes closed, hoping they wouldn't realise she'd woken. Best not to reveal herself until she figured out the situation she was in and what she was going to do about it.

For a moment, though, the only thing she could focus on was not betraying the aching in her head and stomach or the sharp stabbing pain in her ribs from her fight with Ahrin. Her old crew leader had really worked her over.

She took small, slow breaths, mastering the pain, pushing it far enough away she could use part of her focus to pay attention to the conversation nearby.

"We have to move more quickly than I had anticipated." Lucinda's voice. "Those out searching are more competent than I expected. If we remain here much longer, we'll—"

The remainder of her words were drowned out by someone knocking at the door. It opened, and there was a murmured exchanged Lira couldn't pick up. When it closed again, Lucinda's voice was the first she heard. "No, not quite, but enough."

"And what about—" Lira fought down an involuntary start at the sound of Ahrin's voice.

"The Magor-lier will soon be dealt with," Lucinda snapped over Ahrin, clearly impatient. "Now we just need to worry about our biggest problem."

"And who or what would that be?" Ahrin drawled. "It sounds to me like you've got everything carefully arranged."

"Don't make the mistake of thinking I don't know when you're fishing for information," Lucinda said. "You know what you need to. That's all."

A charged silence. "I'm your blade. That's what you've made me. All I ask is that you use me."

"We will. You don't need to worry about that." Footsteps as someone paced. "Go and speak with Dasta, make sure he's getting everything organised."

"As you command." There was a hint in Ahrin's voice that only Lira would recognise as disdain. "What do you want to do with your precious symbol?"

"She's not biddable enough. Her behaviour earlier was proof of that. We can't afford people we can't trust." Lucinda hesitated.

"The rest of the Shadowcouncil might have something to say about you killing her." Ahrin sounded nonchalant. "Not to mention how keen you were to get her on that table. You need something from her, are you sure you've got it?"

"We won't know for—" Lucinda cut herself off, impatience creeping into her voice. "What I do with her isn't for you to question."

"I get it. She's clearly not the follower type." Ahrin's tone was the verbal equivalent of a shrug, dismissing Lira's life in a blink. "Which is a dangerous liability. Especially if the procedure worked."

"As you've already surmised, I had other goals in mind with that procedure, but I now doubt that making her more powerful is a good idea." Lucinda's voice was crisp, dismissive. "We have you. She has become too much trouble to be worth the value she brings."

A pause, then, "Well, you're certainly not going to get any arguments out of me on that."

Lira felt like she'd been slapped in the face. She expected that cold mercilessness from Lucinda, of course, but Ahrin... to throw her life away so easily. Again. It cut deep. Deeper than any wound had before. She hated that it was possible, hated that her impervious shield that kept everyone out failed when it came to her past.

Her thoughts, slower to focus through pain, tried to figure out what she should do. Destroying Lucinda and anyone connected to her remained her ultimate goal—ensuring she did it in a way that helped her advancement amongst the Mage Council.

But to do that, she had to get herself out of this mess while maintaining her access to Underground. Attacking Ahrin earlier had been foolish, and now Lucinda had clearly written her off. It had been a mistake that might cost her everything.

Maybe if she revealed that she was awake, apologised, promised to be more loyal... but no, that wouldn't work. Lucinda would see through it in seconds. Lira just wasn't capable of the type of submission Lucinda wanted. Besides, Ahrin was an additional complication. She knew Lira well enough to know when she was lying.

Another knock came at the door, breaking Lira's concentration. Footsteps moved to open it. Murmured voices that Lira couldn't pick up. Then Ahrin's voice: "Timor thinks he's found them."

Timor. Ahrin had called the other unconscious man that name. Lira swore inwardly at the implications. Another likely mage was present here they hadn't factored in. It also meant he was no longer unconscious, so Jora was probably awake too.

"Send Dasta..." Lucinda's voice faded as two sets of footsteps crossed the room. The door closed, and silence fell. Lira remained still, eyes closed, just in case. But when the silence lengthened, broken only by the popping of the nearby fire, she cautiously opened her eyes.

From where she sat, she could see the edge of the fireplace, the thick rug on the floor. When there were no further sound, she lifted her head to look around properly.

She was in the bedroom that they'd kept her in before, and it was empty.

Urgency set adrenalin flooding her system. There was no way to know how soon Lucinda and Ahrin would be back, and this was her best opportunity to get free. She yanked at her bonds, ignoring the pain from the bruises already there, but the rope was tied tightly. Her magic surged, but she forced it down, not wanting to summon any razak unless it was necessary.

Next, she tried to curl her fingers around to study the knot, see if it could be undone. But Ahrin had clearly been the one to tie it—Lira could get out of basic knots, and Ahrin knew that very well. She wasn't getting out of this one.

Her gaze roamed the room for any potential tool to use to cut through rope. Hope flared briefly when she spotted her mage staff still lying on the bed, but it faded just as quickly when she saw there was no way of getting to it. Or using it.

When no other obvious options revealed themselves, she slumped in the chair, trying to figure out something else. Lucinda would be back, and Lira needed to have a plan before she returned.

Lucinda's power was the main obstacle. She could *probably* talk herself out of the chair, freeing herself to fight, but there was no getting around the fact Lucinda could freeze her to the spot. She'd have to do better than just getting out of the chair. At least if Lucinda came back alone, she had a better chance of fooling the woman, of successfully negotiating with her.

And if she managed to get free... it was hard to know how much time had passed since she'd separated from Tarion and the others, but it was probably safest to assume they'd made it underground. She'd start with following the path they'd taken and hopefully catch up. If what Ahrin had said was right, and they'd been found, they'd need her help to fight their way free, especially now there was an additional mage they hadn't accounted for.

From the conversation she'd overheard, it seemed whatever was happening here, they were being forced to wrap it up earlier than expected.

Lira guessed having a furious mage of the higher order and her Taliath husband hunting the world for their missing son and nephew might have something to do with that. A flicker of a smile crossed her face. She savoured the thought of Lucinda being put in a room with Alyx Egalion after this.

As long as Lira was the one who got to lock the door behind them and watch.

Lira started when the door creaked inward. She braced herself, ready to appear repentant, sincere, apologetic. She planned what to say, repeated it over and over in her head. But when the door swung all the way open, emitting a slight creak, nobody entered.

Something was wrong.

She knew it in the instant before the rattling sounded—inquisitive, anticipatory—and the temperature in the room plummeted until her breath was clouding in front of her face.

They'd sent a razak in to kill her.

Rotted carcasses! When Lucinda decided something, she didn't hesitate to act. A dark tendril of shadow curled around the door, solidifying into hard carapace and pushing it further open.

Lira didn't wait for it to come in. Didn't hesitate to worry that using magic might draw every razak in the place to her. Violet light flashed and she *tore* the ropes binding her wrists off with a brute burst of telekinesis.

The rattle that echoed through the room in response to her use of magic was pitched with ravenous hunger, like chains screeching over metal. The door swung all the way open, writhing tendrils of darkness sliding across the floor and creeping up the wall on either side of the doorway. Silver eyes flashed as the thing's head came into view. The space grew so dark that Lira could barely see, and bitter cold dug deep into her aching body.

Lira dived for the bed, her hand closing around the mage staff lying there and bringing it up swinging to deflect the closest limb—the scaled carapace reaching for her neck. It was an awkward blow, and the collision shuddered through her, her arm twisting under the force of it. Her injured ribs erupted in pain and she grunted, almost dropping her staff.

The limb lifted into the air, more of it solidifying as Lira stared, scales sliding into place to cover inky blackness. The next strike was too fast and all she could do was scramble further onto the bed, rolling off the other side and crashing to the floor as the blow whipped through the air inches from her head.

Another dark tendril curled down from the wall, turning solid as it reached for her ankle. She scrambled forward, kicking out, and tried to make a run for the doorway. The razak closed the distance too quickly, a scaled limb swinging out to slam the door shut so hard it made the frame shudder.

She clutched her burning side, trying to concentrate amidst the pain. The thing was so big it filled most of the space in the room, giving her little room to move, and making everything so dark she could barely make out what was monster and what was just shadow.

She had to focus on the head, where the eyes were visible. Where it was vulnerable.

With a controlled burst, she wrapped her magic around the chair she'd been tied to and sent it flying at the creature's head, following it up with the table, but it ducked both objects with terrifying ease before turning its attention back to her.

Those silver-lit eyes focused on her with a hungry intensity that left her in no doubt of what it would do to her if it pinned her down. It hungered for her with a desperation she could sense. Slowly, its limbs encircled the space around Lira, closing in until there was no gap left for her to escape through. The inky blackness was so deep now she could see only its eyes glowing, and the glint of its long, curving fangs.

She watched it, light on her feet, ready to move when it did, forcing herself to conserve strength, only exert energy when she needed to. She needed those seconds to think, to steady herself, but she wasn't going to survive this by being on the defensive... it was too fast.

So, gritting her teeth with resolve, Lira jerked right, as if preparing to run for the door. The moment the creature's limbs uncurled to stop her, she changed direction and launched herself at its centre of mass.

Carcasses, it was fast. A leg snapped towards her as she closed in on its head, staff raised. She hopped over it, ducked the next swing, then threw herself forward. Her body collided with its head, the creature letting out a frustrated rattle, and Lira managed to drive her fist deep into one of the glowing silver eyes.

Warm, sticky fluid cover her skin.

It screamed and its head reared back, well out of her reach, limbs writhing in distress.

Lira ran, trying for the door. She barely got a step before having to jerk wildly to the left to avoid a swinging blow. Thinking quickly, she dropped to a crouch and crawled for the exit as shadow and scaled limbs waved above her head.

The creature was already recovering before she got to the door, and Lira had to scramble back to her feet, forced to dance around more concerted efforts to capture her, taking far too much time and tiring her exhausted body even further. But she'd gotten just close enough to break through a sliver of a gap in the cage of darkness. Her breath heaved in her chest as she reached the doorway, dived out, then pulled it shut behind her just as the first leg came curling towards the opening.

She pressed her back against the wooden surface, panting from exhaustion and adrenalin both, sweat pouring off her.

It was then she noticed that the door hadn't been barred from the outside to lock her inside after the creature had been let in. The brackets were empty, the bar resting against the wall nearby.

An angry rattling came from the other side of the door, and a slamming blow hit the wood. The second shuddering hit snapped a crack right through the middle of it. Lira picked up the bar, dropped it into its bracket, then stepped away and quickly took stock of her surroundings.

She was in a well-lit, familiar hallway. Several quick steps to the next open door brought her to the experimentation room where she'd fought Ahrin. Her breath escaped in an incredulous huff. They hadn't taken her far.

Behind her, wood splintered. A furious rattle leaked into the hallway. Lira swore, shook herself to try and concentrate. More razak would be coming after her use of magic, not to mention Lucinda or Ahrin.

She forced herself into a painful jog, her entire body one big sore spot at this point, senses attuned to anything ahead. In moments she was passing the room where they'd been strapped to the tables. A quick look inside found the room untouched, and then she turned down the unlit corridor to follow the route Garan and the others had taken.

Urgency thrummed at her, desperation to get clear of this area before someone came back. No more razak stood in her way, and there was no sign of the mage that controlled them, either. It made her uneasy. Why no guards to make sure the razak had done its job in killing her?

She moved as quickly as she could, but her limbs were aching, tired, even though the adrenalin of the fight with the razak still flowed through her veins. Her breath was like fire in her chest, which probably meant she had at least a cracked rib or two. Or maybe it was after-effects of whatever they'd done to her in that room.

A shudder rippled through her at that thought. She pushed it away. Right now she had to focus on surviving. She would worry about everything else once she was out of here.

At the end of the hall was another turn—Lira assessed her mental map, matched it to the vague familiarity of the light and position of doorways, and guessed she was heading towards the library entrance. Which was a dead end.

Too aware the razak could have broken free of the room by now and be hunting her, she began desperately opening doors, trying to find a way off this floor. As she did, she continuously double-checked her magic to make sure it was buried deep where none of the creatures could sense it.

The third door she checked opened into a stairwell. A servant's access, judging by how narrow it was. Relief filled her and she slipped inside, closing it just as quietly behind her. As soon as the darkness embraced her, she rested her exhausted body against the door for a moment as she got her bearings.

If her mental map was right, she was on the same side of the building as the kitchen storeroom, her goal. The others should already be underground, searching for the razak queen. Maybe they'd already found it. All she had to do was get from here to there and join them.

She straightened her shoulders, willing her body to be stronger. But she couldn't take any more than short, shallow breaths because of her ribs, and the lack of oxygen was making her dizzy. Not to mention the unrelenting throbbing in her face.

She started down the steps. They curved around, passing a door she assumed led out into the first floor. Here she paused. If this was a servant's access, it might lead directly into the kitchens, which wasn't ideal—she wasn't going to be able to creep past anyone in her condition. Better to access the storeroom via the office above it on the first floor.

She pushed the door open, froze, but the darkness was still and silent.

Lira turned right, but as she closed in on the end of the hall she already knew she wasn't where she thought she'd be. Instead of the corridor ending at the outer wall, windows set into the stone, a right turn taking her to the office, it simply ended in wall, a left turn the only option.

She peered around into open space, an empty area, too dark to see the opposite end. Wide steps led downwards to her immediate left.

Lira rubbed her eyes, steadied her breathing as best she could, and tried to think. She could go back to the servant's access and chance nobody being in the kitchens. Or she could take these stairs down and hope to be able to find her way to the storeroom.

She'd just decided to chance the kitchens in the interest of speed when a thundering concussive boom tore through the air, making her start in shock. Faint blue light flashed briefly in the complete darkness at the bottom of the stairs to her left.

Lorin's magic.

Another boom exploded through the darkness quick on the heels of the first, larger, more powerful this time. Lira's magic prickled in response. She paused only long enough to summon enough magic to send it flooding through her veins, not enough to let loose and summon the razak, but enough to give her strength and focus.

Then she moved lightly down the stairs, careful in the dim light not to twist an ankle. Her ribs protested the movement, but her simmering magic helped mask the pain. At the bottom she came to a halt, despair curling through the pit of her stomach as she took in the sight before her.

A handful of wide, shallow, steps led down into a cavernous hall. It might have once been impressive, magnificent, but like the rest of this place it was half-destroyed. The centre of the roof had caved inwards, leaving a large gaping hole open to the night sky. Rubble littered the floor, overgrown and charred. Moonlight shone through the gaps to light the interior in silvery shafts.

Directly opposite where Lira stood, on the other side of the hall, large double doors stood beckoning, revealing the entrance foyer and freedom. Mist-wreathed trees were visible beyond the now-open main doors.

Something about the sight stirred a memory, but there was no time to chase it down.

Because the hall was full of razak—at a quick count four or five of the creatures, although it was hard to tell amidst all the dark and shadow—that had arrayed themselves before Tarion and the others.

It looked like the apprentices had been making for the front doors in an effort to escape onto the grounds when the razak had presumably ambushed them—maybe the monsters had been hidden and waiting amongst the rubble. It would explain Dasta's absence at her door if he'd been here setting up an ambush.

They'd been trying to escape. Without her.

She shouldn't be surprised. Didn't know why she was. If they'd found a way to get out, they would have been utter fools to wait for her without any way of knowing where she was. But the bitterness ate at her anyway, bringing stinging tears to her eyes. She shoved that emotion away and roughly scrubbed at her eyes. It didn't matter. None of it mattered.

Because they weren't going to get out.

They fought in a group, trying but failing to get closer to the exit. Garan led, Athira bringing up the rear. Both fought fiercely, but it was Tarion almost singlehandedly keeping them alive as he moved with a grace and skill that had Lira's bitterness turning to momentary wonder.

Pearlescent blue light flashed through the dark space as Lorin let off another concussive burst, but it did nothing to harm the creatures, instead dissolving harmlessly around them.

They weren't going to make it. There were too many razak and without swords or effective magic, there was no way they could kill enough to make it through and escape. Lucinda had obviously finished with them and had ordered Dasta to kill them.

Lira couldn't help them. She *could* use the fact they held the attention of so many razak to get out herself. It was the right call. She had critical information to pass to the council. She owed nothing to these apprentices.

"Lira!"

Lira spun, drawing her staff in an instant at the sight of Ahrin standing on the steps above her. Her chest heaved—she hadn't even noticed the Darkhand's approach, she'd been so caught up in what was happening below. She sucked in a shallow breath and regretted it almost instantly as pain flared in her side.

Ahrin lifted her hands. "I'm not here to attack you."

"You're lying."

"I'm not." Ahrin gestured to the hall where the fighting raged on, a little frown on her face. "You're not considering helping them, are you?"

"That's none of your business." Lira almost screamed the words, forgetting in her hurt and fury that she was supposed to be a member of Underground. "You walked away, Ahrin. We're not friends anymore. I'm not teaming up with you. I don't *need* you."

Her eyes narrowed. "You say you're one of us, but you were wavering just now, I could tell. You were thinking about helping them."

Lira said nothing, not confident she wouldn't betray herself again if she spoke.

"They were escaping without you," Ahrin said, midnight-blue gaze dark and intense. "They left you behind."

Lira's lip curled. "How does that make them any different to you?"

Ahrin took a step down. "Forget about them. I know what you want, what you've always wanted, and Underground can give it to you. You know that already, that's why you joined them. I'll help you figure out a way to make things right with Lucinda."

"You're a liar, Ahrin, and I'm not going to be fooled by you anymore." Lira took a heaving breath, pain stabbing through her chest, but the physical pain was nothing on the grief spilling out of her, grief she'd pushed away too long and now didn't know how to re-bury. "You can't manipulate me into doing what you want, what *they* want, not again. I'll be part of Underground on my own terms or not at all."

"I don't—"

"You tried to *kill me*. You let Lucinda try to kill me without a word of protest. You served me up to her to be experimented on without my knowledge," Lira shouted. She didn't want to feel hurt, to feel betrayal, but the emotions rose up in a tide, banishing the anger, making her what she hated most: emotional and irrational. "You were the *one* person in the world that I..." She trailed off, horrified at her weakness. "I won't make that mistake ever again."

"I gave you the choice. You took it," Ahrin said steadily.

"You didn't tell me the whole truth." Lira's voice shook. "You manipulated me, just like you've manipulated everyone your entire life. I was such a fool to think I was different."

"I gave you what you wanted. What you've always wanted."

Lira let out a bitter laugh. "And sending the razak to kill me in that room. That was what I wanted?"

A brief silence fell, and for the life of her, Lira couldn't read the expression on Ahrin's face.

"You asked me once, back in Dirinan, why you were my favourite." Ahrin took another step closer. Another concussive blast went off in the background, the blue light flashing over her beautiful face. "Why I treated you differently than the others. Do you remember?"

Lira only half-heard the words. Her gaze shifted between Ahrin, alert for sudden attack, and the fighting in the hall. Part of her was frantically wondering where Lucinda was, whether she was waiting nearby to use her magic if Ahrin failed to bring Lira back this time.

While those thoughts tumbled through her exhausted brain, her searching gaze caught sight of the razak mage. Dasta. He stood in the shadows off to the side of the hall, barely visible in the darkness. She couldn't read his features from so far away, but he held himself rigidly, as if he were concentrating. Making sure the monsters fought together as a unit rather than as individual creatures. Ensuring Tarion and the others would never be able to defeat them.

If she wanted to survive this nightmare, she had to use the distraction they were causing and sneak away. She could get to the back entrance via the kitchens. With most of the razak here, not patrolling the grounds outside, she could get a horse and ride for the road. Escape before the razak could come after her.

Lira swung her attention back to Ahrin, some focus and clarity returning as she forced herself to slow her breathing. All she had to do was get past Ahrin before Lucinda showed up. Yet standing around debating with her was giving more time for Lucinda and the others to work out where she'd gone. Which was probably Ahrin's plan.

"Lira." Ahrin's voice was soft; she'd gotten closer than Lira realised, only one step away from her now. "Do you want to know the answer?"

Lira lifted her staff in warning. "No."

"Liar," Ahrin accused. "You were my favourite, Lira, because you were the one person in the world *I* ever cared about."

Lira stilled, shaking her head to try and dispel those words. Ahrin was lying, of course, like she always did, doing Lucinda's bidding. Manipulating her.

"I don't believe you."

"Then I'll prove it," Ahrin said, holding her gaze. She closed the remaining space between them, one hand lifting to tuck a strand of hair behind Lira's ear, before lingering, hovering so close Lira could *almost* feel her touch. Her breath was warm on Lira's cheek as she breathed, "Go. Help them or escape on your own. It's your choice. I won't stop you."

Lira glanced back to the fighting. Garan and the others had drawn closer together, desperate now, weariness making them slower, prone to mistakes. They weren't going to last much longer. She was surprised none were down already. They were tough, these coddled mage apprentices she'd only ever thought of with contempt.

"She'll kill you if you let me go," Lira murmured.

Ahrin smiled wryly. "I'm the Darkhand. I've learned how to survive Lucinda and the Shadowcouncil."

Lira was rigid with indecision. She couldn't trust Ahrin, not for a second. If Ahrin was truly letting her go, then there would be a greater purpose in it that Lira didn't understand. But she had to get past her. Lucinda could be there any second.

"Forget them. Go back up the stairs to the first floor. Take the servant's access down to the kitchens—they're empty right now. You know the way out from there. Make for the southern valley wall. Once you're over, there's a town not far away, you just need to follow the road." Ahrin's voice was steady, brisk. Relaying orders like she once had all the time.

Lira closed her eyes. If she tried to help the others, the razak would sense her magic. They might turn and come after her. Her clean escape would be gone.

"Go, Lira, and then we're done. I told you, together we can turn Underground to our purposes." Regret filled Ahrin's voice. "But I won't let you stand in the way of what I want. I won't let the fact I care about you make me weak."

Another burst. This one not as strong. Someone cried out in pain. She thought it might be Fari. Her heart sank.

She couldn't walk away from them.

More weakness. But she couldn't overcome it, even though she knew how stupid it was.

Lira lifted her gaze to Ahrin's. "You're right about what I want, but I told you, I don't need you to help me achieve it. And I won't let you stand in my way either."

Unbelievably, a smile spread across Ahrin's face. "Then I very much look forward to the next time we meet, Lira."

She lifted a hand to trail her fingers down Lira's cheek, the touch light as gossamer, and for a heart-stoppingly dizzying moment, Lira thought Ahrin was going to kiss her. She swallowed, almost swayed forward into the touch, but then Ahrin dropped her hand and walked away, long strides carrying her into the shadows.

She didn't look back once.

Lira turned away before she stayed, before the traitorous part of her that wanted to go with Ahrin won the internal battle she was fighting.

But instead of going up the stairs, she moved across the landing, her gaze going straight to where Dasta stood in the shadows. He was facing the fight, features in shadow but shoulders set and both hands slightly raised.

She was the heir to the Darkmage.

That had to be good for something.

CHAPTER 34

L ira straightened her shoulders, took a deep breath, and summoned her magic. It leapt through her veins, alive and true. She pushed away all thoughts of Ahrin, of Lucinda and Underground, and she thought about the sheer reckless danger of what she was about to do.

And that seductive thrill rose up again. The rush of pitting herself against the darkness that wanted to consume her, fighting to defeat it every single time.

She let it flood her, combining with her magic, filling her senses, soaking into her muscles, replacing exhaustion with strength, dimming the pain. A smile curled at her mouth, anticipation tasting heady on her tongue.

Then she threw out her magic and wrapped it around the hall doors. She flicked her hand, like yanking a rope toward her, and the doors tore away from their hinges with barely any resistance. Grinning now, she sent both doors flying at Dasta—using every bit of strength and skill she had left to hurl them so fast that he couldn't move away in time. He didn't even see them coming.

He crumpled, buried under the splintered wood, and didn't move again. Unconscious or dead, it didn't matter. He was out of commission for now.

The razak all screamed at once, their connection with the mage lost, and for a few precious seconds they milled around in disarray, limbs whipping everywhere.

Chest heaving, she turned to the others, satisfaction filling her at the sight of Garan sweeping his staff at the creature in front of him, sending it skittering away, then pushing through the gap towards the exit. "After me!" he bellowed. "Hurry!"

It wasn't long before the razaks' screeches changed to furious rattling and they turned back towards their prey, angrier than they had been. Fari, Lorin, Athira, and Tarion ran after Garan, desperately swinging their staffs to force the path through.

Garan leapt up into the doorway and turned back, waving Fari through as she reached him next. He stayed to keep the path clear, and Fari made it across the outer foyer and into the outdoors.

Lira told herself to go. To run now while everything was in chaos. Lucinda could be right behind her, especially if Ahrin really had been trying to stall her. She blinked, holding on to the remnants of strength that her magic had given her, and turned, preparing to force her body into a run.

She'd gotten two steps away when Lorin screamed.

The sound froze her mid-stride and she spun around, gaze searching the interior of the hall without even thinking.

The initiate had made it most of the way to Garan and the front doors before a razak leg had wrapped itself around his ankle and yanked him back into a pack of them. Another scream rang out as a second razak slid towards him and used one of its scaled limbs to wind around Lorin's calf. Blood soaked into the ground under his leg.

The initiate struggled bitterly, pain and panic combining in another cry.

Lira dimly heard Garan's bellow. Registered Tarion turn around and begin fighting his way back to Lorin. Had a brief moment to feel scorn for both of them—why would they be so stupid? They needed to leave Lorin and get out, get away, or they all would die with him.

And then Lorin screamed again. His leg was pinned to the floor, bloodied and torn. The limb wrapped around his calf was crushing the leg, holding him in place while fangs lowered towards his chest. More razak were closing in on him, their rattling hungry.

Lira tried to turn again, to flee. There was nothing she could do.

But she couldn't get the story out of her head. Lorin telling them about when he'd broken his leg as a boy. How terrified he'd been. How it had been the worst day of his life. Not because of the break, but because it had threatened the life he wanted more than anything.

Rotted carcasses, she was as soft in the head as Tarion!

Instead of running away, Lira turned back and launched herself down the steps into the hall, pulling together the remains of her draining magic, wrapping herself in it then leaping into the air.

It was blunt, an exhausting and rapid drain on her strength, but Lira's body hurtled across the room to crash to the floor beside Lorin. The whole time her brain was screaming at her not to be an idiot. That she was going to get herself killed. That Lorin, the others, they weren't worth her life.

She hit the floor hard, her shoulder taking most of the impact. Her breath escaped her in a gasp, then pain roared in an agonising fire through her broken ribs. She cried out from the intensity of it, slapping a hand on the hard floor.

What was she doing?

A razak leg stabbed down at her chest. She rolled away just in time, then brought her staff up to swing wildly. More pain ripped through her. The razak backed off momentarily and she turned, gasping and biting back tears, to begin hacking at the leg pinning Lorin to the ground.

Eventually the creature pulled away with an annoyed rattle. Lorin let out a sobbing cry and curled up, cradling his injured leg. Lira thought she saw bone sticking out through the still-flowing blood. Her stomach turned.

"Lira!" Relief filled Garan's voice as he bellowed across the space between them. He'd left the doors and was following Tarion in trying to fight his way back to them. They were all insane. "We were looking everywhere for you."

"Oh yeah? And how long did you spend doing that before making a run for it without me?" She wasn't looking at him, busy thrusting her staff at the nearest razak to try and keep it away from Lorin.

"They found us while we were looking for you, chased us in here." Garan's shouting voice grew closer, but he was still some distance off.

His words sounded sincere. Was it possible they hadn't abandoned her?

That thought blew out of her head when another creature came at them. She backed up rapidly, swinging her staff to keep it at bay, but was forced to abandon Lorin in doing so. The razak immediately tried to close in around both of them and cut them off from each other.

A blur of movement crossed her vision and then Tarion was there, expression calm and focused, body moving like a dancer's as he forced the razak away from the space around Lorin, keeping them together in a cleared circle.

"Where did you learn to fight like that?" she asked, gasping for air. Her arms were leaden—she wasn't sure how much longer she could hold her staff, let alone swing it. Already her blows were limited because of the blinding pain in her chest. Her magic was gone after throwing herself across the room, dry as a well in a desert.

"Da taught me." Tarion smiled across the space between them, hazel eyes alight at the mention of his father.

Envy stabbed at her then, and she pushed it away with a huff. She was clearly delirious if she was allowing herself to feel envious of Tarion Caverlock.

She was about to die.

As if to emphasise that point, Tarion barely avoided a swinging leg, then fell sideways as another leg wrapped itself around his right arm and yanked. Lira swung at it, trying to force it to let go. When it did, blood soaked the arm of his tunic.

And then another body crashed into the floor nearby, just as grace-lessly as Lira had. Garan scrambled to his feet, hair askew, eyes wild, mage staff spinning in his right hand. "Nice trick there, Spider. I might need to work on it a little though, that was a rough landing."

"You shouldn't have come back," she snapped. "You should have gotten free while you had the chance."

He'd come back for her and Lorin. Tarion too. She didn't know what to make of that.

He ignored her, going to drop beside a shivering Lorin. "Can you both cover me while I try and stop this bleeding?"

"Where's Fari?"

"With Athira. Escaping to go and get help," he said grimly as he dragged off his tunic and began tearing it into strips.

Tarion hadn't stopped to debate with Garan—he was already swinging his staff to try and force the razak back, seemingly unhampered by his wounded arm. Lira stared between them both... they weren't getting out of this. All they were doing was prolonging the inevitable.

A leg swung at her head and she was broken from her thoughts as she swung to bat it away. The move was slower than she liked, her arm too tired to do much more.

"Could you distract some of them by throwing things around?" Tarion called over to her.

She shook her head, ducked desperately. "I used the last of my magic getting to Lorin."

"Me too," Garan called up. He was swiftly binding Lorin's leg to make a tourniquet, using cloth from his robe to staunch the bleeding. The initiate was clearly in terrible pain, blood beading on his lip as he bit down on it and endured Garan's ministrations in silence.

"What about you, Lorin?" Lira asked. If Garan and Tarion wanted to give in to insanity and behave like they might escape this, then why not join them? "Think you can set off a concussive burst or two? Maybe the noise will help distract them."

Lorin nodded gamely.

"He's losing a lot of blood, Spider. The effort might kill him," Garan said grimly.

"He's a warrior mage, Garan," she said. "He can do it."

"She's right," Lorin said fiercely. "You've slowed the bleeding. I can summon enough for two or three bursts."

"Then you get him out of here with your magic." Lira looked at Tarion. He'd been able to escape this whole time. He'd just chosen not to. He'd chosen to stay and help. To risk dying with them.

"What about you and Garan?" he asked.

She ducked another blow, swung out with her staff, then glanced at Garan. He flashed a smile at her. Nodded. Accepting their fate. The certainty they wouldn't get out.

She almost smiled back. The rush of danger was stronger than ever then, hot and fierce. One last dance with death before it would all be over.

"We'll bring up the rear." She turned back to Tarion, breathing hard. "You make sure you get the others clear, you hear me?"

"I will," he said, the words confident and firm. "I swear it, Lira."

"It was nice knowing you, mage-prince." She held his gaze for a moment, then turned back to the fight.

In the next moment, Lorin sent two concussive bursts exploding just over the heads of the nearest razak. It didn't harm them, but the deafening noise was enough to distract them for the briefest of moments. While Tarion swooped down to pick up Lorin and then vanish from sight, Lira and Garan moved to try and fight through the razak between them and the door.

"Bet our grandparents never thought *we'd* be fighting side by side one day." Garan's smile flashed warm and bright. There was fear shining in those eyes, too, fear of their death, but he was controlling it. "Astor and Egalion, huh?"

Lira grunted as she just barely managed to duck a swinging leg, then jabbed her staff forward to try and clear space. She didn't want to die. Everything in her rebelled against it.

"I'm glad I'm not alone, Lira," he said then.

She barely heard him over the rattling of the closest razak, but she spared a moment to glance over, give him a little nod, and tell the truth. "Me too."

And then a leg curled around her ankle and yanked hard till she hit the floor, the breath whooshing out of her. Her staff clattered to the ground and rolled away and she had no magic to call it back with.

She rolled to her stomach, tried to scrabble away, but the grip on her leg tightened, crushingly hard, sharp scales cutting into muscle, sending agony tearing through her calf.

Before she could yell in pain, something hard slammed into the back of her head. Everything went out like a light.

She supposed this was dying.

CHAPTER 35

L ira slowly rose to consciousness.
Everything was off, but it took her a while to work out
why. She was sprawled against something rough and knobbly.
And she was outside. Cold air bit into her skin and a light snowfall
landed damp kisses on the skin of her bare hands and face.

Daylight pressed against her eyelids. That was the change.

She'd become so accustomed to darkness that daylight seemed...
unreal. Dreamlike. Memory came back then, and her heart thudded.
She'd been fighting in the dark, with Garan, then one of those *creatures*
had gotten hold of her. Something had hit her in the back of the
head...her leg! Despite the brightness, she forced herself to open her
eyes properly.

Her right leg was stretched out, her calf bound neatly in bandaging,
blood seeping through in spots. She lifted a hand and gingerly palpated
her aching face. Pain throbbed through her entire skull in response. So
she still had a broken nose and swollen cheek. She slid her hand around
to the back of her head. No soreness. No sign of a wound there.

Lira took a long, shuddering breath, then promptly swore, curling
over, at the stabbing agony in her right side. The cracked ribs hadn't

gone away either. Ignoring the pain as best she could, she pushed her attention outwards. She'd been left sprawled against a tree.

The trees around her were familiar, as was the pebbled drive not far off. Her heart thudded in shock.

She was inside the walls of Temari Hall. Not in a half-falling down mansion or abandoned army barracks. There was no thick forest nearby. Only the familiar and distant sounds of carts, carriages, and horses moving along the northern causeway out of Karonan.

A city that had been deserted the last time she'd seen it. Her head ached in confusion.

Another flake of snow landed on her cheek, its cold touch serving to convince her that she wasn't dreaming. Somehow she was back at Temari Hall.

A glance down. She still wore the apprentice attire she'd been taken in. It was ripped and torn in places, splattered with dried blood too. Her staff was gone. Memory flashed back, dark and vivid, of it rolling away from her as she desperately reached for it, a scaled limb wrapping around her calf to hold her in position.

She lifted her right hand to her face again, then looked at her wrist. Dried blood spatters encrusted her skin.

Ahrin's blood. From where Lira had driven a knife into her shoulder.

It hadn't been a dream. Or a hallucination.

Then how had she gotten here? And where were the others? Her stomach twisted... Lucinda said she hadn't planned to leave any alive. Had they just returned Lira? Fari and Athira had gotten clear, hadn't they? And Tarion's magic should have saved him and Lorin. Garan...

Shivering set in, from cold and shock both. Somehow, she managed to drag herself to her feet. The breath hissed out of her as hot pain tore through her right calf and ribs, but as soon as the throbbing settled to a manageable level, she lurched into a walk, limping through the trees and onto the pebbled driveway. The movement stirred her other injuries—throbbing in her shoulder from where she'd landed hard throwing herself towards Lorin, tearing in her ribs from Ahrin's boot. Exhausted, trembling legs. An aching face.

Shudders racked her frame as she left the cover of the trees and an icy wind swept around her. She hunched over her right side, trying to breathe through the pain in her leg, and kept moving.

She stumbled to a halt at the sight of the two apprentices on guard at the front entrance doors. They looked as shocked as Lira felt. But when she started moving again, they just stood there, watching her approach and doing nothing.

"Spider, is that you? Where have you been? Everyone's been looking, it's been..." The male apprentice trailed off, clearly stunned. She didn't know his name, but recognised the fear in his expression as his gaze travelled over the dried blood splattered on her hand, face and clothes.

She took a step towards them. "Are the others back too?"

"The others? You mean—"

The second apprentice's words were cut off as shouts spilled out from inside the tower. It sounded like multiple people, all calling out in shock and surprise.

Lira took off at a limping run, ignoring the agony in her ribs and the fresh blood leaking through the bandage on her calf, pushing past the two apprentices and going inside. Other curious students trickled into the main foyer from rooms and corridors close enough to hear the shouts.

Lira weaved through the throng and headed up the stairs, ignoring the looks being thrown her way, ignoring the shakiness of her legs as she reached the first floor landing, gasping for air, and turned in the direction of the shouting.

Several grey and brown-robed figures were huddled around something in the hallway. Lira limped in that direction, trying to see around the huddle, forcing away the dizziness that was now threatening her ability to stand upright. When one particularly tall apprentice was jostled out of the way, she could briefly see through the gap.

Lorin.

He lay sprawled on the floor, his eyes open but glazed over. His chest moved in shallow breaths. Blood seeped heavily from several bandaged wounds in his leg. Garan's tourniquet was gone. Lira's heart leapt into her throat and she moved faster. On reaching the huddle, she tried to push her way through.

Lorin caught sight of her, his brown Shiven eyes widening. He tried to sit up, but then she lost sight of him as she was yanked away. She almost tripped, went stumbling into the wall. Pain flared in her chest and she bit her lip, desperately trying to stifle tears.

"Stay away from him, Spider," a voice snarled.

She blinked, staring at the angry face of a vaguely familiar female apprentice. "I was just trying to—"

"Clear the way at once!" The voice was stentorian, loud, and filled with magic that forced instant obedience.

Lira found herself shuffling aside with the others as quickly as she could, every single student moving to line the sides of the hall so that Alyx Egalion could stride through to Lorin. Furious anger snapped in her green eyes, and when they shifted in Lira's direction she pressed further into the wall in an effort to escape that gaze.

This was a mage of the higher order in full fury.

Behind Alyx came Finn A'ndreas. He immediately dropped beside Lorin, pressed a palm over the worst of the boy's wounds, and closed his eyes. Alyx watched, body so still she had to be holding back her anger with an iron-fisted grip. A hush fell over those gathered as they watched the renowned healer work.

After a few moments Finn opened his eyes and looked around, searching the students' faces. "Alon, Ressa. I'd like your help please. The rest of you clear away."

"There will be an assembly tonight and I will discuss this with you then." Alyx used that magic in her voice again when nobody moved. Instantly every student not named Alon or Ressa scrambled away. "Go!"

As exhausted and disoriented as she was, Lira couldn't do anything but obey. She didn't get very far though before her name was called. "Lira, not you!"

"Master?" She turned, tried to straighten her shoulders. Hissed with pain instead. She swayed on her feet, an odd blurriness coming into her vision. She blinked but it wouldn't go away.

Egalion's voice shook with frustrated fury. "What the hell happened to you?"

"We were taken... I..." Horrifyingly, tears rose in her eyes and her throat closed. "I don't know. I didn't..."

"I need better than that. Who took you? Where? Why?"

Lira swayed on her feet. "I... a barracks... buildings. Shadowcouncil wanted...Tarion... Garan, where..." There were others too, she couldn't quite recall their names. Were they here? Were they okay? But she couldn't grasp...

"Alyx!" Finn's voice was firm and authoritative. "She's going into shock. She needs a healer mage."

"I'm fine," Lira insisted, but then the world tilted alarmingly.

The last thing she remembered was the floor coming up to meet her face, and then gentle magic cradling her right before she hit it.

CHAPTER 36

Lira stirred back to consciousness as she was carried into the healing rooms, stubbornly remaining awake as Master A'ndreas' strongest fourth-year apprentice worked on her. Once he was done, she stared up at the ceiling above her bed, unable and unwilling to close her eyes despite the aching exhaustion in her body. She'd been forcibly put to sleep too many times to willingly put herself there again. Even though she was back at Temari.

They'd taken her from here before. They could do it again.

The door finally opened, admitting A'ndreas. He took one look at her, frowned, then placed his palm lightly on her forehead.

She was out before she knew what happened.

Lira woke to silence.

Her body soaked up the warmth of the blankets around her like a starving child—no matter how far removed from the streets of Dirinan, she would never get enough of feeling properly warm.

When she opened her eyes, she took in the familiar surroundings of one of the handful of private rooms in Temari Hall's healing wing. They were mostly used for infectious patients, but Lira supposed they didn't want to let her anywhere near the other apprentices or initiates until they figured out whether she had anything to do with their precious students being kidnapped.

A'ndreas or his apprentice had obviously worked more on her while she slept though, because she felt right again, back to her normal self. Complete with the faint pressure in her chest that came with being back inside Temari Hall.

Cautiously, she reached up to probe her face. It was still sore but nothing like the aching throbbing it had been. The swelling seemed to have gone down too. She sat up slowly, relieved when no more pain spiked through her, then tested standing. Soreness rippled though her left calf but it was bearable.

Even her magic felt back at full strength. For a long moment she sank down into it, eyes closing, letting it soothe and restore her.

How long had she been out? Where were the others? Had they all come back at the same time? She refused to admit to being worried about them. About Lorin's leg. Or whether they'd all made it out. Besides, whether they were back or not, there was nothing she could do for them right now. Still... she let out a breath, acknowledging to herself that she'd at least like to know if they were okay. Then she could put them out of her thoughts and move on.

She was debating whether to open the door and see whether a guard had been left to watch her when a hubbub outside the window caught her attention. She limped slowly over to it to stare out.

The main gates were swinging open to admit three riders galloping through at a frenetic pace. A fourth rider followed close behind. Pebbles from the neatly-kept driveway sprayed into the air behind them with the speed of the racing horses.

One of the front riders was Zandian, wearing the royal blue cloak of a council mage, the other two dressed like lords but with Taliath swords at their hips. She gave an indrawn breath when she recognised the blades, even at a distance.

Mageson and *Heartfire*.

And then two familiar apprentices came into view, walking quickly from the tower's front steps towards the riders. Without thinking Lira pressed a palm against the cold glass to steady herself against the unexpected rush of relief that flooded her.

Tarion and Garan were alive and back too. And they seemed okay.

She watched as Dashan Caverlock leapt from the saddle to run to his son and pull him into his arms, as Tarion threw his arms around his father and they clung fiercely to each other. The grim-faced Ladan Egalion was a little more reserved in greeting Garan, but his relief and the love between them was palpable. The final rider—a young woman with a flashing grin and the grace of a Taliath—joined Dashan and Tarion, one hand reaching up to rustle Tarion's too-long black hair.

The familiar emptiness opened inside Lira at the sight, the same one she'd kept at bay for years until Underground had kidnapped her and ripped open her shields, laying her bare and exposed once again.

She pressed her palm harder against the glass, using the cold to focus her mind. She'd built those shields once before, and she'd do it again, no matter how hard it was. She'd go back to being the perfect student, what the mage council wanted, and she'd figure out a way to rip that smirk from Lucinda's calculating face and make everyone remember *her* name instead.

And then she'd be fine. Then everything would be fine. Finally.

"Alyx flew straight back here with Finn and I when we heard you were missing to coordinate the search." Dawn A'ndreas' voice spoke suddenly from behind her. "Dash and Ladan have been out looking. We've all been worried sick."

Lira started and spun away from the window, one hand lifting to scrub away the wetness gathering in her eyes. She berated herself for not having noticed someone enter the room—that was stupid.

Rionn's lord-mage looked awful. She was beautiful as always, but there were shadows under her eyes, and lines of exhaustion and worry were furrowed deep into her skin. Garan's kidnapping had hit her hard.

"Lord-Mage Egalion," Lira managed, keeping her voice polite. She stayed where she was, wary, making sure there was distance between them. She checked and re-checked her mental shields, ensuring the woman wouldn't be able to read anything in her head. There was too much there she had to keep hidden.

"How are you, Lira?" Dawn entered the room and closed the door behind her. "From what I hear, you've been through an awful experience."

"Before you ask, I don't know what happened," she said quickly. It was already taking on a dreamlike quality. Being back here in Temari Hall made the razak and the half-ruined estate and Lucinda... *Ahrin*... feel like they had been a dream of some sort. "It wasn't me."

Dawn halted, a frown flickering over her face. "Nobody thought you had anything to do with this."

"Then why am I shut up in this room?"

"Finn thought you'd prefer privacy over being stared at by everyone else in the main healing ward."

"I..." Lira fell silent. That had been thoughtful of him. Her shoulders relaxed, weariness weighing them down. Sometimes it was unbearably hard, being constantly on guard.

"He says you had a concussion, a broken nose, torn shoulder, three cracked ribs and were suffering from dangerous levels of magic overuse." Dawn spoke matter-of-factly. "He's surprised you survived, not least because of the amount of blood you lost from the deep cuts in your leg."

"I'm hard to kill," Lira said with a trace of bitterness, then, before she could stop herself, "Lorin's leg?"

"Badly crushed. The healers are still working on it. Garan and Tarion are fine. So is Fari."

Unexpected worry climbed up the inside of her stomach at Dawn's hesitation. "Athira?"

"She wasn't returned with the rest of you." The kindness on Dawn's face filled her voice, as if she felt sorry for Lira. It made her hackles rise.

"I'm fine. Stop looking at me like that. I don't even like Athira," she snapped, then began pacing, trying to hide her limp. "How did they get us back on the grounds without anyone noticing?"

"We're unsure, but Finn's guess is that a mage capable of illusions could have pulled it off... a powerful one. Do you think that's possible?"

Lira nodded, a breath escaping her at such a simple answer. "Nothing happened to Karonan, did it?"

"Tarion told us what you saw the night you were taken." Dawn frowned. "But no, nothing happened to Karonan. That's what made Finn think of an illusionist, though it doesn't begin to explain why they'd want to make you all see a deserted Karonan."

"What about the other students who were in here that night, staying at the tower for mid-winter break?" Lira asked.

"Drugged like you. Including the apprentice on guard shift—his body was dragged away from the entrance and locked in the kitchens. They didn't start waking until morning, at which point Derna's body was found in the library and then the dead guards and dogs, and the alarm was raised."

"And Master Alaria?"

Dawn looked grim. "Killed the same way as the Shiven soldiers on the main gates. Throat slit cleanly."

Lira frowned, lifting a hand to rub at her forehead. "So the monster killed Derna in the library, but our captors left the apprentice on guard alive?"

"Yes."

"There were mages amongst those who took us." Lira hesitated. "They said they were Underground."

"Garan and Tarion have said the same. I feared as much when we heard you'd been taken." Dawn sat on the room's only chair. "Did you know the kidnapping was coming?"

"Sure. Weeks ago. I didn't think to mention it, that's all," Lira snapped as her heart sank and some of her despair returned, tightening in her chest. Had Dawn really thought she wouldn't warn them?

"That's not what I meant, Lira. It's just that your last report to me indicated you were scheduled to attend a meeting right before the kidnapping. I wondered if perhaps they'd revealed their plans and not given you an opportunity to warn us."

"There was no warning." Lira stopped pacing as her leg began to throb. "The meeting went exactly the same as all the others I've been to."

"All right." Dawn seemed to accept that, and her blue eyes roved Lira's face. "I've been so worried. About why they took you too, whether they knew that you were spying and intended to kill you for it."

"There's no need to be worried about me," she said sharply, unease making her start to pace again. "And they don't know I'm spying for you." At least, they hadn't. Lucinda or Ahrin might suspect it by now. Lira would have to figure out a way of dealing with that.

Dawn's gaze tracked her pacing. "What is it?"

Something about the calm understanding in Dawn's voice removed Lira's reticence. "The one in charge, she claimed to be a member of the Shadowcouncil."

Interest sparked on the telepath's face. "What can you tell me about her?"

"She called herself Lucinda. She was... calculating, highly intelligent, controlled, and she knew a lot about me. And she was cold. Ruthless." Lira hesitated. "Something is wrong, Lord-Mage. Really wrong. The Underground I know? The Underground you asked me to infiltrate? They're nothing like the people that took us from here."

Fear flashed over Dawn's face, some of the worry she must have been feeling these past days surging to life in her expression. "Were any of your captors familiar to you from the Karonan cell?"

"No, but Lucinda knew enough to convince me she was telling the truth, and she mentioned Greyson." Lira took a breath. "She told me I'd been kidnapped with the others to strengthen my cover, make the council trust me more, remove any suspicion I might have had anything to do with the kidnapping."

Dawn's frown deepened. "What can you tell me about the Underground members with Lucinda? You said there were mages?"

Lira was about to reply when a soft knock came at the door and it opened.

"Magor-lier!" Lira straightened her shoulders in shock, then promptly winced in pain from her ribs, as Tarrick Tylender entered the room, his height and broad shoulders making the space seem suddenly small. Dawn gave him a worried smile.

"I'm glad you're here, Tarrick. You should hear what Lira has to say."

Lira spun, eyes narrowed. "He knows?"

"Tarrick is the Magor-lier, Lira," Dawn said. "He needed to know of my suspicions about Underground, of what I asked of you. I told you I planned on telling him. There's no need to worry, not even Dash knows where the reports I give him come from."

"Nobody else knows it from me, either, Lira," Tarrick assured her as he sat on the bed. "Not even Councillor Egalion. Your safety is my highest priority."

Dawn smiled wryly. "Probably best to keep Alyx and Dash in the dark for the moment. Alyx is likely to destroy an entire town in fury after what happened to Tarion. If we admit to using one of her students as a spy, she'll probably kill us too. Her tempers are terrifying."

Tarrick's little smile of agreement softened his serious face.

"Will you tell us everything you know, Apprentice Astor?" Tarrick said, his voice deep and authoritative.

The Magor-lier will soon be dealt with. Lucinda's voice rang through Lira's head. What had she meant? Tarrick Tylender was a war hero, a mage warrior who'd been instrumental in helping Alyx Egalion defeat Shakar. And ever since then, he'd been a strong Magor-lier, doing what he could to work against the old mage traditions to improve the way mages interacted with the world.

"Is something wrong?" he asked, noting her hesitation.

She swallowed, glanced at Dawn. She looked untroubled. If a telepath of Dawn's skill trusted Tarrick implicitly, then so should Lira.

"No, not at all." She took a steadying breath.

And she told them. *Almost* everything. The whole time, she wrestled with herself. They would want to know the Darkhand had been there too, and her identity even more. She wasn't sure why she was hesitant about naming Ahrin. She shouldn't be. She deserved whatever came for her. Lira should serve her up to the Mage Council just like Ahrin had served her to Lucinda.

But something held her back. An old loyalty that had once been so strong that even now, after years and abandonment and betrayal, she was reluctant to break it.

"Lucinda was the leader, and you believe there were three other male mages," Tarrick clarified once she was done. "One could control these creatures. What could the others do?"

"I don't know. I never saw them use magic, but there was a thick mist surrounding the property the whole time I was there, as if to hide it, so I think one of them could manipulate weather or water. If I had to guess, the third was the one doing the experiments, so maybe he is some kind of healer?"

"And there was nobody else?" Dawn pressed.

Lira shored up her mental shield, then made a split-second decision to give them half of the truth. "The Darkhand was there too... but whoever it was wore a hood and loose cloak. I didn't get a good look."

It wasn't just old loyalty holding her back. If Lira admitted to Ahrin's presence, then that would lead to a lot of awkward questions that would require more lies. The mages could never know that Lira had once been close to the Darkhand, as close as family, that she'd run in Ahrin's crew. Dawn would pick up that something was amiss. And Lira couldn't afford to lose their trust.

Because she wanted Underground destroyed. And that meant she needed Dawn and Tarrick to allow her to keep spying inside the group.

Tarrick glanced at Dawn, clearly worried by this news. "I find it interesting that a Shadowcouncil member and the Darkhand were present at this location. It suggests whatever they're doing there is highly important to the group."

Dawn nodded agreement, turning to Lira. "Do you have any idea what sort of experiments they were doing? Or why?"

Lira hesitated. If Dawn and Tarrick knew that the granddaughter of Shakar had willingly submitted herself to an experimental treatment to give her more magic? Even they wouldn't believe she meant no harm then. A shiver of fear went through her at the reminder of what she'd done. She didn't feel any different. Not yet anyway.

"Lira, we need to know everything you do, even if you don't think it's important," Dawn said softly.

"Lucinda said something about being able to give normal people magical abilities," she said, hedging. "But she wouldn't explain it any further."

"That's absurd, and impossible." Tarrick chuckled. "You must have misheard."

Lira glanced between him and Dawn. Hesitated. Then she nodded.

"Maybe. Did Fari tell you her theory, about them deliberately making us feel scared and hopeless as part of an experiment?"

"We'll have Finn check you all over very carefully, make sure you're all okay." Dawn bit her lip. "As relieved as I am that you're all back, I wish I understood why they willingly returned you."

So did Lira. Lucinda had been very clear that she didn't intend to let them leave alive, but that had been a lie. The razak had had them all in that hall. If Lucinda had truly wanted them dead, they would be.

The question became why she'd wanted them hunted, attacked, injured even, but not killed. More fear? Perhaps the experiments hadn't worked as they were supposed to.

A chill ran through her. Had they been experimented on *after* being stopped by the razak? It was more than likely. And either having them almost killed had worked, so Lucinda released them to watch the results of a successful experiment unfold, or they hadn't, and Lucinda had returned them to avoid the consequences of killing the children of such powerful mages.

She needed to get back to the group, find out which it was. Find out what they'd done to her.

"There's something else too," she said, remembering. "They have access to Temari Hall. One of the kitchen deliveries the day before the kidnapping delivered the candles used to drug us."

"How do you know this?" Dawn asked.

Again, Lira hesitated, though she cursed herself for it and tried to pass it off as tiredness. It had been Ahrin that had delivered those candles. It was why the delivery person had caught her attention in the middle of a duel, why it had nagged at her. Some deep part of her had recognised her old crew leader from Dirinan. "A delivery came the day before. The delivery person seemed... odd. I talked to the servant in the kitchens, and he said they'd delivered candles. I thought nothing of it at the time, but now..." She shrugged.

Dawn and Tarrick shared a look. "Master A'ndreas had guessed as much, though we weren't sure about when or how the candles had arrived," the Magor-lier said. "Councillor Egalion has already instituted more security around deliveries at the academy. Everything coming in is now thoroughly searched."

Dawn leaned forward. "Can you tell us any more about Lucinda? Any small detail could be helpful."

By the time she was done with Tarrick and Dawn, night had fallen outside and the room was cheerfully lit. A tray of food had mysteriously appeared at the door. Tarrick—the Magor-lier of the entire mage order—had taken the food from a servant, making a wry remark about the usefulness of telepaths.

He'd deftly split the food three ways and handed Lira a plate with her portion. She'd hesitated before taking it, instinct warning her that it must be some trap. But it wasn't and the food had been delicious.

Once her words trailed away and her voice turned raspy, a long silence settled over the room. Lira took the opportunity to finish the leftover food.

"Do you think your cover with Underground is completely blown?" Dawn asked eventually.

At the very least it was badly damaged. She'd outright attacked Lucinda and tried to help the apprentices escape. But if Lira admitted that to Dawn and Tarrick, they'd pull her out. And she couldn't afford that. She'd figure out a way to get back in, to convince them she was a useful asset.

Lira shrugged, again bending the truth. "I played it like I wasn't sure they really were Underground, like I wouldn't trust them unless they told me more information. I attacked Lucinda, but only when my life was threatened. And she seemed oddly impressed every time I did something aggressive. I can talk my way back in."

Tarrick and Dawn shared a glance, but it was Dawn who spoke. "Lira, I don't think you should, it's too dangerous. From what you've told us, a Shadowcouncil member actively tried to kill you."

"She's not part of the Karonan cell. Greyson trusts me. I can do this," Lira insisted.

"If you tried going back, they might just kill you outright," Tarrick said with an air of finality. "You're still an apprentice, not even a fully trained warrior mage."

Lira gave him a scornful glance. "Is that really what you think of me after everything we just survived? You're telling me the trials are more difficult?"

"You haven't finished your education," Tarrick said patiently. "I—"

"You asked me to spy, so let me finish the job," she said coldly. "I can help you destroy Underground. I *want* to do this."

Another shared glance. It made her want to scream. They thought they knew what was best for her and they didn't. It was infuriating. A heavy silence fell, both clearly still reluctant.

"You'd have to be beyond careful here in Temari Hall," Dawn warned. "You said they made it clear they had spies inside the walls."

"Nothing could change," Tarrick added.

Lira almost rolled her eyes. "What do you think is going to change? I'm still the one everyone looks at like I'm about to turn into a murderous Darkmage any second. Anyone watching me is going to see exactly what they want to see—an outcast with the perfect motive to help lead Underground against the Mage Council."

Dawn looked at her. "Are you sure this is what you want? Neither of us would blame you now if you wanted to walk away."

"I said I was in, and I meant it. They want me. They can have me." She hesitated when they still didn't look convinced, then added more incentive. "Besides, if I go back, I might be able to find out where Athira is."

A small thrill of triumph went through Lira when Dawn's frown cleared. "You'll write weekly reports without fail," she said. "You miss one and I will contact Alyx and Finn immediately and then come straight here myself. Is that clear?"

"Understood." Lira stifled her smile and kept a sober look on her face.

"Dawn and I will remain in Karonan a few more days, but we won't contact you again unless you need us," Tarrick said. "Best not to chance it. They'll expect us to have spoken to you today to get your account of what happened, but any further meetings might look suspicious."

"If anything happens that makes you uneasy, you go straight to Finn or Alyx. Promise me, Lira," Dawn added.

"I will," Lira said, again serious, even though she had no intention of doing any such thing.

Tarrick rose to his feet, then bowed slightly. "The Mage Council formally thanks you for your help and your sacrifice, Lira Astor."

She huffed a breath. "The Mage Council doesn't even want me in its ranks, Magor-lier. I'm not doing this for you."

The sharp words were out before she could snatch them back, but he merely smiled. His dark eyes twinkled with the same good humour as Fari's as he offered his hand. "Maybe not, but I do."

She took his hand and shook it, not knowing what to say to that.

The Magor-lier is taken care of.

She shuddered, wondering what Lucinda had meant. She thought about telling Dawn and Tarrick about that overheard comment now, but instinct checked her... best to figure out what was going on before revealing it. As friendly as they were being, she didn't truly trust Dawn or Tarrick. No, she'd have to find out herself what those words of Lucinda's had been referring to. The shiver rippled through her again. For all Lira's tough words, Lucinda wasn't going to be an easy adversary to face again.

Although... the beginnings of an idea came to her. Of how she could regain access to the group, or at least get some leverage to earn their trust again. They'd wanted that letter after all, the one Councillor Duneskal had written to Master A'ndreas.

Lira would get it for them and prove her loyalty in the process.

CHAPTER 37

By nightfall, a large throng of students had gathered outside the tower entrance, forming an impromptu celebration of sorts to welcome back their returned comrades.

Lira doubted it had been any of the masters' idea—they all looked far too worried about the implications of what had happened to be thinking of celebration. But Garan and Fari were highly popular students, and Tarion was Alyx Egalion's son, so a large bonfire now burned in the grassy centre of the circular drive near the willow tree. Students clustered in a thick throng around it, eating and drinking and laughing.

Several wreaths of flowers had been placed by the steps for Athira —another popular student—as if to say she hadn't been forgotten, even though she was missing. It was a nice gesture, but that's all it was.

Lira's skin crawled with discomfort at the sight of the party. All she could see when she looked at the tree was the shadows where a razak had hidden, leaping out to chase her back inside that night. A shiver ran through her, the echoes of a rattle rippling through her mind like nails on a chalkboard.

What had happened wasn't worth a celebration. Relief, yes, at returning safely, at surviving. But seven students had been kidnapped from the grounds and nobody had been able to find them. Two students and a master were dead. Nobody knew what had been done to those who were taken. Nobody knew how they'd gotten back. One was still missing. Another was in the healing ward and might lose a leg.

The masters were right to be worried.

Lira had no intention of joining the party. After her long talk with Tarrick and Dawn she'd come downstairs to the stores area on the ground floor to fetch a fresh set of apprentice clothing, intending to slip across the main foyer and upstairs to a hot bath and then her room to sleep.

After everything that had happened, she longed for her narrow bed and quiet. Just her alone. Time to process her thoughts and figure out how she was going to steal a letter from Master A'ndreas' office while everyone was back in residence and there was extra security everywhere.

She was halfway across the foyer when she spotted the tall figure loitering in a pool of shadow by the front doors, hands thrust in his pockets, shoulders hunched.

Tarion.

No doubt he was expected to be out with the others, the son of Alyx Egalion and Dashan Caverlock returned safe and well, a symbol that everything was okay now. Even if it wasn't.

And she was equally certain it was the last thing he wanted—that the thought of all those eyes on him, all those voices, made him curl up inside the way she did whenever she met someone's gaze and saw their fear of her grandfather.

She took two more strides. Stopped. Turned back. He still stood there, clearly working up the courage to go out. She dismissed him with an annoyed huff, kept walking.

Her steps slowed.

Then she abruptly turned around, crossing back over the foyer in quick strides. He glanced up in surprise when she appeared beside him. "Lira, you're okay! They said you were, but Uncle Finn wouldn't let us in to see you. I was worried maybe they were lying about how hurt you were."

They'd tried to see her? Warmth blossomed at that, and she was suddenly glad she'd turned around. "I'm fine."

"I'm glad," he said, earnest. "What happened to you after we separated? We managed to get down into the cells where they held us, but there was nothing else down there. No razak or razak queen. We'd barely gotten back upstairs when they caught us, herded us into that half-destroyed hall, and, well... you know the rest."

She couldn't help but smile. "So many words. Don't tell me, almost being killed multiple times has cured you of your inability to talk like a normal person?"

He chuckled. "I wish."

"Lucinda grabbed me before I could kill the mages," she said quietly. "Long story short, I got free, ran for it, then heard you all fighting so I came to help."

He reached out, squeezed her shoulder in silent support, then let it drop quickly, as if instinctively understanding it might make her uncomfortable.

"Why are you even contemplating it?" she asked, breaking the silence.

"What do you mean?"

"You hate the idea of going out there, don't you? So who cares that it's what they all expect. Why do it? Just turn around and leave and go to your room, or wherever it is you'd rather be right now."

"It's more complicated than that." He stared out into the party, eyes dark, voice miserable. "Besides, the place I truly want to be is far away from here."

"It's really not that complicated. You just turn around and walk away."

"What I do reflects on my parents, whether I like it or not. And I love them more than anything. I won't shame them by hiding away in corners, even if that's what *I* want."

"They'd want you to do what made you happy."

"But I want to make them happy," he said softly.

She still didn't understand that sort of caring between people. Had no frame of reference to understand it. But she understood that this was who Tarion Caverlock was. So she bent to place her pile of new clothes on the floor, then stepped closer and tucked her arm into his. He started, hazel eyes flashing in surprise.

She shrugged, smiled back. "Walk out there with me, and they'll all be staring at me, not you. I can handle a few stares, I've been doing it all my life. Once you're in the huddle they'll stop looking."

Relief and gratitude filled his face. "Thank you, Lira."

"I don't want thanks. Let's go."

They walked out together, down the steps and into the crowd of students. And Lira was right. They all stared at her. Whispering. Wondering.

And also as Lira had predicted, they were barely three or four steps into the crowd when two apprentices came over to Tarion, shouting greetings and dragging him away with them, barely even sparing a glance at Lira. "Hey Tar, a new student started while you were gone. Come and meet her. She's gorgeous."

Tarion threw Lira an apologetic glance and allowed himself to be led away. She shrugged, glad to be free of him quickly so she could leave. She didn't even know why she'd helped him—she was supposed to be maintaining a low profile in case Underground spies were watching.

But even though she told herself to leave, she watched him anyway, an annoying part of her wanting to make sure he was okay before she left.

So she watched as his friends dragged him over to meet the new student that had recently started at Temari Hall. Lira's eyes shifted from Tarion to the girl, wearing the brown of an initiate.

Her gaze locked on Ahrin's midnight blue eyes.

Ahrin grinned as she caught Lira's shocked stare, lifted the cup of whatever she was drinking in a little salute.

And she winked.

TO BE CONTINUED...

CONSIDER A REVIEW?

'Your words are as important to an author as an author's words are to you'

If you enjoyed this book, I would be humbled if you would consider taking the time to leave an **honest** review on Goodreads and/or Amazon (it doesn't have to be long - a few words or a single sentence is absolutely fine!).

Reviews are the lifeblood of any book, and more reviews help my books achieve greater visibility and perform better in Amazon's ranking algorithms. This is a MASSIVE help for an indie author. Not to mention a review can absolutely make my day!

Review on Amazon

Review on Goodreads

Want to delve further into the world of *The Mage Chronicles?* By signing up to Lisa's monthly newsletter, *The Dock City Chronicle,* you'll get access to exclusive, free, bonus content, including:

- An exclusive forward from the beginning of *Heir to the Darkmage*
- A short ebook with a collection of short stories from *The Mage Chronicles* universe;
- A pronunciation guide;
- Exclusive content from Lisa's other fantasy series;

The Chronicle will also keep you up to date with all the details on Lisa's upcoming books, special content for her followers, and invites to her events (as well as her advance reader team).

Head to Lisa's website (tatehousebooks.com/Lisa-Cassidy) to sign up!

If you haven't read Lisa's *Mage Chronicles* series yet, then read all about Alyx, Dawn, Tarrick, and Finn's war against the Darkmage by diving into *DarkSkull Hall* now!

ALSO BY LISA CASSIDY

The Mage Chronicles

DarkSkull Hall

Taliath

Darkmage

Heartfire

Heir to the Darkmage

Heir to the Darkmage

A Tale of Stars and Shadow

A Tale of Stars and Shadow

A Prince of Song and Shade

A King of Masks and Magic

A Duet of Sword and Song

ABOUT THE AUTHOR

Lisa is a self-published fantasy author by day and book nerd in every other spare moment she has. She's a self-confessed coffee snob (don't try coming near her with any of that instant coffee rubbish) but is willing to accept all other hot drink aficionados, even tea drinkers.

She lives in Australia's capital city, Canberra, and like all Australians, is pretty much in constant danger from highly poisonous spiders, crocodiles, sharks, and drop bears, to name a few. As you can see, she is also pro-Oxford comma.

A 2019 SPFBO finalist, and finalist for the 2020 ACT Writers Fiction award, Lisa is the author of the young adult fantasy series The Mage Chronicles, and epic fantasy series A Tale of Stars and Shadow. Her brand new series, *Heir to the Darkmage,* debuted in April 2021.

She has also partnered up with One Girl, an Australian charity working to build a world where all girls have access to quality education. A world where all girls — no matter where they are born or how much money they have — enjoy the same rights and opportunities as boys. A percentage of all Lisa's royalties go to One Girl.

You can follow Lisa on Instagram and Facebook where she loves to interact with her fans. And make sure you go to her website, where you can sign up for her mailing list and get spoilers, bonus content, and advance info on all her new books!

tatehousebooks.com/Lisa-Cassidy

Printed in Great Britain
by Amazon

15957238R00214